T0354893

# The
# Memory Keeper

# The
# Memory Keeper

Marilyn Land

# THE MEMORY KEEPER

*iUniverse books may be ordered through booksellers or by contacting:*

*iUniverse*
*1663 Liberty Drive*
*Bloomington, IN 47403*
*www.iuniverse.com*
*844-349-9409*

*ISBN: 978-1-6632-6170-0 (sc)*
*ISBN: 978-1-6632-6172-4 (hc)*
*ISBN: 978-1-6632-6171-7 (e)*

*Library of Congress Control Number: 2024906135*

*Print information available on the last page.*

*iUniverse rev. date: 04/09/2024*

## THE MEMORY KEEPER

is a work of fiction.
Any and all references to actual people, events, places, or business establishments are intended solely to give the fiction a sense of authenticity and a reality of the times. All names, characters, and non-historical incidents are the product of the author's imagination, and any resemblance to anyone living or dead is purely coincidental.

History laced throughout the story was compiled from public information made available by Wikipedia Free Encyclopedia, Google, and a multitude of articles that have appeared in miscellaneous newspapers and magazines.

## MEMORY

The recollection of past experience.

## MIRROR

A polished or smooth surface (as of glass) that forms images by reflection; that which gives a true representation or in which a true image may be seen.

## PROFILE

A biographical or descriptive essay presenting the subject's most remarkable characteristics and accomplishments.

## PORTRAIT

A painting, photograph, sculpture, or other artistic representation of a person, in which the face and its expressions are predominant.

## WHAT IF?

The question most asked when one is second-guessing a decision in order to determine a different conclusion.

## GODWINK

An event or personal experience often identified as coincidence, so astonishing that it is seen as a sign of divine intervention, especially when perceived as the answer to a prayer.

To my grandchildren:

Haley (Ryan), Andrew, Jillian (Josh), Chase (Suzy),
and Zachary

You are a window to my past, a mirror of today, the door of the future,
and the keeper of my heart.

My request is that as you go through life. . . .

You pause to take *A Look In the Mirror*
Hoping that you are pleased with what you see and
Never finding the need to ask *What if?*

# New Amsterdam to New York

The Dutch first settled along the Hudson River in 1624, and established the colony of New Amsterdam on Manhattan Island; over the next forty years, the Dutch colony continued to grow. In 1664, the English Fleet arrived, took control of the colony, and renamed it *New York*.

When the thirteen original colonies decided to rebel against Britain and declare their independence, New York was in the midst of the action. The largest battle of the Revolutionary War was the Battle of Long Island fought in 1776; the British defeated the Continental Army and gained control of New York City. The Battle of Saratoga in 1777 was a turning point. General Horatio Gates led the Continental Army to victory and the surrender of the British Army under General Burgoyne.

On July 26, 1788, New York ratified the new U.S. Constitution and became the 11th state to join the Union. New York City became the nation's capital, and George Washington was inaugurated as the first President of the United States in front of Federal Hall in 1789, where the United States Bill of Rights was drafted, and the United States Supreme Court sat for the first time.

New York rapidly became a center for advancement—in trade, education, transportation, agriculture, manufacturing and medicine—becoming a center for progressive causes, including supporting abolitionism and women's rights.

In the first half of the 19th century, New York culture set the stage for the future. Reflected by its size and ethnic diversity, it was the birthplace of many cultural movements. Music, art, film, theatre, and literature expanded. It is home to the Metropolitan Museum of Art, the Museum of Modern Art, and the Brooklyn Museum—one of the premiere art institutions in the world.

New York is one of only five cities in the United States with permanent professional resident companies in all the major arts disciples: the Metropolitan Opera, New York Philharmonic, New York City Ballet, and the Public Theatre. The Lincoln Center for the Performing Arts is the largest art institution in the world.

The second half of the 19th century saw New York strengthen its dominance in the financial and banking industries. Manufacturing continued to rise and giants such as Eastman Kodak, General Electric, and Endicott-Johnson Shoe Company emerged. Immigration increased starting with refugees from the Great Famine of Ireland, but the estimated eight million immigrants coming to America during this time included German and Eastern European Jews, Poles, and Italians.

As the century drew to a close, New York City's population outnumbered that of London, making it the most populous city in the world. New York's most identifiable symbol was *Liberty Enlightening the World* (the Statue of Liberty), a gift from France for the American Centennial completed in 1886.

The turn of the century saw New York as the richest and most populous state whose new emblem was becoming the skyscraper—the Woolworth Building (1913), 40 Wall Street (1930), the Chrysler Building (1930), the Empire State Building (1931), and the World Trade Center (1974). Over a dozen major railroads and electric interurban rail networks serviced the state.

While New York enjoyed a booming economy during the Roaring Twenties, it suffered greatly during the Great Depression, which began with the Wall Street crash on Black Tuesday in 1929. The Securities and Exchange Commission was established in 1934 to regulate the Stock Market.

WWII reestablished New York's great industrial ability. The state supplied more resources than any other having manufactured eleven percent of the total military armaments produced during the War.

The New York City that emerged from the war was a dramatically different place than the one that had entered it four years earlier, due in large part to the war itself, which finally lifted the city out of the Depression and ushered in an era of unparalleled prosperity. The explosion in commercial activity brought on by the war reignited the city's economic engine propelling it to a level of economic power and dominance like nothing before or since.

By the late 1940s, New York City became the world's largest manufacturing and wholesaling center, the world's biggest port, and the world's financial capital. Above all, it was home to the immense corporations that now dominated life in the United States and increasingly around the world. One hundred thirty-five of the Nation's five hundred largest industrial companies called it their *Headquarters City*.

Although many cities vied for the honor of hosting the United Nations

Headquarters site, by the end of 1946 New York City had been selected. The groundbreaking ceremony September 14, 1948, for the magnificent new complex along the East River was completed on October 10, 1952.

In the late 20th century, telecommunications and high technology industries employed many New Yorkers. Entrepreneurs created numerous small companies that drew many young professionals to the city. This in turn led to a surge in culture as once again, New York City became *the center for all things chic and trendy.*

New York City increased its already large share of television programming, home to network news broadcasting, as well as two of the three major cable news networks. The *Wall Street Journal* and *The New York Times* became two of the three national newspapers read throughout the country on a daily basis.

Today, New York is a mecca for sports fans. It is host to the headquarters of the National Football League, Major League Baseball, National Basketball Association, National League Hockey, and Major League Soccer. The New York metropolitan area boasts the most sports teams in these five professional leagues, two minor league baseball teams—the Brooklyn Cyclones and the Staten Island Yankees, and five of the most expensive stadiums ever built.

The New York Knickerbockers were one of the first baseball teams formed, and professional baseball's Hall of Fame is located in Cooperstown. Queens hosts one of the four annual grand slam events—the US Open Tennis Championship; and the New York Marathon is one of the world's largest.

New York is home to West Point, Columbia, Cornell, Colgate, Julliard, and the New York Performing Arts Academy, representing a fraction of the universities, colleges, and specialty education venues in the state.

New York is the birthplace of five US Presidents, eleven US Vice Presidents (four became president), three Chief Justices and fourteen Associate Justices of the US Supreme Court, many statesmen, and an epic corps of writers and entertainers.

The state offers a variety of choices to its millions of visitors each year. Ranked #1, New York City has long been a favorite vacation destination. Aside from the arts, eclectic dining, and shopping, a visit to the 9/11 Memorial is a must. It is the heart and sole of New Yorkers.

On September 11, 2001, the worst terrorist attack in United States history occurred when two of four hijacked planes were flown into the Twin Towers of the World Trade Center in New York City. The attacks carried out by nineteen members of the Islamic terrorist group Al-Qaeda caused the collapse of both the North and South Towers, killing nearly 3,000 people.

Among the victims deployed to the scene when 121 engine companies and 62 ladder companies responded to the World Trade Center were 343 members of the FDNY. There were 75 firehouses in which at least one member was killed, including its department chief and first deputy commissioner.

In addition, 37 police officers of the Port Authority of New York and New Jersey, 23 officers of the New York City Police Department, and 8 emergency medical technicians and paramedics from private emergency medical services lost their lives.

# Prologue
## New York City—January 2011

Sam Meyerson stood impatiently waiting for the elevator. He had just left the offices of New York's PBS affiliate station, and his meeting couldn't have gone better. For over two years, he had been working on an idea for a new show, and now it looked as if all of his hard work, late hours, missed meals, and the demise of a longtime relationship might have been worth it.

The show—*Profiles of New York*—had been rattling around in his brain for as long as he could remember. He was a born and bred New Yorker and couldn't have come up with a better catch phrase than *I Love New York* to describe exactly how he felt. He prided himself on his knowledge of everything and anything New York and wanted to share it all.

His pitch for the show was to profile persons, places, or events that were significant and native to New York. He proposed a September 11, 2011 premiere airing to commemorate the 10th Anniversary of the attack. The show dedicated to the 9/11 Heroes would include a history of the World Trade Center, an update on construction of the new Freedom Tower Complex, and interviews—to be determined. If well received, a two-hour episode would air on a monthly basis September through June.

It had been five years since Sam Meyerson graduated from Columbia with a degree in Journalism. He had never been without a job, and although he had worked for several media organizations, he soon realized that what he enjoyed most was interviewing people, human-interest stories, and history. He wasn't interested in getting mixed up in the quagmire of politics, crime, or celebrities.

When the idea for *Profiles of New York* came to him, his first thought was the unending amount of resources available that could be accessed and researched without leaving the state. He viewed it as a slam-dunk, and to his surprise, so did Bill Franklin when he presented it to him.

It was a go! He had already done a good deal of research, and felt it would only take a couple of months to tie everything together. Quite confident that the show would be a success, he produced three additional episodes allowing them to hit the ground running and carrying them through the end of the year.

When the elevator finally arrived and opened its doors, the occupants made room for the man standing before them with the huge grin on his face.

# New York City—January 2021

It was hard to find anyone that wasn't relieved to see 2020 come to an end. A year ago, before we were introduced to COVID-19, Americans for the most part were living what they called normal lives. However, in mid-March, all abruptly came to an end. Lockdowns, masks, and social distancing coincided with schools, businesses, and entertainment venue closures, quickly followed by weddings, funerals, and houses of worship services being cancelled. ZOOM became the only means to socialize and keep in touch with family and friends.

With the New Year came optimism that the vaccines rolled out in December, along with a plan to get everyone vaccinated as soon as possible, would reopen everything in a safe and efficient manner and reunite us with our loved ones, allowing us at long last to see a light at the end of the tunnel.

On September 11, 2011, PBS debuted a new show *Profiles of New York* to correspond with the 10th Anniversary of 9/11, and the unveiling to the public of Michael Arad's *Reflecting Absence* featuring the names of all 2,983 people who perished that day. The original episode although centered on profiling the brave heroes who lost their lives running selflessly into the towers to save others, wound up including family members and friends of the victims who voluntarily came forward offering their stories.

The premiere was so overwhelmingly received that PBS continued the show, airing it once a month for 10 months of each year, expanding their profiling to include buildings, landmarks, and events, as well. New York offered an infinite amount of subjects to profile; and with all that was available they hadn't begun to scratch the surface.

The show and its success belonged solely to Sam Meyerson whose idea ten years ago produced a show that captured the hearts of not only New Yorkers but millions around the world, emerging more popular today than when it first aired. Sam remained involved in all aspects of every episode, and although he had put together an excellent team to research and produce the broadcasts, he remained hands on.

Sam had recently hired a young journalist from the west coast who had worked on a few of the episodes behind the scenes, but he was quite impressed by her ability to dig deep for any and all background information that *first and foremost* produced excellence in broadcasting. In September 2020, the LA Times published her heartfelt personal experience article she had written about the loss of her father to COVID. Sam came across the piece quite by accident; it captivated him. His first thoughts were to hire her for the 20th Anniversary episode, but after speaking with her, he offered her a permanent position with the show.

September 2021 was fast approaching, and Sam was steadfast in his belief that *Profiles of New York* marking the 20th Anniversary of 9/11 had to be a blockbuster. The show was scheduled to air on the evening of September 11, 2021, and not only would it mark the 20th Anniversary of 9/11, and the 10th Anniversary of the show, but would be the 100th episode.

For months during the long shutdown, Sam had been racking his brain to think of a person or persons to profile. He felt it should be someone with a powerful story of how that day affected their life from that day forward, and where they were now. He had several ideas, but unfortunately, his list had grown shorter after contacting the first few people he approached. Hit particularly hard by the pandemic, perhaps New Yorkers were not quite ready to leave their safe havens and venture out just yet.

Vaccinations had just begun. Many places had not yet reopened, and those that had were only partially opened at best. Most that could were still working from home, and the many who fled the city left an abundance of office space and apartment rentals in their wake. To complicate things further, each new day seemed to bring a change in regulations, in mandates, and in conflicting advice from the *powers that be* both political and health wise to the point where New Yorkers didn't know who to believe.

It was already January, with Thanksgiving, Christmas, and in fact all of 2020 a part of history. As Sam sat in his office thinking about what was turning into somewhat of a dilemma, his eyes came to rest on a portrait of himself that had been a gift to him from his dear friend Lily Asher. Lily was a portrait artist who was quite noted in New York for painting many of the state's most famous and important people including not only celebrities, but also politicians and visiting dignitaries.

Her story was briefly profiled on the premiere show by sharing her heartfelt memories of losing her only child, her son Noah, when the first plane flew into the North Tower. The episode was dedicated to the emergency workers—the Heroes of 9/11. It was her appearance on that show that prompted her to extend an invitation to each emergency worker's family to provide her with a photograph of their loved one, and she in turn would gift them with a portrait. Her studio—*Portraits by Lily*—had long been a fixture in West Village, a section of Manhattan's Greenwich

Village neighborhood, on the same corner spot where in 1948 she opened for business only months after coming to America.

Through the years, Sam and Lily remained good friends, and he never failed to drop by whenever he was in the neighborhood. There were times that she wasn't there, but when she was, they often grabbed a coffee or a quick lunch and caught up. He suddenly realized he hadn't spoken with her in some time—well over a year.

He reached for his phone, searched contacts, and called her home number. On the third ring, he heard her cheerful and upbeat, "Hello."

"Lily, Sam Meyerson here. How are you? It's been quite some time since we've spoken, and I humbly apologize. I should have called sooner to make sure you were okay."

Lily laughed. "Thank you Sam; I'm just fine. I hope you know that if at any time I needed your help, I would not have hesitated to call you. I find that for most of us, the last year has gone by in a blur, and I haven't ventured out except when necessary. Unfortunately, all this down time has slowed me down quite a bit."

"I'm glad to hear that you're well, and have no doubt that you'll be back up to speed in no time. I hope you have someone nearby who can lend a hand if needed."

"Yes, I'm very fortunate to have good friends. I do enjoy my terrace when the weather allows, and I have my groceries delivered; that proves to be the easiest and best for now. However, I do manage to do a little walking in the neighborhood, and with more and more places reopening, I occasionally stop at the local coffee shop for a treat."

"I don't know if you're accepting visitors, but I would love to meet with you. I have an idea I'd like to run by you, and I prefer to do it in person. Of course, all precautions will be used; although I have been getting tested regularly, I will get tested before we meet, and I assure you my supply of masks is endless."

Lily laughed. "Sam that would be wonderful. I would love to see you. I had my second shot last week, so I am fully vaccinated. We can have lunch here, and it will give me something to look forward to. You know, I've never been one to let grass grow under my feet. Walking around the neighborhood, getting my exercise, and stopping to visit with friends is what I've missed the most the past year. But thank goodness for the computer; at least I can remain involved with the Asher Foundation and keep up with what's happening. I haven't been hands on at my studio for some time now; in fact, it's been closed to the public for almost a year."

"Well then, shall we say next Tuesday at 11:00 am? I'm due to get my second shot on Saturday, so I'll be fully vaccinated, as well."

"Perfect! I so look forward to seeing you Sam. Thank you."

"Thank you for taking the time to see me. I really need some Lily advice and insight—I will be at your door promptly."

They hung up simultaneously—both looking forward to Tuesday 11:00 am.

# Chapter 1

Sam's call to Lily Asher could not have come at a better time. For the past twenty years, she had been unsuccessful in getting one final aspect of her life in order. She was in her nineties and the last in her family with no known living relatives. During the yearlong plus shutdown, she became keenly aware of the importance of tying up the one loose end that had managed to evade her every effort to do so for almost two decades.

In early December, she received word—not from the latest private investigator she had been working with—but from a dear friend—*out of the blue*; his call confirmed what she felt deep in her heart all those years. This time the answers were not elusive; there were no disappointments thus far.

The self-imposed title she had given herself long ago—*The Memory Keeper*—was on the verge of being passed down, giving her closure and lifting the burden from her shoulders.

Throughout the years, her good memories had sustained her but she learned there was little she could do to stop the bad memories from creeping into her mind when triggered by an event or a date that cruelly brought them into the present. Sometimes, they passed quickly while other times they lingered for days eroding self-worth and making one wonder *What If?* things had turned out differently.

Her name was Jodi Jerome, the daughter of Dr. Henry and Julia Jerome of Los Angeles, California. Her mother had lost her battle with cancer three years earlier, and her father had been one of the early COVID-19 deaths reported in LA. She was an only child, thirty years old, unmarried, and a journalist who in her short career had won several prestigious awards for her human-interest stories before and during the Pandemic. She had recently relocated to New York City.

Since receiving the news, Lily had spent endless hours on her computer learning all she could about Jodi Jerome. She had given great thought about how to proceed with her endeavor to meet and get to know her when

Sam Meyerson called. Coincidence or fate or perhaps a *Godwink*, it didn't matter. She would ask Sam for his help.

Lily Asher lived on the Upper East Side of Manhattan that has long been known for it's impressive and expensive residences. Located in the Historic District, it is one of eight in a row of limestone townhouses designed by architects Buchanan and Deisler. The five-story townhouse on East 74th Street, built in 1890, is comprised of 8,000 square feet whose entry through iron grille doors is followed by a roof terrace overlooking Central Park, an elevator for all floors, a garden in the back of the property, a master suite, numerous bedrooms, and an office that encompasses an entire floor.

Although it was mid-January, the weather had been relatively mild and on most days Sam would have walked from his condo to Lily's, but a last minute phone call had delayed him so he decided to call an Uber.

Lily awaited his arrival with anticipation. She had no idea why he wanted to meet with her—only that he wanted to *run something by her*. She hoped that whatever it was, it would allow her to ask a favor from him in return.

He arrived promptly as promised. She answered the door herself. "My goodness Sam Meyerson, you are a sight for sore eyes. It has been far too long since anyone not normally a part of this household has walked through these doors. And since we are both fully vaccinated, I want a big hug."

He hugged her longer than he intended before releasing her and stepping back. "You look pretty damn good yourself, and I'm thrilled that you have gotten through all this none the worse for wear."

"It's a little early, but lunch is ready, and I thought we might start by enjoying a bite to eat, catching up a little since we saw each other last, and then we can talk business—if that is what you want to speak with me about."

Sam chuckled. "That sounds perfect. I can't remember the last time I actually had a lunch date; probably last summer when they briefly opened outdoor dining."

The banter between them seemed like old times. Sam didn't realize how fond he had grown of Lily. He met her ten years ago when he interviewed her for the premiere show of *Profiles of New York*. They had managed to stay in touch through the years, and he often sought her perspective and advice for some of the ideas he had for various episodes.

Once when he visited her studio in the Village, he was amazed to see the many paintings she had done of landmarks and buildings. When he reacted in surprise at her having painted so many, she responded: *although a portrait is defined as a likeness of a person, why shouldn't the likeness of a building not be considered a portrait, as well?*

He realized he knew very little about Lily Asher—she lost her son Noah on 9/11 when the first plane flew into the North Tower. His interacting with her had been purely business in the beginning, but he found it hard not to be drawn to her warm and welcoming nature.

Her studio, *Portraits by Lily* was well known throughout New York City and beyond; she was considered by many to be *a local treasure*. She had opened the small studio in Greenwich Village in the late 1940s having relocated to America after WWII. She introduced her style of painting— portraits from photographs—and became an immediate success. Whether taken by her or supplied by the client, these photos dispensed with the need of time-consuming posing sessions, in particular for the many well-known individuals with hectic schedules to contend with.

In her first appearance on the show, she invited the emergency workers' families to take her up on her offer to paint a portrait of their loved ones simply by dropping off a photograph at her studio. Although not every family responded, many did. There were several showings of the portraits throughout the years, and in the eyes of New Yorkers, she emerged a Hero in her own right. She developed friendships with some of the families and encouraged those with artistic ability to come by her studio for lessons especially the children.

Sam felt deep down that there was much more to Lily Asher than met the eye. He knew nothing about her life in Europe before coming to America; and he knew nothing about her husband other than the fact that he was an attorney. Although, he was alive when they lost their son, it had now been several years since Joe Asher passed away. He thought it time to profile Lily Asher, an immigrant to this country, who loved and knew more about New York than anyone else he knew. His gut feeling told him that the best part of her story was yet to be told, and that it was somehow tied to 9/11. He would do just about anything to convince her to agree.

Over dessert, Sam told Lily his idea for the upcoming 20th Anniversary 9/11 episode of *Profiles of New York*. Much to his surprise, there was no convincing to be done. But—*and there was a but*—she had a few requests.

"I don't know why you picked me; surely there are many New Yorkers more worthy and deserving of the honor. Perhaps, I've been unable to mingle with real people far too long, but I do greatly appreciate your wanting to tell my story. Although it may not prove to be the story you are seeking, if things turn out the way I hope they do, I am certain you will be more than pleased.

"On the other hand, it will give me the opportunity to plug my art students and the Asher Foundation. The fact that the show airs on PBS is also to my liking because as you know, my foundation primarily supports PBS and education. So I see it as a win for everyone.

"Will you be doing the interviewing? I hope you're not suggesting that I just speak into a recorder."

Sam laughed. Lily might be ninety something by his calculations, but she was as sharp as ever. "You will be telling your story in your own words to a real live person, however, we would like to record you while you are doing so simply to facilitate the editing process. You will have the final say on every word that is broadcast, and if you include something that you later wish to delete, we will do so. Together, we shall decide on which format is best—you about you in your own words or a narrator telling about you from your own words, or perhaps a combination of the two. We'll just see how it goes and what you are most comfortable with."

Lily thought for a moment. "Well it all sounds good to me, but you haven't answered my question as to who would conduct the interview. Have you decided on that as yet?"

"No, we haven't. I don't know if you've watched many of the shows, but we've had many different journalists, known people, unknown people, and others do the various narrations, which have all contributed to the show's success.

"As icing on the cake, the 20th Anniversary show will be the 100th episode— having been aired once a month, September through June since September 2011. During that timeframe, it was easier to concentrate on buildings and landmarks. Being able to continue producing the shows during the pandemic by maintaining the required distance between the camera and lighting crews and the narrators worked out well. The men appreciated being able to work; it wasn't something they could do from home.

"Our upcoming shows through May are either complete or in the final stages, and include Hudson Yards, Central Park, and the Museum of the City of New York. We decided to cut this season short by dropping June, allowing us several months to concentrate on making the 20th Anniversary show the blockbuster we anticipate.

For a moment, Lily grew quiet. As of late, her life had been comprised of fate and coincidences. How could that possibly be? September 11, 2021 would mark her 100th Birthday. Once again, a *Godwink* came to mind—always a sign of hope.

"Sam, I think our meeting has gone quite well. You have given an old lady something to look forward to. We all need that after the last year we've had while we hope for a better year to come. I will do everything I can to uphold my end of the bargain and deliver the outcome you are aiming for.

"However, there is one more thing I would like to ask of you. Have you ever come across or heard of a young journalist from California that has made quite a name for herself—Jodi Jerome? I understand she has recently relocated to Manhattan."

Now it was Sam's turn to grow quiet. Perhaps another time, he would not question her inquiry, but after being cutoff from just about everyone and everything for over a year, how on earth did Lily even hear about Jodi Jerome?

"Yes, Lily, not only have I heard of her, I just hired her. Would you like to meet with her? I presume you're asking because you'd like to have her conduct your interview. I must tell you that I hired her as a producer, and she would have to be agreeable, but from what I've learned in getting to know her, she's definitely a *people* person, and I don't visualize her not wanting to hear your story firsthand."

Coincidence and fate be damned. "Yes Sam, meeting her would be splendid! I thoroughly understand your position, and it's not my intention to make things difficult for you."

The afternoon had passed all too quickly. They both had the same thought—how nice and normal it was to be having lunch and conversation with a real live person sitting across from you.

Lily walked Sam to the door. She gave him one last hug. "Thank you again for thinking of me, and don't be a stranger. Come have lunch with me whenever you have time or drop by for supper if that's better for you."

"That I will; I promise. I'll be in touch to set up a time for you to meet Jodi. I think we should get started as soon as possible."

Sam decided to walk back to his condo. His thoughts were all over the place, and he just wasn't up to idle conversation with an Uber driver.

On the Upper East Side of Manhattan that night, Sam Meyerson tossed and turned again and again as over and over in his mind he recalled his conversation with Lily. Had he spoken too soon? He told Lily he had hired Jodi as a producer; what if she didn't agree to do the interview? What did Lily have up her sleeve? He began to feel he had been played by a sweet ninety-something little old lady, but he quickly reconsidered his thoughts. Lily Asher might be ninety something, but she was anything but your stereotype of a little old lady, and he knew it. As he watched the sun come up, he remained wide-awake, his thoughts unchecked.

Also on the Upper East Side of Manhattan several blocks away, Lily Asher slept like a baby.

# Chapter 2

When her father died, Jodi was devastated. For as long as she could remember, it was the three of them—Mom, Dad, and Jodi. When her mother lost her battle with cancer three years ago, it became Dad and Jodi. They clung to one another, growing closer by the day if that was even possible, but after spending their third Christmas sad and still grieving, Jodi decided, the time had come to move on. She talked her father into taking some time off from the hospital, and all their plans were set. She was in between assignments, and in two short weeks, they would be on their way to Hawaii for some much needed rest and relaxation.

It was the beginning of March 2020. COVID-19 was about to rear its ugly head and encompass the world, plunging us all into an unimaginable downward spiral for over a year before hope and anticipation once again would begin to replace the fear and desperation that had overtaken us.

When the family arrived at Los Angeles International Airport on the way home from what had been a short-lived and unpleasant Mexican vacation, they were exhausted. The father was battling a nasty stomach bug, and even before they settled into their Cancun hotel, they received word of the sudden death of the wife's mother in their hometown of Wuhan, China.

The couple and their small son were planning to be at LAX just long enough to switch planes allowing them to get to Wuhan for the funeral. However, as they passed through Tom Bradley International Terminal on January 22nd, the father, overcome with a fever and body aches, approached a customs officer for help.

The family did not make their flight that Wednesday evening and, indeed, would not return to China for more than a month. The father, Qian Lang, became the first confirmed case of COVID-19 in Los Angeles and the fourth in the United States. He remained the hospital's sole patient diagnosed with the virus for five weeks, passing most of that time in top-secret isolation at Cedars-Sinai Medical Center.

The 38-year-old salesman played an important role in what quickly became a frantic race to understand and learn about the deadly new virus before it hit the United States in full force. He emerged as a real-time, flesh-and-blood case study, allowing public health officials and researchers to glean early insights into the protection of healthcare workers, contact tracing, and treatment. He was the second virus patient in the world to take the drug Remdesivir, which was then experimental but would eventually become standard therapy for those seriously ill with the virus.

For the Qian Family, his illness and recovery meant a strange and frightening sojourn in California. Though his wife and son tested negative, they stayed with him at Cedars-Sinai in the closest proximity of a domestic life-infection protocol allowed.

Dr. Henry Jerome was a neuropsychologist who had been at Cedars-Sinai Medical Center for almost twenty-five years. He was widely known for his treatment of brain trauma patients—his most profound and baffling case being his daughter. Often recruited for consultation in severe and difficult cases, he never turned a request down, travelling frequently to do so.

It was uncertain how he contracted COVID-19; he was not an attending physician, but he, of course, was in contact with numerous healthcare workers throughout the hospital on a daily basis before the virus was revealed to the public, before lockdowns and quarantine procedures were put in place, and before the dire consequences of the deadly virus were learned.

In preparation of their impending trip to Hawaii, Jodi called her father to see if he was free to have dinner with her that evening. She was excited about getting away from Los Angeles, chilling out on a beach without a care in the world, and dining out on good solid food unlike her usual fast food and takeout when she was on assignment. She left several messages and was beginning to worry when he finally returned her calls.

She noticed immediately, his voice was strained, and he spoke softly. "Hi honey. I'm sorry I didn't get back to you sooner but I've been swamped trying to cover all my bases before we leave for our trip. What's up?"

"Nothing really. I was just calling to see if you were free for dinner. Are you okay? You sound really tired and down; that's just not like you."

"You're right. I am tired, extremely tired. I've been trying to rearrange my schedule and cover my commitments while we are away, and we've been unusually busy at the hospital. I've been called in on a couple of new consultations, and that has only added to my frustration. Having to deal with the seemingly unending delays in preparing for our departure has stressed me out a bit, but I'm just about to the finish line, and I am so looking forward to our trip.

"For the past couple of days, I've felt like I was coming down with a good old fashioned cold. I've been achy all over, coughing, chills, and a slight fever, and no appetite at all. I'm going to be working from home tomorrow and try to shake this by filling up on chicken soup, tea, and lots of bed rest.

"Sorry I can't join you for dinner, but I think it best, and I don't want you coming over here and catching anything from me. We can keep in touch by phone, and if I'm up to it, I really should start packing."

Jodi had never known her father to be sick, even with a cold. He was the doctor, the person in charge to make everyone else better. But she agreed with his decision to work from home, and although she was worried about him, she felt confident he was handling the situation in the manner he thought best, and she told him so.

"I can't say I'm not disappointed, we won't be having dinner together, but you're the doctor and I trust you to know what's best. I do plan to check up on you frequently, and I hope you're okay with that. I don't want anything to stand in the way of our much-needed vacation.

"I'll let you go. Please call me when you get home and let me know if you need anything at all. I can call the deli and have some chicken soup delivered along with anything else you might want."

"Thank you, but I called Rosy and she took care of everything before she left. She's off the next couple of days, so it works out well. That way, hopefully I won't pass this cold onto her either. Suppose, I call you right before I retire, and then I'll call you when I get up in the morning."

"Sounds good. Please take care. I'll wait for your call. Love you."

"Love you back. Bye."

As promised, her father called before retiring. He said he only had a little of the soup and was just tired and wanted to get some sleep. He promised to call in the morning.

By 9:00 am, Jodi was frantic. She hadn't heard from her father, and her calls to him went unanswered. Finally, she could wait no longer. She left her apartment and headed to his house. Without ringing the doorbell, she let herself in with her key. Finding him unconscious in bed she called for an ambulance immediately.

Dr. Henry Jerome was diagnosed with COVID-19 on March 5th. When Jodi found him, he had already been unconscious for hours; he was alive, but barely, and if he had not been placed on a respirator immediately, he would have certainly died within hours.

For two weeks, it was touch and go. In and out of consciousness, Jodi refused to leave his side. When the national lockdown and quarantine protocols were announced and they attempted to bar her from staying with him, she adamantly refused citing that she had been with him since the beginning, and that leaving after the fact was ludicrous. They allowed her to stay.

She asked Rosy to go to her apartment and bring her clothes, and during the entire two weeks, not once did she leave Cedars-Sinai Medical Center—until March 19th—the day her beloved father, Dr. Henry Jerome died.

Jodi had never been so lost. Both of her parents were gone; she was numb with grief, with sadness, with loss, with no one to turn to—her future unknown.

Dr. Henry Jerome's passing was a great loss to not only the Cedars-Sinai Medical Center and the greater Los Angeles Community but to many institutions and medical personnel throughout the country. Although he died during the first two weeks after the pandemic had been officially announced publicly, the outpouring of support for Jodi was unprecedented.

The Cedars-Sinai staff—from the doctors and nurses to the orderlies, from the cafeteria workers to the volunteers, from management to donors and supporters of the Center, offers of condolences and assistance poured in—all for Jodi.

The letters and notes from far and wide continued to arrive for weeks that turned into months, without showing any signs of stopping.

It wasn't until September that Jodi began to emerge from mourning both of her parents. She had been working with Lloyd Buchanan her father's best friend and attorney. He and Lloyd had grown up together, attended UCLA together, and with their respective wives were good friends and often vacationed together. Lloyd and his wife Leslie never left her side throughout the months following her father's passing. They wanted her to come stay with them, but respected her wishes that she wanted and needed time alone to come to terms with the magnitude of her loss.

During the months following his death, Jodi found herself confronted with life altering decisions that would affect the rest of her life. Her parents' estate was extensive. She learned that her father had only recently, at Lloyd's urging, finalized the updating of his Will following the death of her mother. This in itself made things somewhat easier; however, there were certain items that needed to be managed day-by-day. In addition to their main residence, stocks and bonds, a vacation house in Malibu, a small office building that housed his private office and several rental suites, multiple cars, a boat, and so much more was a lot to deal with.

Lloyd further advised her that during the rewriting of her father's Will, he had indicated that upon returning from their Hawaii trip, he intended to make some additional decisions about selling some items such as the two antique cars, the boat that they never seemed to use anymore, and several smaller investments. He intended to discuss this with her while they were away.

She was overwhelmed simply learning about the vastness of the estate, let alone having to consider what to keep and what to sell. She certainly had no need for any of it. The house was much too big for her to consider living there; she was perfectly happy in her condo. The fact that since her mother's passing, her father hadn't used most of it simply proved her point.

Jodi purchased her condo in a new building in downtown Los Angeles shortly before her mother became ill. Upon graduating from college, working for the Los Angeles Times and a couple of short stints with several independent media groups, led her to the realization that as a freelance journalist, she could control her own destiny.

It turned out to be the right decision at the right time, and her career took off. Once she began earning what she considered a substantial salary, she decided to declare her independence. She wanted to do it on her own and that she did. Her parents were proud of her, and she and her mother embarked on furnishing her new place—a gift from her parents that she finally agreed to accept.

It turned out to be the last mother/daughter project they did together.

After her mother's passing, just being surrounded by pillows and furniture and trinkets that were her mother's choices was bittersweet.

Following a great deal of thought, sleepless nights, and sound advice and guidance from Lloyd, her final decision was to sell everything, keeping only her condo. Her father left a moderate sum to their longtime housekeeper, who offered to stay on as long as Jodi needed her to help sort things out; no one knew the house better than Rosy.

In addition, nothing would be sold until current conditions of the pandemic improved. She would take her time going through the items in the big house and with Rosy's help they would be ready when the time was right.

Jodi's last assignment had been prior to COVID-19, but before she was ready to re-enter the workforce and begin uncovering strangers' stories again, she had one last item to check off her list.

Her father's funeral had been private with only a handful in attendance due to the restrictions of the pandemic. She planned to have a memorial service when it was allowed, but in the meantime, she had given great thought to how she could honor both her father and her mother.

Every fiber of her being was urging her to put her feelings into words—something she was extremely good at—hoping that it would give her closure and allow her to move on.

# Chapter 3

Six months following the death of Dr. Henry Jerome, the following article appeared in the Los Angeles Times.

## Mourning, Memories, and Moving-on
### Jodi Jerome
### September 19, 2020
### Los Angeles

In my short life, I have come to look at death as having three phases of M—Mourning, Memories, and Moving-on.

*Mourning* affects each of us differently. We grieve in different ways, for different reasons, and even for different periods of time. Grief is somewhat precarious, often tending to render us helpless in the face of it; a helplessness where time is our only ally. To some—time passes quickly; to others—time lingers. The stronger and deeper we love—the greater the sorrow we bear.

*Memories* is the most often used word in messages of condolence. We are wished and told that our memories will sustain us. This very thought is the basis of eulogies delivered by Clergy, family, and friends the world over. While there is a great deal of truth in this, memories are not all good, and unfortunately, we have no control over keeping the bad ones from creeping in.

*Moving-on* is totally personal and an individual choice. For some, it comes quickly, and is the most practical option; for others, it is a burden plagued with uncertainties. Of the three, moving-on is the most age related. When one is older, one is not necessarily required to move on; moving-on simply means life as usual, but alone. However, for the young, moving-on is a necessity; without it, there is no future.

We find ourselves in the midst of a COVID-19 Pandemic that has claimed over 600,000 lives in the United States to date, and shows no visible signs of slowing down. Millions are dealing with not only their loss of a loved one but also the lockdown of an entire country that encompasses every single aspect of existence. We are all in a state of mourning our losses.

As a journalist tuned into the pulse of the public, I have seen firsthand the hardship and heartbreak thus far, that will undoubtedly have lasting affects on not only the next generation but also future generations to come. Feelings that a *normal way of life* is no more and may never return again have begun to take root.

As an American, I cannot and do not support this theory. We are fighters, always have been. As we have in the past, I feel certain we will get through this, and we will come out of it stronger than we were. We have all faced crises and emergencies both large and small, both nationwide and personal, and our steadfast adherence to a course of action and belief that we would emerge victors, not victims, has seen us through each and every one.

Henry and Julia Jerome were my parents. Although my mother passed away three years ago, I had not quite relinquished mourning her death when I lost my father, Dr. Henry Jerome. He died March 19, 2020; he was one of the first COVID-19 deaths reported in Los Angeles.

For twenty-five years, Cedars-Sinai Medical Center was his home base. Quite renown for his treatment of brain trauma patients, he often referred to me as his most challenging case. My mother was a pediatric nurse, and although she did not work alongside my father on a daily basis, he enlisted her help when he became my attending physician.

In the wee hours of the morning, December 18, 2001, a 911 call reported a vehicle engulfed in flames on Interstate 10 just outside the city limits of Los Angeles. No one knew how long the car had been there, but by the time the emergency vehicles arrived, the heat of the flames was so intense that only a shell of the car remained. It was uncertain if anyone was in it, but if they were, they surely could not have survived. To make matters worse, just as the hoses began delivering water to douse the blaze, the car exploded.

It took almost two hours, before the blaze was totally extinguished. The vehicle had been reduced to a mangled heap of metal and ashes revealing the remnants of a body.

In an effort to clear the area before the morning rush hour traffic, firefighters scouted the brush along the road in the hopes of recovering any debris from the explosion. Fifty feet or so down the road, one of the emergency workers suddenly called out, "Over here, hurry over here; we found a child."

I was that child. I was unconscious, but I had suffered no burns. At first, it was uncertain if I had been in the vehicle; but if not, what was a child of about 10-12 years of age doing on the side of the Interstate at that time of night? I had suffered a harsh blow to my head rendering me unconscious.

I was taken to Cedars-Sinai Medical Center where I was evaluated and treated for my head injury. Again I was checked for burns and broken bones; I had none. However, I remained unconscious in a coma for three months into the New Year 2002, and into the beginning of spring.

When I awoke on March 21st, the first person I saw was Julia Jerome at my bedside. I did not know her or where I was; I was confused, but her voice was gentle as she said, "Hello, we've been waiting for you to wake up." I will never forget her smile; a smile that seemed to remind me of someone else but I had no idea who that someone else was.

She summoned Dr. Henry Jerome who arrived with an equally warm smile, and who also commented that he had been waiting for me to wake up.

Although I had been in a coma for three long months, very little had been learned about the vehicle that had been destroyed, and nothing had been learned of the identity of the person who died. It was a female; according to DNA, she was my biological mother; but the list of what was unknown was far longer. The body was so severely burned that no fingerprints were available. DNA was taken from the bones and teeth. In order to identify the body by dental records or x-rays of other body parts, there had to be contact with a family member.

Their conclusions were not certain, but investigators believed the fire was ignited by a leak in the fuel line. Why the car was stopped along the side of the road, how I had gotten out of the car, what caused the injury to my head, and the fact that no one was looking for us remained a mystery.

To complicate matters further, the car and its entire contents were destroyed. Any identifying papers, car registration, clothing, and anything that could identify where the car was licensed or purchased did not survive the fire or the ensuing explosion.

The consensus was that when I woke up, I would have the answers to all their questions, and I could return to my family who was probably sick with worry.

None of their hopes was realized nor mine. I had no memory of my name or age, my mother, where we lived, why I was not in the car. The harder and more intense questions, such as—Why was no one looking for us? Did we belong to no one?— were too sad and too overwhelming for me to comprehend.

I had no memory of anything that happened before that night. I had physical therapy to help me walk again after being in a coma for so long, and after going through a series of cognitive tests, I was pronounced healthy. When the time came for me to be released from Cedars-Sinai, the question arose—where would I go?

Because my memory hadn't returned, I still needed to be monitored medically. I needn't have worried; if anything good came out of that terrible night that changed my life forever, it was my two guardian angels—Julia and Henry Jerome.

They petitioned the court to have me legally placed under their care and took me to live with them in their beautiful Los Angeles home. In the beginning, they had tutors come to the house to evaluate and determine my grade and age so that I could attend school in the fall.

There were little things, bits and pieces that came up from time to time but nothing that could be considered a breakthrough. They had a baby grand piano in the living room, and one day I sat down and began to play. To their delight—I chose to play Clair de Lune indicating that my skill was definitely not that of a beginner.

Our biggest problem was what to call me. I had to have a name if I went to school, and a birth certificate, which proved to be a more complicated matter. When I first went to live with the Jeromes, I began having dreams. I never awoke remembering any of those dreams, but Julia said that I had spoken the name Jodi repeatedly at times in my sleep, so we decided to call me Jodi.

In the fall I entered seventh grade at the local Junior High School, listing my age as 12. They thought it best if I attended a public school, and I agreed. I thrived in my classes and made friends easily; I even had a beau or two. I participated in school activities excluding sports because of my head injury. I went on to high school, graduating with honors.

In all those years, my memory never returned. The dreams stopped long ago. All investigations and searches for a family I might have had gone cold. As a graduation gift, Julia and Henry Jerome became my adoptive parents; my name was now legally Jodi Jerome, and I was issued a Birth

Certificate from the State of California. I looked forward to attending UCLA with the hopes of becoming a Journalist.

I'd like to say that was the happiest day of my life, but I had so many happy days, a great life, and good memories to last a lifetime. But as I grew older, there were always those unanswered questions why was no one looking for me, missing me, or wanting me? When I graduated, finding my early positions as a Journalist unfulfilling, I decided to go freelance, and my career took off. I found my niche in inspirational human-interest stories; stories about real people that I could learn from and help.

The years passed yet my memory failed to return. My father never stopped trying to find new methods or revisit old ones, anything that would possibly prompt me to recall a person, place, or thing. He firmly believed that I was not from the Los Angeles area. He felt strongly that if I returned to where I originally came from, familiar places and things would play a big part in restoring my memory. At one point, we even tried hypnosis. It didn't produce any insight into my past, but once again I mentioned the name Jodi. And as before, I kept repeating the name over and over as over and over I giggled.

I lost my father to COVID-19. I am well aware that I am now alone, but Julia and Henry Jerome will live in my heart forever. I could not have loved them more if they had been my biological parents. Since I have no memory from my past, I owe my very existence to everything I learned from them.

They dedicated their entire lives to helping others, and that is what I have decided to do moving-on. They had the gift to medically help others while I have been blessed with the gift of words—words to help, to heal, to comfort, to hope, and to relate our experiences so that we all know no one is alone; we are all in this together.

As we look to the future, signs are promising that there will be at least one and possibly two vaccines by year's end, and we will be able to move on with our lives.

A part of me will always mourn, just as a part of me will always have memories. I am moving-on to make my mark on the world just as Julia and Henry Jerome did—just as they would want me to do.

There is no better way for me to honor them.

In a matter of days, newspapers all across the country picked up her article. What the investigators and Henry Jerome had strived to do for twenty years, Jodi managed to accomplish with her tribute to her parents.

Sam Meyerson read her article with great interest. While delivering a heartfelt tribute to her parents, she managed to convey to hundreds of thousands across the country that she equated her loss to theirs. He hadn't contacted her when news broke of Henry Jerome's death, but after reading her article and learning that he was her father, he called. Speaking with Jodi at length, he offered her a position as producer for the upcoming year of *Profiles* with emphasis on their 20ᵗʰ Anniversary episode. At her hesitation, he urged her to give it a try for a year, adding that she could continue to freelance articles at will. She agreed.

The promised packet arrived following a phone call Lily Asher had received the previous day from a friend. She anxiously opened it and removed its contents—a copy of the Los Angeles Times dated September 19, 2020, highlighting Jodi's article that she had read with great interest online along with several articles written by Dr. Henry Jerome on blunt force trauma memory loss. She read and reread them with the fervent hope that her twenty-year quest for closure could at long last be coming to an end.

# Chapter 4

One of the most instantly recognizable backdrops in the world, the Manhattan skyline is New York City's shining beacon, designed to impress and inspire. From historical fixtures like the Empire State Building, the Chrysler Building, and the Freedom Tower, this man-made masterpiece dazzles at any time of day or night and from any vantage point in the New York City area.

Lily never tired of waking each morning and looking out onto the city that she called home for most of her life. Even at her advanced age, there was something about the honking cars, the sirens, and the hustle and bustle of the start of a new day that was invigorating.

For the past nine months, the eerie quiet of the most *alive* city in the world was disheartening at best while undermining one's confidence by indicating that there was nothing one could do about it. We dwelled on every broadcast word, every mandate, and every bit of advice from those who were qualified, as well as those who were not. Masks, social distancing, hand sanitizers, COVID testing, and quarantines dominated our new way of life.

When 2020 delivered the promised vaccines, New Yorkers were eager to get in line, get their shots, and start living again. The pulse of the city was ready to start beating once more. Slowing but surely as more and more places began to open—the sounds and sights of the city began to return.

Lily rose early as she usually did. Her meeting with Sam Meyerson had gone better than expected. If her instincts were right, she was about to deliver the blockbuster 20th Anniversary show that he was aiming for and then some. In return, he was enabling her to tie up some unfinished business that had eluded her for two decades. Briefly, it occurred to her that if her instincts weren't right, the outcome could be disastrous, but she quickly dispelled those thoughts. Her gut feelings had seldom been wrong, and what about all those coincidences and fate that she felt brought Sam to her before she approached him?

She planned to spend her day going through what she called one of her *memory boxes*, which was nothing more than a file box filled with papers and objects she saved that were part of certain memories of another time. She had several of these boxes, and from time to time she would reminisce about happier times, when Joe was alive, when Noah was a baby, and even when she first came to America and settled in New York City—it was this box she chose to revisit.

She began taking pictures out of the box and as she leafed through them, she began to smile. There were so many, and she had taken every one of them with the Kodak Camera her mother had given her so many years before, and which was also in the box. Every aspect of her life in America was captured in these very pictures from the very first day she arrived.

September 1947, Lillian Austin arrived in the United States in the city that she would never leave. Arrangements had been made by her uncle in Switzerland to have a friend meet her and help her any way he could. A bank account had been opened in her name at Chase National Bank, and an apartment had been secured for her at The Barbizon, a well-known residential hotel for women on East 63rd Street.

John Shepherd, manager of the largest Manhattan branch of Chase National Bank was a longtime friend of her uncle's. As well as handling her financial affairs, he agreed to help her get settled. Since Lillian was a young lady, he decided to ask his wife to meet with her in an effort to make her feel more at ease in a new country where she had no friends or relatives; it was an excellent choice. Grace Shepherd and Lillian hit it off immediately. Any reservations Grace may have had soon evaporated.

Grace began her indoctrination of the city by starting out on a tour of the immediate area and then branching out beyond Manhattan. During the time they spent together, Grace learned that she was an artist, and that she wanted to open an art studio where she could paint, as well as teach. She learned that for someone so young she was quite accomplished having been educated in Switzerland at the best schools, and that she was fluent in three languages—German, French, and English.

Grace learned that her parents and younger brother had been killed in a rail disaster in Germany in the late 1930s, and that she went to live with her aunt and uncle in Zurich where she lived until the war ended. Her aunt and uncle had discussed going to America, but after her aunt passed, her uncle decided it would be best for him to remain in Switzerland. Europe after the war was not a good place to be, prompting her uncle to urge her to move on and leave the past behind. He emphasized that he was not getting any younger, and pointed out that she had her entire life ahead of her.

Grace was touched by her story. Taking an instant liking to her, she offered to help her accomplish whatever it was she set out to do. They became fast friends, forming a friendship that would last a lifetime.

As Grace escorted Lillian around Manhattan, she quickly observed that she never came to meet her without her Kodak Camera in hand. As they visited each and every landmark, park, museum, other points of interest, or simply the small café where they had lunch, she snapped away capturing it all, leaving none of it to memory.

After they had been on their outings for a couple of months, Lillian showed up with a gift for Grace. It was a small portrait she had painted of her from a photograph taken in Central Park. Grace was amazed—at the likeness, at the detail, and at the depth of her talent. Noting that although the picture was taken in black and white, the painting captured the colors of her facial features and the outfit she wore to a tee, including the background of the park.

Right then and there, Grace announced, the time had come to look for the perfect spot for her studio. She invited her to dinner so they could present their plans to John and seek his advice and support.

At their first meeting, John was impressed by her plans to open her own studio, although she was highly qualified to seek a position at one of the many museums in the city. Lillian's uncle had transferred the account bearing all funds from her parents' assets, and he advised her that if she made good choices, he felt she could afford to carry her expenses until she established a following. He assured her that he was available at all times to discuss and/or explain any questions that may arise.

Grace offered to make inquiries and set up an appointment with a real estate agent to show them what was available. In the meantime, she would ask John for guidance along the way to help determine their boundaries. Of course, they would not commit or sign anything before clearing it with him.

Their first appointment did not go well. Grace wasn't happy with the agent, an elderly gentleman too set in his ways; he clearly looked unfavorably on women who aspired to become proprietors. He felt they lacked the business acumen to be successful and were merely pursuing a whim. To make matters worse, he so much as told them so. Grace politely thanked him and firmly told him they had no further need of his services.

Their second appointment was a complete reversal. Rich Harrison was young and the newest addition to his family's real estate business. He had recently leased several properties to up-and-coming entrepreneurs, and when he heard what they were looking for, he immediately told them that West Village was *THE* place for Lillian's studio. He knew of a couple of spots that were currently available, but if one of the two was not to their liking, he assured them that new listings came on the market daily.

Grace picked up on the fact that his priority was finding the perfect location for his clients. They left Rich's office and set out for the Village. Lillian was totally excited, and had her camera in hand so she could capture it all. And that is exactly what she did, actually running out of film. When she asked Rich if there was a place nearby where she could purchase more, he reminded her that she could return at any time to take more shots, if in fact she chose the area for her studio.

West Village is a neighborhood in the western section of Greenwich Village in Lower Manhattan, New York City. In the late 1940s, West Village was well on its way to becoming an important landmark on the map of American Bohemian culture.

The area was known as an artist's neighborhood with eclectic and avant-garde residents, and the alternative culture they propagated. Due in large part to the progressive attitudes of many of its residents, the Village was destined to become a focal point of new movements and ideas, whether political, artistic, or cultural, where small presses, art galleries, and experimental theater thrived.

Known as *Little Bohemia*, West Village became the epicenter for the American Bohemia movement of the early and mid-20th century. Home to quaint tree-lined streets you would never imagine in New York City, an overabundance of restaurants, bars, cafés, and so much more. Washington Square Park was so delightful, they chose to stop for a brief rest, and then it was on to Caffé Reggio for lunch.

The two properties that Rich showed them were both good choices for what Lillian was seeking. However, the corner location had much more to offer. In addition to the exposure of the larger corner location, it offered an ample area for her gallery, a back area on the ground floor where she could set up a workplace to paint, and a loft above where she envisioned setting up her art classes.

As she walked about the space, she thought that she could perhaps make the front gallery portion smaller allowing a larger work area in the back, as well as setting up a dark room where she could develop her own film.

In addition, the second floor of the building housed an apartment currently under lease, but when it became available down the road, could be considered for expansion or living quarters. As she shared her enthusiastic envisions for her studio, Lillian's excitement soon encompassed Grace and Rich. She deemed the location and the property as close to perfect as she could get. As they hugged and danced around the room, she kept thanking Rich and Grace for all they had done for her. It was only the beginning.

Rich told her he would draw up the papers, and he would be in touch once he finalized everything with the owner of the building.

Lillian stared at the next picture—Bonnie's Stonewall Inn where they had made one last stop for a celebratory toast, recalling she had taken the picture on a return trip because she had run out of film that day.

In the weeks that followed, she returned often to West Village to take pictures. A brief rest, lunch at Caffé Reggio, and back to photographing shops she had missed on that first visit became routine. These pictures represented the subjects of the first paintings that she displayed in the gallery for her opening.

The next pile of pictures revealed those she took at her first Thanksgiving dinner with John and Grace, her first Christmas Season in New York, and the Christmas Party at the Barbizon with her very first friends in her new home.

Rich Harrison actually met with John Shepherd before delivering the papers to Lillian. He wanted to be certain that what he presented to her would not be shot down, disappointing her. He recalled her excitement at first seeing the space and how her eyes lit up as she described how she envisioned her studio. She had even chosen a name—*Portraits by Lillian*; she had faith in him, and he was determined not to let her down.

Rich went all out for Lillian with the owner of the building stating that his proposed tenant was a good investment with long-term possibilities. For the most part, properties came on the market daily, and he was well aware of that. John's suggestions to slightly reduce the rent, sign a one-year lease, and an option to extend the lease for an additional four years with no increase were ultimately agreed upon, and Lillian was on her way to realizing her dream.

It was November, and with the Thanksgiving and Christmas holidays coming, Lillian made a spring opening of her studio her goal. Although she was given access to the space as soon as the Lease was signed, her rent would not commence until December 1st. She was well aware it was not a good time to be looking for contractors to create her studio, but Rich had a few people in mind who just might be interested in earning some extra cash for Christmas.

He called a friend whose father ran one of the biggest construction companies in New York and asked if he could help. They had ample company employees, but whenever additional help was needed, they hired independent workers to pick up the slack.

With list in hand, Rich set out to help Lillian interview prospects. She particularly liked a young man who seemed to grasp what she envisioned for the space and even offered a few suggestions that she definitely thought about considering. She also liked the fact that he gave her a price to complete the job, as opposed to an hourly wage, and felt that he would be more apt to finish in a timely manner. Donny Collins was her choice.

For the next couple of weeks, she spent a lot of time with Donny making decisions about flooring, wall coverings, and furnishings for her workplace and the loft where she would be holding classes. Following Thanksgiving weekend, work began in earnest.

The Kodak Company in Rochester, New York, debuted its first Kodak camera in 1888. It came pre-loaded with enough film for 100 exposures and could easily be carried and handheld during operation. *"You press the button, we do the rest!"* became the company's promise in their advertising slogan.

After the film was exposed—all 100 shots taken—the entire camera was returned to the Kodak Company in Rochester where the film was developed, prints made, a new roll of film inserted in the camera and returned to the customer for the cycle to begin anew.

In 1935, Kodak revolutionized color photography with their refined coloring process using three layers of emulsion on a single base that captured the red, green, and blue wavelengths—labeling it *Kodachrome* film. The processing of the film was quite involved, but Kodak kept with their motto of *"You press the button, we do the rest!"* and simply had their customers mail back their finished rolls for prints/slides.

By the late 1940s, Kodachrome film could be purchased and developed locally.

For her very first Thanksgiving, Lillian was invited to Grace and John's for dinner with all the fixings. It was a wonderful day; a day like she had never experienced before. There were twenty people at the table, friends and relatives, and the food was so delicious, she savored every bite.

Lillian was slightly embarrassed when Grace made an announcement about the upcoming opening of her studio, but everyone seemed genuinely interested, and she quickly found herself speaking openly and easily conveying her excitement in becoming a proprietor.

When the evening ended and everyone had gone, Grace and John told her they had a present for her. It was a new Kodak Camera and an ample supply of Kodachrome film. Lillian was overwhelmed. John told her he would help her with directions if need be, but he was certain she was more than capable of figuring out how to insert the film herself. It also came with a flash attachment for indoor shots.

Donny was true to his word. He hired a helper to reconfigure the layout of the space, but once the walls were in place, and the new flooring was laid, he completed the remainder of the work himself. Christmas was still a week away when he called Lillian seeking her approval of *Portraits by Lillian*—her new studio in West Village.

They made plans to meet the next morning at 10:00 am. Lillian eagerly called Grace and asked her to join them; she in turn urged John to come, as well. She then placed a call to Rich, whose help and advice had been invaluable. She never could have accomplished so much so soon without his guidance. She considered him her new friend, the first real friend she made in America, other than Grace and John and the few women she met at the Barbizon.

What a wonderful morning it was. December in New York was usually colder and many days could even be overcast, but not on her special day—the sun was brightly shining and the temperature was in the mid-forties. Donny unlocked the door and stepped aside allowing them to enter. Everyone was in awe at the beautiful job he had done.

*Portraits by Lillian* from the beautiful new double front doors with coach lanterns on either side to the big picture window to the polished wood flooring to the ornate wood railing leading up the steps to the loft—to the back rooms which included her workplace to paint, a small bathroom, and kitchen area. It was perfect, even better than she had envisioned. It was simple yet classy; it was elegant yet welcoming; it was her dream; and now, it was reality.

At first, everyone was quiet simply absorbing it all, and then all hell broke loose. They were laughing and crying and couldn't believe how wonderful it had all turned out. Without warning, bottles of champagne appeared out of nowhere as toast after toast continued until the last one from Rich declared Lillian had officially become *Lily* and her studio had become *Portraits by Lily.*

There was still the matter of paint supplies and canvasses for her work area, and furnishings and supplies for her art classes, which she planned to take care of as soon as possible.

With her new camera and film in hand, she returned to West Village day after day taking color photographs of the places she chose. While the film was being developed, she purchased her art supplies, chairs and easels for the loft, and searched for a framer to work with once her paintings were finished. She found a small shop two blocks from her studio; Louis turned out to be a real find becoming her one and only framer.

The weeks flew by and into the New Year, Lily spent endless hours painting. She chose the eclectic makeup of West Village as her subjects; and by the time spring approached, the walls were filled with the storefronts of many of her neighboring merchants, Washington Square Park, theatres, schools—all in and around *Portraits by Lily.*

The last pictures she removed from the box were taken at the Grand Opening. They were all black and white. Because color photography was quite expensive, she only used it for her portraits. It was early March 1948, not quite spring, but it was a beautiful day. To say that the opening was a success could hardly describe what happened. Beyond everyone's wildest imagination, there was a steady stream of visitors from noon when the doors opened until 6:00 pm that evening when the last guest left.

Lily stared at the very last picture in the box depicting three of her paintings. They were all that were left. Once the first merchant inquired if the paintings were for sale, everyone who was fortunate enough to have had their establishment included purchased their own. Even the schools and other galleries followed suit.

Everyone had gone including Grace and John, but Rich offered to remain and help her clean up. There had been light refreshments and champagne throughout the afternoon, but a quick trip to the trash bin out back and clearing out the table and few chairs only took a short time.

Lily began returning items to the box—the photographs each in their separate groupings including the color photos of the paintings she did for the opening, and of course the Kodak Camera her mother had given her so long ago. What wonderful memories they all were, but she didn't need to go through the contents to recall any of it. Those wonderful times would forever be etched in her mind.

There were no pictures of later that evening. After closing up the studio and joking about having to get back to painting to refill the walls of the gallery, Rich insisted on taking her to dinner. He opted to go to one of his favorite spots in Manhattan where the drinks were generous and the food amazing.

It had truly been a wonderful day.

As they were leaving, Rich ran into a friend. He introduced them— Lily as his new friend to his forever friend having grown up with him—Joe Asher.

# Chapter 5

Sam Meyerson fondly recalled meeting Jodi Jerome at a wedding he attended in Los Angeles. He was standing at the bar with a friend, when he looked up and saw her approaching them. It turned out she wasn't approaching them at all; she was simply approaching the bar for a drink. As she walked past them, Sam's eyes followed her.

She was quite beautiful, tall, long dark hair, piercing blue eyes—not in the least how one envisioned a California girl who was usually blond whether it was natural or otherwise. Maybe she wasn't a California girl, just a visitor from out of state like he was.

As luck would have it, they were seated at the same table. Finding himself seated next to her allowed him to open a conversation and much to his surprise, learned she was a journalist. She seemed fascinated by his work at **PBS**, and she told him so, adding that she was a fan of *Profiles of New York* even though she had never been to New York.

She further told him that she had recently gone freelance, and had written several articles that were picked up by New York media outlets. Although Sam's first incline towards her was anything but, they spent the entire evening discussing business. By the time the evening ended, he convinced her to have dinner with him the next day where they continued their discussion, and learned they were both Dodger fans—Sam through his avid Dodger-fan father and all the memorabilia that he passed on to him. Albeit he was a Brooklyn Dodger fan in absentia while she was a Los Angeles Dodger fan, he viewed it as another connection.

Sam flew back to Manhattan the following day with Jodi's promise to contact him if she ever found herself in New York; that never happened. It didn't stop Sam from thinking about her or wondering what she was up to. In turn, Sam had no occasion to travel to Los Angeles.

It had been almost five years since his last relationship had ended. He dated from time to time, but there had never been anyone who caught his eye; that is until the wedding. Considering his last breakup was a result of his 24/7 work ethics, he began to mull over the fact that since they were in the same line of business, this time things could be different. He began instead searching for a way to get her to come east—on business of course.

Nancy Reagan died of congestive heart failure on March 6, 2016, at the age of 94. She was laid to rest at the Reagan Presidential Library with her husband.

For the first time since *Profiles of New York* aired in 2011, Sam received requests to dedicate an episode—all were for Nancy Reagan, citing a little known fact that she was born Anne Frances Robbins in New York City.

When her Mother remarried a prominent neurosurgeon, Loyal Davis, in 1929, she moved to Chicago. In 1931, Loyal adopted *Nancy*, a nickname she acquired early on, and she became Nancy Davis.

The show's determination to steer clear of politics left Sam with somewhat of a dilemma. After thinking it through, he decided that he would dedicate an episode to Nancy Reagan the private citizen, not the First Lady, excluding all politics. It would be about her contributions to women's causes, her drug awareness campaign, and after her husband's diagnosis of Alzheimer's disease, her strong advocacy for finding a cure. Her causes were far reaching and touched many Americans.

Immediately, Jodi Jerome came to mind. Hoping she could provide some input about her life in California, he gave her a call. She was quite happy to hear from him, and without hesitation accepted the assignment. Ten days later, she called to tell him she was sending him ample background that he could choose from, and asked him to let her know if there was anything else he needed.

Not only was he impressed by the detail of her research, but also by the fact that she had gathered so much more than he anticipated, managed to tie a good deal of it to New York, all in such a short period of time. He called her to thank her, and ended up by inviting her to come east to observe firsthand what it takes to produce an episode of *Profiles*. She accepted. By the next morning, he emailed her travel itinerary, and told her he would personally be there to meet her at JFK Airport.

Since that first visit, she had collaborated on two additional episodes. One was profiling *The Tonight Show*; a longtime New York staple broadcast from NBC Studios in Rockefeller Center—a tradition interrupted by decades of originating from various studios in Los Angeles until finally returning to New York in 2014. The other was profiling *The Honeymooners*; one of television's first shows to portray working-class married couples set in the Kramden's kitchen in a neglected Brooklyn apartment building. The Stars of the show were born in New York—Jackie Gleason was a Brooklyn-born comedian, and Art Carney was born in Mount Vernon.

It had been over three years since he had seen Jodi in person. On his way to the airport to pick her up, he wondered if she had changed. Since he had seen her last, she had lost both her parents, and had to deal with settling their estate during a pandemic that was ongoing and unending. Now she was moving on with her life and moving east at his request. He fervently hoped everything would work out for the best and that she would find her niche and happiness in New York.

He spotted her immediately as she came down the escalator to the baggage area where he told her he would meet her. She was as beautiful as he remembered even with a mask on her face, and her hair was shorter. They collected her luggage and exited to the car Sam had waiting for them.

They had both tested negative for COVID 24 hours previously, and once they were in a private car, they removed their masks.

Sam sat back and said, "How was your flight?"

"The best way I can describe it is *empty*. We had to wear masks, but we were served drinks, and I spent the time alternating between reading and sleeping. There was no one in the seat beside me, so I could spread out a little. It wasn't the greatest but it wasn't that bad."

Sam responded, "I haven't flown since the pandemic. With the show based in New York, my travel is mostly for vacationing. The onset of the pandemic with all it's restrictions and mandates took care of that."

"So Sam, tell me a little about what I've gotten myself into. Where am I going to live? I hope you're planning on giving me a tour of what's going to be home for at least the next year."

Sam laughed. "It doesn't sound too good the way you describe it, but I promise you I have not taken your faith in me lightly. I think you will be happy with the living arrangements I have made for you, and not only do I plan to give you a tour of the area where you will be living and working but where accessible, I plan to take you to some of the New York landmarks we have profiled, as well as some we are considering for future episodes.

"After you're settled and rest up a bit, we will have dinner. I also have someone I want you to meet who is very special to me. I've done my homework, and you can rest assured that for the rest of 2020, I will be showing off my city at the best it can be for now.

Next week is Thanksgiving, and then comes the Christmas season and New Year's Eve and Day which is when New York is at its finest. Of course, everything will be scaled back, way back because of the pandemic. We will be watching the Macy's Thanksgiving Parade on television, but we will be able to see the annual tree lighting in Rockefeller Plaza in person, and New Year's Eve and Day are yet to be determined."

"Wow. Looks like I'm going to be pretty busy which honestly is what I hoped for. Losing my Dad hit me pretty hard. When my Mom died, my Dad and I had each other to lean on, and we were only days away from leaving on a planned trip to Hawaii. I have begun the process of settling the estate; working with his attorney who was also his best friend made it a lot easier for me to make some hard decisions that I never anticipated having to deal with. When the time is right, we will sell."

"Dare I say that you are planning to stay in New York longer than a year?"

It was Jodi's turn to laugh. "Not so fast. I'm keeping my Condo for now. I feel good about what I did decide to sell: my parents' house is much too big for one person, the upkeep alone is expensive; I don't think I'll have any need for the house in Malibu, our getaway place; or a number of other items like our boat that we hadn't used since my Mom died. Holding on to things I will never use just doesn't make any sense, especially when his attorney told me my Dad had made plans to sell some of his holdings when we returned from our trip."

Suddenly Jodi grew quiet. "I'm sorry for going on and on. There's no way that you could have known that we had planned a trip to Hawaii for some much needed rest and relaxation. We were due to leave only days after Dad was diagnosed with COVID, and on the day he died, we would have been in Hawaii. In truth, neither of us had stopped grieving the loss of my Mom, and the trip was our first step in moving on."

Without thinking, he reached for her and drew her into an embrace; realizing he may have overstepped; he quickly released her and moved back over on the seat.

"I am so sorry for your losses. Though it is in no way comparable to what you have endured, when my Dad died, I was lost for a long time. He was fit and healthy, never smoked or drank to excess yet at the age of 55, he had a massive heart attack and died two days later. We were not only father and son but also best friends, and I was extremely close to him. It was my wise Mom who finally set me straight although I'm quite close to her as well.

"I gave a lot of thought to the promise I made to find you a place to stay that would be convenient to the office yet in an area I thought you might enjoy. I considered location, amenities close by, and above all privacy. In truth, we don't know each other very well, something I hope will be a part of the past in short order, so at first it was a bit perplexing second-guessing myself every inch of the way.

"Thankfully, my #1 go-to advisor came through for me, as always, and I hope you will be pleased with my choice. If not, there are endless vacancies in the city since the pandemic, and you can pick and choose until you find a place to your liking."

"Sam when you get to know me better, you'll learn that I'm really quite down to earth, and although I've led a privileged life, my parents raised me to appreciate what we had and not take anything for granted. Their words were certainly not wasted on me, considering how they came into my life and gave me a life filled with love, happiness, and support. I can't even begin to imagine what my life would have been like without Henry and Julia Jerome."

Sam felt the sincerity in her words. "Well that is one more thing we have in common; I too have led a privileged life. Growing up, my parents' involvement in and commitment to endless charity organizations and community events never ceased to amaze me. Losing two dear friends on 9/11 prompted them to get involved wherever they were needed, and though my father is no longer here, my mother continues their dedication and support.

"I mentioned wanting you to meet someone who is very special to me; that person is my Mom—Trudy Meyerson; she is also my #1 go-to advisor. A couple of weeks ago at dinner as we were catching up on things, I asked if she had any suggestions to help find you a place. Without hesitation, she did; it all made sense; and just like that my dilemma was resolved.

"My Mom lives at the Pavilion on the Upper East Side, one of the finest rental residences in New York City. After Dad died, she decided to sell their house in Westchester and move to the city where she has many friends. She also purchased a condo in Naples, Florida where she spends at least four months of the year, and she's usually in the Hamptons for a month during the summer. I'm here, and she thinks there's no place better than Manhattan in the fall and during the Christmas season, so she rents a condo at the Pavilion. No matter where she is physically, she is constantly working on her *projects*, as she calls them.

"It was her suggestion that you stay at her condo. The location is perfect; it's a fully furnished two-bedroom unit with a study, and virtually has everything you need including a cleaning service. Thanksgiving is about two weeks away, and she will be leaving for Florida the following weekend. With you staying at the apartment, she won't have to cancel anything while she's away, and in turn, everything is ready and waiting for you.

"The building's amenities are endless: 24-hour Doorman, Shopping Arcade, Grocery Store, Fitness Center, Cleaning and Laundry Valet, Spa Salon, and a shuttle to the Lexington Avenue and Second Avenue Q subway stops. Oh, and did I mention the awesome views?

'How does that sound so far?"

"How does that sound? It sounds magnificent, extremely generous, unbelievable, like you're doing your very best to get me to stay in New York City permanently, and like I'm going to owe you big time!"

They both laughed and the banter between them for the rest of their ride was light and uplifting and just what Jodi needed.

Their car pulled up in front of the building, and as Jodi walked through the door that Lester the doorman held open for her, she took it all in trying her best not to appear like this was her first-time visit to the big city. After all, she came from Los Angeles, which was not exactly a small town.

In the elevator, Sam pressed the button for the 23rd Floor. They walked to Trudy's condo at the far end of the hall. She greeted them with open arms, asking a million questions. "How was your flight? On your ride in, did Sam point out any landmarks, restaurants, or take you by his office?

"Just listen to me. You must think I'm terrible. Please come in, and make yourself at home. Sam, please put Jodi's things in the guest room and show her around the apartment. Then Jodi you can freshen up a bit, and we can visit awhile, have a drink, and enjoy a few snacks."

"That sound like a plan. Follow me Jodi; right this way."

After taking her through the apartment, he left her to freshen up or rest for a while, telling her that they would be in the living room waiting for her whenever she was ready.

When Sam walked into the kitchen where Trudy was busy putting an assortment of cheeses, crackers, dips, and fruit on a platter, she was humming. She looked up smiling and simply said, "I like her. Considering all you have told me she's been through, at first glance there seems to be nothing pretentious about her."

Handing him the platter she prepared, she said, "Sam you can put this on the coffee table; I'm right behind you with napkins and glasses. We can sit and chat a bit until Jodi joins us."

They didn't have to wait long. "Trudy, your condo is not only beautiful but warm and welcoming, as are you and Sam. I don't know how to thank you for your generosity and hospitality or how I can ever repay you."

"No repayment necessary; learning to love New York as we do would be the best *Thank You* of all." Picking up a glass, Trudy asked, "May I pour you a glass of wine? And please, have some snacks. I don't imagine you've eaten since earlier today."

"You're right. Actually I haven't eaten anything. Coffee and juice is about all I've had. Wine sounds great." She reached for a small plate and filled it with cheeses, crackers, and fruit.

"I'm certain that Sam has a full schedule planned for you, but as woman-to-woman, I have a suggestion that's going to delay his plans a bit. I don't know if he told you his nickname for me—#1 go-to advisor—but I'm invoking it here and now."

Neither Sam nor Jodi said a word; Trudy continued. "In ten days, it will be Thanksgiving and shortly thereafter, I will be leaving for Naples, so this is what I am proposing with the hope of accomplishing everything I have in mind in two days.

"First and foremost, a shopping spree. It's colder here in New York than in LA, and about to get much colder. You definitely need sweaters, jackets, a coat, shoes, and boots, etc. The weather can be quite pleasant today and a snowstorm tomorrow can shut down the city in a New York minute!

"Although we're never finished shopping, when we have what we feel is good for now, I'd like to point out places such as hair and nail salons, and the like that you might like to try. And, I'd like us to get to know each other a little better before I leave. Am I being selfish?"

Sam and Jodi both laughed. "Mom, Thank You. I think your suggestions are spot on. I wouldn't know where to take Jodi shopping, and I think you're quite aware of that."

"You both are quite amusing. I have to admit that I never thought about a shopping trip with Sam; on the other hand, a shopping spree with you Trudy sounds like an adventure—an adventure that I haven't had since my Mom died. I could really use one right now as I embark on my new job in my new city. It sounds amazing, and I can't wait. Thank you for offering."

For the remainder of the afternoon, they talked about so many things. They just drifted from one subject to another with such ease one would think they were longtime friends.

Since most of the restaurants in the city were operating at 50% or less and the weather was no longer conducive to dining outdoors, they ordered in. They were never at a loss for words; Jodi asked many questions about New York, about the show, and even about the building that she would call home for the next few months.

It had been a long day. Sam noticed that Jodi was growing tired, so he decided to bid them goodnight. "I'm taking my leave. Hope you have a super day tomorrow shopping and enjoying lunch at one of the many great eating spots that are open. I'll touch base with you tomorrow, and we can plan to meet up for dinner."

Sam let himself out, and walked down the hall to his condo.

"Jodi, come with me and I'll show you where the towels are, the shampoo, and anything else you might need. Please feel free to make yourself tea or coffee; there's bottled water in the fridge, and there's yogurt too. If you have a sweet tooth, there's leftover dessert, and I always have chocolate chip cookies in a jar on the counter—an old habit from when Sam was a little boy.

"While we're out tomorrow, we can stock up on your favorites, if you like."

"Trudy, it seems as though you've thought of everything. I'm perfectly happy; yogurt and chocolate chip cookies are high on my list of favorites too. I know I've had a long day and with the time change, I am ready for bed. But with that said, I'm an early riser, so whenever you want to get started tomorrow is fine with me. I'm really excited about getting to see and know New York.

"I feel a little guilty about abandoning Sam on my very first full day here, and I hope we can get together for dinner tomorrow as he suggested. What I would really like to do is take the two of you to dinner. I know it's not easy dining out, but if there's a certain favorite place where we could get a reservation, I would be most appreciative."

"There is, and I will give them a call right now. If I'm successful, I'll call Sam."

"How far does he live? Would he be home yet?"

Surprised, Trudy said, "Oh, he didn't tell you? Sam lives down the hall."

# Chapter 6

One of the most widely distributed and imitated images in the world, the *I Love New York Logo*—consisting of an upper-case *I*, followed by a *red heart symbol*, and then the upper-case letters *N* and *Y*, set in the rounded slab serif typeface American Typewriter—was created by graphic designer Milton Glaser and first introduced in 1977 to promote the city and state.

New York had gone through hard times in the 1970s—crime was at an all-time high, while tourism was at an all-time low; in 1975, President Ford denied federal assistance to save New York City from bankruptcy; and 1977 saw a widespread blackout that led to extensive looting and 4,500 arrests. Tourists stayed away from the city as a result of the negative publicity that followed.

The New York State Department for Economic Development tapped Madison Avenue advertising firm Wells Rich Greene to create a tourist-friendly campaign to encourage visitors to *The Big Apple*.

The Agency quickly developed the central components of the campaign—they had a slogan, a jingle, and a television commercial yet they lacked a logo. Enter Milton Glaser whose portfolio up to that point included Bob Dylan enclosed in the singer's greatest hits album; the design of *New York Magazine*, which he founded in 1968; and the visual identity of the restaurant in the World Trade Center.

Glaser was recruited by the Department for Economic Development to meet with Wells Rich Greene about logo options for the new campaign. During the meeting, Glaser pulled a crumpled piece of paper from his pocket with a doodle he'd done on the back of an envelope during a recent cab ride where he had scribbled the logo we know today. Glaser did the work entirely pro bono, to help the city rise again.

Sam was determined to put the next couple of days to good use while Jodi and his mother were off on a mission to take care of getting Jodi settled into becoming a New Yorker.

He was working from home. Piles of scripts from past episodes, testimonials from a myriad of anyone and everyone who had any connection to 9/11, and historical facts about the buildings and events lay spread out before him. In reality, it was a great opportunity to get organized and come up with a plan for him and Jodi to begin working on the all-important 9/11 episode of *Profiles of New York.*

Sam was too organized not to have a plan all along, but after meeting with several people on his original list that didn't materialize, he felt the need to change his perspective and come up with one person whose blockbuster story could deliver the show he was seeking. With Thanksgiving only ten days away, he decided to bring Jodi into the loop, go through previous episodes dedicated to 9/11, and hopefully a new set of eyes would see what he was missing. This would allow his mother and Jodi ample time to accomplish their errands, and allow him to have an office set up for Jodi in Trudy's study.

Plans for a nice quiet Thanksgiving Dinner at home were already in place; and his mother was due to fly to Florida Sunday following the holiday, leaving that Monday as the perfect day for Jodi to begin her new job.

As he began leafing through the first pile of papers, he came across an article about the State Anthem of New York. *I Love New York* was written and composed by Steve Karmen in 1977 as part of the advertising campaign. In 1980, Governor Hugh Carey declared it as New York's state anthem, although it was not officially enacted into law. Karmen, who was well known for retaining the publishing rights to his songs, gave the rights to the anthem to the state for free. He wrote a new verse for the song during the height of the COVID-19 Pandemic in New York City to emphasize the city's resilience. It was never commercially recorded or used.

As he tackled pile after pile, he jotted down notes of how to open the show, musing all the while just where to put the emphasis. Of course, first and foremost, he had to come up with *the person* whose story would be profiled; he would ask Jodi for her input—a good place for them to begin. In the meantime, he would take Jodi to the office, introduce her to everyone she would be working with, and give her a feel of how an episode materializes.

Glancing at his watch, he decided to take a lunch break. Anxious to begin going through the boxes he had brought home, he had bypassed having breakfast. Throughout the morning, all that he had consumed were three large mugs of coffee.

He made himself a roast beef sandwich and grabbed the bag of potato chips placing them both on the Island in the kitchen. After retrieving a beer from the refrigerator, he sat down, and as he ate, he began going over in his mind where New York was when 2020 began and where New York was now.

There was no doubt about it, 2020 was a tumultuous year overtaken by a presidential election during a global pandemic and racial injustice protests. What made 2020 unprecedented wasn't that it was a year of a pandemic—we've had pandemics before and handled them far better with far less resources—or that a President was impeached, or that there were massive marches for racial justice across the country, or that there was a disputed election. What made it unprecedented was that they all happened in the same year. From the tragic to the confounding to the ongoing and seemingly unending, Sam could never remember a time when we needed hope more than now.

In early January 2020, the World Health Organization confirmed a coronavirus-related pneumonia in Wuhan, China; days later the President's Impeachment Trial began in the Senate; days later the first case of COVID-19 in the US was confirmed; days later Trump established the White House Coronavirus Task Force; days later WHO announced a COVID-19 global health emergency; and the month ended with Trump imposing travel restrictions to and from China.

February brought an acquittal of Trump's Impeachment Trial; the DOW began its coronavirus crash—its drop over the following six weeks would result in the most devastating since 1929; and the first COVID-19 death in the US in CA.

March 11th, WHO declared COVID-19 a *Pandemic*. The lockdown, business and school closures, cancelled sports and entertainment venues, and people mandated to stay home, distance themselves from others, and wear masks at all times ushered in our new norm. Sam recalled standing outside his office building and looking down an empty street one would never believe was New York City.

What was thought would be a short lockdown until we got a handle on things dragged on and on with no end in sight. By the end of May the COVID-19 death toll in the US surpassed 100,000. In early June, the number of confirmed COVID-19 cases in the US hit 2 million and within a month reached 3 million.

The first case of COVID-19 in New York was confirmed on March 1st, and the state quickly became an epicenter of the pandemic, with a record 12,274 new cases reported the beginning of April; by the 10$^{th}$ of the month New York had more confirmed cases than any country outside the US, and had the highest number of cases than any state until July when they were surpassed by CA. Approximately half of the state's cases were in New York City where nearly half of the state's population resides.

The state's response to the pandemic began with a full lockdown from March-April 2020, followed by a four-phrase reopening plan by region from April-July 2020. Modifications were imposed as the state learned more about the pandemic and dramatically increased its testing capacity through both public and private labs. The workforce that could work from home was encouraged to do so, as was remote schooling.

Throughout the summer and into fall, tensions were high, and everyone's frustrations came to the forefront. Crime was up all over the state; demonstrations for and against everything were rampant; and although many places had opened at reduced capacity, the people wanted more. When news came that two vaccines were approved and vaccinations would begin in December, it was viewed as a Christmas Miracle—the hope long awaited.

Sam realized that his lunch break and mental analysis of what happened in 2020 had stretched into an hour. It was the first time he actually looked at the past months in such a way, and he thought about what parts if any should he include in the program he was planning.

He cleaned up from lunch and returned to the background information he had neatly placed in piles. Try as he may, he found it impossible to focus on how to proceed with the show. Instead, for the remainder of the afternoon, he could not shake his thoughts about how the pandemic had affected New York and so many people he knew and loved, which now included Jodi.

Unable to get back to the job at hand, he suddenly realized that his thoughts had veered way off course. COVID-19 was not an issue; *Profiles* continued to air new episodes throughout the lockdown. He was well aware that every major network had *specials* in the works for the 20$^{th}$ Anniversary, and truthfully, he expected no less. In all probability, the ceremonies and events that would be downsized and scaled back were those involving large gatherings even though they were held outdoors.

He began straightening up a bit by returning the files he wasn't planning on using back into one of the boxes, and arranging the remaining files into three piles that he planned on sharing with Jodi, outlining introductions, formats and closings in previous episodes. He glanced at the time and decided to take a shower and get dressed for dinner. It was after 5:00 pm, and their reservation was at 7:00 pm; he should be hearing from them soon.

When his mother and Jodi returned to the condo, he was quite pleased with what he had accomplished even though he had taken a slight detour. Jodi called to tell him they were home, and that their reservations had been made at Doc Watson's. It was a clear brisk evening and since the restaurant was a little more than half a mile up the street, they decided to walk.

Doc Watson's was a favorite of Sam's—European pub style American dishes—that never disappointed. Since the pandemic, both their limited indoor and heated outdoor settings were winners.

Once they were seated and had ordered drinks, Sam said, "OK, let's have it. Tell me all about your day and how much of New York you got to see."

Jodi laughed. "Well, I got to see more than I would have imagined, however, Trudy tells me we've only just begun. I did get in some much-needed shopping for warmer clothes, and we had lunch at L'Avenue."

"Great place. You couldn't have had a better guide. My Mom knows all the best places in the city. I was certain she would take you shopping to her favorite store—Saks Fifth Avenue.

"I'm pleased that you had a nice day and that the two of you got the chance to know one another a little more before Mom leaves for Florida.

"I wouldn't describe my day as having fun, but I did get my thoughts organized and I'm ready to begin working whenever you are. I have decided, however, that part of your orientation to becoming a New Yorker should be to see as much of, and get as much of a feel for the city that will be your home for the next year as possible. There are limitations because of the pandemic and some places may still not be open, but many are and we can concentrate on those.

The following two weeks flew by, and true to his word, Sam took Jodi to many of the places they had profiled; some were open while others were not, but she absorbed it all and learned much more than she thought possible. In doing so, they grew closer each and every day—which was good for both of them.

Thanksgiving Dinner was relaxing and fun, and to Jodi, it felt like *family*. She really needed to feel that *feeling* again, and amazingly although she had only been in New York a little more than two weeks, she was pleasantly surprised that it was beginning to feel like home.

After Trudy left for Florida, they began working on the show in earnest. Sam took her to the office and introduced her to Greg and Carol—the in-house producers, to Lou, Frank, and Edie—their researchers, and to Sandy—their girl Friday. Greg and Carol were husband and wife, as were Frank and Edie, and Lou and Sandy, as well. Greg, Frank, Lou, and Carol were longtime friends of Sam's; they grew up together. It was only natural that he sought them out when he began assembling a team for *Profiles*.

The beginning of December saw the rollout of the Pfizer vaccine followed soon after by Moderna as New York led the way—the elderly and health workers were at the top of the list. Both Jodi and Sam were among the first to be vaccinated, Jodi for underlying medical reasons—Sam because of his volunteering at one of the local clinics since the onset of the pandemic.

Sam hosted Christmas Dinner at his condo for his office staff—anyone whose family wasn't local or didn't want to put up with the hassles of travel restrictions, and it turned out to be a great day. They exchanged silly gifts; ate and drank the day away; and had so much fun that they decided to do it again for New Year's Eve.

All in all, 2020 ended on a high note, with hope that COVID would soon be a thing of the past. In two short weeks, they would be fully vaccinated and hopefully, businesses would begin to reopen at higher capacities.

It was the first week of January 2021, while Jodi was working with Greg and Carol, that as Sam sat in his office thinking about what was turning into somewhat of a dilemma, his eyes came to rest on a portrait of himself that had been a gift to him from his dear friend Lily Asher.

Lily, who lost her son Noah when the first plane flew into the North Tower of the World Trade Center, had participated in previous episodes but had never been profiled. Sam always had a gut feeling that there was much more to her story, but until now, he had never pursued it. Maybe, just maybe the time had come to test the waters and learn if his gut feeling was right.

# Chapter 7

Sam's meeting with Lily had gone better than he expected, and once again, he gave all the credit to his gut feeling. Although, he and Jodi had dinner the previous evening, he decided to gather his thoughts before he discussed Lily's requests for the show.

He woke early and decided to go for a long walk to clear his mind and outline a strategy to move forward. He and Jodi had made plans to meet around 9:00 am to discuss her meeting the previous day with Greg and Carol, after which he planned to tell her about his meeting with Lily.

On his way back from his walk, he stopped at the corner coffee shop, and picked up two lattes and two blueberry muffins. He texted Jodi that even though it was not yet 9:00 am, he came bearing *goodies* and asked if she was available to meet in five minutes. She texted him back immediately: lol—for goodies, absolutely!

As they sat sipping lattes and nibbling blueberry muffins, Jodi filled Sam in on her meeting with Greg and Carol, Sam's in-house producers, who introduced her to what actually went into producing an episode. She was quite excited, stating that she had never produced anything—her experience having been solely in writing. However, although she was certainly up to learning something new, she added that she was such a big fan of *Profiles of New York* that she was willing to offer her expertise and experience wherever it was needed to assure that the Anniversary Show of 9/11 became the blockbuster Sam envisioned.

For the next half hour, Jodi sat quietly, as Sam filled her in on Lily Asher and the meeting he had with her the previous day. He told her how they had met ten years previous, and how a friendship between them had grown. Truth be told, Sam admitted that he was somewhat fascinated by her story—how she had come to America, a young girl with no family or friends with only a dream to build a life for herself after losing her family in Austria during the early months of the war.

She was fortunate that her uncle had friends in New York whose hearts she captured. They guided and supported her by offering friendship and help in making lifelong decisions. They soon learned that she had a mind of her own. Her decisions proved that although she was young, she possessed the talent, the desire, and most importantly the acumen to succeed, which she did in short order making *Portraits by Lily* one of the most well-known landmarks in West Village.

As Sam paused, Jodi sat overwhelmed at what he had related to her. What an amazing story about an amazing person—exactly the type of story she based her career on and with which she had the most success. "I can certainly say that any episode profiling Lily Asher would be a blockbuster, but is her tie to 9/11 strong enough to base the entire show on her? I know she lost her son, her only child, but nothing further has ever come forward or has it?"

Sam was impressed. "You're right. All I have going for me is my gut feeling. I've struggled with putting this episode together, and Lily was not even in the running for my early choices, each of which by the way turned me down. Lily only came to mind a couple of week's ago, and I set up a meeting with her for yesterday. Honestly, I really expected her to turn me down as well.

"I was more than surprised when she didn't hesitate to say she would be thrilled to work with me. She did have a few questions about the format of the interview that I answered to her satisfaction, adding that her approval to the content was paramount.

"Here's where Lily turned the tables on me by challenging me with a request. First she asked if I had heard of a new young journalist making a name for herself on the west coast. The name she offered was none other than Jodi Jerome. She had read the tribute you wrote to your parents and was quite taken with it. Having learned that you had recently relocated to New York, she asked if there was a possibility that I could hire you to do the interview with her.

"When I told her I had already hired you to work on the show as a producer, she was quite pleased and reiterated her request to have you do the interview. I was somewhat taken aback, but I told her it could be arranged.

"I never questioned how much she knew about you. She did tell me that she read the article you wrote about your parents, but I don't know how she learned that you had relocated to New York. I guess I was too excited to have averted another dead end, and I was selfishly delighted with her interest in you."

For a few moments neither spoke. Jodi's response was simply "Wow!

I'm speechless. Of course, I will do the interview. I'm all in. This is a dream come true for me, and now my gut feelings are beginning to kick in like yours, although I've never met her or heard of her prior to coming to New York. Perhaps there just might be more to Lily Asher's story than either of us imagines.

"I'm still having a problem with thoughts of how this ties into 9/11, but maybe when I meet her and start the interview, it will come together and fall in place. Perhaps losing her son was so unbearable it has taken all these years for her to be able to address it."

Once again Sam could not believe that everything was breaking his way. "I told Lily I would get back to her in a couple of days and I will. Let's agree on a date and time, and I will call and set up the appointment. If I guess correctly, Lily would prefer sooner than later, and truth be told, so would I."

Sam's call to Lily confirmed a meeting for Lunch on Friday at noon.

The Pfizer vaccine was approved on December 10, 2020, and vaccinations began in earnest less than a week later on the 20th. Among the first vaccinated was an intensive care nurse at Long Island Jewish Medical Center, who received the vaccine live on camera. The first three million doses were distributed to dozens of locations across all 50 states. One week later on December 21st, distribution of the Moderna vaccine began.

This was particularly fitting since New York was the epicenter of the pandemic in the first wave of infection in early 2020.

Many places remained in lockdown mode; the majority of those that were open for business were not operating at full capacity. The streets of New York City remained deserted for the most part, and Sam found himself wondering how long the vibrant, most *alive* city in the world could continue to lie dormant proceeding at a snail's pace at best.

Since Jodi had come to New York and into his life, Sam found himself in a place where he had never been before. Although he had met her years earlier, there were long in-between gaps where they were not in contact at all. Now, working together on a daily basis and living down the hall from one another presented quite an unusual situation. In addition, they spent more time together than a married couple or a couple who were in a romantic relationship.

They shared all their meals together; they made plans for each and every day together; and they were slowly getting to know one another to the point where they each knew what the other's likes and dislikes were. All of this had totally escaped his notice until his Mother's call over the weekend.

For as many years as Trudy had spent her winters in Florida, they made it a point to touch base on a weekly phone call on Sundays. Of course, there were many times when they spoke at will if either sought the other's advice or something urgent or newsworthy came up. The past Sunday, when Trudy asked him if he had made any progress on the anniversary episode, he had to admit that he was still working on it. That was before his meeting with Lily. Then when she asked what he and Jodi had been up to, he couldn't stop talking. When he finally did, there was complete silence, prompting him to ask, "Mom, are you still there?"

Trudy had laughed and said that it was wonderful that they were so in sync and getting along so well. She further stated that she thought his choice to hire Jodi was a good one and that the final outcome of the show would definitely benefit by it.

However innocent his mother's remarks had been, they seemed to be invading his every thought and were constantly on his mind.

At bedtime, he found himself lying awake for hours questioning his feelings for Jodi. It was an entirely different situation than meeting someone you're attracted to and asking them for a date. He made all their plans, and she seemed to have no problem accepting any of it, albeit most of it was business. On the other hand, she didn't know anyone in New York other than Sam and the *Profiles* crew.

Now that he was solidly on track to put the show together and working closely with Jodi would be all about delivering a blockbuster episode, he set his thoughts aside.

After two nights of tossing and turning, and their lunch with Lily still two days away, he planned to spend that time offering his suggestions how to conduct the interview. He planned to tell Jodi about what they had discussed when he met with her, adding that nothing had been decided. Since interviews were Jodi's strong suit, he would defer to her to take the lead and present whatever she thought best to Lily. He had no doubt whatsoever that they would work well together.

Their individual thoughts about the interview were coming from two different perspectives. Sam knew Lily and a lot about her life in New York City and *Portraits by Lily*. Jodi knew only what Sam had told her. She planned to approach the interview open minded with no preconceived notions. It was Lily's story and only Lily could tell it. First and foremost, she had to meet with her and get a feel for the type of person she was as she did with everyone she interviewed.

Once again, she felt the need to learn the personal side of Lily Asher as a wife and mother and what affect the events of 9/11 have had on her life for the past twenty years. This was what the episode was all about, and she was determined to not only deliver a blockbuster show to Sam, but also in the process help Lily come to terms with her loss.

Friday came and although it was cold, the brisk walk to Lily's was stimulating and invigorating. For the most part, they walked in silence, each lost in their own thoughts. They arrived a little early, but Lily answered the door and welcomed them warmly.

"Come in. Come in. I have the fireplace going and you'll be warmed up in no time. After they removed their coats, Sam said, "Lily, I would like you to meet Jodi Jerome. Jodi, this is my dear friend Lily Asher."

Lily grasped both of Jodi's hands in hers and looked directly into her eyes. "It is my pleasure to meet you dear. Since Sam called to set up our lunch, I have been looking forward to this very moment. Now please, let's move away from the door, and into the library where I have a table set up for lunch in front of the fireplace.

"Lunch is ready, and if both of you will help me bring everything in, we can get acquainted while we eat. There is wine as well as an assortment of drinks in the refrigerator. Please help yourselves. Sam, if you would be good enough to open the wine that would be splendid. There are glasses in the Library."

Once they were seated, Sam opened the wine and they began lunch with a toast. Lily raised her glass. "To friends old and new. The gift of friendship is priceless."

Lunch was easy and relaxing, and Jodi began to feel as though Lily was an old friend. Her warm and genuine nature was encompassing. Sam did not know her exact age, but felt certain that she was in her nineties. Her sharp wit, recollection of the past, and optimism for the future belied that the years had taken any toll whatsoever on Lily Asher. She was awesome; she was cool; she presented a challenge that Jodi accepted unconditionally.

Lily eyed the beautiful young girl sitting across the table from her with heartfelt admiration. According to the article she had written about her parents, for someone so young having endured such immense loss and pain, she emerged selfless and only wanted to help others through her writing. She felt an instant connection to Jodi as though she was an old friend.

As Lily sat across from them, she observed their easy interaction with one another and saw them as a couple, although she had no idea if they actually were. Sam had hired her to come clear across the country to New York to work, so maybe, just maybe her instincts were right.

Sam sat quietly as Lily and Jodi exchanged questions about one another. None had anything to do with the show; they were more of a personal nature. Lily asked about Jodi's life in California; Jodi asked about Lily's non-business life and how she came to live in such a beautiful home.

Jodi reiterated her story of how she was found on the side of the road where her biological mother perished in their car when it exploded. "Although I was unconscious having suffered a bad blow to the head, I had no other injuries. When I awoke three months later, I had no memory of anything prior to the accident.

"Weeks stretched into months; months stretched into years; no one came forward looking for us. Henry and Julia Jerome came to my rescue eventually adopting me as their own. My memory never returned. It was my father's opinion that I was not from the area and that perhaps if I ever ended up where I had originally come from, someone, something, or someplace would spark me to recall my past. As yet, that hasn't happened."

Lily briefly related her coming to America to New York, starting a business, and how *Portraits by Lily* led her to meeting Joe Asher and eventually marrying him. "Rich Harrison the real estate agent who helped me find my studio's location was a friend of Joe's and recommended that he stop by to get me to paint a portrait of his parents as a gift for their upcoming 50th Wedding Anniversary.

"Joe's father Lou was in the construction business and was hired to renovate several brownstones in the area. This particular house was among them and just happened to be Lou's favorite. When work was completed, and the owner decided to sell, he made a deal with the owner taking into consideration the cost of the renovation, and he purchased the home as a 50th Anniversary gift for his wife Arlene.

"Joe and I were married in this house; it was a wonderful and lavish affair for the times. Upon returning from our honeymoon, we moved into their brownstone in Brooklyn Heights. When Joe's parents passed away, we moved into this house, and our son Noah moved into the house in Brooklyn.

"This beautiful home has hosted celebrations from weddings to holidays, to any event that arose calling for an assembly of family, friends, and business associates that often included the rich and famous, as well as local politicians.

"This home has been too much for one person for a long time, but I have no intention of leaving or downsizing. The Asher Foundation's offices are upstairs, and I have a staff that sees to the everyday needs of running such a large property. I convinced my dear friend Nina to move in when her husband lost his long battle with cancer. She works for the foundation, and keeps me apprised of any new developments or problems. In addition, we're good company for one another, and her help ordering groceries and the like during the pandemic has been invaluable.

"Hopefully, she will return home before you leave and I can introduce you. Now if you will help me clear the lunch dishes and just get everything into the kitchen, I will put coffee on, and take you on a tour of the house. We can have dessert afterwards. I made something special—my Lindy's New York Cheesecake."

As the elevator took them from floor to floor, Jodi was surprised to find that the home was not in the least over furnished. The rooms' contents were tastefully and beautifully coordinated down to the very last pillow, lamp, and knick-knack. The windows were covered with light and airy draping beckoning sunshine in, and allowing visibility of the New York skyline day or night from the upper floors.

The Asher Foundation's offices on the second floor were precisely appointed for both comfort and use. The largest of the rooms was furnished with a sofa, chairs, and tables surrounding the majestic antique desk that stood in the center across from the gas fireplace. Above the sofa, was a portrait of Lou and Arlene Asher painted by Lily. On the desk, was Lily's computer; it was Lily's office.

Other rooms on the floor housed an accounting office, an administrative office, a file room, and a memorabilia room. The walls throughout the floor were filled with posters featuring the many **PBS** productions funded by the Asher Foundation over the years, and Lily's numerous paintings of scholarship recipients.

The master suite was extensive. There were other bedrooms, though only Nina occupied one. Another of the rooms was furnished for a young child, and Jodi assumed it had been Noah's although it leaned more towards a young girl's room.

They glanced at the roof terrace through glass doors and saw that it overlooked Central Park. Taking the elevator back down to the first floor, Lily led them to the back where they could look out at the garden area telling them that they would have to return when it was in full bloom to appreciate it.

"Well my tour is over. I don't give tours of the house to just anyone, and since the pandemic Sam, you were my first visitor in almost a year. I hope you're ready for dessert and coffee. I certainly am."

Jodi brought plates, cups, saucers, and silverware to the table. She returned to the kitchen to retrieve the freshly brewed coffee carafe, cream and sugar with Lily close behind carrying a large tray bearing her version of New York Cheesecake and small bowls of fresh fruit for toppings. Sam stood and quickly took the tray from her placing it on the table.

The cheesecake was delicious. Sam remembered Lindy's famous cheesecake with sour cream topping from when he was growing up and their frequent trips to the city. Jodi remarked, "This is awesome and although I've had what was touted as New York Cheesecake, I don't think it was this recipe."

As they sat savoring every bite, they were quiet, each lost in their own thoughts. Lily pronounced, "I am so full, I can't take another bite. In fact, I think I'm going to skip dinner."

Sam and Jodi nodded in agreement, and San said, "I can't thank you enough for this wonderful day that you have managed to make magical. You have generously shared a preview of what we have gotten ourselves into, and I am certain I speak for both of us when I say *let the adventure begin.* Here is where I bow out. I'm going to leave it up to you and Jodi moving forward to decide on format, how often and how long your meetings will be and mainly content which as I promised you will be based on your final approval.

"I want you to proceed at a pace that is comfortable for you, and I have every confidence that Jodi is the interviewer that can tell your story the way you want it told."

"Thank you Sam, I appreciate your comments. And thank you Jodi for accepting the job. I don't know if Sam told you, but it was actually I who requested you to do the interviewing after I read your article in the LA Times. It was so beautifully written—each and every word flowed from the heart. As I read it, I felt your loss, your pain, your sorrow, your love, and your commitment to move on and live. My first thoughts were if your words could affect me so deeply, and I didn't even know you or your parents, I could find no one better to *spill my guts to!*"

They laughed. Lily continued. "What I didn't tell you Sam was when I received your call I had actually been contemplating calling you and offering my story whenever it could be worked into your scheduling. Although what I have to relate begins with 9/11 and comes to an end twenty years later, it was your offer to air it as the sole subject of the Anniversary episode that I couldn't believe. The icing on the cake was when I asked if you knew of Jodi Jerome, and to my surprise learned that you had recently hired her. Never in my wildest dreams could I have imagined that everything would come together in so neat a package.

"Now I have had the great pleasure of spending a few hours with you Jodi, and I sincerely hope you are as delighted with me as I am with you. Since the pandemic restrictions set in, my schedule is virtually non-existent, and I stay pretty close to home especially in cold weather. I do venture out up the street to the coffee shop on nicer days. I've known the owners since they opened the shop years ago, and their baked goods and lattes are to die for."

Jodi had tears in her eyes. She leaned over and hugged Lily not wanting to let her go. When she did, Lily was crying too. Even Sam brushed a tear from his eye.

"I have both of you to thank immensely. To Sam for offering me a lifeline to move to New York and a fresh start on the rest of my life, and to you Lily for having such faith in my writing and me before we even met. It seems as though I have once again been blessed with two guardian angels.

"I assure you that I am as anxious to get started as you are. If you're up to it now, I can give you a few of my initial thoughts as to how I see everything coming together. In that way, you will have the time to gather your thoughts and any visuals you would like to present when we have our first meeting and actually begin the interview."

Lily readily agreed. So for the next hour, they sat at the table discussing how and when to move forward. Jodi made notes on her yellow legal pad of everything they discussed and agreed upon.

Sam cleared the table. In the kitchen, he loaded the dishwasher, found the detergent under the sink, and turned it on. He covered the remaining cheesecake and placed it in the refrigerator along with the coffee cream. Wiping down the counter, he stood back surveying his cleanup with satisfaction. He retrieved a bottle of water from the refrigerator and returned to the library where he took a seat on the sofa not wanting to interrupt Jodi and Lily's discussion.

As they were finishing up, Nina came home and they got to meet her, as well. Before she would allow them to leave, Lily asked them to wait and went into the kitchen. When she returned, she thanked Sam for cleaning up after lunch and returned with two servings of cheesecake to take with them.

There were hugs all around in spite of COVID. They were all vaccinated and assured that they were safe, and they had spent most of the afternoon eating without wearing masks.

It was dark, and it had grown colder but they decided to walk back to the apartment anyway. Finding it almost impossible to contain her excitement, Jodi offered to throw something light together for dinner. She couldn't wait to talk to Sam and run her ideas by him. Of course, and as a bonus, they did have cheesecake on hand for dessert—thanks to Lily.

January 2021 was a month of ups and downs. With the rollout of the vaccines, priority to get everyone vaccinated, and ongoing testing, hope ran high, only to be tamped down January 6th when utter chaos broke out at the Capitol in Washington, DC. Rioting and the escalation of crime mired in political rhetoric that had begun the summer before spread to all major cites across the nation.

Wednesday, January 20, 2021, the world watched as the 46th President—Joe Biden was inaugurated promising to unite us, heal us, and defeat our #1 Enemy—COVID-19, as the cloud of FBI warnings of potential protests and continued unrest in all 50 state capitals hovered above us.

For the most part, lockdowns and mandates remained in place.

# Chapter 8

As promised, Jodi had no problem preparing a light meal for supper. Grilled cheese sandwiches and roasted red pepper soup (store made) was quick and easy; it was perfect. They decided to eat first, contemplating that once they started delving into a plan to move forward, it would be difficult to apply the breaks to their thoughts.

With her legal pad in hand bearing the notes she had taken earlier, Jodi opened the conversation. "I have never had the pleasure or good fortune to meet someone like Lily Asher. On the other hand, I don't think many of us ever get that opportunity. She absolutely captivated me, and what little I've learned about her has actually inspired me.

"I don't know what I expected, but from the moment she opened the door, I knew that if I did expect anything, it wasn't what stood before me. What I saw was a woman of average height; her gray hair coiffed short; she wore winter white slacks, a bright red silk blouse, and short boots. Except for diamond stud earrings, the only jewelry she wore was a wedding ring. It was easy to see that with no effort whatsoever, she exuded elegance and class. I assure you, her warm welcome was not wasted on me.

"You did say that she was in her nineties, right?"

Sam laughed. "That I did. I reached that conclusion on my own. I learned early in our friendship that when she came to New York after the war she was in her twenties, so I did the math and that would definitely put her in her nineties and possibly more towards her mid-nineties. I absolutely agree with you; she takes elegance and class to a whole new level.

"The fact that she is so *with it* amazes me. I think that you're about to conduct the interview of a lifetime, and I predict that you are going to nail it while enjoying every minute of it."

Jodi smiled. "Thank you Sam. I owe you big time for everything. All I know is that I am more determined than ever to deliver the blockbuster episode you have entrusted me with. In the process, I plan to let Lily take the lead and proceed at her own pace. I'm sure that you picked up on the fact that she answered my main concern before I had a chance to ask by confirming her story's tie to 9/11. My gut feeling is now that she has decided to share her story, she knows precisely how she wants to do it. I intend to give her that freedom.

"Although she stated that her story began 9/11 and would end twenty years later, I feel there is no way it can be told without encompassing almost every aspect of her life including how Noah's death affected Joe. When she spoke of him at lunch and how they ended up living in that magnificent house, I noticed a sentimental look in her eye, almost as if she momentarily returned to happier times. It is quite evident they cared deeply about one another.

"I envy her. The one thing missing in my life is that I am unable to go back to my beginning. Since my parents passed away, the void looms larger than ever. But, I'm getting off track here and that's not my intention. I made an excellent choice to accept your offer to come east. I love it here so far even with the lockdowns and mandates, and I can only imagine how wonderful it will be when everything opens up again. I owe all of that to you and to your mother for letting me stay in her apartment."

Sam's lighter side couldn't resist. "Does that mean I have a shot at your staying in New York longer than a year and possibly permanently?"

Jodi laughed. "You do, absolutely. I meant it when I said I love it here although I could do with a little less cold weather. We've had quite a day. We are on schedule with the show and not wanting to over think every small detail of the interview before it takes place, I say we are finished here. Time for desert, and I can brew some coffee if you like."

"I like; sounds good to me. Can I help?"

"No thanks, I have it. Why don't you see if there's something on TV—anything but the news."

They started watching a movie but there was no interest on either's part. Sam turned to Jodi and said, "It's getting late, and I can see that you're tired. Like you said, it's been quite a day, a day that I don't think either of us anticipated. We're certainly not going to work on the show over the weekend and Martin Luther King Jr.'s Birthday observance is Monday. Not that having a day off makes a difference during the lockdown, so I've been thinking."

Jodi frowned, "Uh oh should I be worried?"

"No, not at all. I'm merely suggesting some ways to just relax and chill out.

"I have a few ideas that I think you might enjoy. The weather is quite cold, so I'm opting for a driving tour of the city and a little beyond. We can start on Saturday in and around Manhattan and finish what I started when you first moved here, while I try my best to fill you in on the history of some of the landmarks we've profiled. Although it might have to be carryout, we can start with breakfast from a nearby coffee shop, possibly a corned beef sandwich for lunch from Katz's deli, and a little more upscale fare for dinner where perhaps we could snag a reservation and eat in.

"On Sunday, I'm going to introduce you to Sam Meyerson and take you on a tour of places personal to me, like Westchester County—city of Port Chester where I grew up. I hope you won't be bored, but I'll give you the full picture of what I was like back then including a little background on the people who raised me, Al and Trudy Meyerson. We can savor the foods of my youth and there is one fantastic restaurant that I have in mind for dinner. Hopefully you won't be bored.

"Monday will be my ace-in-the-hole. I'm leaving the best for last, and it will be a surprise. That's all I'm going to divulge except that there is no doubt in my mind that it will be your favorite."

Jodi was delighted. "Oh Sam that sounds wonderful; I can't wait. There is nothing for me to do anyway until the interview gets underway, and it will do me good to clear my mind and think about other things. I will give Lily a call in the morning to set up our first meeting for some time next week, if she agrees."

Sam rose and as he started to clear the dessert dishes, Jodi said, "Sam please, I can do that. We're both tired, and you've given me a wonderful long weekend to look forward to especially piquing my interest about Monday. What time do you want to get started tomorrow?"

"There's no need to leave super early. How does 9:00 am sound?"

"Great, but we definitely have to stop for coffee immediately."

"I'll say goodnight then. See you in the morning."

As he walked down the hall to his apartment, Sam's thoughts wandered. He would have liked nothing better than to hug her, perhaps draw her into a kiss; what was he thinking? It was certainly not professional. He realized how vulnerable she still was, particularly with the first anniversary of her father's passing a few weeks away. To some extent he felt he was vulnerable as well; his concerns of how his previous relationship ended continued to surface. No, he would do nothing to jeopardize their friendship. She would have to make the first move that is if she felt the same way about him, although deep down he felt that was something the Jodi he had come to know would never do.

When Sam left, Jodi remained with her back against the closed door as her thoughts wandered. She would have liked nothing better than to hug him, and thank him once again for all he had done and continued to do for her. And if on the outside chance he might have kissed her, she would have definitely kissed him back. She had dated somewhat but had never been in a relationship. The feelings she was experiencing were totally new to her, and she wasn't sure quite how to deal with them. No, she would do nothing to jeopardize working with Sam. When was it ever a good time to get involved with your boss? NEVER!

A few minutes before 9:00 am, Sam knocked on Jodi's door. Even though they would be in the car, he had urged her to dress warmly. She opened the door with a smile on her face. "Good morning! I am so ready for our adventure; just let me grab my coat."

He noticed she was wearing a bulky white sweater that he hadn't seen before. When he complimented her on it, she replied, "OK, you got me. Since the weather has turned so much colder than when I arrived here and what I'm used to, I've been doing some online shopping at night when I can't sleep. You said to dress warmly, and this sweater is the warmest I have along with my wool slacks. I also purchased some gloves and a hat for my walks to Lily's."

When they reached the Lobby, Lester told them their car had arrived. Sam opened the door for Jodi and once she was buckled in, he went around to the driver's side and slid behind the wheel.

"I don't drive very often especially around the city, are you sure you want to go on this adventure?"

Jodi laughed. "Too late now. There's no chance whatsoever that I'm backing out. I'll just tighten my seatbelt and hang on for dear life. Admit it. You might be just a little disappointed if I cancelled out on all the plans you've made, wouldn't you?"

"That I would. Besides, our first stop is just a few blocks away. We're having breakfast at Alice's Tea Cup on East 64th Street, and once I've fed you and plied you with coffee, I happen to know that you will be as eager to go on our adventure as I am to take you on it."

In short order, they were at Alice's, and Sam found a parking spot right out front. The small café had lowered its capacity by spacing the tables, and patrons were required to wear masks until their food was served. Fortunately, there were only two other people seated. They practically had the place to themselves.

Jodi chose pancakes; Sam opted for waffles; both ordered regular coffee. As they ate, all Jodi's efforts to learn what lay in store for their Saturday were in vain.

Sam paid the check and picked up two bottles of water for the car. They were on their way. Since Jodi was not very familiar with the city as yet, she had no way of knowing where they were heading.

As he drove, he began to speak. "Oftentimes this entire region of Manhattan is referred to as the Upper East Side. The Pavilion and Alice's Tea Cup where we had breakfast are both on the Upper East Side. Even taking into account the many separate and distinct districts that comprise the area, it represents an expansive, scenic section of New York City. The neighborhood is a historic Manhattan enclave, featuring classic storefronts and residences.

"However, the emerald jewel of New York City is Central Park. It is simply a priceless slice of immaculately designed nature—the very heart of Manhattan. Although it seems like a well-preserved snapshot of natural origins, Central Park is, in fact, manmade, designed and constructed by architects Calvert Vaux and Frederick Law Olmsted in the 1850s and 60s officially opening in 1873.

"To date, there have been many additions and renovations, including the ice skating rink where my Dad taught me to ice skate. Central Park is a compelling, vital, vibrant part of Manhattan. From its artwork to its natural beauty, there's little wonder why it remains such a priority attraction for not only the millions of tourists who visit the city each year, but to native New Yorkers alike.

"Although they only occur a few weeks each year in spring and autumn, *In-the Park Events* are not to be missed.

"Once the pandemic broke out, in an effort to keep the show up and running, we decided to profile landmarks especially at the onset of the lockdowns. Central Park was the subject of our last show in June 2020 before our summer hiatus.

"When we returned to the air in September, our 9/11 episode for 2020 focused on the Tunnel to Towers Foundation founded by Frank Siller to honor the heroic life and death of his brother, Stephen Siller, a New York City Firefighter who lost his life on 9/11 running through the Brooklyn Battery Tunnel to the Twin Towers where he gave his life to save others.

"Subsequent shows for the remainder of 2020 continued to exclude direct interviews. October's episode gave an overview of the reopening of Broadway, as well as other shows scheduled to go on tour or were cancelled. November's episode profiled Thanksgiving Day in America, and as you know, December's episode that we watched together profiled Christmas in the city with the 88th annual tree lighting at Rockefeller Center, and included the history of the Rockettes and their annual Christmas Show.

"Our January episode profiles a relatively new addition to the city and is due to air a week from Sunday. We will be visiting the site later today, so I won't say anything further about it now."

Sam drove through the park, pointing out various points of interest including the ice rink offering to teach Jodi at another time if she wanted to give it a try. She said she would consider it.

Pulling out of the park, he drove until he found a spot to park. "Are you hungry? There's a great sandwich shop in the next block, and then I'm going to take you to one of my favorite places in all of New York City."

"I'm not asking where that might be because you're not going to tell me, right?"

"Right. It's a surprise."

Again, they were lucky. The sandwich shop was mostly carryout since the pandemic, but the three small tables were all empty. Having had a big breakfast, they decided to share a sandwich and an order of fries.

They left the restaurant and walked up the street coming to a stop in front of William Greenberg Desserts. Sam noticed Jodi's eyes light up. "I am so glad you didn't give into me and spoil this surprise. Desserts are my weak spot. I don't think you realize you may never get me out of here."

Known for their Black and White Cookies that are #1 in New York City, Greenberg's goes far beyond that. The Black and White's just happened to be Jodi's favorite; how on earth did Sam know or was it just a lucky guess? Either way, she was in heaven.

By the time they left, they had spent $75 on several different delicacies in addition to the #1 cookie. Carrying the two bags filled to the brim, they laughed all the way back to the car. Sam put their precious cargo in the back so they wouldn't eat anything until they got home—where they could savor every bite.

From the Upper East Side and Central Park, they headed to the West Side of Midtown South. Jodi sat quietly taking everything in that she had seen and that Sam had related to her.

After glancing her way a couple of times, it prompted him to ask,

"Are you OK? You're awfully quiet and that's not like you. Do you have any questions other than asking me what's next?"

"Oh Sam, I can't begin to tell you what a wonderful day this has been so far, and it's only half over. Your every word, your every description, and the tone of your voice when you speak about the city shows how much of a New Yorker you are and how much you love it and everything about it. *Profiles of New York* was your baby and it is evident to me that its success leads directly to you and your input. I know you will defer to your staff and yes, they have contributed, but now that I have gotten to know you, I view the episodes with a different perspective—your heart and soul is the basis of every one."

Sam didn't know what to say. He reached for and squeezed her hand. "Thank you. It's exactly how I felt when I read the article you wrote about your parents. You poured your heart and soul into writing it; I imagine it touched many people the same way, even those who don't know you personally. And not only did it get my attention, it seemed to have had the same affect on Lily who admitted just that when we had lunch with her. Perhaps reading your article was what she needed to finally come forward with her own story."

"Thank you for being so candid. I was pleased with the article; it was actually easy for me to write because it was so heartfelt. I owe my life to Henry and Julia Jerome and losing both of them devastated me. I really want to start the interview process with no preconceived ideas. It's Lily's story, and I'm going to let her tell it. My feeling is that neither of us will be disappointed.

"By the way, your driving hasn't frightened me one iota, so what say you step on it! I'm anxious to see what you have in store for me next."

"We're just a few minutes away from our destination—a 28-acre real estate development in the Chelsea and Hudson Yards neighborhoods of Manhattan. Upon completion, 13 of 16 planned structures on the West Side of Midtown South will sit atop a platform built over the West Side Yard, a storage yard for Long Island Railroad Trains.

"The first of two phases of Hudson Yards opened March 2019, consisting of a mall, a public square, eight structures that contain residences, a hotel, office buildings, and a cultural facility. However, the opening was short-lived when a year later, the onset of the COVID-19 Pandemic caused everything to close down. As of today, there is no construction completion date for Phase 2, which has been delayed indefinitely by COVID.

"Although scaled back by mandates and restrictions, as businesses began to reopen throughout the city, Hudson Yards followed suit. I don't know what is actually open, but we have all afternoon to explore and see what we can.

"Hudson Yards is our profile for next Sunday. We originally planned to give an overview of the complex and face-to-face interviews with both the developers and select merchants. However, when in-person contact proved to be a problem during the pandemic, we improvised with more in-depth coverage of the amenities. When everything gets back to 100%, we can revisit with interviews.

"Hudson Yards boasts a seven-story mall with 100 shops and 20 restaurants; The Plaza—a 6-acre public square with 28,000 plants and 225 trees rooted in *smart soil*; The Shed—an events and performing arts center; the *Vessel*—a permanent art sculpture challenging visitors to climb 2500 steps to the top to enjoy an aerial view of Hudson Yards; Mercado Little Spain—an all-day destination market for the very best of Spanish food, drink, and culture; Edge—the highest sky deck in the Western Hemisphere suspended in mid-air giving one the feeling of floating in the sky with views you can't get anywhere else, and I could go on and on."

As Sam pulled into the garage, he said, "We're here so I can stop talking and you can see everything for yourself."

Jodi was absolutely blown away. "Wow. This is all so totally awesome and unbelievable. If I wasn't actually here, I might not have believed your in-depth description."

For the entire afternoon, they wandered every level of the mall. There were places that were closed, and they agreed it would give them a reason to return in nicer weather. They stepped into many of the unique shops, visited the Mercado Market, and as if the cookies and sweets from Greenberg's weren't enough, visited Li-Lac Chocolates and didn't leave empty handed.

Their evening ended with dinner at Hudson Yards Grill. Sam would have preferred Queensland Restaurant, but felt they weren't dressed for it. That too would be a reason to return.

Exhausted, they made their way to the car. As Sam pulled out of the garage onto the street, he looked over at Jodi who was fast asleep. He smiled to himself thinking what a truly nice day it had been. His intention was to show her the city he loved, hoping she would learn to love it too and stay in New York. In the process, he had enjoyed the day immensely himself. It had been far too long since he had such a great time and someone to share it with.

When they arrived at the Pavilion, there was a place to park on the street so he took it. That way, the car would be there in the morning when they were ready to leave.

He hated to wake her up, but he didn't think lifting her out of the car and carrying her upstairs was a good idea, and he mused there was no way he could carry Jodi and their multiple bags of goodies up to the apartment. Nudging her gently, he said, "Wake up sleepyhead; we're home."

Rubbing her eyes she looked up, and for a moment she was unsure where she was. "Don't tell me I slept the whole way home; this is so embarrassing. I think I should have passed on that last glass of wine."

He retrieved the bags from Greenberg's and Li-Lac Chocolates, and they walked to the apartment. Taking the elevator to their floor, Sam said, "If you want to leave a little later in the morning we can. There's no rush; we're not on any schedule. I think I wore you out today, and I didn't intend to. I promise tomorrow will be more laid back and easy going, definitely a lot less walking."

He walked her to her door, waited for her to unlock it, and as he handed her the bags, she said, "Please come in for a little while. We didn't have dessert, so I can brew a pot of coffee, and we can enjoy some of the goodies we bought. Now that I've had my nap, I don't feel tired anymore."

Sam hesitated. "If you're sure you don't just want to go to sleep, I would love a cup of coffee and definitely some of the cookies. I can also fill you in on the upcoming episode on Hudson Yards, that is unless you consider that *work talk*. Do you?"

"Of course not, I don't consider that *work talk* at all. And you're not leaving here without taking some of the cookies and pastries from Greenberg's along with some of the chocolates, as well."

They were like two kids in a candy store sharing bites of several kinds of cookies and pastries and refills of coffee. Jodi said she had never seen anything like Hudson Yards, and considering she wasn't able to see everything, she definitely planned on going back.

It was only 9:00 pm when Sam left, so they agreed leaving the same time in the morning would be fine.

She walked him to the door, but this time she didn't hesitate to hug him and thank him for the best day ever—again.

Maybe he held her a little longer than he should have, but she didn't seem to mind. She fit into his embrace perfectly. A broad grin spread across his face when he suddenly realized she had made the first move after all.

Sunday began as the day before with Sam walking the hall to meet Jodi before taking the elevator down to the car. However, the minute she opened the door things changed. Instead of grabbing her coat so they could be on their way, she invited him in.

"I'm altering our plans slightly without knowing what our plans are. I hope you won't mind or that it doesn't mess things up."

Sam walked into a set table for two—orange juice, pastries from Greenberg's, and that all-important *coffee*. "No, this is perfect. I was going to suggest picking up a light breakfast that we could eat in the car because after starting out in the area, our destination is a 45-minute ride away from the city."

They didn't rush but they didn't linger. Once they cleared the table, they were off on the second day's adventure. Sam kept having second thoughts. Was he being presumptuous to think that Jodi was interested in learning all about him, or was he simply hoping that she was? At any rate, it was too late now. They took coffee in travel mugs and bottled water for the trip.

After they were in the car, Sam said, "You already know how much I love New York, so my choice to make today about me is to show you why.

"Al Meyerson and Trudy Caruso—both born and bred New Yorkers— are my parents. My Dad's parents although they were first-generation American-born Jews, raised their children traditionally in all things Jewish.

62

When they married, without a second thought, they settled in Brooklyn to be near their parents. They had two sons—Edward and Alvin—both born of the same genes; both reared in the same household conditioned to be nothing less than 100% Jewish.

"In their eyes, Edward, who was six years older than my father, was the perfect son in every way. He was of average height with a stocky build, not particularly athletic with okay looks. He attended religious school to prepare for his Bar Mitzvah and continued with his religious studies afterward at a time when most boys are so elated that *it's over*, they're never to be seen in a religious class again. He was also a straight-A student, and attended Columbia University where he earned his law degree. He married a *nice Jewish girl* and blessed them with three beautiful grandchildren—all girls.

"My Dad Alvin showed no signs whatsoever of having inherited a single Meyerson gene. His genes came entirely from his mother. In a nutshell, he was tall, dark, and handsome with a fabulous personality. He was an awesome tennis player who at one time was urged to consider becoming professional. Although he was a good student, he barely made it through his Bar Mitzvah. It just wasn't *his* thing. When it was time for him to attend college, he applied to Columbia to earn a degree in Business.

"After almost flunking out his very first semester, he switched courses and earned a BA Degree in Theatre—without his parents ever knowing about it until he graduated. They were horrified. What was a degree in theatre? Could one make a living with such a degree? My Dad was determined to show them he could.

"He decided he wanted to try his hand at acting. His charm and personality won him the hearts of many, and he remained close friends with a number of his fellow students from his college days. Although his initial attempts at acting were rather disappointing, only managing to secure a few minor parts, he refused to let it deter him. He continued to attend every casting he learned of whether he was attending to try out or simply to observe. During the process, he became acquainted with two directors in particular that were on their way to becoming big names in the business, and their friendship grew into a business partnership that benefitted the three of them.

"On an offhand chance, he offered the name of a fellow student at Columbia for a role in an upcoming musical, and she landed the part. After a few more fortunate recommendations, they approached him with an offer to become a talent scout. He accepted. Though his dream had been to become an actor himself, he found using his expertise to help others realize their dreams even more satisfying.

"One day, on his way to a casting, he tripped on the curb exiting his taxi. By the time his meeting was over, his foot was so swollen, he could barely remove his shoe. A friend insisted on taking him to Lenox Hill Hospital where the nurse who pulled back the curtain to his ER bed was none other than Trudy Caruso. From that very first moment, he was smitten.

"He left the hospital with a cast on his foot, and instructions to see his personal doctor to remove it in three weeks from the beautiful young woman bearing the nametag—Caruso. She was never out of his thoughts. When the cast was finally removed, he returned to Lenox Hill with a bouquet of flowers to thank her for taking such good care of him, and asked her to dinner. She flatly refused; she didn't know him and vaguely remembered him.

"He did manage to convince her to have a cup of coffee in the hospital cafeteria. After half a dozen more cups of coffee and getting to know him, she accepted a dinner date, and admitted she liked him too.

"By the time he brought her home to meet his parents, he had asked her to marry him, and she accepted. As his success grew, his parents mellowed. Times change, and he had proven that one could make a very good living in the theatre business. His brother Edward had married a *nice Jewish girl*, according to plan; Trudy Caruso was an *Italian Catholic girl*. Against all odds, they loved Trudy.

"The Caruso family was huge. Her parents lived in Queens; she had five siblings and far too many cousins to count and keep track of. Against all odds, they loved Alvin.

"It was my Dad who always said that even though his parents considered Edward the perfect son, in the end, he gave them the one blessing every Jewish parent desires—a grandson to carry on the family name; I was named after my grandfather's father. I grew up surrounded by love, and that was what counted most. Some of my fondest memories are the many times I spent with both sets of grandparents."

As Sam told Jodi about his parents, he drove past Lenox Hill Hospital to show her where it all began, through the theatre district that had been shuttered for almost an entire year, and finally the hole-in-the-wall that had been his Dad's first office until he could afford better.

Leaving the city, he told her they were now on their way to Port Chester where he grew up, urging her to relax and enjoy the ride that would take about forty-five minutes. "Do you have any questions? Am I boring you yet?"

Jodi laughed. "I don't have any questions yet, and I'm definitely not bored. What a beautiful love story. You know I'm a sucker for stories like theirs. It's evident that growing up in such a close and loving family certainly left its mark. I know that I'm not the first person who has been at the receiving end of your kindness and generosity, just as I know I won't be the last. You might even be the most genuinely decent person I have ever met.

"I wonder what difference the pandemic will have on people's views when it's finally over. The current political climate has hit such a fever pitch espousing too much hated and inability to accept others who disagree. Instead of uniting us as in the past, growing resistance to ongoing lockdowns and/or quarantines appears headed for a reverse affect made all too evident by the growing unrest spreading throughout America. Social media has taken our country hostage along with many journalists and broadcasting giants. Getting to know that people like you still exist is definitely uplifting. Being a part of *Profiles* is icing on the cake."

Not quite forty-five minutes later, they reached their destination.

Port Chester is a village in New York in Westchester County and the largest portion of the town of Rye by population. It is one of twelve villages in New York still incorporated under a charter. Nicknamed *The Gateway to New England*, it serves as a transportation hub between New England states and New York. Its economy is stimulated not only by small businesses and local government but by several large national chain stores, as well.

It was a cold but beautiful sunny afternoon. As they entered the village limits of Port Chester, Sam said, "This is where I grew up. My parents often told me their decision to move out of New York City was not taken lightly. It was after all what they had known their entire lives. In the end, they opted to move; the benefits were simply too hard to ignore—a large home with a yard, schools, shopping, and entertainment, all convenient and accessible by walking or if driving was required, parking abounded.

At the end of the cul-de-sac on Hilltop Drive, Sam pulled up and stopped. "This is the beautiful house that we called home until my Dad passed away, and Mom decided to sell. It was much too big for one person.

I was already living in the city, and my parents had considered selling for a while before he passed."

"It's beautiful Sam. I can only imagine how it was decorated after seeing how lovely the apartment is. It appears to be a big house even for three people."

"Actually, there were four of us. I had a younger sister who died when she was twelve. She had a congenital heart defect that wasn't known until she collapsed playing basketball at school. It was a rough spot that took the three of us a while to come to terms with, but family helped, and we have a lot of family.

"The house was big even for four people, but it didn't seem that way when we hosted the Caruso Clan. They had no trouble filling it up. The house was also home to several dogs throughout the years."

Sam pulled away and began driving through the area. "We have excellent schools in Port Chester. I attended the John F. Kennedy Magnet Elementary, went on to Port Chester Middle that ranks as A National Blue Ribbon School of Excellence, and graduated from Port Chester High School with honors—I might add. They had a way of bringing out the best in us at an age when many teens rebel.

"Co-curricular and athletic activities offered are quite varied and the majority of students participate in two or more. The Port Chester High School Marching Band even flirted with fame by appearing in the movies *Spider-Man 3* and *Miracle on 34th Street* (1994 remake), and has performed in Orange Bowls, Disney World Festival of Lights, and the Macy's Thanksgiving Parade."

"Were you a member of the band?"

"Yes, I was. I played the big bass drum. I think I was chosen because of my size. I was tall and you may not know it, but that drum definitely had some weight to it. The only event I participated in was the Disney World Festival of Lights. They actually recruited me to play the drums. I took piano lessons as a child, but it's my Mom who's the better pianist by far. I didn't have a problem picking up the drums, and in the process, I managed to catch the eye of blond-haired, blue-eyed Suzy Davis who marched with the band twirling the baton.

"Now that I've finished showing you around the basics of the town as they pertain to me, we're going to stop for something to eat. I hadn't realized how late it was getting, and we didn't have much for breakfast. After this, we have one last stop to make.

"The Roadhouse Restaurant is one of my favorites—they're known for their fried chicken and ribs. They do have a rather extensive menu and you are free to go through it and pick whatever catches your eye. However, we are not going to eat here. If you're okay with the fried chicken and ribs, I can order for us, and we can be on our way. We're close to where we're going, so the food will still be hot and ready to eat when we get there."

"You've done such a good job thus far, I'm going to go for it. You do the ordering. While we're waiting, I would like to take a peek at the menu, if I can. You make it sound tempting to say the least."

Sam got her a menu and placed the order. Fifteen minutes later loaded down with two large shopping bags filled to the brim, they were once again on their way. Less than ten minutes later, he pulled up to a house on the waterfront across from the marina.

"My Dad loved the water and as long as I can remember, we had a boat that was berthed at this very marina. This beautiful waterfront property belonged to my Dad's best friend, and when he decided to relocate to Florida after his wife died, my parents purchased it—with the thought in mind that they would sell the house on Hilltop Drive, move to an apartment in Manhattan, and spend weekends here. With my Dad's sudden passing, Mom just followed through on plans that were already in motion. The only thing left for her to do was find a place in the city which she did readily."

They got out of the car, each carrying one of the bags. Sam opened the door, and once again Jodi was amazed but for a different reason. This house seemed almost a mirror image of their getaway place in Malibu. It was furnished tastefully with a nautical twist featuring bright colors throughout. Yes, it definitely reminded her of Malibu. The house showed no signs of having been shuttered. She correctly surmised that it had been used all during the lockdown simply as a place to go, and Sam confirmed her thoughts.

As he pulled silverware, plates, and napkins from the cabinet, he said, "This place has been a godsend especially since the onset of COVID and the ensuing lockdown. New York City became a ghost town immediately, and this became my oasis—a mere 45 minutes away. We still have a boat and all during the summer, I found myself spending not only weekends but weeks here as well."

They emptied the bags of food onto the table, helped themselves, and dug in. Sam opened a bottle of wine and for the next half hour they ate, drank, laughed and laughed some more.

"This fried chicken is delicious and the ribs are great. Sensing that you knew what you were talking about, I'm glad I opted to go along with your choices. I can only imagine that pretty much everything I saw on their menu is equally as yummy.

I'll just have to make sure I come back to check it out."

As they were finishing up, Jodi surprised Sam when she said, "You really outdid yourself ordering so much food. Why don't we clean up, put everything away, and wrap the leftovers to take back with us? I can't believe that for the second time today, I'm attempting to alter your plans. Nevertheless, I'm not quite ready to leave this beautiful place, so I'm suggesting we spend the remainder of the afternoon relaxing and enjoying it here. There's something I'd like to tell you."

Sam welcomed the fact that Jodi had a few ideas of her own. "I am impressed that you have captured the true essence of this house and can understand why I often come here not only to clear my thoughts, make decisions that I can't come to terms with in the city, or simply to get away. In fact, I must admit that I had another motive for bringing you here. I can't begin to tell you how many episodes of *Profiles* I have put to rest in this very room, and they turned out to be some of the best. When you reach the point of finalizing your interview with Lily, I just want you to know, that if needed, this place is yours for the asking."

"Sam that is so sweet and considerate; thank you. I'll certainly keep that in mind.

"You have been so open and warm sharing your history with me, I want to do the same with you. Throughout the day as your story unfolded, I have been amazed that although there are differences between us, there are many similarities. This house is one of them. Our Malibu home is waterfront and it too faces a marina. It was hard for my father to relax or even take time off and distance himself from the workload he constantly carried, but when he did, his boat was his salvation. He was considering selling both the house and the boat when he died, correctly citing that since my mother passed away, we hadn't gone to the house or used the boat even once.

"Although I have no recollection of the first ten years of my life, the past twenty were wonderful. Unlike you, I had no siblings or extended family, but Henry and Julia Jerome engulfed me in love. We did everything together as family. I too grew up in a big house that welcomed their many friends and medical associates who they entertained on many an occasion.

Like Trudy, Julia was a nurse. Once they petitioned the court for me to become their ward, she became a stay-at-home parent who was always there for me.

"I also play the piano; it's one of the mysteries of my past. Months after the accident, Henry and Julia took me home to live with them. In their parlor stood a beautiful baby grand piano that instantly drew my attention. I sat down and began playing not just any simple melody mind you, but Debussy's Claire du Lune. When I finished and looked up, I saw the stunned look on their faces. They were not only elated but told me they saw this as a sign that my memory was returning.

"Julia hired a piano teacher to assess my playing and arrange to give me further lessons; she wasn't prepared for her recommendations—she saw no benefit in giving me further lessons unless the goal was to prepare me for a recital. She noted that my advanced ability to read music indicated that I had begun playing at an early age. She suggested that Julia spend time playing with me hoping that the pieces I chose to share would help me recall. Unfortunately, we hit yet another dead-end.

"When I saw the piano at Lily's, everything stopped. It was all I could do to remain quiet and not mention that I played or ask her if she played. I don't know why after all these years, I reacted the way I did.

"I attended public schools and graduated from UCLA. They supported me in every way and only wanted me to be happy, and I was. Whenever I wished for my memory to return, it was more for my father than myself. At times he felt as though he failed me having helped so many others yet unable to help me, but that was not the way I saw him. To me, Henry and Julia Jerome were my saviors, my guardian angels, my parents—who could ask for more? My biological mother brought me to life; they gave me a life.

"I must admit, since I lost both of them, I do think about the first ten years of my life more often; where I came from; who I belonged to? Was my father onto something with his thoughts that I wasn't from California, and that if I ever returned to where I was from originally my memory would return perhaps sparked by a person, place, or thing? I remain optimistic that someday that will happen, but I can't live in a past that's unknown to me. I owe my parents so much; my way of repaying them is to live a good life and help as many people as I can.

"Unless my feelings change, I plan to stay in New York. I truly have come to love it here. I'm well aware that the city today is a scaled down version of what I experienced on my first visit, but having seen all that it can be, I have no doubt that it will be back, and I want to be a part of it. I really have no one to return to in California, and as soon as my parents' assets have been sold, only my condo will remain. I've made up my mind to rent it out in the meantime.

"I love my job and for me that is paramount. It's why I came here, at your behest I might add. I hope you realize that my interviewing Lily is going to be a tough act to follow, so my friend, you better start looking for my next assignment!"

For a moment or two, Sam sat speechless. To be honest, second guessing himself about planning an entire day about *Sam Meyerson* had kept him up most of the previous night. Was he being too pushy? He neither wanted to turn her off nor scare her away, yet he did not sense the time was right to reveal his feelings for her. At times, he definitely felt the vibes between them, though it had barely been three months since she came east. The one question at the center of it all loomed large—*did she feel the same way about him?*

"You've made my day! I hope I haven't pressured you into making your decision. I planned this weekend to acquaint you with not only the city, but with me, not only as your boss, but also as a friend and admirer of your talent as a writer. I do want you to get to know the *Profiles* team better. We may be small in number but we're large in delivering an award-winning show to millions of viewers who overwhelmingly support us locally and across the nation.

"The week ahead is a big week for all of us at *Profiles* as you embark on your interview with Lily. By the way, were you able to reach her and set up your first meeting?"

"I did, and I apologize for not mentioning it. We've chosen 10:00 am on Wednesday. At what point she chooses to begin makes no difference. I'm going to record everything, take notes, reserve questions I may have for last, and simply let Lily tell Lily's story. It will be up to us to produce the finished product through editing and verifying. I can't even begin to guess how much material we will have to work with and how long it will take to condense it into a two-hour episode. Then, of course, we will have to allow time for any changes Lily may want to make.

"After our first couple of meetings, I'm hoping to get a better feel for the timeframe we're working with, as well as hoping that we can wrap this up by June at the latest. Since the show goes on hiatus for the summer, it will give me time to look for an apartment, have my things shipped east, and depending upon the status of the pandemic restrictions, have a memorial service for my Dad in California.

"I'm going to be quite busy for the next few months, but I welcome it. At any rate, it should make the time go faster. When does your mother come back from Florida? I don't want her to return to her beautiful apartment only to find my work mess everywhere."

Jodi's phone pinged. She looked down at the text and smiled.

"Not to worry, my mom usually returns sometime in late May or early June. If need be, we can simply move your computer and all work-related items to my apartment allowing you to work from there. By that time, I hope we'll be spending more time at the office anyway. Your staying on with her until you find a place of your own won't be a problem, I assure you. Knowing my mom, I'm certain she will want to pick up where she left off and plan more shopping and lunch outings for the two of you."

Jodi felt good having made decisions she was pleased with. "Somehow we always end up talking *business*. But that's not a bad thing, is it? I find myself so excited about interviewing Lily, and I'm anxious to get started. Dealing with the feeling that I've come home is new for me. The only home I know has been clear across the country and quite different in every aspect starting with the weather.

"Okay Sam, my last interference of the day. Let's head back to the city where you will be at the guessing end of my plans for the evening. A change out of our jeans to dressy casual is in order; I've taken care of everything else. A car will pick us up at 6:45 pm to take us to our 7:00 pm reservation, so we better get a move on."

A pleasantly surprised Sam asked, "Where are we going?"

Earlier, Jodi had texted Greg from *Profiles* asking if he could help set up a dinner date at one of Sam's favorite places. She was beginning to think it wasn't going to happen when her phone pinged. They were all set; he had taken care of everything. Her response was smug. "You don't really think I'm going to tell you, do you? In case you do, I'm not!"

With little traffic on the road, they made it back to the city in record time, allowing them plenty of time to shower and change. Jodi turned the tables on Sam by walking down the hall to his apartment. Just as she was about to knock, he opened the door. They both laughed.

Taking the elevator to the Lobby, just as she had yesterday, Sam again asked where they were headed. "We are headed to the car that awaits us in front of the building. That's all I will say for now, but our destination is nearby so your suspense won't last for long."

Two miles away, they pulled up to *Match Brasserie*. Sam was surprised; it was high on his list of favorites. The food and service were excellent. Early days of the pandemic had reduced their business to *takeout*—but with the easing of restrictions and the arrival of warmer weather, spaced indoor and outdoor seating began drawing loyal customers back. Now that cold weather had returned, their limited indoor reservations were normally booked solid especially on weekends, while many chose to continue ordering takeout.

Sam was a frequent diner and knew the staff well. When Greg called, they were happy and eager to welcome their old friend who they hadn't seen in a while. Consolidating two tables for a party of eight had opened a table safely spaced in a private corner of the dining room that was perfect. Greg's instructions were to *take good care* of Sam and his guest who had sought his help in setting up the evening.

They were shown to their table and seated. "I'm impressed. How do you know about this place? Are you aware that it's very close to being my favorite?"

Quite content she had pulled the evening off albeit with Greg's help, Jodi replied, "In case you haven't noticed, everything you planned for this weekend has blown me away. I have learned a lot about the city you love in such a short time, and in the process I have learned so much about you, it seems as though we've known each other forever.

"I made several important decisions going forward in my life—the least of which is remaining in New York permanently. My upcoming interview with Lily is a dream come true for me, and I just happen to have the best *Boss* ever!

"Wanting to do something *nice* for you was a no brainer—you've gone overboard for me. As you might suspect, I had help. I called Greg; so actually we both owe this evening to him."

A little celebrating was definitely in order. It was a wonderful end to an awesome day.

# Chapter 9

Monday morning arrived and Sam was unable to contain his excitement. This was, after all, the day he considered his *ace-in-the-hole*; the day he felt certain Jodi would like best—it was all about Lily. On the spur of the moment, he had come up with the idea of a weekend dedicated to unwinding and distancing themselves from the business at hand. Thus far, it had turned out better than he anticipated, largely due to the fact that Jodi's few surprises had made it a joint endeavor and that pleased him to no end.

As they had the previous two days, they started out at 9:00 am, and took the elevator down to the Lobby where their car awaited them. The short drive to Sarabeth's East for a quick light breakfast gave Jodi the opportunity to once again inquire about their destination. Expecting to get the same *wait and see* reply, she was pleasantly surprised when Sam said, "We're going to start in Brooklyn."

He headed toward DUMBO (Down Under the Manhattan Bridge Overpass) filling her in on the neighborhood's history as he drove. "DUMBO encompasses two sections: one located between the Manhattan and Brooklyn Bridges, which connect Brooklyn to Manhattan across from the East River; and another that continues east to the Manhattan Bridge to the Vinegar Hill area.

"In the late 20ᵗʰ century the area was gentrified into an upscale residential and commercial community—first becoming a haven for art galleries, and currently a center for technology startups earning it the nickname of—*the center of the Brooklyn Tech Triangle*. Today, DUMBO has become Brooklyn's most expensive neighborhood, as well as New York City's fourth richest community overall. The area is the corporate headquarters for e-commerce retailers Etsy and home furnishing stores company West Elm.

"Lily told me that in the late 1970s, she considered opening a second studio in DUMBO but ultimately decided against it. During that time, the area itself was very inclusive, serving mainly as an enclave for artists and young homesteaders seeking relatively large and inexpensive loft apartment spaces for studios and homes. In 1978, the acronym DUMBO was coined when new residents believed such an unattractive name would help deter developers. Many believe the area is one of the last of what could be considered a true arts community in New York."

Sam drove until he found a parking spot and pulled over. "It's a little chilly but the sun is bright, and you can get a better feel for the neighborhood on foot.

"The DUMBO Archway where we are standing is a popular location for film shoots, art exhibitions, live music, large-scale events, and watch parties—for events like the World Cup. The Archway also hosts the Brooklyn Flea every Sunday from April to October. A favorite of locals and tourists alike, the outdoor market features 80 vendors, selling products ranging from secondhand goods to custom-made jewelry.

"The pandemic's slowdown and pushback has been particularly hard on the many small businesses up and down the streets throughout this entire area. As one of my favorite places, I have faith that it will be back to the hustling and bustling community it once was. There is no better place to spend an entire day, and then some, visiting the many shops with unique restaurants offering every kind of cuisine one can imagine."

They walked up and down the side streets—many businesses were closed or opening late; eateries that were open offered takeout only. It was just past noon when they walked back to the car.

Sam turned to Jodi. "You said that you've watched some of our *Profile* episodes. If you happened to see the one we did on Brooklyn, you would have learned that Brooklyn is referred to as the twin city of New York in the Emma Lazarus poem *The New Colossus* that appears on a plaque inside the Statue's pedestal.

"In 1883, the same year the poem was written, the Brooklyn Bridge was completed, transportation to Manhattan was no longer by water only, and the City of Brooklyn's ties to the City of New York were forever strengthened.

"It is the second largest of the boroughs by land area; its water borders are extensive; and its neighborhoods are dynamic in ethnic composition. My family is a perfect example. My father's heritage is rooted in the historically Jewish area of Bensonhurst, while my mother's heritage is rooted in the historically Italian area of Dyker Heights.

"After being priced out of certain types of living arrangements in Manhattan, Brooklyn became a preferred site for artists and hipsters to set up *living and work spaces* not only in Dumbo, but Williamsburg, Red Hook, and Park Slope.

"By the late 1970s when these areas in Brooklyn evolved into preferred sites for artists, Lily had already been successfully established for 30 years. It was no wonder she decided to remain with her studio in West Village.

"The one place we won't be able to visit today is the Brooklyn Botanic Garden; it remains closed since the onset of the shutdown in March of last year. It is at the top of our list of upcoming episodes. In a word, the place is awesome, and we felt we couldn't do the profile justice without personal interviews."

Sam turned onto Vanderbilt Avenue named after Cornelius Vanderbilt—the builder of Grand Central Terminal in Midtown Manhattan. It carries traffic north and south between Grand Army Plaza and Flushing Avenue at the Vanderbilt Avenue gate of the Brooklyn Navy Yard.

Midway down the block of stately manicured homes, he pulled over and stopped. Directly across the street stood the brownstone he wanted Jodi to see. "You are looking at Lily and Joe's Brooklyn home—the first home they moved into after they were married; and the very same home they gave to Noah when they moved into the house on the Upper East Side where Lily still lives."

Jodi did not say a word. She sat staring in silence at the beautiful and evidently well cared for home. There was a wrought iron fence at the front property line. An ornate wrought iron railing on both sides of the wide cement staircase led to the entrance of double doors with wrought iron grilles. Behind the fence at the front of the property were two dirt beds indicating where in spring and summer there would be flowers in full bloom. For a brief moment Jodi closed her eyes and envisioned flowers—of red and yellow and pink and orange and purple and blue.

She opened her eyes, and looked at Sam. "Is anyone living in the house now? It's been almost 20 years since Noah died. Has it been unoccupied all this time? If it has, it is quite obvious the outside of the house has been well cared for and maintained. And I think it's a sure bet that in the warm weather there are flowers growing in those two dirt beds."

Sam agreed. "I think you are right on all accounts. I really don't know the answers to any of your questions. I just thought you might like to see where Lily and Joe started out as a married couple. Remember when we had lunch with her, she told us that they moved from this house to where she lives now."

"Yes, and Sam, she also told us that this used to be Joe's parents' home. His father bought the house on the Upper East Side for their 50th Anniversary."

"You're right. Lily and Joe weren't married until a year or so later. Perhaps they refurnished or remodeled the house before they moved in. Noah would have been born while they lived here and in all probability grew up in Prospect Heights."

Sam pulled back onto the street. At the corner of Sterling Place, he once again pulled over and stopped. "The two red brick buildings facing one another are the old Public School 9 and Public School 9 Annex buildings. Noah probably went to school here."

A million thoughts were whirling around in Jodi's mind. Once again, she closed her eyes and pictured Noah's red brick brownstone with flowers, lots of flowers of bright colors in the dirt beds in front of the house. Now she began picturing children, lots of children that were laughing and playing in the schoolyards of the two red brick schools—Noah may have attended.

"It's getting late, and I still have places to show you. Are you hungry? I'm going to take you to a Brooklyn landmark—Junior's—for a corned beef sandwich that is too big not to share; potato latkes that are as big as breakfast pancakes; and if you have the room, cheesecake that is almost as good as Lily's."

Lunch was great and served as a diversion. Their conversation as they ate was all about the food. For most of the ride back to the city, Jodi was quiet. Sam hoped he hadn't upset her in any way, but if he did, he couldn't figure out why; he simply thought it would be helpful background information for the interview. He wasn't prepared for her reaction first when seeing the house and then the schools; he had expected excitement and curiosity and a million questions, not silence and closing one's eyes as if trying to remember another time or place.

Sam drove in silence giving her space to gather her thoughts. He was certain when she was ready, she would start asking away. She didn't.

The ride took twenty minutes from Brooklyn to West Village. Sam looked over at Jodi to see if she was sleeping; she wasn't. "We've reached our final destination—Greenwich Village. I thought a visit to the *Portraits by Lily Studio* might interest you. Though we can't go inside, you can get a pretty good idea of the gallery, as well as see samples of her work through the large display windows.

"We don't know where her story will begin. However, her studio and

West Village were the biggest part of her early years in New York so I imagine she will speak of them at the very beginning. Are you up to walking around and getting a feel for the area?"

The Jodi that responded was the Jodi he had come to know. "Absolutely yes; I would love that. I can definitely picture Lily here."

They were back to trading quips. Jodi was blown away by the detail in the portraits on display in the large front window certain that Lily had painted them all. They surmised that in all probability, students painted the portraits and landscapes in the smaller side windows, although they did not appear amateurish in the least.

Jodi revisited the large front window staring intently at Lily's work. She was good, very good, if not excellent. The details made the subjects come alive and made one feel as if they knew them. In particular, one painting caught her eye—a couple holding an infant. The pink sweater and bonnet indicated that the pale blue eyes, rosy cheeks, and dark curls were that of a girl. The couple—perhaps the parents—was unidentifiable. Their heads were tilted down looking at the child—showing only a slim side view of their faces.

Jodi was entranced. "Sam, look at this painting. What a beautiful little girl. Although the couple's faces aren't visible, one can feel their love for the child."

Sam agreed. "That's one of the best I've seen. Her paintings have a way of telling stories of their own. Having introduced her portraits not only as paintings of people, but also paintings of buildings, laid the solid groundwork for her success that was almost immediate. She once told me that although a portrait is a painting of a person's face, she considered a descriptive painting of a structure a portrait of that building.

"In that regard, she and I thought alike. When I introduced *Profiles of New York*, I had the exact same concept. Although profiles are generally of people, I envisioned including profiles of structures, events, and even tragedies as long as the subject matter was unique to New York. When I made my *Profiles* pitch to Bill Franklin at PBS, he told me that profiling beyond people was what excited him the most and ultimately sealed the deal."

They walked around West Village for over an hour with Sam pointing out some of the businesses that were still around after all these years, and telling her amusing stories of some of the places that were there in the beginning but had long been a thing of the past.

The sun was setting and it was getting quite cold as they headed back to the car parked near Lily's studio. "Well, what do you think of West Village?"

Jodi thought for a moment. "It reminds me a lot of some of the small beach towns in the Los Angeles area, and Sausalito. These towns were also home to many artists and craftsmen who sold their wares on the boardwalks and wharves up and down the coast.

"My mother had a keen eye for decorating, and she was always looking for something new and original. She took me to many of these outdoor markets, and I was always eager to go. They were a lot of fun. Sometimes when my father took us out on the boat, we would pull into one of the small towns, have lunch, and visit the outdoor market in progress going from booth to booth up one side and down the other. On one occasion, my mom bought me a small Statue of Liberty. We had just studied all about Lady Liberty in school, and I was fascinated by the story. I still have it among my things in California."

Sam smiled. "I hope I made good choices for our weekend. I've had the best time in a long time, and I owe most of it to the person I spent it with. My goal was to acquaint you with your new hometown, and lay some groundwork for your upcoming interview with Lily, while allowing us the opportunity to get to know one another better. I hope you've enjoyed it as much as I have."

"I have enjoyed every minute of it. Your knowledge and love of New York is amazing. Have you ever thought of being a tour guide?"

Sam laughed. "Okay, so now you're making fun of me."

"I'm sorry Sam. I would never make fun of you. I couldn't resist; forgive me? I can't believe that you put this whole three-day weekend together on the spur of a moment. You thought of every detail and you included so much; as far as I can see, you omitted nothing while including everything."

"I forgive you. My mind just works in overdrive constantly. A good deal of the facts that I know about New York are from living them; I owe the rest to researching episodes of *Profiles*, and facts have a tendency to stick with me. But that's a good thing, isn't it?

"We've had such a full day, I thought we might return to the apartment and order in Chinese food. I'm definitely through with talking business. After dinner we can just relax and unwind, maybe watch a movie if there's anything you want to see."

"That sounds like a plan. I love Chinese food. San Francisco's

Chinatown has long been one of my favorite places. I spent an entire month there once when I was on assignment, and I think I ate some type of Asian food every day. On Sundays, there was a Chinese Restaurant near Fisherman's Wharf that had Dim Sum to die for."

Sam called and ordered the food from the car. By the time they arrived at the apartment, it had been delivered. And as promised, no business talk arose. They were both in a good mood. As they ate, they began trading stories of people they dated. A few were quite funny causing them to laugh at themselves and causing them to conclude they were two misfits nobody wanted. This could not have been further from the truth.

They had little interest in watching TV, and Sam decided to call it a night. "I think I'll leave and let you get some rest. Tomorrow I have to go to the office. If you would like to come with me, you can pick up whatever you need for the interview on Wednesday—tape recorder, pads, pencils, etc. I'd like to show you the office I chose for you. You can set it up to your liking, ordering anything I may have missed. We've pretty much worked from home since the pandemic, but when you are finished with Lily's interview you may prefer to work from your office; it's totally up to you.

"I don't know how long I'll be tied up in my meeting, but if you're ready to leave before I am, I can have a car bring you back to the apartment."

"I'd like that. My plan is to tape Lily's every word. When I have finished the interview, we can discuss how we want to present the episode, and then the editing will begin. Since 9:00 am seems to work, is that good?"

"Yes, definitely. We can stop for coffee and breakfast rolls on the way. We have a kitchen at the office, but we haven't used it for almost a year. I can't believe it's been that long."

Jodi walked Sam to the door. As they hugged, she leaned back and said, "It seems like I'm endlessly thanking you and I guess I am. You've been good and extremely generous to me. I'm going to give this interview everything I've got."

Sam responded, "I have no doubt whatsoever that you will." He kissed her on the forehead and he was gone.

Jodi spent the morning just as Sam had suggested. She was quite impressed with the office he had chosen for her. It was quite large, beautifully furnished, and left no doubt that it was professionally decorated; in fact it looked and smelled new. She learned that indeed it was. After she accepted Sam's offer, he placed a call to his friend who was a decorator and gave her carte blanche; he was pleased with what she had done. Jodi was over the moon.

She had never had an office other than a small cubby somewhere when on assignment. The office space she set up in her condo was a small part of her second bedroom. Her new office had windows all around with a beautiful view of the area; a handsome antique desk and chair, a small conference table and chairs; two plush visitors chairs facing the desk, and paintings on the wall.

She gathered everything she needed to begin the interview with Lily, and placed it all in a small box. Sam was still behind closed doors on his conference call. She left him a note asking him to bring the box home when he came. As she was putting on her coat, the door to his office opened. "Hi, I was just leaving you a note; I'm finished here so I've decided to spend the afternoon doing a little shopping. I'll meet up with you later at the apartment."

"Good decision. You deserve some time for yourself. Enjoy!"

Jodi called an Uber and waited patiently in front of the building. Her first stop was the hairdressers; she desperately needed a haircut. She normally wore it short because it was easier especially when she was on assignment. Her last cut had been months before she came east.

Staring at herself in the mirror, she couldn't believe what she saw. She left the shop not only feeling like a new person, but she also looked like a new person. Her hair was naturally curly when it was short and the chic new haircut had done the job—her short dark hair accented her pale blue eyes and flawless complexion giving her an air of sophistication. The girl that had gone into the hairdressers had come out a woman.

Thoroughly pleased with the new Jodi, she went shopping for some much needed clothes. Slacks, sweaters, blouses, even new underwear and pajamas were on her list. She caught sight of *a little black dress* on a mannequin as she headed towards the escalator; an additional bag soon held that dress and a pale blue one that had also caught her eye. The next and last stop was the shoe department.

Loaded down with bags, she called an Uber to take her to the apartment. After spending the better part of an hour removing tags and putting all her purchases away, she realized all she had all day was coffee and a Danish. As she warmed up the leftover Chinese food from dinner, she gave thought to her final plans of the day.

First she placed a call to Sam. When he looked at his cell to see who was calling, he was surprised to see that it was Jodi. "Hi. How was your day? Did you buy out the stores?"

"No, I left a few things. I'm back at the apartment, and I'm calling to see if you have any plans for this evening. If not, I would love to have you join me for dinner."

"No, I don't have plans, and yes, I would love to join you for dinner? Nothing would please me more. Where are we going?"

"I'm not going anywhere; you will be coming here. Is 7:00 pm good?"

"Yes, that's fine. Shall I bring wine?"

"Thank you. Red wine will be perfect. By the way, dress code is casual. See you then."

Sam hung up. As he sat smiling and gazing into thin air, Greg walked by and stuck his head in the door. "What's the smug look on your face? Does it happen to have anything to do with Jodi?"

Sam wadded up a piece of paper and threw it—missing Greg by a mile—as he walked down the hall laughing.

Jodi made a call to Westside Market and placed her order: Prime Rib Roast, salad fixings, baking potatoes, loaf of French bread, fruit flan for dessert, and an assortment of cheeses. She had crackers, condiments, and whatever else she needed on hand. It would be delivered within the hour. She was a good customer, and this was the first time she had placed an order that she needed as soon as possible. They were happy to accommodate her.

She placed a call to Lily confirming their appointment in the morning. It was all set for 10:00 am. They each heard the excitement in one another's voices. "I'll have coffee and plenty of food to nibble on however long our day is. I'm just so anxious to get started."

Jodi replied, "I second that; I can hardly wait. See you in the morning."

She set the table, readied a pan for the roast, a salad bowl and tongs for the salad, and a breadboard for the French loaf. Next she set aside sour cream and butter for the potatoes, caviar butter for the bread, and salad dressing for the salad in the refrigerator.

The knock on the door indicated that the delivery from Westside Market had arrived. Checking the clock, she was good; it was 5:30 pm.

She began by making the salad. Next she wrapped the potatoes in tinfoil and placed them in the oven, seasoned the roast and placed it in the pan ready to take its place with the potatoes. She refrigerated the fruit flan, and placed the cheeses on the counter next to the serving dish and crackers.

It was 6:00 pm; she was right on schedule with enough time for a shower and change of clothes. She was in the kitchen finishing up the cheese platter when Sam arrived.

She opened the door to a speechless Sam holding a bottle of wine. Facing him stood a fascinating young woman with the most beautiful pale blue eyes he had ever seen. She wore a pale blue sweater and winter white slacks. She was stunning. "Wow! You look fabulous."

"Come in; don't just stand there. Thank you. I just had my hair cut. It was longer than I normally wear it; shorter hair has always worked better for me. I don't know how busy I'm going to be when the interview gets started so I decided to have it cut today.

"If you would be so good as to open the wine and take the cheese and crackers into the other room, I'll put the roast in the oven and join you. We're having Prime Rib, and if I recall correctly, you like yours medium to medium rare."

He couldn't take his eyes off of her. "I have to say, I think your new look is fantastic and quite complimentary. It definitely suits you."

He poured wine for both of them, handing her a glass.

"To Jodi, you never fail to amaze me. I can't believe I was fortunate enough to convince you to come east and be a part of *Profiles*. We have a relatively small staff, but we consider ourselves family, and I can't think of anyone I would rather have as family than you, both professionally and personally."

Now it was Jodi's turn to be speechless. "Sam I feel the same way about you. My circumstances are different because I have no family, and that's probably why I'm having such a hard time dealing with the feelings I have for you. I don't want them to be feelings of gratitude or feelings of thanks for all that you have done and continue to do for me. And then there's that little fact that you're my boss. How am I supposed to deal with that?"

He took the glass from her hand and placed it on the table. Drawing her into his arms, he kissed her with all the longing he had carried inside since he was first attracted to her at the wedding in California where they first met. She kissed him back; it was not a kiss of gratitude.

Sam released her and looking into her eyes said, "I've waited so long for this moment; it was worth the wait. I've agonized how to deal with my feelings for you just as you have for me, but I had no intention whatsoever of professing those feelings for you tonight. Now that I have and you have, as well, I'm glad we did.

"This doesn't change anything except the fact we no longer have to keep our feelings in check bottled up inside. We'll take things slow and let fate take its course.

"Something smells delicious! Do you have to check on anything?"

"Oh no, I hope dinner isn't ruined." It wasn't. The roast and potatoes had a few more minutes to go; together they moved the untouched cheese platter to the kitchen. Sam helped bring the salad and condiments to the table; Jodi asked him to carve the meat and put it on the platter with the potatoes.

"Well I learned something new about you today and I'm impressed; you're quite a cook or shall I say *chef.* Even with a little distraction, dinner turned out excellent."

"I definitely do not qualify as a cook or a chef; my menu is extremely limited. My Mom was always working so the dinners she prepared tended to be ones that could be put together at a moment's notice. She didn't have any hand-me-down family recipes, or the time to prepare them, so she made meat and potatoes with a salad on the side; they worked for her, so I learned to make them work for me. I'm so glad you liked it.

"I have a fruit flan in the refrigerator for later with coffee, but it came prepared, ready to enjoy. I can't take any credit for that."

When the dishes were cleared and all the food wrapped and refrigerated, they retired to the living room and talked the evening away.

The kiss they shared cleared the air and opened the door to the future whatever it held. They felt good about each other; they felt comfortable with each other. They were embarking on producing an episode of *Profiles* that they hoped would be a blockbuster never imagining the affect Lily Asher's story would have on not only the show but also their lives.

# Chapter 10

It was a cold crisp morning, a morning that Jodi would have preferred to walk to Lily's if it wasn't for the box of supplies she was taking with her for the interview. When she went through the box she had asked Sam to bring to the apartment for her, she discovered that he added a few items, items that included a backup tape recorder and a camera. Sam offered to have their car service pick her up, but she declined opting to call for an Uber instead.

She was glad that it was only a short distance from the Pavilion because her thoughts were rampant. How would Lily begin her story? Where would Lily begin her story? She would soon know—the car pulled up in front of her house.

Lily opened the door. "Come right in Jodi; it's a bit chilly. I heard on the news last night that a snowstorm is headed our way over the weekend. How are you adapting to our cold weather? I imagine coming from sunny Southern California, it's a big change."

Suddenly Lily stopped speaking and stared. "You look fantastic. I see you got your hair cut, and I must say it is quite becoming. It accents your blue eyes and gives you a totally different look. What did Sam think? I'm betting he liked it as much as I do."

Jodi laughed. She had no idea her haircut would be so well received, and found Lily's reaction a bit awkward. "He did like it, and much the same as you agrees that it is quite flattering. Thank you.

"As far as the weather, I haven't had a problem so far, as long as I'm warmly dressed when I'm outdoors. My parents and I used to go up to San Francisco regularly and it's colder up north. We also used to go skiing every winter with friends that owned a place in Breckinridge, Colorado. They had twin daughters my age, and we had so much fun."

Lily led the way to a large room she had called *the relaxing room* when she took them on a tour of the house. It was tastefully and comfortably furnished; the warmth coming from the gas fireplace was cozy and welcoming—Jodi looked about the room approvingly. She made a mental note that meant absolutely nothing—there were a lot of gas fireplaces in the house; it seemed as though there was one in almost every room.

There was a small table set up with coffee, sweet rolls, juice, yogurt, and—bringing a smile to her face—energy bars. The plush sofa and chairs appeared eager to indulge anyone seeking comfort and relaxation. There was a medium size box on the floor next to the lounge chair that Lily would occupy.

"I thought this would be a good place for us to start today. If it doesn't work for you, we can certainly find another room or rooms in this big house. Is there anything else you need? Anything I've forgotten? Please help yourself to coffee or whatever you would like and we can begin."

"No Lily, you have thought of everything. I'm a bit of a coffee junky, and since I haven't had any coffee as yet this morning, I will pour myself a cup. Thank you.

"Before we begin, I'm going to share my thoughts on how we should proceed. Every interview I have done has been different; some may be similar but none are exactly alike. You are the subject of the interview; it is your story to tell so you should tell it. Sam has gone over several *Profiles*-episodes with me to acquaint me with the many different types of presentations. As an example, some are first person as told in their own words. Others are a combination of an introduction, the story as told by the subject followed by a summation conclusion. There are many options. What we look for is whatever is best for the story being told.

"I plan to record the entire interview in your own words. At its conclusion, it is my job to review and edit the material laying a background extending up to and including the events of 9/11, and the significance those events had on your life. I want you to be candid yet comfortable with whatever you relate. We encourage you to begin *Lily's Story* as early in your life as you feel it impacts leading up to 9/11, and end by including the last 20 years up to the present.

"Although I usually ask questions at times, they are not recorded, but are asked mainly to clarify. As my boss, Sam would normally have the final say, but we both agree wholeheartedly that the final say is yours; allowing you to speak freely without hesitation and rest assured that you can retract or delete anything that we tape. What are your thoughts?"

Lily was quite impressed; Jodi had done her homework. "I think my decision to request you as my interviewer was the right choice. When I read your article, it made me feel as though I knew you. I felt if anyone could do my story justice, it would be you. You are quite accomplished for someone so young. You are a talented writer, a heartfelt writer, and that comes from within not from experience.

"The one thing you didn't mention is a timeline. Are you on a deadline of any sort? I can't say how long it will take to tell my story, which would depend on how often we meet and the length of the sessions. I have many pictures and items I would like to show you as we move through the process that is if you have an interest in seeing them. And we do have to consider breaking for lunch, do we not?"

Jodi laughed; she was really something! "Your points are well taken. *Profiles* breaks for the summer—July and August. Their show in June ends the season; however, Sam told me that this year there would be no June episode. The new season begins in September with the two-hour 9/11 Anniversary Episode airing on the exact date. We are not on a deadline by any means. We just want to produce a blockbuster show for the 20th Anniversary, and if we go into the summer months, we are up for it. Do I want to see your pictures and items; you bet I do—no matter how many there are.

"We can meet as often and for as long as you like. Let's just see how it goes. I'm at your disposal; it is my job and a dream come true for me. It's the type of journalism I chose to pursue after my early media associations left me totally empty and unfulfilled. The one thing I learned early on was that I connect better with people than with events. My mother actually encouraged me to go freelance—pick my own subjects on my own time.

"I might suggest that we just proceed at a pace that suits us both. We also don't have to do the interview every time we meet. I think it would be extremely interesting and informative to spend days in between going through your memorabilia at times when it fits into your story or just chatting about odds and ends that come to mind. This would also allow us to get to know one another better which is equally as important to me as telling your story.

"Breaking for lunch is a given. We do have to eat."

Lily was elated. "I assumed we would begin today. I'm going to sit here in my lounge chair. Pick your spot, set up the recorder, grab your coffee, and we can get started. Let our adventure begin!"

Jodi refilled her coffee cup and took an energy bar. Lily's chair faced the sofa where Jodi sat with pad and pencil in hand to take notes. The tape recorder sat on a small table between them—Jodi flipped the ON switch. And so it began—*Lily's Story*.

"My father was a Professor of Art History at the University of Vienna when he met my mother; she was a student in his class. Although their attraction to one another was immediate, he was fifteen years older than she was, and they agreed it best to proceed slowly and surely. Standing the *test of time* they were married only days after she graduated.

"Shortly thereafter, my father accepted an offer from the Museum of Art History in Vienna—it was an extremely prestigious and generous offer he could not refuse. By the time I was born two years later, they brought me home from the hospital to our beautiful and elegant home.

"During her pregnancy, my mother studied and worked hard perfecting her knowledge of art restoration which she had chosen to pursue as her career. My mother was an artist and although she chose to pursue a career in art restoration, she painted whenever she had the chance mainly as a form of relaxation. Needless to say, she taught me a great deal, not only about painting but also about life.

"She noticed early on in my childhood that I had a flair for drawing, and much to her astonishment—drawing people's faces with precise detail— although I had not yet reached my fifth birthday. She was determined to support my innate talent by assuring that I had every opportunity to reach my full potential; that is, if that was what I wanted.

"My mother continued to purchase art materials for me to work with, and we often went to a park or other secluded place to spend time together drawing. On these outings she always brought along a picnic basket filled with a variety of goodies. The outings are among the fondest memories I have of my mother.

"In our parlor stood a magnificent baby grand piano. Another of my mother's talents was playing the piano. On days when the weather was bad and we couldn't go to the park, we turned to indoor activities. She taught me to play when I was quite young. To this very day, I find playing very relaxing unless my arthritis interferes.

"When I was five, my brother's birth grew our family to four. Months later, my mother was hired by the Museum of Art History to join their in-house restoration team. I had started school, and a Nanny was hired to care for my baby brother.

"My childhood was wonderful. I grew up loved in a close family that spent what today one would call *quality time* together. We vacationed several times a year, and holidays were a big deal in our house always, especially Christmas. My parents were not religious to any degree; the rare times that found us in church were to attend christenings, weddings, funerals, and the like.

"When I was sixteen, my parents presented me with a choice of schools. My mother had researched schools that offered dedicated art programs and found one in Zurich that stood out above the others. Although It was a boarding school, having an aunt and uncle that lived nearby would allow me to spend weekends with them, making it easier on me leaving home for the first time. I was quite excited.

"I loved my aunt and uncle; we often spent holidays with them, and having no children of their own doted on both my brother and me. They owned a small art gallery in the Zurich business area, but my uncle was better known as an Art Dealer brokering the sale of valuable paintings and art collections worldwide. His clients were the wealthy, the famous, the museums, and the institutions that paid him handsomely for finding what they sought.

'My life was far removed from politics and world problems in general. In March 1938, Nazi Germany occupied and annexed Austria. I was at school in Zurich. I came home for the summer to Vienna and my mother had a surprise for me. She gave me a camera. She came upon the idea while using one in her art restoration process. It was an American-made Kodak—made right here in New York, a fact that I didn't learn until I moved here.

"With the Nazi presence throughout the city of Vienna, my parents urged caution wherever I went. My mother's concern stemmed from noticing the attention the young soldiers paid the young women they encountered on the streets. Although they kept a close watch on both my brother and me, it was nice being home and seeing my friends; all too quickly, the summer was over.

"In the fall of 1938, I returned to school in Zurich; Hitler's anti-Jewish policies fell on fertile soil in Vienna on Kristallnacht November 9th. The city began changing overnight and though hostilities to-date were solely against the Jews, my mother grew wary and worried constantly.

"As Christmas and the end of the year approached, my parents made a decision about our holiday plans. Our normal routine was to spend Christmas at home in Vienna, and the week following skiing in the Swiss Alps with my aunt and uncle. They were family vacations that all of us looked forward to.

"My mother called my aunt and uncle to tell them that I was to stay in Zurich when school closed. They were hoping to spend Christmas with them, and then leave for our ski trip together. I never forgot the hesitation in my mother's voice when she called me at school to tell me the change of plans. By the time the holidays were over, and my parents and brother returned to Vienna, I had set my worries aside. We had a wonderful time together as always.

"At the end of June 1939, I returned home to Vienna for the summer break. I wasn't prepared for what I observed. The Gestapo, along with Austrian Nazis and sympathizers seized Jewish businesses and looted their belongings, while leaving in its wake shuttered stores and buildings, streets scattered with debris, and Austrians who hurried on their way with heads lowered.

"I was seventeen years old that summer yet I felt as if I had grown up overnight. I was horrified at what I saw; a feeling of dread came over me. I worried for my parents, for my brother who was attending school in the city, and the only way of life that I had known. I stayed close to home. When I told my mother I planned to call my friend Tessa and see if we could get together, she told me they had moved to Berlin months earlier. Her father, who had once worked with mine at the museum, had been transferred.

"I returned to Zurich in late August. September 1, 1939, WWII began with Hitler's invasion of Poland. We called my parents as much as possible; greatly relieved when we learned all was okay. With Christmas approaching, my parents agreed with my aunt and uncle that the previous year's plans would be best. The only difference would be a trip to Berlin for my father's business meeting; my mother and brother would accompany him, spend the night in Berlin, and the three of them would travel from Berlin to Zurich the following day.

"On December 22, 1939, they boarded a heavily laden D180 Express train from Berlin to Genthin, Germany, where they would change trains and travel on to Zurich. Christmas Day 1939 fell on a Monday, which many families and soldiers used as a long weekend.

"As the D180 Express train approached the Genthin Station, the preceding D10 Express train was late leaving, having been delayed by patchy fog. The engineer of the D180, intent to keeping on time, failed to heed a stop signal and misread the clear signal intended for the preceding train, causing the engine to strike the rear of the D10 with such force that coaches were hurled upwards, landing on top of the locomotive. There were 453 injured and 278 fatalities, my parents and brother included. To this day, it remains the worst train disaster in Germany's history.

"It wasn't until the next morning, that my uncle learned what had happened. As we waited for them to arrive, and it grew later and later, there wasn't much we could do. The electronics we take for granted today were unavailable, a part of the distant future.

"Upon learning of the accident, the options open to us were equally as limited. We had but one option and that was to wait. Waiting gave us time to think, and thinking although rational was not always positive. If they were unhurt, they would have contacted us. That meant they were either injured or perished in the accident. Days later we finally learned they were not on the injured list. My uncle announced he was going to make arrangements to go to Genthin. He did, but not without my aunt and me.

"The next few weeks were a blur. My uncle was a godsend; he took care of everything. Our decisions, greatly hindered by the war, were a well thought out process. We agreed to cremate the bodies to be buried or scattered at a later time in Switzerland. The long week we spent in Genthin seemed endless.

"We returned to Zurich, and my aunt and uncle encouraged me to return to school. I did so reluctantly but it helped. I threw myself into my art; it kept me close to my parents. I agonized about the times I called my brother a pest and told him to stop bothering me. The least little thing brought me to tears. But time passed, and although I don't believe that time heals everything, I do believe that it lessens the burden we carry.

"The war dominated the headlines, and made it difficult to make any plans whatsoever. WWII had been declared only months before, yet no one could predict what tomorrow would bring. Though there was a presence of thousands of Nazi soldiers in the country, Switzerland was neutral, and for the most part life went on as usual. My uncle's contacts at the bank advised him to settle things in Austria as soon as possible before it was too late. After weeks of red tape, submitting form after form, and endless hours waiting at the travel office in Zurich, he managed to secure rail tickets for us.

"After my graduation in the spring, the three of us traveled to Austria to settle my parents' affairs, empty the house, and decide what items I wanted to keep. My uncle was the Executor of their estate and had taken care of the financial issues. When he contacted the museum to arrange pickup of any personal items my parents left behind, he learned that they had someone who was interested in purchasing our house. This was the first good news we received. When we returned to Vienna, although I had little to do except go through the house, it turned out to be a much bigger job than I anticipated.

"I soon learned that there were many things I wanted to keep that I couldn't. It took me almost two weeks to come to the realization that my life was never going to be the same. My parents and brother were gone; the life I knew as a family was gone. No amount of items to remember them by would ever suffice. Items could never replace what I lost nor did I need them to remember. My memories might be all I had but they were mine to keep forever.

"Once I arrived at these conclusions, my job became easier. We boxed up the personal items to be shipped, and filled a small box that included jewelry and smaller sentimental pieces to take with us. It broke my heart to leave my mother's beautiful baby grand piano. Before leaving the house, I sat down one last time and played Debussy's Claire du Lune, my mother's favorite; my aunt and uncle stood listening with tears streaming down their faces.

"We returned to Switzerland where I enrolled in art classes at the University of Zurich. I lived with my aunt and uncle and although business at the gallery had definitely declined because of the war, I helped whenever I was needed. In early 1942, my aunt was diagnosed with cancer and died two months later.

"After the war, my uncle began talking about the two of us going to America. He was quite convincing when he said he wanted me to have a good life and pursue my art in a place where opportunities and possibilities were infinite. After the war, Europe was broken and had nothing to offer the young or the old; it would be good for both of us. Having only each other, he wanted us to be together while assuring my wellbeing above all else.

"He had several contacts in New York City that he reached out to,

91

and he shared their conversations with me. There was a big art world in Manhattan, and they assured him that I could find a place that suited my abilities and ambitions.

"It had been a long time since I had given any thought to the future—where that would be; what it held for me; what I wanted it to be. The idea of relocating to the United States was both daunting and quite exciting. In the end, exciting won out.

There was much to be done before we left Zurich. My uncle had seen to my affairs when my parents died. Selling the gallery and settling his affairs was a much larger undertaking.

"After almost three years of working with lawyers and banks and clients, he suggested that we make plans for me to go to New York alone, assuring me that he would follow as soon as possible. He transferred my funds to Chase National Bank and put me in touch with the branch manager, John Shepherd. John and his wife Grace were my first friends in America; we remained good friends until they passed.

"I arrived in New York in September 1947 and fell in love with the city and everything about it. I wrote to my uncle telling him that *I Love New York* long before the saying became popular. John enlisted his wife to show me around, and it was Grace who arranged for the real estate agent who found the location for my studio in West Village.

"There was but one downside to my new life, my uncle never came to America. Somehow deep down, I knew when I left Zurich I would never see him again."

Lily stopped talking and sat quietly lost in her thoughts.

Jodi sat quietly lost in her thoughts taking no notice that Lily had stopped talking. When had she stopped listening—when she heard that she played Debussy's Claire du Lune. She didn't recall hearing anything after that.

Suddenly realizing that Lily had stopped speaking, she reached over and turned off the recorder. "Lily, are you okay?"

Snapping out of her momentary trance, she replied, "Yes, I'm fine. Memories are all I have and sometimes that makes me sad. I think we've reached a stopping point. Let's take a break and have a snack, and then I have some things in this box on the floor that I want to share with you."

Moving the box closer to the sofa, they sat side-by-side as Lily removed item after item from the box. There were small portraits of her parents, her brother, and herself. "I painted these. I mentioned that my mother had given me a camera, and I started taking pictures of my subjects.

Painting from the photographs was her suggestion, and from that point on, it became my signature method. When I opened *Portraits by Lily* my clients loved the idea of not having to pose, allowing them to bring in a favorite photo of themselves or surprise someone with a gift painted from a favorite photo taken in the past."

She removed a few additional larger paintings. "This one is a front view of our house in Vienna; this one is the park where we often went to draw together and picnic; and these are all paintings of my brother and I at the Vienna Zoo. It was his favorite place, and we went there many times. All of these paintings are my mother's. There are larger paintings of hers that hang throughout this house."

Next she removed the Kodak camera her mother had given her. This is what started it all, and I continued to use it until John and Grace gave me the Kodak color camera made to use Kodachrome film. It was my first Thanksgiving in America and they invited me for dinner. When all the guests were gone, they gifted me with this beautiful camera. It still looks good today, except it's much bigger than the new ones. There's really no reason to own a camera today; smart phones took care of that."

Lily continued to remove items until the box was empty. "I think that does it. These few items are from my life in Vienna except for the camera John and Grace gave me. There was just so much I could take. I wish I had some pictures of the rooms in our house, but there aren't any. It was such a beautiful home; I can still picture every single room and how it was furnished."

Jodi absorbed her every word and description. "That was wonderful. Let me help you put everything back in the box. It's growing late, and I think we're off to a good start. Do you agree?"

"I do. As I told you when you arrived this morning, they're expecting a sizeable snowstorm heading into the beginning of the week. Even though you're not far from here, I see no need for you to come if the weather is bad. Since that might mess with plans for our next meeting, are you available Friday? That will give you a couple of days to go over today's material."

"Lily, if you're up to it then so am I. Shall we say 10:00 am; it worked fine today."

"Yes it did; we are all set. Thank you for the refreshments, and I look forward to seeing you Friday. Today was wonderful Lily."

Jodi called an Uber and they chatted until it arrived.

Jodi sat quietly lost in her thoughts on the ride home. If her Uber driver said anything to her, she wasn't aware. Pleased at how their first session had gone, she hoped Lily was also. Arriving at the Pavilion, she quickly disappeared into the building and took the elevator up to the apartment.

It was early, not quite 4:00 pm. She hadn't made plans with Sam although since her arrival in New York, it had become routine to share meals together. She knew no one else; he lived right down the hall; and they were working together.

Removing her coat and shoes, she collapsed onto the sofa collecting her thoughts. Everything was just fine as she sat listening and absorbing Lily's every word—until she mentioned playing Debussy's Claire du Lune before leaving their home in Vienna for the last time. She heard nothing after that. She would have to play the tape to learn what she had missed.

She was at a loss as to how to proceed. Should she tell Sam? Was it a coincidence? What was happening? Today was her very first day and she was unsure as to how to continue right off the bat. The pictures and items Lily had shared were wonderful. A picture is truly worth a thousand words. Her mother's paintings were windows to her world—the world she was born into and where she grew up.

After going over and over in her mind the day's interview, she decided that Lily had started her story at the beginning, which is exactly where she should have started. Whether we used all of the material, some of the material, or none of the material, made no difference. When one tells a story, one starts at the beginning. And she had told Lily it was her story to tell as she saw fit.

Jodi decided to call Sam and leave the decision to him. Did he want to hear the interviews as they were recorded or would he prefer Jodi do the editing and present him with the finished product. She would simply leave the decision up to him. She smiled to herself knowing exactly what it would be.

She reached for the phone; he picked up on the second ring. "Hi! Where are you? You're not still at Lily's, are you?"

"No, I'm in the apartment; I got home a short while ago. Today went well and I feel as though we're off to a good start. We plan to meet again on Friday, since the weather next week looks bleak.

"I'd like your thoughts about how to move forward. Do you want to listen to the tapes as I get them, at various intervals, or at the end? I'd prefer your input as we go along; this will allow me to give you my thoughts on how we should proceed.

"Anyway, we don't have to discuss it over the phone. If you're up to having breakfast for dinner, I'm offering Western omelets, hash browns, coffee, and blueberry muffins. We can talk about it then, and if you like, listen to the tape as well. Are you home?"

"I am; I got in about 10 minutes ago and was just about to call you. I haven't had a Western omelet in some time, and it sounds good. Is there any wine that goes with breakfast fare? Or is there anything else I can bring?"

"Do you happen to have any Vodka? I have tomato juice, and we can have a Bloody Mary instead of wine."

"I'll check, but if I don't, I think my mom does. I'll show you where she keeps her private stock. We can always replace anything we use. What time should I be there?'

"Let's say 6:00 pm. We can eat first and then have the whole evening to go over today. See you soon."

They ate first, enjoying breakfast for dinner immensely. With a second Bloody Mary for each in hand, they settled in to listen to the tape.

When the tape ended, they both sat quietly deep in thought. To Sam, the tape revealed new insight to Lily's early life in Austria and Switzerland, and how she ultimately came to America. Most of what he knew about her was from 1947 forward when she arrived in New York, and the opening of *Portraits by Lily* in West Village. He was unaware of her privileged life before the loss of her family, unaware of her parents' background, and totally unaware of the bond between her and her mother whose influence and support so obviously shaped her destiny.

To Jodi, the tape was just right. Lily started at the very beginning of her life, and this indicated to Jodi that she meant to leave no stone unturned. She had laid a strong foundation for telling her story with the perfect mix of detail and feeling allowing the listener to envision both the environment she grew up in and the relationship with her mother. She heard for the first time, Lily's account of leaving Austria and moving to Switzerland to live with her aunt and uncle until ultimately coming to America.

It was at the point in the tape where she spoke of playing Debussy's Claire du Lune that she had frozen and stopped listening. For some reason

Jodi once again pictured the brownstone on Vanderbilt Avenue with colorful flowers in full bloom, and a schoolyard where three young girls held hands as they danced around in a circle. She divulged none of these feelings to Sam.

"Wow! I would say your first session went extremely well. It's off to a good start, and if Lily continues along these lines in future tapings, our job to edit and format the show will certainly be easier and far less time consuming. What are your thoughts?"

For a moment Jodi did not answer; when she did, she shared Sam's feelings. "Wow is right. I loved that she started at the very beginning and not when she first came to New York. It indicates to me that she's going to take us on the ride of our lives, and we better buckle up and be ready."

Sam thoroughly agreed. "Did you schedule another meeting or are you going to wait for Lily to call you?"

Jodi laughed. "Sam if there's anything I've learned about Lily Asher in the very short time that I've known her is that she is in the driver's seat and will set the pace going forward.

"She suggested that we get together again on Friday. There is a pending snowstorm coming up the east coast over the weekend, and if the prediction becomes reality, she saw no reason for me to venture out in bad weather— even though I assured her I was well equipped with hat, scarf, heavy coat, and boots. We set up the second session for Friday at 10:00 am.

"I'm quite excited, and I'm eagerly looking forward to Friday. In the meantime, I'm going to listen to the tape again and make some notes.

"Now, are you ready for coffee and blueberry muffins? I know breakfast is usually not followed by dessert, but I believe that desserts are good anytime."

# Chapter 11

True to her word, Jodi listened to the tape, not once but several times. Not only couldn't she dismiss the Claire du Lune part, she couldn't understand why she kept returning to images in her mind of the brownstone on Vanderbilt Avenue with a multitude of brightly colored flowers in the dirt beds that were bare. Most concerning were the images of children on the playground of Public School 9 filled with the laughter of children playing—laughter that she could actually hear.

At last Friday arrived and with a cup of coffee in hand, Jodi walked to Lily's arriving on time for their meeting. It would become their routine. There was no reason for idle chatter; both were anxious to get started and they did without delay.

Lily picked up where she left off—arriving in America. "I arrived in New York in September 1947. My only sadness was that my uncle had not come with me, but he had seen to my every need. John and Grace Shepherd became my guardian angels—John took care of my financial affairs and Grace became my friend. I lived at The Barbizon, a popular residential hotel for women on East 63rd Street.

"At John's behest, Grace agreed to show me around the city and orient me to my new surroundings, my new home. When she learned that I wanted to open my own studio, she became determined to help me realize my dream and that she did.

"She retained a real estate agent to show us properties for rent and when the first one didn't materialize, she found another who turned out to be a true gem—Rich Harrison. He took us to West Village and showed us two spaces that he thought I might like. The first location was nice but the lighting wasn't good. The second one was my choice and what a choice it turned out to be. It was to become *Portraits by Lily*—and to this very day remains in the same location.

"Through the years, the original studio has seen minimal changes. I leased the upstairs when it became available, and ultimately moved from The Barbizon to my new apartment. I lived there for a brief time before Joe and I were married. Years later, Joe purchased the building for me when the owner decided to sell.

"With Rich's help and recommendations, John and Grace's never wavering support, and my relentless drive, *Portraits by Lily* opened in the spring of 1948; it became an instant success. John and Grace had managed to spread the word among their friends and business contacts, as did Rich among his many friends throughout West Village, who welcomed their new neighbor with open arms.

"Actually three lone paintings remained at the end of opening day—all the others were sold. After everyone had gone, Rich insisted on staying and helping me clean up and discard the many empty champagne bottles and trash. As we were closing up, Rich announced he was taking me to one of his favorite restaurants in Manhattan to do a little celebrating.

"Still over the moon as to how the day had gone, I was definitely up for it. As we were leaving the restaurant, we bumped into a friend of Rich's and he introduced us—me as his new friend to his forever friend having grown up with him—Joe Asher. To someone who never drank but had been drinking for the better part of the day, I did manage to notice how handsome he was and what a nice smile he had.

"With so many paintings sold at the opening, my work was cut out for me. I displayed some of my old paintings just to fill the walls until I could catch up. All of the paintings for the opening had been various businesses in and around the studio. My new paintings were portraits of people. My subjects were varied; I chose mainly locals—the cop on the beat, the Chief of FDNY Squad 18, and even a few local politicians. The one that stood out above the rest was my portrait of Rich Harrison.

"After being on display in my gallery for a time, I gifted him with the portrait. He was quite moved and profusely thanked me. I felt otherwise; I had him to thank for the part he played in making my dream a reality. In short order, I would have another reason to thank him.

"On a cold crisp December day as 1948 was nearing it's end, a young man came to my studio seeking a portrait of his parents as a 50th Wedding Anniversary gift. He looked vaguely familiar but I couldn't place him at first, and then he smiled. Even if he had not introduced himself, I knew—he was Joe Asher.

"He explained that he had seen my portrait of Rich, and it had actually been his suggestion that he contact me knowing that there was a big celebration in the works for his parents. Joe brought several photographs with him, but decided to look further before making his final decision. We later joked that he wanted a reason to return to the studio to see me.

"Before, the portrait was finished, Joe asked me to dinner—several dinners, ice skating, and just hanging out—as though we had been doing these things together for years. We both fell hard; in a matter of three brief months, we had declared our love for one another.

"Lou and Arlene Asher's 50th Anniversary Celebration was held in this very house at which time, my future mother-in-law learned that the house was their new home when Lou presented her with the key. It was the first of many gatherings, both personal and business related, hosted in this house by my in-laws, as well as Joe and me, when abruptly 9/11 ended it all. Their portrait in the foyer is the very one I painted for Joe—the thought never entered our minds to replace it.

"I was a guest, Joe's date for the party, and attending the very first of many celebrations held here; this house became a part of me long before I actually lived here. Perhaps that's the reason I cannot imagine living anywhere else.

"At times when I reminisced about our house in Vienna, I realized that the possibility of our remaining in that home throughout the war was unrealistic. By war's end, Vienna had suffered vast destruction in and around where we lived and the museum stood. I was eighteen when I lost my parents and brother; losing the house and my family only enhanced my feelings of insecurity that proved to be a lot for me to deal with. I never wanted to experience those feelings again; yet another reason I'm so determined to remain here.

"Joe's parents were very good to me. They welcomed me into their hearts, into their home, and into their lives. Although we were in love and impatient about moving forward, we decided to take it slow; get to know one another; plan for our future.

"My studio had been open over a year, and there were still additions I had planned and not yet executed. Attendance for my art classes doubled; the number of commissioned portraits was overwhelming at times; and I had even picked up two corporate accounts that were quite lucrative, thanks to John and Grace Shepherd.

"When the upstairs space became available, I leased it and moved from The Barbizon. Living above the studio was amazing, even at Joe's insistence that I keep to my business hours. Once the studio was closed for the day, I was off the clock, and my personal life took precedence.

"Joe had his own schedules and goals to contend with. He had started a new job only a month before we began dating. As an attorney who had been in private practice since graduation, his new position with New York City Department of City Planning was a complete one-eighty. He had taken his father's suggestion to apply for it. To his surprise, they offered him the job immediately.

"Lou Asher founded AAA Construction in the summer of 1929. When the stock market crashed, it looked as if the business had no chance of surviving. He managed not only to survive but also to grow during those bleak years doing mainly renovations on old brownstones throughout Brooklyn. Although many had lost everything, there were still many who hadn't. If one had the means to buy a property well below market value and renovate it, they could end up with a piece of real estate that doubled and tripled in value as times improved.

"He named the company AAA Construction—A for Lou **A**sher, A for Marty, **A**sher, A for Joe **A**sher. He envisioned his sons in the business, as they often worked alongside their father during school breaks growing up; Lou relished not only their close relationship but also their enthusiasm. After graduating from high school and having no desire to go to college, Marty began working with his father fulltime.

"On December 7, 1941, following the attack on Pearl Harbor, he enlisted in the Navy, along with many of his friends who had also chosen not to attend college; reasoning it was only a matter of time before he was drafted anyway.

"When Joe was fourteen, he was diagnosed with Rheumatic Fever that left him with heart-related problems. Although they were minor in nature and not life threatening, there were changes that had to be made: 8-10 hours sleep a day, no contact sports, avoid over exertion. Exempt from being drafted due to his medical history, upon graduating from high school, he chose to remain local by attending Columbia University to earn a law degree.

"The end of the war saw the end of Lou Asher's dream. Marty was killed in the final days of fighting in the Pacific, and Joe was an attorney in private practice. He found himself the sole owner of AAA Construction, based in Brooklyn and having solely conducted business there since its onset. He realized AAA needed to be updated and put instep with the current needs of the community if it was to remain viable.

"After the war many were convinced that Brooklyn's Golden Age had come to an end. Hundreds of thousands of white middle class residents abandoned Brooklyn for Queens, Long Island's Nassau County, Staten Island, and New Jersey. In 1957, the final blow was dealt when the Brooklyn Dodgers moved to Los Angeles.

"Once vibrant neighborhoods fell into disrepair, decay, and poverty. Not until the final decade of the 20th century did we witness neighborhoods like Brooklyn Heights, Fort Greene, and Clinton Hill spring back to life—a gentrification that continues to give Brooklyn her due to this very day.

"Lou Asher knew Brooklyn and construction inside and out. He knew how to keep a business up and running during the worst of times. Once he determined it was time to expand beyond Brooklyn, he was determined to also find a way to include Joe in the business. He often sought his son's help and advice with certain permits and legal snags in the early stages of a project; Joe had never let him down.

"The time had come; Lou Asher seized the day. He told Joe about the position at NYC City Planning and pointed out to him that his interest in the city's history would serve him well as he worked on projects setting the framework of the city's physical and socioeconomic planning. Joe didn't admit to his father that he was more than a little interested—just in case he didn't get the job—but he did.

"As time passed, we became more and more comfortable with one another and deeper in love. *Portraits by Lily* was doing extremely well; he was happy for me. Joe's job with NYC City Planning was more than he ever envisioned, while allowing him to work with his father on a regular basis. He often came home overly excited about a project he was working on; I was happy for him.

"Joe proposed to me New Year's Eve, December 31, 1951. Of course, I said *Yes* and our journey began. We planned our wedding for September 7, 1952. Our gift from Joe's parents was the brownstone on Vanderbilt Avenue in Brooklyn undergoing renovations, but projected to be finished and ready for occupancy by the time we were married.

"We became man and wife in this beautiful home, and I can still picture every minute of it. The food, the music, the flowers, the guests, and the love that encompassed it all—I couldn't believe it was all happening to me. The announcement in the paper read: *Lily and Joe Asher were married September 7, 1952 on Manhattan's Upper East Side. The newlyweds will reside in Brooklyn, New York.*

"I had invited my uncle to attend the wedding, but he was not well enough to travel. He wrote me a long heartfelt letter professing his love for me and how happy he was that I had found such happiness and wellbeing in America. He took no credit for anything that he did for me, but I gave him all the credit for giving me a life, a future. He died two weeks later.

"Our home on Vanderbilt was ready and waiting when we returned from our honeymoon. We spent a week in Lake George being tourists. We dined on lobster, enjoyed ice cream every day—at least once, and relaxed lakeside sharing picnics and our dreams for the future—no cares, no worries.

"We were married! Yay! I didn't realize how much I wanted to marry Joe until we were finally husband and wife. Never had anything felt so right but it was so much more. We shared a deep love, a love that never faltered nor lessened throughout all the years we were together or since.

"We wanted to start a family and saw no reason to delay. Although it took me a while to get pregnant, it was short lived; I had a miscarriage in my third month. Three months later I became pregnant again, and this time everything went well. After an easy pregnancy and an easier delivery, on May 31, 1955 at 9:55 am, Noah Martin Asher was born.

"Joe and I couldn't have been happier. Lou and Arlene were overjoyed with their grandson. He was a beautiful and happy little boy. I stayed home for three months, and then I started taking him to the studio where he never lacked for attention from my students or my clients. Once he started walking, our routine changed again.

"I cut back on my time at the studio. I hired a manager for the gallery and an art teacher for classes. Most of my time was allocated by appointment only and it worked out just fine. There were times when my appointments were at a client's home or place of business so having someone at the studio allowed me the freedom to book these appointments at will.

"Arlene offered to watch Noah any time she was needed. Knowing how she loved spending time with him, I asked for her help often; she never turned me down. We thought about hiring a nanny, but Joe preferred leaving Noah with his mother. He had his own room here in the house with toys and books and games galore, and he knew there was an unending supply of chocolate chip cookies in the cookie jar on the countertop in the kitchen. There was nothing he liked better than spending time with Nana and Pop and spending the night made it perfect.

"The fifties seemed to fly by and before we knew it, Noah was starting school.

Joe and I both took him to his first day of Kindergarten, and as we stood there teary eyed, he ran off to be with his friends without looking back. On the walk back home, we both agreed; it was better that we had cried than Noah.

"I became pregnant once again when he was six, but I had another miscarriage. We were in our thirties when we married and once we were in our forties, we decided that having a baby at that point was not something either of us wanted. We were quite content with our lives. We loved Noah who was growing up faster than we could imagine and though our family was small in number, it was over the top in love and happiness.

"The Ashers were Jewish. When I married Joe, I told him that I had not been raised in any faith, and if he wanted us to be married by a Rabbi, it was fine with me. Although we didn't attend services on a regular basis, we joined his parents' temple and Noah began taking lessons to prepare for his Bar Mitzvah.

"In May 1968, according to Jewish tradition, Noah became a man. We were so proud of him. He looked more like Joe than me, tall for his age, and quite handsome. He had his father's dark hair and winning smile and my blue eyes. He excelled at everything he tried. He played basketball and baseball in school, but enjoyed a game of tennis more. He took up golf, a sport he could share with Joe.

"Throughout his high school years, his interest in engineering grew and upon graduation, he left New York to attend MIT in Massachusetts. For the first time since he was born, our house seemed terribly empty; and although there was an abundance of phone calls, weeks went by without our seeing one another. Noah seemed to handle it better than Joe and I did, but he was growing up, and we soon realized that it was only a matter of time before he would be on his own. Above all else, we wanted him to be happy. We never thought to influence his choices in any way whatsoever.

"When Noah was in his second year at MIT, Joe's mother Arlene passed away in her sleep. She had not been ill; we felt fortunate that both of his parents had enjoyed good health throughout their lives. When Arlene died, a part of Lou died with her. In the days and weeks following her funeral, he seemed lost and without purpose, although he had not officially retired.

"Each day, no matter what the weather, he arranged for a car to pick him up and take him to Mount Hebron Cemetery where he spent hours on end at her gravesite. He passed away four months later.

"Life goes on. Of course, we were sad, but we couldn't deny that they had a wonderful life. Joe and I inherited everything including this house. They had set up a Trust Fund for Noah shortly after he was born. There was but one stipulation in their Will: This house was to become our home, and the brownstone on Vanderbilt was to pass to Noah. We had long known that the Vanderbilt property was Lou's last tie to Brooklyn, and he felt a strong attachment to it.

"Joe and I met with our attorneys, and established the Asher Foundation. We felt it the best way to honor his parents while doing good for the community.

"We embarked on a partial renovation of the house, mainly upgrading appliances and lighting fixtures, and a major renovation to refurnish and redecorate.

In the interim we determined it would be a good idea to establish office space for the Asher Foundation on the second floor. When the work was finished, Joe and I were quite pleased. The few rooms that were the least used were on the upper floors and were furnished as guest rooms.

"By the time Noah graduated from MIT, we had been living here for a year. We left the brownstone on Vanderbilt in tact. Noah knew that it was now his and when he was ready to move in, whatever changes he wanted could be made. We retained a cleaning service to come in from time to time, and in the spring I had flowers planted in the front beds, just as I had done each and every year we lived there. Nothing pleased me more than to see the multitude of bright colors each time I entered or left the house. When Noah was a little boy, he actually learned his colors from some of the flowers."

Once again, Jodi pictured in her mind the brownstone with multicolored flowers. How could she have known they were multicolored? They could just as easily have been a single-color bush of perennials that died down but came back each year.

Suddenly, Lily said, "Why don't we take a break? Could you use another cup of coffee?"

Jodi snapped out of it. Stopping the tape recorder she replied, "That sounds good. I think we should stretch our legs a bit too.

"Have you heard anything more about the storm moving in over the weekend? The last I heard, it was still headed our way, and they're expecting some areas to be hit hard. In a way, I'm a little excited. It will be my first snow event in the city since I came east."

Lily chuckled. "Most people don't look forward to snowstorms. The last I heard is pretty much the same as you did. I think it's supposed to hit New York Sunday night into Monday. We'll just have to wait and see.

"When you're ready to get back to the interview, I have another box of items I'd like to share with you. I'll just grab a bottle of water and I'm good to go."

"I'm ready. A good stretch and the sandwich hit the spot."

"This box of items has mostly mementoes of Noah. These are pictures that I took of him through various phases of his growing up. There are so many taken when he was a baby, but he had no choice. However, he didn't seem to mind; whenever he looked up to see me with my camera poised, he never failed to give me a beautiful *Joe smile*.

"As he grew older, many of the photos are sports related and include school events like dances. Here's one with his date for senior prom. He looks so much like Joe in this picture.

"These are shots of the brownstone. As I told you, I have no photos of the inside of our beautiful home in Vienna; they exist only in my mind. So with my trusty Kodak in hand, I took pictures of all the rooms starting with the Nursery we prepared for Noah and following up with all the other rooms. The only changes we made along the way were to Noah's room as he went from the baby phase to the big boy phase to the sports phase— with posters of New York teams and athletes and rock stars. He always had photos of the three of us taped to his mirror."

Suddenly Jodi was blown away again. "Here's a picture of the front of the house with all those colorful flowers I told you about."

She could not believe that she was staring at a perfect match to the picture in her mind—the picture she had first envisioned when Sam took her to see the brownstone. It was eerie, unsettling, and totally unexplainable.

"It's just as I described it; isn't it Jodi? I love the beautiful colors and the abundance of flowers bursting in bloom. They remind me of when I was a child and my mother and I would picnic in the park that was near our home."

Lily began replacing the items in the box. "If you want to flip the switch, I have just a little more to add, and then we can call it a day."

Jodi sat back and pushed the ON switch.

"Noah had many girlfriends growing up and we knew some of them because they were local neighborhood girls, but when he went away to MIT, we didn't know much about his social life or who he was dating. We only met the one girl he brought home and introduced us to right before graduation—Allison Adams. She was not only beautiful on the outside but even more so on the inside. Joe and I saw the same spark of love in their eyes that Arlene and Lou told us they had seen in ours.

"May 1977, Noah graduated from MIT with a degree in civil engineering, the company he had worked for during two summer internships offered him an entry level position for an upcoming project offering great potential. The construction firm had been awarded the contract to begin preliminary work on the Jacob K. Javits Center, a large convention center on Eleventh Avenue between 34th Street and 38th Street in Hell's Kitchen, Manhattan. The space frame structure was due to begin in early 1980, with the projected completion three to five years down the road.

"There were no downsides to the offer; it seemed almost too ideal to be true. Through his internships, he was acquainted with the team he would be working with and shared the company's vision for the future. He saw the Javits Center project as a long-term commitment allowing him the opportunity to prove himself further. The job location in Manhattan would make it easier for him to proceed with plans to update the brownstone in Brooklyn, and he saw no reason why he couldn't live there during the process, commuting to the city each day by train.

"To sweeten the pot further, Allison and Noah were planning a future together. Although negotiations were still under wraps, the cosmetics company she worked for was in the process of merging with another company and rebranding the two as one. The company agreed to accommodate her transfer request to New York City.

"The 1970s were among the toughest times endured by New Yorkers. The city already in an economic decline, rising crime rates, and the Son of Sam murders all combined to make many refer to that time as New York's Dark Ages. On July 13, 1977, lightening struck and the city went dark *for real*. By the time the power was restored 25 hours later, arsonists had set more than 1,000 fires and looters had ransacked 1,600 stores, as reported by the New York Times.

"By the end of the summer, they were all settled in. Updating the brownstone had been minimal, and when Allison's transfer came through, she moved in with Noah. Both were happy in their jobs. Joe and I were happy because we got to see them regularly, and they often invited us for an impromptu get together for dinner. I treasured those times getting to know Allison while getting reacquainted with our grown and matured son. We were so proud of him.

"Joe was impatient and often asked me, *What are they waiting for?* It was then that I reminded him that we had waited over a year, and we were older. In the spring of 1979, we were invited to dinner at the brownstone. As we were having our dessert, Noah told us that he asked Allison to marry him and she accepted. They were both beaming.

"Allison's family lived in Illinois. They made plans to fly to Chicago in May, ask for her parents blessing, and get engaged officially upon their return to New York. In the interim, Noah met with the jeweler and ordered her ring. All went according to plan until the day before they left. A last minute request from her company to attend an opening in Los Angeles would keep her in Chicago two additional days. She would fly to LA, attend the opening, and return to New York.

"At first Noah was upset. It meant that their engagement over Memorial Day weekend would have to be postponed. When Allison told him that she would be flying back to New York late Saturday evening, he realized a minor adjustment to the plans—moving up the festivities to Sunday in lieu of Saturday—would avoid a total postponement. He would return to New York as scheduled, pick up the ring, and move their plans forward one day thereby keeping everything on track.

"The afternoon of Friday, May 25, 1979, the beginning of Memorial Day weekend, passengers including Allison Adams boarded American Airlines Flight 191 at Chicago's O'Hare Airport bound for Los Angeles. The DC-10 jet took off without incident but after rising to only 400 feet, stalled, rolled to the left, plunged, and crashed. The plane, loaded with fuel, exploded on impact killing all on board instantly. The heat was so intense that firefighters could not approach the crash for close to an hour.

"It's hard for me to talk about it even after all these years. I don't know how we got through those horrible days, weeks, and even months following the crash. The hardest was watching Noah sink into a deep depression. We didn't know how to help him, how to ease his pain. We were hurting along with him. In the end, it was Joe who got through to him recalling his father's comforting words when they were notified his brother Marty had been killed in the final days of the war.

"Eventually Noah began to emerge from his depression. He went back to work fulltime and became obsessed with working long hours and being involved in anything that kept him from returning home. In retrospect, I was relieved that they had not picked a wedding date, and since they were never officially engaged, there was no engagement date. I didn't want him to go through life hanging onto the onus of what might have been.

"It took a long time, two years to be exact, but Noah was a survivor. He finally reached the point where he gave Allison's things to charity. He saw no reason to offer them to her parents and open old wounds. He decided to renovate and redecorate the brownstone, top to bottom. When he was finished, it was beautiful. He worked with a young decorator who seemed to know exactly what he had in mind.

"He invited Joe and I to dinner and to our surprise, there was a fourth person included. But before we got too excited assuming that he was dating again, he introduced her—Victoria Nolan was his decorator. Noah did all the cooking, and it was a wonderful evening. It had been quite a while since we had seen our son as optimistic about the future as he was that evening."

Lily stopped talking and grew quiet. Jodi turned the tape recorder off. "I think we've done enough for today. You look tired. Can I get you anything?"

Lily sighed. "No, thank you. Memories are both good and bad. In order to enjoy the good ones, we have to learn to deal with the bad ones. It's true you know; losing a child is the worst possible loss as is the heartache that comes with it. But, there's another pain that's right up there; it's when your child needs your help and you don't know how to help him. In the end, Noah did it all himself.

"I agree. I think we accomplished a lot today. We'll have to see what the weekend brings with the storm. Let's plan to touch base the beginning of the week."

"That sounds like a plan." Jodi stood and removed the tape from the machine. She reached for her phone to call an Uber.

For a moment, Lily was lost in thought trying to remember if she had mentioned the fact—*That sounds like a plan*—had long been Noah's favorite expression going way back to when he was quite young.

"Jodi, before you leave, I want to the take a picture of you and a selfie of the two of us. By now, I'm sure you've learned that I'm a hopeless shutterbug, still snapping away at my age."

# Chapter 12

Jodi got back to the apartment, took off her coat, put her bag and briefcase on the table, and plopped onto the sofa. Her head ached from all the thoughts whirling about in her brain—thoughts she couldn't explain. She couldn't help wondering what their next meeting would uncover. She had no memory of her past; she couldn't possibly be clairvoyant. Of course not, but she wasn't ready to dismiss the images as coincidences either.

The two interview sessions had both gone well. Lily's story had captivated her, making her want to hear more. She was quite pleased with the way Lily began her story and now in only their second meeting, she had covered her life in America from her marriage to Joe leading up to Noah as an adult. Could their next session encompass the events of 9/11 so soon? Things were progressing at a much faster pace than she anticipated.

At times her story was told in great detail; at other times she seemed elsewhere lost in her memories. It was, however, her story and she knew how she wanted to tell it. Both Jodi and Sam had agreed to that from the beginning. Thus far, that is exactly how the tapings had gone; she told it the way it was—not as she viewed it.

Jodi would have liked to have someone to talk with about her strange feelings and images, but she hadn't decided if she wanted to divulge them to Sam, just yet. The interview was about Lily; the feelings and images were about her—she couldn't and wouldn't let them interfere with the promise she made Sam to go above and beyond to deliver the episode of *Profiles* he entrusted to her. She decided that for the time being, she would deal with them on her own.

Her cell rang; it was Sam. "Hi! Are you still at Lily's?"

"No I'm not. I Ubered back to the apartment a few minutes ago. It was certainly another eventful day, and if you're up to it, I'd like you to listen to the tape.

"With the storm predicted to come in over the weekend, we left our next meeting up in the air; we're going to touch base early next week. I'd like to use the next couple of days to go over the tape and get your thoughts on her story and on our progress. We've entered new territory, and I am quite certain that today's taping will be as eye opening to you as it was to me.

"I thought we could order in Chinese Food for dinner. What do you say?"

The excitement in her voice was contagious, and Sam easily picked up on it. It pleased him that she wanted to share each taping as soon as she came home. "I'm all in; can't wait to hear Lily's next chapter. By the time the order arrives, it will give you time to relax and unwind a bit. I'll order from Pig Heaven and see if they can deliver by 7:00 pm."

"Perfect. I love that place; everything we've ever ordered from there has been delicious. See you at seven. Bye."

Sam was just about to walk down the hall to Jodi's, when his phone rang. "The food has arrived and true to their name, the aroma is *sooooo pig heavenly*. The table is all set; we can eat first like we usually do, and during dinner, I can fill you in on a couple of my thoughts so we can relax and listen to the tape uninterrupted. Come now."

"I'll be there in a sec. I'm walking down the hall as we speak."

Dinner was indeed heavenly and delicious. Although Sam had ordered extra with the thought that they could have leftovers for lunch, they were both so famished that they managed to leave only a couple of ribs and barely a serving of wonton soup.

With the table cleared, the dishwasher filled, and everything put away they sat down to listen to the tape.

They were both lost in their own thoughts and neither spoke as Lily's story unfolded. When at last Jodi, turned the recorder off, she turned to Sam and said, "Am I right to assume that you weren't aware of anything she spoke of today?"

"Yes, you assume correctly. I didn't meet Lily until 2011. Through her contacts at PBS, she learned about *Profiles* early on. Quite taken with the concept of the show and the possibility of it becoming a monthly series, she was the first to come forward to offer funding from the Asher Foundation. I learned through our talks that she had lost her son in the North Tower, and asked if she was willing to be a part of the premiere. She agreed.

"My friendship with her and any further input she had in various subsequent episodes, which I might add were not about 9/11; all came years after the timeline she recorded today.

"If I'm figuring correctly, today's taping ended somewhere in the early to mid-eighties. If I'm right, she still has to cover 20-25 years to get to 9/11. I don't think she's going to get there before the fourth taping at the earliest."

"Your point is well taken. Although I'm anxious to hear what comes next, I don't want to rush her, as if I could. So far, her story has been told without embellishments. I feel the history and events she has included are intended to give us a feel of the times they were living in, and not in the least meant to draw out her story. The years she has to cover leading up to 9/11 could very well center on Noah.

I can only imagine how difficult it was for both of them to lose their son after watching him battle depression when he lost Allison in the plane crash. Although she and Joe had experienced the loss of loved ones previously—when Lily lost her parents and brother in a train collision in Germany, and Joe lost his brother in the war—no doubt their biggest loss of all was losing Noah, their only child on 9/11. How does one come back from that?

"Lily Asher is a survivor. My gut feeling tells me she's going to keep her promise and deliver a *Profiles* episode that's going to be hard to beat."

Jodi put the recorder away and turned to Sam, "Are you ready for dessert? I have several different kinds of ice cream, and I'm sure I can scrounge up some toppings like nuts, syrup, and whipped cream. As we pig out, we can check on updates about the storm."

Sam turned on the TV and went into the kitchen to help with the sundaes. The news remained steadfast about the storm moving up the east coast and due to arrive in the city Sunday evening with overnight accumulation of a foot or more. Everyone was urged to prepare for several days of staples especially if there were children or seniors involved.

"Tomorrow is Saturday, and I'm sure the grocery stores will be swamped. Why don't we plan to get an early start and pay our friends at Westside Market a visit? We only need to shop for food, and I'm thinking a few items for breakfast and lunch, and 3-4 dinners should be plenty. The market is only a short walk from here, and I'm certain we will be able to get out by Wednesday. If the storm turns out to be as bad as predicted, the restaurants will undoubtedly close down early and delivery won't be an option.

"We can prepare dinner together; that should be fun. It's something we've never done before. When I place my usual Sunday call to my mom, you can be in on it. I'm sure she'll have a million questions about how the interview with Lily is coming along. She never fails to ask me about it each and every time we speak. I'll let you answer her questions this time.

"You've more than earned the weekend off, but maybe we could listen to the tapes again and see if our thoughts change. Sometimes I get the feeling that you're holding back on me; do you have some kind of ace-in-the-hole you're going to surprise me with?"

Jodi was totally surprised. It appeared they were getting to know one another quite well; well enough for Sam to pick up on her *holding something back*.

"No to both. I am not holding anything back about the interview— you've listened to the tapes and heard Lily's words the same as I did. I have no ace-in-the-hole; that belongs to Lily. There is one thing that I forgot to tell you. Before I left today, she asked to take a picture of me, and then she took a selfie of the two of us."

Sam laughed. "She's been snapping away for most of her life. I'm sure there's nothing to read into it. She's taken pictures of me from time to time, and I've never given it a second thought."

The next morning as planned, they left early for Westside Market and returned with several bags of provisions to see them through the storm. Sam spent the afternoon in his apartment making phone calls and finishing up some paperwork he brought home from the office.

Jodi spent the afternoon on the computer researching. Her first search was American Airlines Flight 191 that crashed just after takeoff May 25, 1979. She wasn't fact-checking or second-guessing Lily; she was more interested in learning what the investigations revealed.

She learned the plane had gone through maintenance two months earlier; the pilots were more than qualified; and takeoff appeared normal when suddenly the left engine fell off the plane. One report stated their findings determined the crash *an extremely rare and dramatic malfunction that was eventually determined to be due to and exacerbated by the very design of the plane.* America's deadliest plane crash unfolded in 31 harrowing seconds at Chicago O'Hare International Airport killing 258 passengers, 13 crew members, and 2 individuals on the ground at the site of the crash.

She could only imagine the pain families of the survivors felt over and over again as each investigation was finalized and the reports were published. If Noah read them all, it was a good possibility that those reports only added to his frustration while trying to make sense of it all, prolonging his state of depression in the process.

Her next search was the brownstone on Vanderbilt. She learned there were two previous owners prior to Lou purchasing the home. Last sold in March 1910, the house was currently listed as Off Market.

For the most part, Sunday was a chilly overcast day with low hanging clouds. Sam suggested they take a walk to the nearby coffee shop to pick up some muffins and surprise Lily with a visit. Detecting the sadness in her voice after listening to the tape, and a looming snowstorm threatening to shut down the city for a couple of days, he wanted to cheer her up a bit and make sure she was okay. He was worried about her and the effect visiting her past might be having on her.

Nina answered the door. "What a lovely surprise. Come in; come in where it's warm. Let me take your coats, and I'll go upstairs and get Lily. She's been on the computer all morning. Why don't you make yourselves comfortable in the library in front of the fireplace?"

Minutes later Lily entered the room. "What a wonderful surprise. We didn't have anything scheduled, did we?"

Jodi laughed. "No we didn't, but Sam thought since we might be snowed in for a couple of days, we would surprise you and drop by. We come bearing goodies. We stopped at Alice's Café and picked up some of her over-the-top muffins. We're counting on you to provide the coffee and please have Nina join us. This is strictly a social visit, and we'd like to get to know her better."

They spent the better part of the day at Lily's. She regaled them with stories of the many portraits she had painted and the different personalities she had to deal with over the years. At times they laughed so hard they cried. Every time they started to leave, she would begin anew, and the afternoon flew by. At one point, Nina made sandwiches and put on another pot of coffee. By the time they left, it was dark out and light snow had begun to fall.

When they returned to the apartment, Sam placed his weekly call to his mother. For a while she was on speakerphone, but when her questions became solely directed to Jodi, who was promptly answering them in return, he opted out saying he would talk to her next week, and went into the kitchen to start dinner on his own.

What a wonderful day it turned out to be. Their impromptu visit was pure genius, and Jodi was glad Sam had suggested it. She too felt Lily's sadness when she spoke of Noah's losing Allison, only to be followed by the hard time he had dealing with it. Sam's ability to sense someone's needs was yet another one of the things she liked best about him.

New Yorkers went to sleep Sunday night only to wake up Monday morning to a winter wonderland. New York City was hit by the 17ᵗʰ biggest snowstorm in the city's history with more than 16 inches being recorded in Central Park.

Ordinarily, New York traffic would play a big part in dissipating the snow on the city's streets, but traffic had been reduced considerably during the pandemic lockdowns and bumper-to-bumper traffic was yet to make a comeback. By Tuesday, progress had been made clearing the streets and sidewalks, but with nowhere special to be, Jodi and Sam continued to work from home.

Jodi placed a call to Lily just to make sure they were okay, and asked if she and Nina needed anything. After assuring her they didn't, she thanked her once again for their visit, adding she greatly appreciated their concern for her wellbeing.

They tentatively set up their next meeting for the following Friday at the usual 10:00 am.

Lily couldn't pinpoint when she started rethinking her course of action. She had grown quite fond of Jodi and Sam; they seemed more like family than friends. On their recent visit, she had noticed a special closeness, a familiarity between them that had not been there when Sam first brought Jodi to meet her. She now saw them as a couple, yet she had no idea if they shared anything other than work. She sensed that they spent the majority of their time together aside from work, but that could easily be explained by her recent move to a city where she knew only a handful of people. The fact that she was living in Sam's mother's apartment in the same building where he lived made it all the more a possibility.

She thought about asking Sam to join them for the tapings, but reconsidered since they had decided that Jodi would do the interviews alone. She had no idea if the tapings had been shared with him or if they were waiting until they ended and were ready for editing.

She hoped she hadn't bitten off more than she could chew and needed some sound advice. After spending two sleepless nights in a row, Lily placed a call to Dr. Charles Hurwitz. When learning the reason for her call, he opted to come by the house to speak with her in person. She was pleased that he did. His visit lasted well over an hour; by the time he left, she was back on track to continue the interview as planned—albeit with a few minor changes.

By Friday, the city's streets were cleared, and New Yorkers began emerging from their latest home confinements. This included Jodi as her Uber dropped her off just before ten for their third meeting. Nina opened the door and let her in as she was leaving to run a few errands. After getting a cup of coffee, they went into the library where she settled in to listen to the continuation of Lily's story.

"On schedule, the Javits Center's space-frame structure began in early 1980 and was completed in 1986. Topped out in December 1984, the center opened to the public on April 3, 1986 with little fanfare—a five-minute ribbon-cutting ceremony. One of the first events held at the Center was an Art Expo of emerging young artists. I worked with the promoters of the event to spread the word with the hopes of getting a good turnout; it was a big success. I was very proud of each of the six students that represented *Portraits by Lily.*

"Noah had, of course, moved on to numerous other projects by then, having received several promotions along the way. He was happy at work and relished knowing that his input and expertise had made a difference each time a project was finalized. He felt fortunate to have had the opportunity to work on a project like the Javits Center immediately upon his graduation from MIT.

"Not long after the renovations were completed on the brownstone, our foundation's accountant decided to retire, and we began our search to replace him. Joe met with several applicants to no avail; frustrated, he decided to turn the task over to me. I hired the very first person I interviewed.

"It was a *she* not a *he* and although she was relatively young, her resume was extensive—and I took note that she had passed the CPA exam on her first try. I was quite impressed. She pointed out that she was loyal, hardworking, and dedicated, and welcomed the chance to prove it by offering a fresh new perspective to the Asher Foundation. I hired her in a New York minute.

"Nicole Robins was a breath of fresh air with an upbeat personality and a smile that could melt the coldest heart. Thanking me for taking a chance on her and anxious to prove herself, she came to work each day, with enough energy and commitment to run a giant corporation. She was instrumental in not only growing the Asher Foundation but also introduced new and worthy recipients. It was at her suggestion that we became involved with PBS ultimately becoming sponsors of many of their Masterpiece shows—of course, *Profiles* is one of them; it's how I met Sam.

"The Asher Foundation offices have always been located on the second floor of this house. Nicole loved the atmosphere here—the warmth, the quiet, and the convenience—she thrived.

"She had been working for the foundation for three months when Noah stopped by one afternoon and met her for the first time. I wasn't at home when he came looking for me. Thinking that I might be upstairs, he wandered up to the offices on the second floor.

"They took instantly to one another, and soon began dating. Noah asked how Joe and I felt about his dating our employee, but we didn't have a problem with it. We didn't foresee it having any bearing on her work, and it didn't. We established the foundation while Noah was at MIT, and he had never been involved in anything to do with the foundation. Of course, Joe and I were well aware that at some point we would turn it all over to him, but that was down the road.

"Over the next year, we got to know one another. Nicole was from California, raised by a single mother who worked several jobs to support them. When she was five, her mother enrolled in night school to improve her secretarial skills so she could land a better paying position that would allow her to spend more time with her daughter.

"She purchased a small dilapidated cottage in Redondo Beach, and managed to turn it into a cozy home for the two of them doing most of the fix-up work herself. When Nicole graduated from high school she went off to college to pursue a degree in accounting. Math had always been her best subject, and she felt an accounting degree could also serve her well if she decided to pursue a career in finance.

"Unfortunately, her mother was diagnosed with lung cancer when she was a senior in college. She lived to see Nicole graduate, but passed away two months later. Nicole sold the small cottage for a hefty sum to a developer who had begun buying several other properties in the area to develop. With the proceeds from the cottage and a small insurance policy her mother left, she decided New York was the best place for her to seek a position in finance. She pulled up stakes and relocated to New York City.

"After finding an apartment, she set out to study for and take the CPA exam. In the meantime, she landed a job with an estate attorney working in the accounting department. Impressed with her work ethic and loyalty, he allowed her time off to study for the exam, and when she passed on her first attempt, he gave her a raise and additional duties. He and his wife took her to dinner at Chez Pascal to celebrate.

"She had chosen well; the top four accounting firms in this country are in New York City. She had also done well; she aced the four-part exam on her first try—a feat only 20% of all applicants manage to do. At least half must retake one or more parts before passing. She continued to work for the estate attorney while she looked for a new position without realizing she was learning a great deal about establishing foundations. She was instantly drawn to families wanting to share vast sums of money to help others less fortunate.

"When she learned the Asher Foundation was seeking a replacement for their accountant who was retiring, she jumped at the chance to arrange an interview. We often joked about the fact that I hired her, wondering if Joe would have done the same. We soon realized that he most certainly would have; how else would she and Noah have met?

"We knew that Noah would never rush into a relationship having gone through his ordeal with losing Allison; he didn't. They took their time, but once she moved into the brownstone, we knew they were serious about their future together.

"In September 1986, they were married in this house. It was a smaller wedding than ours but that didn't make it any less wonderful. Noah's friends and business associates, Nicole's friends, the attorney she previously worked for and his wife, and her business contacts through the foundation managed to result in 125 guests that also included several of our friends.

"They honeymooned in Hawaii, and returned two weeks later.

"The years following their wedding turned out to be some of the happiest in our lives. Joe was still working; he wasn't planning on retiring any time soon. I was also still working; I managed to go to the studio a couple of days a week, and I continued to paint and even teach a few classes. I also worked closely with Nicole and the foundation. Knowing the close bond that had grown between us, Joe opted out and let me make most of the decisions knowing that I would continue to seek his advice from time to time.

"Joe and I were beginning to think we were never going to be grandparents when Noah called one day and asked me to invite them to dinner at the house. He thought it more convenient to have dinner here because Nicole worked upstairs, and we could get together right after her workday ended.

"I didn't think too much about his request; it was not unusual. He had often invited himself to dinner on the spur of the moment. It was May and the weather was beautiful. Although it was only the four of us, I always jumped at the chance to entertain family. I decided to serve dinner in the garden where the early perennials were in full bloom knowing that many would be gone in a matter of days. As in previous years, I had already ordered the annuals, and our landscaper was scheduled to begin planting the following week.

"We enjoyed a nice and relaxing meal over casual and upbeat conversation. Noah offered to help me clear the table and bring in the cheesecake he brought for dessert—it was both Joe's and my favorite. Having kept their news in check throughout the evening, he could wait no longer. As Nicole sat by his side, brimming from ear-to-ear, he announced we were going to be grandparents.

"We were over the moon. The baby was due in mid-December, and although they had only learned that they were expecting the previous day, they couldn't wait a moment longer to tell us, but urged us to keep it under wraps until she was further along.

"Not the least bit superstitious, we moved forward without delay to ready the nursery and stock up on essentials all newborns needed. It was too early to learn the sex of the baby, so we chose a myriad of pastels that were all reflected in the wallpaper, bedding, and clothing we selected. The crib and chest were white, as was the rocking chair that sat in the corner of the room.

"Later, when we learned they were expecting a girl, a hand-knit pink sweater set that included a bonnet and booties was left at my studio. Upon opening it, we learned it was a gift from one of my students.

"Our granddaughter arrived on schedule in December—they named her Olivia Aileen Asher. To our eyes she was not only perfect in every way, she was beautiful. Dark curls framed her rosy-cheeked face and deep blue eyes; and by the time she was three months old, her dimpled smile added the finishing touch.

"Nicole took a month off, but by mid-January, she was ready to return to the foundation. Her working here at the house made it convenient to continue nursing Olivia, and bringing her to work each day allowed me precious time to spend with her.

"Once she began walking, Joe used to tease me by calling her my shadow. Everywhere Nana went Olivia was sure to follow. She didn't like playing with her toys alone; the activities she favored were those we did together. I purchased crayons and drawing materials, but she showed no particular interest or talent for art.

"We played games; I read to her everyday, and we often visited the bookstore to pick out a new book or two to read. She was naturally drawn to books, and looked forward to the adventures we took reading them. As she grew older, writing turned out to be the one activity she enjoyed doing alone.

"What she liked best was to listen to me play the piano. She would climb up onto the bench and sit next to me as my fingers moved across the keys producing a soothing magical sound. About the time she was three years old, I began teaching her to play as my mother had taught me. She was a natural. By the time she started school, not only could she read, she could play the piano like a pro. I think we were all a little in awe of how she had taken to it so handily.

"I don't want to give you the impression that I was totally one hundred percent hands-on with taking care of Olivia, because I wasn't. I had the studio to oversee; I was still painting; and there were times when my corporate accounts were demanding. I discussed the time I was spending with her with Noah and Nicole, but they were not concerned. She was a happy, good-natured child totally unspoiled regardless of having lived in an *adult world* since she was born.

"From time to time she came with me when I went to the studio, and she soon stole the hearts of my students and clients just as Noah had done. She may not have had any interaction with children her own age before she started school, but that didn't deter her from making friends easily when she began kindergarten. Naturally once she started school, she spent more time in Brooklyn, and weekends became our time to *catch up*.

"In school, she blossomed. She was an outstanding student who never missed an opportunity to become involved in school projects. When she was in fourth grade, she started a school newspaper with a staff of two— her best friends. Their goal was to report special class projects and field trips from kindergarten thru sixth grade, ending with both teachers' and students' plans for the summer. It was a huge success. The faculty as well as the students eagerly awaited each edition.

"When the school year ended in June, she had already begun making plans for improvement and expansion during the next semester. At the top of her list was—increase her staff and find a name for the paper."

At this point, Lily signaled Jodi to stop the recording. "Let's take our usual break, and as during our previous sessions, I have another of my memory boxes to share with you. After we have gone through it, I would like to speak with you about our meetings going forward. I have a suggestion I'd like you and Sam to consider."

Jodi was slightly caught off guard. It appeared as if Lily had been *thinking and planning* as opposed to her original *let's just see how it goes* approach in telling her story. She turned the recorder off, removed the tape and put it in her purse.

"I think I'll have something cold to drink. I don't know why I'm so thirsty when it's you who has been doing all the talking."

"If it's any consolation, my throat is a bit dry also. Nina and I made a salad for lunch with chicken and/or shrimp to add if you like, as well as a bowl of fruit. I set up a table in the library so we could be seated and have a proper meal without juggling plates on our laps. When we are through eating, I'll clear the table, and we can go through the box of photos and other items I have to share with you today."

As they enjoyed lunch, they talked about the weather, about how Jodi was settling in as a New Yorker, and suddenly Lily asked if she had made a decision about staying permanently?

"I have, and I've discussed it with Sam. I really don't have anything urging me back to LA. I'm still waiting for the right time to have a Memorial Service for my Dad, and I plan to include my Mom in the service as well. In addition, our attorney is waiting for the right time to sell the estate. For the time being, I plan to hold onto my condo and rent it. As the weather gets warmer, I'll ask Rosy our housekeeper to pack up some of my clothes and ship them east.

"Once I start the process, what follows becomes a domino effect. I can't have my clothing and personal items shipped until I get my own place. Staying in Trudy's apartment has been convenient, and I love it, as well as the neighborhood. She normally returns in late May, and I'm hoping to find a place by then somewhere in the general area.

"Although we've been working primarily from home, at some point that will definitely change. My office at *Profiles* is beautiful; Sam had it professionally decorated especially for me and is by far the biggest and nicest office I have ever had. The staff's involvement is paramount in the final stages of wrapping the show; as are the resources and ample space required. We have already discussed approximately when that move will take place.

"My real problem is the timeframe. First and foremost is my interview with you. I can't let anything deter me from the business at hand—it is why I am here in the first place. For now, it's a waiting game to see how soon the show wraps; when the COVID mandates begin to expire; when Trudy plans to return from Florida; and I could go on and on.

"If I botch your interview, Sam may send me *unemployed* back to LA. If that happens, then my decision to stay in New York won't matter. For now, he seems quite pleased that I've already made my decision to stay."

Lily smiled and with a twinkle in her eye, she said, "I don't see even the slightest chance of Sam sending you packing. From what I've observed, you're good together; he's good for you and you're good for him. Everyone deserves someone special in his or her life; when he or she is extra special, it's even better. I've never seen Sam happier, and since I've come to know you better, I'd say coming here was a good move. He gave you a lifeline when you needed it most; you took it; and as a result, you've come into your own."

Jodi blushed. "Thank you for your generous compliments. You're good! Your observations are quite accurate. In the beginning, I thought what I felt for Sam was gratitude. I soon learned it was more, and that he shares my feelings. As you can see, this created yet another problem. I was torn between retaining my professionalism and acting on those feeling which were growing stronger by the day. In the end, we agreed that the show comes first; it made me all the more determined to stay focused on our interview and deliver my promise to Sam."

When lunch was over and everything put away, Jodi picked up the box and placed it on the table. Lily wasted no time reaching in and pulling out photos and various items. "As usual, I was quite busy with my trusty Kodak Camera. I continued to use it long after new and more efficient cameras came on the market until it literally died. When I took it in for repair and learned that replacement parts were hard to come by, I had no choice other than purchasing a new camera.

"Knowing it was a big decision on my part, Joe set aside a day for us to go shopping. It was fun. It had been a while since we had taken a day for ourselves. We looked at so many different cameras, manufactured by so many different companies, it made my head spin. In the early 1990s, digital cameras began nipping at the heels of many photographers, although the technology had not been perfected and the costs ranged upwards into the thousands.

Photography was not my profession; all I wanted was an uncomplicated compact camera. I finally settled on a Polaroid 35mm model that was not too different than my Kodak—just new and more up to date. I'm happy to say, it still works even though I tend to use my cellphone like all you young people."

Jodi had expressed her thoughts to Sam that going forward Lily in all likelihood would concentrate on Noah leading up to the events of 9/11. She was only partially right; it was more about Olivia. But in all fairness, it was before she learned that Noah had married and had a daughter.

Lily spread out a handful of photos on the table; all baby pictures of Olivia. "I don't believe I'm being prejudiced at all; she was truly the most beautiful little girl."

Thoroughly enjoying the task at hand, she placed photo after photo on the table, made remarks about some and stared distantly at others as she continued to replace them time and again with a new batch. As Olivia grew older, the photos included Noah and Nicole, their home on Vanderbilt Avenue, shots of Olivia at PS9, family vacations, and several of just Noah and Olivia or so Jodi thought.

She was mesmerized. Two of the last photos Lily produced were of Noah and Olivia. While one depicted a father and his child with arms wrapped around his neck as they looked adoringly at one another, the other showed only the father's back, and like the painting at the gallery, looking into the face of the child who in this instance was laughing. She suddenly realized she had tears in her eyes as a warm feeling spread throughout her body.

She heard Lily's voice in the distance although she sat right beside her. Handing the two pictures back for her to return to the box, she commented. "I don't think you give yourself enough credit; you're really an excellent photographer. These two shots of Noah and Olivia are awesome."

"Thank you, dear. I've certainly had enough practice. Only one is Noah and Olivia; the other is Joe with Olivia. Though his back is to the camera in this photo, he and Noah were often mistaken for one another in pictures. As he got older, he not only looked more and more like Joe, their builds and demeanor were identical."

Lily said, "I'm almost finished. I saved the best for last." She placed three small paintings face down on the table.

She turned over the first painting and Jodi found herself looking at a smaller version of the one she and Sam had seen in the gallery window—that of a couple holding an infant. The pink sweater and bonnet indicating that the pale blue eyes, rosy cheeks, and dark curls were that of a girl and showing only a slim side view of the faces of the couple who was perhaps her parents.

"Olivia was only weeks old when I painted this picture. I painted a larger one for their home first and Joe loved it so much, I painted a smaller one for us. It was the only time that I produced two portraits from a single photo."

Lily turned over the second painting. "This is another favorite of mine—Olivia at the baby grand piano in the other room; she had not yet turned five. Joe and I often watched her small hands as they moved across the keys in utter amazement. We often mused about having a *prodigy* in our midst. She proved all of us wrong in assuming that as she grew older, she would lose interest in playing the piano. So once she started school and spending less time here at the house and more time in Brooklyn, Nicole arranged for her to take lessons."

She picked up the last painting and held it to her breast. "Before I show you the last painting, I want to tell you that it's the first one I've painted since before the pandemic. Truth be told, I didn't know if I still had it in me, but when you have feelings for the subject, the process becomes quite natural, and it didn't take long at all. I couldn't get out to have it framed so I removed a painting from a frame I had. Nina will take care of getting a replacement."

She turned the painting around, and Jodie found herself looking at the image of the photo she had taken of her the previous week. She was amazed at the detail she had captured from the cellphone photo taken on the spur of the moment. "It's beautiful Lily. I can't believe you did this so quickly."

"When you and Sam dropped by on Sunday, I was actually upstairs working on this painting. Knowing what I was up to, Nina made sure you waited for me in the library instead of just sending you up. I'm glad you like it; it's my gift to you."

Although their taping session had been shorter than previous ones, going through all the photos and paintings had proven time-consuming, and it had already grown dark.

"Lily, thank you for today. Each time we meet, I think things can't get better but they do. In spite of the snowstorm, we've made good progress. Before I call for an Uber, you said you had a few suggestions for the interview going forward. Do you want to discuss them now?"

"Yes, it won't take long. First I have a couple of questions. I'm curious as to how you and Sam are moving forward. Are you sharing the tapes following each of our meetings, or do you intend to wait until the end to go over them together, do the editing, and ultimately decide on the format?"

"I do share each and every tape following our sessions. We decided it would be easier and more productive to know upfront what we would be dealing with as far as editing, while leading us to the best format. We are in total agreement—you are an excellent interviewee. Thus far, the only editing we foresee is time wise depending on the length when the interview is finished. As far as format, your story in your words has captivated us to the point where we feel it will do the same for our audience."

Lily smiled. "Thank you. Since I view this as my first and last interview, it's nice to hear that I'm doing a good job. Now my suggestion, which is really a request, is that Sam be present at the remaining sessions. I don't know how many more there will be, but I'm thinking three at the most. Our next meeting will cover the events of 9/11, and though almost twenty years have passed, at times it's as though it were yesterday.

"I would like to ask Sam myself, and I will call him prior to arranging for our next meeting. I wanted to apprise you of my thoughts and give you a heads-up. Are you okay with my request?"

"Absolutely. I was open to Sam joining us all along. However, his feelings were a one-on-one between us would allow us to get to know one another better. I believe it was the right decision; I feel as though I've known you forever, and I've grown quite fond of you, as I hope you have of me. I envy Olivia—what a wonderful Nana she had."

With tears in her eyes, and without saying a word, Lily pulled Jodi into a tight hug before letting her go.

As the story unfolded, Jodi found herself somewhat bewildered by her own reactions to a number of things. Their agreement was to table any and all questions until the interview was finished. She had taken very few notes because Lily's story in her own words was turning out to be more than they hoped for. At the rate they were progressing, it could be a wrap by the end of June.

However, beginning with the images brought on by Sam's tour of the area, which occurred before they began the interview, each of their three meetings to date had revealed numerous—similarities, recollections, and/or coincidences—she simply could not dismiss. With no explanation for the feelings or the many unanswered questions that accompanied them, she found herself in the difficult position of having to make a decision.

Previously, she had second thoughts about burdening Sam with her uncertainties, unwilling to chance compromising the interview. She now feared the possibility of that happening if she didn't.

# Chapter 13

When Jodi returned to the apartment, she showered and put on sweats. She found it mandatory to clear her head of the pervading thoughts overwhelming her before she called Sam, hoping to do so before he called her. Uncertain as to just how to proceed revealing her personal concerns, she decided it would be best to maintain their usual routine of listening to and discussing the tape first. Once that had been put to rest, she would find an opening to vent her concerns.

She called Sam; he picked up on the first ring. "Hi, where are you?"

"I'm just leaving the office. Today was jam packed, and felt like old times. Our small staff enjoyed being together for the day like old times, and we were in total agreement that we are all looking forward to once again working from the office to wrap the anniversary episode and including you in the mix.

"In addition to a tape of the entire episode broadcast, certain PBS shows generate the production of various related items offered for sale to the public as an ongoing way to raise funds. We had a preliminary meeting today via the Internet to give them a heads up as to whom we were profiling. Even though we divulged as little as possible, they were quite excited. Lily is quite well known in New York City and there are many who consider her *a legend in her own time*.

"When they come up with a few ideas, we're going to meet again. Although the choices are not mine to make, they always run them by me as a courtesy and appreciate any suggestions I may have.

"I'm assuming you're at the apartment. When did you get in? And how did today go?"

"I'm not going to *spill* any of it; just get ready to get blown away. I'm suggesting we order in pizza. That way, we can listen to the tape while we eat. It's shorter than the last two tapes because the box of photos and items she shared with me was quite full and took us the better part of the afternoon to go through. She gave me a gift as I was leaving; I'll show it to you when you get home. See you soon."

Sam's curiosity was getting the better of him, but he had put in a full day's work for the first time in almost a year, and he decided to take a shower and unwind before meeting up for dinner. He wanted to listen to the tape with his mind clear of the many things that had come up during the day.

It had been over a month since he had placed an order for the COVID home tests that became available in January, and they had finally been delivered. Since public testing became available, they had been testing regularly for their own benefit, as well as Lily's prior to each and every meeting. Home testing would be far more convenient than having to go to one of the many sites setup throughout the city. Masks remained a must everywhere. They relaxed the rules only at home and at Lily's. Thus far, they had all remained symptom and COVID free.

Sam ordered two large pizzas, garlic bread, and six oversized chocolate chip cookies. He hadn't eaten all day, and he was famished. He liked Jodi's choice of pizza for dinner allowing them to listen to the tape as they ate. He forgot to ask if she had wine. He enjoyed a good red wine with anything Italian, and gave credit to the Caruso side of his family for that. If per chance she didn't, he could easily return to his apartment for a bottle or two, which he always kept on hand.

Jodi opened the door to Sam standing before her loaded down with packages. "Wow! What did you order besides pizza? Let me take something before you drop everything."

"I'm good. Don't touch anything, or I will drop something. I forgot to ask if you have wine."

She laughed. "Of course I do; red, am I right? I've set everything up. All we have to do is bring in the pizza and pour the wine."

Without interruption, they listened to the tape. From time to time, each stole a glance at the other to see if there was any reaction to Lily's words. There were none. When the tape ended, Jodi reached over and turned off the recorder. For a few moments, they sat without speaking, lost in their own thoughts.

Sam spoke first. "In the midst of the pandemic with lockdowns and mandates in place, my initial attempts to get the anniversary episode up and running all resulted in disappointing dead ends. With COVID-19 rampant, New York soon led the world in coronavirus cases having more cases than any country. It wasn't long before Manhattan had the highest transmission rate.

"You had been here for two months, and the job I hired you for was non-existent. Here I was trying to persuade you to remain in New York permanently, and for the first time since *Profiles* premiered, I was at a loss as to what to do.

"With the holidays, behind us, and my mother in Florida for the winter, I decided to spend a day at the office determined to come up with someone that I could pursue for the show. As I sat there gazing into space, my eyes fell on the small portrait Lily painted of me from a photo—a photo I was totally unaware she had taken. It sits on my desk; I don't know if you noticed it or not, but the next time you're in the office, I'd like you to see it. It portrays me in a pensive mood, deep in thought, and I took it as a sign.

"I have never been superstitious or someone who searched for signs or omens to bring them luck. I'm more of a hardworking, loyal, and dedicated sort of guy who just happens to believe in gut feelings. As I looked at the portrait, the thought crossed my mind that it portrayed my very mood that very day, and I immediately thought of Lily. I hadn't been in touch with her since before the pandemic, which was well over a year.

"I liked Lily from the moment we met. She was what I call *genuine*. What you saw was what you got—there was nothing pretentious about her. Although I met her ten years after she lost her son, as I got to know her better, it was evident that she had not yet come to terms with her loss. At times when we were engrossed in conversation, she would momentarily become lost in thought of perhaps another place, another time, or another someone that seemed to haunt her.

"I had long believed that Lily had a story to tell. That day, my gut feeling confirmed it. When I called to see if she would meet with me, I was pleasantly surprised that she agreed so readily adding that she was planning to call me.

"By the time we met, Joe had passed away, and until I listened to today's tape, I was unaware that Noah had married and had a daughter. Where are they? Was his wife with him in the tower on 9/11? I know there were no children killed in the towers. The children who were victims that day were on the planes.

"I'll have to listen to the tape again to be certain, but by 9/11, Noah and Nicole would have been married more than ten years, maybe fifteen, and their daughter would have been at least ten. I don't believe they're alive; if they were, wouldn't they be here in the city? It's where they lived.

"At any rate, she and her story definitely have my attention. I cannot begin to imagine what the next tape will reveal, but without a doubt it will cover the events of 9/11."

At first Jodi sat quietly. Although she had tried and believed she was succeeding in separating her weird feelings from the interview, listening to Sam's take on the tapings thus far proved otherwise.

"Sam, kudos for your synopsis. It was excellent. I've put off sharing something with you that I believed I could resolve on my own, but after listening to your thoughts, so precise yet inquiring, I feel as though Lily may have chosen the wrong person for the interview."

Sam immediately apologized. "I am so sorry. I have no intention of taking your place. Why do you feel that way? You told me you enjoy the time you spend with Lily and you seem to get along splendidly. Is there a problem that I'm not aware of? Did something happen today?"

Jodi stood up and went into the other room returning with the painting Lily had given her. She handed it to Sam. "Remember when I told you she took a picture of me last week? She painted this portrait of me from that photo on her cellphone. She told me she hasn't painted in quite a while, but I love it. She certainly hasn't lost her ability to create an amazing likeness of her subject.

"I've grown to love Lily; and I have thoroughly enjoyed every minute I have spent with her. It seems as if I've known her my entire life; honestly, I wish I had. As I was leaving today, I told her I envied Olivia the wonderful Nana she had. She began to cry. We hugged, my Uber arrived, and I had to leave. I felt bad that I had made her cry. I can't imagine what happened to Nicole and Olivia, but I agree it is unlikely they are alive or they would surely be in her life.

"Once we have finalized the show, I'm going to ask Lily to share with you the part of our meetings that aren't taped. Each time we've met, she has produced what she fondly calls a *memory box* that contains photos and various items that represent different times in her life, such as the first Kodak camera that her mother gave her in Austria shortly before she died.

"Her photos are quite extensive; they include the museum where her parents worked and their home in Austria, as well as pictures and paintings of her and her brother when they were young painted by her mother. She has photos of the brownstone on Vanderbilt, inside and out, wedding pictures, and pictures galore of Olivia.

"You and I presumed today's taping would be centered on Noah, but it turned out to be more about Olivia. Her attachment to the child was profound. They were far closer than a mother and child relationship in spite of the fact the child's mother was alive and very much a part of her life. However, it didn't seem to deter from the fact that Olivia was close with both of her parents and Joe as well.

"This afternoon after Lily went through the box, she set aside three paintings placed face down on the table. For some reason, I had the feeling she was observing my reactions as one-by-one she turned them over. The first one, a smaller version of the couple holding an infant that we saw in the window of her gallery turned out to be that of Noah and Nicole with Olivia. She painted the larger version for Noah and Nicole first for their home. Joe liked it so much; she painted the smaller version for him. I have no idea at what point, she moved the larger painting to the gallery.

"The second one showed Olivia in a party dress and patent leather shoes seated at the baby grand piano, poised to play. The third and last one turned out to be the painting of me. We sat for a while staring at the three paintings, neither of us saying a word.

"When I got back to the apartment, I found myself facing a puzzling situation requiring attention sooner rather than later. I took a shower to unwind, and sat down to collect my thoughts before calling you to come listen to the tape. I wanted you to be brought up to speed with the interview since several things that concern me occurred during today's meeting.

"The past three weeks have flown by. The three days you planned to show me around the city and beyond were awesome. Since I arrived, you have gone all out to make me feel at home, to make me feel wanted, and to assure I have everything I need. Your mother's beautiful apartment, my fantastic newly decorated office, and the opportunity to produce the *show of a lifetime* indicates to me the faith you have in my ability. I would have never accepted your offer to come east to join the staff of *Profiles* if I had harbored any thoughts otherwise or doubts that I was not up to the job.

"Lily Asher is a bonus I neither foresaw nor expected. I felt honored that she requested me, Jodi Jerome, to do her interview; someone relatively unknown and living clear across the country, during a pandemic no less. She told both of us that after reading my article in the LA Times on the loss of my father, she felt a connection, and saw me as someone who would tell her story the way she wanted it told.

"Everything miraculously fell into place. You had already hired me; I was already living here; and through you and *Profiles* she was more than ready to tell her story hoping to ease the burden she had carried for almost twenty years. In return, you had found your subject for the show.

"Each of the three days you planned was special in its own way. The first introduced me to the city that was to be my home for a year and showed me that in spite of the lockdowns there was much to see and do in the city that everyone loves.

"The second introduced me to Sam Meyerson as you openly shared your history; before it was over, I made my decision to stay permanently. I shared with you my history or what I know of it, and the similarities at times endeared me to you.

"The third introduced me to *Profiles* and what I had signed on for— interview of a lifetime with Lily Asher. I was delighted to no end to visit Brooklyn to see the brownstone on Vanderbilt, the school Noah may have attended, and the *Portraits by Lily* studio and gallery. Riding around Brooklyn and walking through West Village was a real treat. I was brimming with anticipation of our first meeting only days away.

"As you pulled over, and we sat in the car looking at the brownstone, images came to mind of brightly colored flowers in the dirt beds on either side of the entrance. When we went further up the street to the school and annex, the images were those of children playing in the yard accompanied by laughter I could actually hear. Momentarily, I froze in both instances. You didn't seem to notice how quiet I had grown; if you did, you didn't say anything.

"The day ended. We had a big week coming up. Before my meeting with Lily, you took me to *Profiles* to pickup what I needed for the interview, and showed me my office; I was totally overwhelmed by your generosity. I've never had anything like it or even close to it. I left to do a little shopping and ended up getting my hair cut, meeting you later at the apartment for dinner.

"The day for my first session with Lily finally arrived. The Uber dropped me off in front of the house; Lily opened the door and urged me to come in out of the cold. As she took my coat, hat, and scarf, she complimented me on my haircut adding that it was not only quite becoming but gave me a totally different look. She continued to stare at me almost as though she was comparing me to someone else.

"I loved every minute of our first meeting. The taping and the contents of her memory box were mostly about her coming to America and opening the studio in West Village. Although she began her story in Austria, her arrival here, her early days in the city, and the opening of her studio were fairly well known. It began to give me insight to who she was. We were in agreement when you listened to the tape that evening; we were off to a good start.

"Our second session was more in-depth and covered the unknown—her marriage to Joe, the birth of Noah, the house on Vanderbilt, and the house on the Upper East Side. In hindsight, and perhaps growing a tad complacent, I continued to be quite pleased at the progress we were making.

"Following our usual break, she once again produced one of her memory boxes filled with photos and items to share. There were photos of everything she spoke of on the tape from their wedding to the brownstone, to Noah's birth, to the nursery they prepared for him, and every phase of his life growing up. She had photographed their home inside and out.

"As she held up a picture of the front of the brownstone, showing a profusion of multicolored flowers in the beds on either side of the entrance, I found myself staring at an exact match to the images I had envisioned. Again I froze. I looked up as she handed me additional photos, and once again I became confused. There in the schoolyard of PS9 stood Noah with his friends, but the images that appeared in my mind contradicted. It showed instead three girls holding hands and laughing as they danced in a circle. Again, I heard the laughter loud and clear.

"Today's taping ended early. We normally take our break around noon, stretch, and have a snack before sharing her memory box of the day. We didn't break until 1:00 pm, and instead of a snack, we had lunch—salad with chicken and shrimp and a delicious bowl of fresh fruit for this time of the year was a treat. While we ate, Lily spoke her mind.

"She started our conversation asking if I had made a decision to stay in the city permanently, as yet; I told her that I had. I told her that the timeline was my biggest challenge since everything hinged on the end of the pandemic and the lifting of the mandates.

"Suddenly, she switched to the two of us. She was curious to know if we shared more than a work relationship, noting that from what she had observed, we were good together, adding that she had never seen you happier. She went on to say that everyone deserves someone special in his or her life. I admitted that we have grown close and enjoy one another's company, but for now, the *Profiles* anniversary show remains our priority.

"She began taking photos from the box in batches. The number of pictures she had taken of Noah paled in comparison to those of Olivia. There was one of Noah and Olivia with her arms wrapped around his neck that instantly brought tears to my eyes. There was another of Noah's back, like the painting at the gallery, looking at Olivia who was laughing. I felt the bond of love and admiration they shared as a feeling of warmth spread throughout my body.

"When I complimented her on her photography skills citing the two photos of Noah and Olivia, she told me the second one was not Noah; it was Joe.

"By the time she individually shared the three small paintings at the end, she appeared to be observing my reactions as I observed the paintings. At that point, I lost control of my pent up thoughts and feelings that I so desperately had tried to dispel. I realized I could no longer consider them coincidences. My greatest concern is how all of this will affect the outcome of the show. I simply cannot and will not allow that to happen."

Sam rose from the chair he was sitting in and sat down beside her on the sofa. Encircling her in his arms, he tenderly kissed her, holding her close without saying a word, mulling over and over in his mind what she had told him. He was about to speak when he looked down and saw that she had fallen asleep. Slowly he released her and lifted her legs onto the sofa placing her in a horizontal position. Retrieving a pillow and blanket from the other room, he carefully placed the pillow under her head and covered her with the blanket.

After dimming the lights, he took what was left from dinner and put everything away. Not knowing what state of mind she would be in when she awoke, and unwilling to leave her alone, he decided to spend the night in the chair opposite the sofa to keep an eye on her. She appeared to be in a deep sleep, sleeping soundly without stirring.

As his mind continued to focus on what Jodi had told him, he could see no clear-cut way to approach her concerns nor explanations for what she was experiencing. Though he wracked his brain again and again, he came up empty handed. One thought that did occur to him was her father's belief that her memory hadn't returned because she was not from the Los

Angeles area, and if she were to return to what had been home, certain people, places, or objects would in all likelihood spark a memory. This same reasoning might also account for the fact that no one was looking for them.

Flashes in her mind of flowers at the brownstone and children playing on the playground of the school could be anywhere in any neighborhood. But—and there was that but—there was a good possibility home had been on the east coast. The makeup of Los Angeles was a far cry from Brooklyn. The images invading her mind were definitely not from the life she knew; they had to be from before the accident.

His thoughts turned to her concerns about Lily. Was she actually observing her reactions to certain photos, and if she was, why was she?

Not for one moment did he entertain the thought that Jodi was in any way connected to Lily Asher. He felt if she were, she would have certainly reacted to Lily's house especially when she took them on a tour of each and every room, not to mention the many times she has been there since.

Her reactions to certain photos of Noah and Olivia were also puzzling. She described feelings of melancholy when she viewed them; was it because the bond between father and daughter was broken when her father died causing her to equate with that loss? He recalled how wistfully she stared at the painting in the gallery window at the couple holding the beautiful little girl, although at the time, he thought nothing of it.

Unable to get comfortable in the chair, Sam returned to the kitchen and emptied what was left of the wine into a glass. He grabbed a blanket and returned to watch over Jodi. The wine helped; he finally dozed off only to be awakened by Jodi's murmuring—*Jodi, Jodi*—over and over as she giggled in her sleep.

# Chapter 14

The following day was Saturday. Jodi awoke to find herself on the sofa. As she stared at Sam across from her sound asleep in the chair, the first thought that came to mind was how uncomfortable he looked; the second was why was he sleeping in the chair; the third was why had she slept on the sofa? Slowly she began to recall the previous evening—reviewing the tape and sharing her concerns with Sam.

Trying her best not to wake him, she stood and headed towards the bathroom when Sam called out to her, "Jodi, are you okay?"

"I'm good, but I'll feel better after I've showered and changed clothes."

Sam headed to his apartment to do the same offering to return to make breakfast. The shower felt good as the hot water soothed his aching back. He was dressed and just about to walk out the door when suddenly his phone rang; it was Lily. "Hi Sam; I hope I'm not calling too early. If you have a minute or two, I'd like to run something by you."

Her usual and cheerful voice in sharp contrast to Jodi's concerns of the previous evening came to mind. "This is a surprise. I always have time for you. I hope all is well."

"Oh yes, everything is fine. Thank you for asking. I offered a suggestion going forward with the interview to Jodi yesterday, and she said she had no problem with it. She told me that you listen to the tape following each meeting. As you are aware, we've had three so far, and I'm hoping we can arrange for the fourth early next week.

"My suggestion is that you join us for the remainder of the tapings. With our progress thus far as a guideline, I anticipate that a total of five will bring us to the present. Since the remaining tapes will reveal the most important part of my story and provide the core of the show, I think you will find it beneficial to hear them firsthand."

Sam immediately agreed. "I like your suggestion; it certainly makes sense. I look forward to joining you and Jodi as eagerly as I have looked forward to listening and discussing each tape so far. Make your plans as you normally do with her, and I will rearrange things on my end if I have a conflict. We listened to the tape last evening, and I find it odd that she made no mention of your idea."

"Don't be angry with her; I told her I would like to extend the invitation to you myself."

"I could never be angry with Jodi; I'm rarely angry with anyone. Thanks for the call, and I'll have her get in touch with you about next week. It will be good to see you."

They hung up and Sam headed down the hall to make breakfast. Lily's call had come at a good time. His presence at the tapings would allow him to observe both of their reactions as he tried to make sense of Jodi's concerns. He planned to be upfront with her and tell her what he planned on doing.

When he got to the apartment, he found Jodi in a lighter mood, and breakfast well in hand. The table was set, juice poured, and the smell of coffee brewing permeated the air. "You started without me. What else is on the menu?"

"I have a quiche in the oven, a bowl of fruit, and blueberry muffins. Not bad for the spur of the moment, if I have to say so myself."

During breakfast, Sam addressed her concerns, shared his thoughts, and although he could only offer hypothetical explanations at best, he assured her that he did not take her concerns lightly, and that they would figure everything out together.

He reiterated that there was not the slightest possibility of anyone else interviewing Lily Asher for *Profiles,* pointing out that she had chosen her. He told her about the call suggesting he be present at the remaining sessions, adding that the thought had crossed his mind, as well. And finally, he told her about his plan to do some observing of his own.

He had come through for her once again. She was in total agreement with everything he said and planned to do while putting her fears to rest—at least for the time being. They shared a common curiosity as they anxiously awaited their next meeting and what it would reveal.

Sam decided they could both use some time for themselves. By now, there was no doubt in his mind—he was in love with the beautiful Jodi Jerome. He loved everything about her; she was everything he ever wanted; he had never met anyone like her. At times, he saw her as a female version of himself—though only as it related to work. Lily was right; they were good together, and he had never been happier.

Earlier in the month, Governor Cuomo announced the reopening of

New York City indoor dining at 25 % capacity. Since her arrival, the city's pandemic restrictions and ultimate inclement weather limited their outings, and they found themselves in a rut, opting to order-in or cook-in, especially once the interview got underway. So far, he was batting a thousand. It was obvious that Jodi thoroughly enjoyed each and every activity he planned for them, not to mention that he had enjoyed them too. He was at it once again. He decided to make the next couple of days all about the two of them and only about the two of them, by making dinner reservations for Saturday and Sunday at two of his favorite upscale restaurants.

To make their plans even more special, he suggested a dress code of his own making. He found it hard to recall the last time he had worn a suit. Observing his image in the mirror, he was pleased that he had made the decision to *dress up*. It felt good.

Jodi was equally pleased. She had purchased two dresses on her shopping trip weeks before, and had as yet found an occasion to wear them. She chose *the little black dress* for Saturday night.

She opened the door for Sam; momentarily they stood staring at one another. Dark hair, deep brown eyes, and a boyish grin—he was so handsome. She had never seen him in a suit; he looked fantastic. How beautiful she was. Her haircut only made her more so. He had never seen her in a dress; she did more for the dress than it did for her; she looked awesome.

They were soon on their way to Columbus Circle for an evening at Per Se. The restaurant's intimate environment enhanced by their table near the fireplace was perfection. Breakfast had been filling and an earlier than requested reservation at seven prompted Sam to suggest that they not eat the remainder of the day. He was glad he had. They opted for the Chef's Tasting Menu and enjoyed every morsel.

Tired from the night before, they decided they could both use a good night's sleep. Sam drew her close and tenderly kissed her goodnight; he walked down the hall to his apartment. Leaning against the closed door, Jodi smiled contentedly. It was an amazing evening; she considered it their first real date. She wondered how many others had been in love with their first date on their first date.

They spent a laidback Sunday together doing pretty much nothing. They decided to walk to one of the neighborhood cafes for breakfast. Back at the apartment, they discussed the show but only in general. They each offered their thoughts on the format, and soon realized that they really couldn't make any decisions until they knew how much editing would be required to accommodate the two-hour time slot.

Jodi chose her pale blue dress for Sunday, making a mental note to get in some shopping to expand her wardrobe. Accenting her eyes, the blue dress was actually more flattering than the black one. Sam wore pale grey slacks and a Navy blazer. Their destination for the evening was Mastro's Steakhouse on 6th Avenue. When she commented on the ambiance and décor, he promised to bring her back when they once again had live music.

He wanted desperately to take her into his arms and kiss her on the way home in the Uber, but wearing masks prevented that from happening. When they arrived back at her apartment, he accepted her invitation to come in.

It wasn't clear who made the first move, but it didn't matter. They were in love, which is all that really mattered.

Jodi woke up encircled in Sam's arms. She smiled to herself, suppressing the urge to shout to the world—*I'm in love with Sam Meyerson and he's in love with me!* And just how did she know that, because he had told her repeatedly as they made love.

It was Monday, the beginning of a new week. Neither was expected anywhere; neither had anything scheduled. Sam decided they should talk.

Taking her hands in his and looking directly into her eyes, he said, "In case I didn't get my message across last night, I love you from the depths of my being. I think a part of me fell in love with you years ago when we met at the wedding in Los Angeles. Timing is everything, and it just wasn't our time.

"I'm a firm believer that if something is meant to be, it will eventually become reality. Reading your article and learning that you had recently lost both your parents, made me want to reach out to you to see if there was any way I could help you through what was obviously a difficult time for you.

"I began looking to increase our staff at *Profiles* just as COVID reared its ugly head; everything was put on hold. The thought crossed my mind that if I could bring you on board to produce the anniversary episode, not only would I be getting a highly qualified employee, but you would be doing what you do best. I thought a new environment might also help to ease your pain. Unconsciously, I had an ulterior motive. I wanted to get to know you better.

"As things worked out, and you agreed to interview Lily, we continued to spend all of our waking hours in one another's company. When you first arrived in New York, the time we spent together stirred up old feelings, and they began to grow stronger by the day. Sensing your vulnerability was the only thing that kept me in check.

"I rationalized time and again—there was no way you shared my feelings. On my part nothing had ever felt more right. Falling in love with you was easy: you're smart and savvy, honest and warm, a darn good journalist, and as genuine as they come. In fact, you possess a lot of the traits I would use to describe Lily. That's why the two of you are such a perfect fit.

"When we shared our first kiss, and I realized you had feelings for me, I felt I was the luckiest guy in the world. Our decision to take things slow was the right one, but we didn't stand a chance abiding by it. We fell fast and we fell hard.

"I no longer want to rein in those feelings in favor of what we initially considered more pressing issues. My priority is our love and happiness. There's no reason why we shouldn't continue to work together now and in the future; one has absolutely nothing to do with the other."

Jodi leaned over and kissed him. "Well said, but far too serious. My first thought when I woke up this morning was to shout to the world *I'm in love with Sam Meyerson and he's in love with me!* You're absolutely right; our love has nothing to do with working together. And because we both agree on that, there's no reason to deny that we're involved; everyone seems to think so anyway."

Sam raised an eyebrow. "What do you mean by everyone?"

Jodi laughed and threw her head back. "Oh Sam, I do love you. Greg for one—when I asked him to make the reservation for dinner; then there's Lily—I told you what she observed; and your mother—who told me to take good care of you, Wink! Wink! Although, I'm not sure she would have said anything if you were still on Face Time with us.

"Nothing has changed except that I like this feeling of being in love and being loved back by this handsome hunk of a guy who also happens to be the most generous and kind person I know and my Boss!

"Let's not sit here all day doing nothing. I want to call Lily and set up a time for our next meeting. If she can do it tomorrow, that would be great, if it's OK with you. At the rate we're going, we could finish the interview by the end of the month. The sooner we wrap the show, the sooner we can make plans."

Sam look puzzled. "Plans? What plans?"

Jodi threw a pillow at him. He reached for her causing them both to fall back on the bed, delaying for a while longer the start of their day.

On the ride to Lily's, they shared mixed emotions about the fourth session of the interview. Finally Sam said, "I think we should stop second guessing what we're about to learn. It doesn't matter what we think she is going to say; it only matters what she does say. The day we have waited for; the most anticipated day of the interview is here. I, for one, am glad I'm going to be present at the taping.

Nina awaited them at the door as the Uber drove up. It was only 9:00 am. They had been asked to come early. As they removed their coats, Lily called to them. "I'm in the kitchen."

They entered to see the Island set for four. Four glasses of orange juice had been poured, butter and syrup sat in the middle, and mugs for coffee sat nearby. "I'm making pancakes; it was Noah's favorite for breakfast and when Olivia came along, it became hers too."

Nina joined them, and they were soon savoring a real treat. On a warming plate was a stack of pancakes ready to be enjoyed.

Sam proclaimed, "These are the lightest and fluffiest pancakes I have ever eaten. Delicious doesn't begin to describe them. Do they have a secret ingredient?" Lily laughed. Jodi answered. "Room temperature eggs and milk, right Lily?"

"Why yes, that is my secret, although I am sure there are other ways."

Sam was totally surprised. "How do you know that? Have you ever made pancakes from scratch?"

"If I have, I don't remember. I do know it works with pancake mixes too."

When every last pancake was gone, Lily offered to make more, but they opted for a second cup of coffee instead. Nina offered to clean up so they could get started on the interview.

With Lily seated on her lounge chair facing Jodi and Sam on the sofa, she gave the signal to begin taping.

"As we reached the end of the nineties and headed into the twenty-first century, life was good—not just for the Ashers but throughout the city. For the past seven years under the leadership of Rudy Giuliani the city was safer and sounder than it had been in decades.

"FBI statistics named New York City the safest large city in America. Crime across the board was at an all-time low as drug use dramatically declined. He was instrumental in ridding the city, and Times Square in particular, of pornography; and he cracked down on the squeegee men who had long harassed commuters at the city's many bridges. His cleanup of the city was unprecedented.

"For the Ashers, 2001 offered a year of anticipations and celebrations, with the month of September in particular looming large. September 7th was Joe's and my Wedding Anniversary; and September 11th was not only my Birthday, it was Nicole and Noah's 15th Wedding Anniversary.

"To mark the occasion, Noah had spent months planning a special surprise for Nicole. He knew precisely what he wanted, and had taken great pains to bring it to fruition in time for their anniversary, which he finally managed to do the week before.

"In addition, they had a full day of activities on tap: Noah had a 9:00 am meeting in the North Tower with the Port Authority of New York and New Jersey. After confirming their reservation for dinner at Windows on the World, he would head to the hotel. Nicole would drop off their luggage at The Plaza, and head for her appointment at Elizabeth Arden, returning to the hotel afterwards to meet up with Noah for their Plaza Picnic at Gapstow Bridge. The remainder of the afternoon they left at will—to do a little shopping, take a carriage ride through Central Park, enjoy a leisurely walk or simply relax.

"Their reservation for dinner was at 8:00 pm; he planned to reveal his special surprise over dessert—a two-week vacation in Hawaii where they had spent their honeymoon in the very same house they had rented on the beach in Maui. Nicole often wistfully spoke of going back.

"We celebrated our anniversary over the weekend by having dinner together. I stayed overnight at their brownstone, so I could see Olivia off to school the next morning. After school, we had appointments to have our nails done, and return to wait for Joe to come to Brooklyn. The three of us were set to celebrate my birthday in Brooklyn with dinner, ice cream, and a special surprise we had in store for Olivia's 10th Birthday in December—we were taking her to Disney World.

"Everyone in New York on the morning of September 11, 2001 will tell you just how perfect the weather was that day—brilliant sunshine, a deep blue sky, mild temperatures, low humidity, and a light north breeze. As Noah came into the kitchen where I was making breakfast for Olivia, he took one of the pancakes off her plate. When she pretended to want it back, he said, *I'd give it back for a kiss!* She kissed him and told him he could keep it. He did. She hugged and kissed Nicole, and told them to have fun in the city. Noah put his arms around me, kissed me and wished me *Happy Birthday.* At the sound of the cab's horn, they left.

"How could I have possibly known I would never see him again? On that perfect day, our perfect plans off to a good start, and the anticipation of the remainder of those plans being just as perfect at day's end gave no hint of what was to come.

"After Olivia left for school, I cleaned up the breakfast dishes, poured another cup of coffee, and sat on a stool at the Island with the paper. It was early, but I turned the television on to watch Regis and Kelly, that came on at 9:00 am.

"I wasn't really paying attention to the TV. Suddenly, the phone rang. It was Joe; his voice as I had never heard it before actually shouting, *Are you watching television?* I turned towards the screen and found myself staring at a gaping hole near the upper floors of the North Tower as smoke enveloped the building. To this day, I don't remember what we said to one another or how we ended the call. Although later, I vaguely remembered him saying, *I'll try to reach the kids.*

"My first thoughts were of Olivia. Surely the news would spread quickly of what initially appeared to be a freak accident—an American Airlines Boeing 767 crashing into the North Tower at 8:45 am. Well aware of her parents' plans to spend the day in the city would surely concern her when she learned of the accident; I needed to get to her first and assure her that everything was okay.

"As I was preparing to leave and walk up to the school, I grabbed my keys, and just as I reached to turn off the TV, a second Boeing 767 appeared in the sky, turned sharply toward the World Trade Center and sliced into the South Tower. The collision caused a massive explosion that showered burning debris over buildings and onto the streets below. It was now clear that America was under attack. It was 9:03 am. I froze. Thoughts of Austria and the war pervaded my mind.

"Somehow, I pulled myself together and set off to pick up Olivia.

When I got to the school, they were in the process of trying to reach out to the parents. Hand in hand, we walked back to the house, and trying to remain as calm as possible, I told her that we would call Papa Joe when we got home to tell him that we were fine and see if he had been able to reach her parents.

"The thought that Noah was in danger never crossed my mind. I was aware of his meeting at 9:00 am, but I reasoned their cab left Brooklyn at a little past 8:00 am, and considering rush hour traffic, in all probability, he hadn't yet arrived at the North Tower when the first plane crashed into the building, and Nicole was with him in the cab.

"When we got back to the house, against my better judgment, I turned on the TV. It was pure pandemonium. I didn't want to expose Olivia to any of it, but I had to learn what was happening. The morning wore on; the news grew worse as we watched in horror American Airlines Flight 77 striking the west side of the Pentagon.

"United Airlines Flight 93 was the fourth plane hijacked and crashed into the Pennsylvania countryside outside of Shanksville. It was the only plane that didn't reach its target, which remains unknown—theories included the White House, the Capitol, or possibly Camp David, the presidential retreat in nearby Maryland—having been diverted by the selfless and courageous actions of the 40-passengers and crewmembers on board; all perished. What had begun as an ordinary, late-summer day of fair weather and blue skies had been transformed in less than two-hours' time.

"Olivia and I clung to one another. I was the adult; she was the child, yet she comforted me and assured me that Papa Joe was taking care of her parents just as I was taking care of her. We cried. I tried to convince her to eat something but she refused. My attempts to call Joe were futile. The circuits were overloaded; nobody was getting through. Brooklyn was so close yet so far.

"It was late in the evening before I heard from Joe. Olivia had fallen asleep on the sofa; I covered her with a blanket and let her be. His voice was weary, sounding tired and drained. Nicole was with him at our house. There was no word from Noah. She confirmed the cab had dropped him off before the plane went into the building. By the time she reached the hotel, the attack had occurred.

"There was nothing we could do but wait. Again my thoughts returned to another place and time—the train accident that claimed my parents and brother—remembering all my aunt and uncle and I could do was wait. As the evacuation of the twin towers got underway, television cameras continued to broadcast live images of the horror that had overtaken the city.

"In the days following the attacks, we became aware of the grim statistics. With heavy hearts, we also learned who survived and who didn't. When the jets slammed into the towers, stairwells became the sole means of escape for the thousands of occupants and visitors who sought to do so. Overcrowding and congestion in the stairwells contributed immensely to the time needed to descend to the ground floor taking longer than the buildings stood before collapsing. Noah's body was found in a stairwell; mere feet away from escape. At 10:30 am, the North Tower collapsed. Only six people in the World Trade Center towers at the time of their collapse survived.

"How I managed to get through those days, I'll never know. If I didn't have Olivia with me, I don't know what I would have done, or could have done, differently. Three days passed before Joe and Nicole finally came to Brooklyn. Nicole refused to leave the city; Joe had his hands full. She refused to talk with Olivia fearing she would ask about Noah. I worried about Joe and his heart. Stress was not his friend.

"The look on Olivia's face when Joe and Nicole finally arrived at the brownstone was a look I will never forget. She didn't ask where her father was; she knew. I think she had a feeling from the beginning he wasn't coming home, having asked not a single question as we waited for news. She sought more to comfort me.

"As father and daughter alike in so many ways, they shared their love for a myriad of things, including pancakes. The bond between them grew stronger as she grew older. Without saying a word, she went upstairs to her room. Joe and I didn't feel it was our place to go to her, yet Nicole made no move to do so.

"Finally, Joe went to her. I could hear them crying, and it broke my heart, as if my heart could break any more. Joe and I tried to talk to Nicole, tried to make some decisions. We had all lost Noah; we were all hurting, but the only one who counted was Olivia. She was a child.

"We steadfastly refused to leave Brooklyn; leaving Nicole in the state she was in wasn't going to happen. She was in no condition to take care of herself, let alone Olivia. On the other hand, we didn't want to take Olivia home with us and leave her alone, even if she agreed to it. Days dragged by, and we became robots—eat, drink, sleep—and then do it over and over again. I asked Olivia if she wanted to go back to school. At first, she didn't. Then one day, she thought she might try it.

"Joe began commuting to Manhattan a few times a week, I stayed at the brownstone basically taking care of Olivia and Nicole who was in another world. A month passed, and the three of us were coming to terms with losing Noah as best we could; we were there for each other. Joe managed to slowly draw Olivia out of her sadness by doing some of the things she liked doing with her father. I knew his heart was breaking, but he thought it more important to ease his granddaughter's pain; I loved him for it.

"At times, I went to the city with Joe. I dropped in at the studio, and it felt good to be out and about interacting with others. But Nicole never left my mind when I did so. I went by the house to pick up clothes, and to check in with the foundation. With the studio and foundation both in good hands, Olivia back in school, and Joe back to work, I decided the time had come to help Nicole whether she wanted to be helped or not. I suggested she seek professional help; she flatly refused. During one of our conversations, I realized I was seeing a side of her that I never knew existed. She came into our lives as a young, positive woman out to conquer the world with a personality that was infectious. The person I was speaking to bore no resemblance to her whatsoever.

"I decided I was going to shake her up a bit and give her a reality check. I spent the remainder of the day thinking. When I was satisfied with my plan, I set out to put it in action. At dinner, I told her that I had planned a day just for the two of us, stating that it had been a long time since we went on one of our *girl's day outings*. Surprisingly, she took me up on it. I was elated.

"The next day, after Olivia left for school, off we went. We had our hair done, manicures and pedicures, did a little shopping, and stopped for lunch. While we were eating, we had a long talk, and at long last she opened up to me. She knocked my socks off.

"She told me that for weeks leading up September 11th, she suspected Noah was having an affair—citing numerous hush-hush phone conversations when she walked in the room, and the inability to shake the feeling he was hiding something from her. A week before their anniversary, as she was on her way to meet Noah from work and head home together on the subway, she saw him hugging a young woman with red hair. By the time she arrived at his building, the woman was gone; he was alone.

"When Noah died, she was devastated. Now she would never know if in fact she had already lost him long before September 11th. I sat stunned, unable to utter a single word. In my wildest imagination, I could never have guessed what she had agonized over for almost two months; we were approaching the end of October.

"I called the waiter over and ordered two drinks. When they came, I started my conversation by telling her we had received word that they had recovered Noah's remains, and we could move forward and lay him to rest, adding that it was the first step in allowing us all to move on. A step I felt we all needed to take sooner rather than later.

"As I continued, I described the morning of September 11th by detailing everything as it happened, from my spending the night before, to making breakfast for Olivia and seeing her off to school, to their leaving by cab for the city—outlining their plans for the day and evening—and ending with dinner at Windows on the World where Noah was going to surprise her with a two-week trip to Hawaii.

"The hush-hush calls, the halted conversations when she entered the room, the woman he hugged—the travel agent, an old friend—who had gone above and beyond to duplicate their honeymoon trip, and of course, her feeling that he was hiding something from her because he was—all explained in a matter of minutes.

"I guess I knocked her socks off too. At first, a smile crossed her face and then she began to cry. She said she felt like such a fool and asked my forgiveness. I had nothing to forgive her for. I only wanted her happiness. She was the daughter I never had; she was the mother of my granddaughter; and I saw firsthand the love she and Noah shared. Joe and I lost our son; we didn't want to lose her too. Most importantly, Olivia needed the only parent she had left.

"Dinner that evening was like old times. Joe attributed it to our outing until I told him later that night about our conversation. We made plans to bury Noah and laid him to rest in the Asher family plot at Mount Hebron. It was a solemn day, but gave us closure. Less than 300 bodies were recovered in tact from the rubble of the towers; identification of body parts remains ongoing to this day.

"November arrived and with it the weather grew cold. Joe and I were back at our house and both of us were back to our normal routines. Each weekend, Nicole and Olivia either came to Manhattan or we went to Brooklyn. We did everything as a family. We needed one another. Nicole returned to work three days a week at the Foundation. Olivia was back in school happy to be involved in all of her projects, having just announced a contest to name the school paper.

"Thanksgiving was a couple of weeks away, and Joe and I invited Olivia and Nicole to come for the long weekend and stay over. We decided to include Nicole and continue with our plans to take Olivia to Disney World for her 10th Birthday in December over the Christmas break. We never had the chance to tell her about it in September.

"It was a wonderful weekend; just the four of us. Our traditional dinner with all the trimmings was delicious; we went to the movies; we did a little shopping; best of all, Olivia was thrilled with her surprise. It was nice to have something to look forward to. We had been through a rough time. With our concerns for Olivia and Nicole, Joe and I never had a chance to mourn Noah; we chose instead to celebrate his life by going through pictures of happier times. We laughed a lot; it was good for both of us."

"December brought invitations to several holiday parties we had been attending for years. In addition, the Foundation hosted an annual dinner party the first weekend of the month, which was held at the house. It went off without a hitch. A lot of the credit went to Nicole who made most of the arrangements. Olivia didn't attend the party; she enjoyed dinner in her room while going through the contest entries to name her school paper. She planned to announce the results the following week.

"Everything seemed to be returning to normal. It wouldn't be long before we left on our trip to Florida. I was beginning to share Olivia's excitement; I too had never been to Disney World.

"The weekend of December 8th, we had one of our holiday parties to attend so we didn't have our usual family get together. The holiday season was always a slow time for the Foundation, so Nicole sometimes chose to work from home. It was Tuesday when I realized I hadn't spoken to her in days. Olivia called daily and sometimes more than once a day. It was odd; she hadn't called yesterday at all.

"Knowing Olivia was in school, I thought I would call her later. I placed a call to Nicole; there was no answer. Throughout the morning, off and on, I repeatedly called the house and her cell phone to no avail. I left messages; none were returned.

I didn't want to bother Joe, so I waited for him to come home. Throughout the evening, we continued to call; there was no answer.

"As the hour grew late, Joe hesitated to call the police. He suggested driving to Brooklyn while I reasoned, if something had happened at the house, their neighbors would surely be aware. Several knew Joe and I well, and had our contact information. We decided to wait until morning, try calling again, and if there was no answer, drive to Brooklyn.

"It was exactly what we did. On the drive, the thoughts that filled my head were not good. My heart sank at the thought of another crisis that neither Joe nor I was up for. Although I worried more for him, I didn't know how much more I could endure. The house was locked; nothing seemed out of the ordinary. Opening the door with our key, we went inside. There was no sign of anything wrong, and there was no sign of Nicole and Olivia.

"We didn't know what to do. Unable to imagine where they might be, we stopped in at the local police station and told them our dilemma, asking if they thought we should file a missing persons claim. We left their names and descriptions and the officer we spoke with said they would check local hospitals for accident reports to see if there were any matches. They promised to keep in touch.

"Joe and I wearily returned home. A FedEx envelope had been left at the door. We opened it to find a note from Nicole explaining that she and Olivia were taking some time to reconnect and say their goodbyes to Noah. She couldn't say how long they would be gone, but requested that we give her space and time to heal so that she could move on.

"Joe and I were speechless. Neither of us slept that night. It was the one time in my life that I yearned to pray—I didn't know how. Joe called the police station and cancelled the search. When he asked me to go to Temple with him, I jumped at the chance. We spoke to the Rabbi asking for guidance. He advised us to be patient, telling us that we each mourn differently, and although, we didn't agree with the way she chose to deal with her loss, she was doing what she felt was right for her. He made no mention of Olivia. It was the last time I set foot in a house of worship."

Lily stopped speaking; she motioned for Jodi to turn off the recorder. "I'm tired, and I really would like to lie down for a while. I have shared all my memory boxes with you that have bearing on my story, so there won't be one today."

Sam and Jodi sat unmoving on the sofa. When Lily stood up, Sam asked, "Do you want me to get Nina to help you upstairs?"

"You can get Nina to come down, but I'm not going upstairs. I'll just lie back in my lounge chair and close my eyes. I find the warmth from the fireplace relaxing.

I'll have Nina make me a cup of tea, and I'll be all set."

Sam went upstairs to get Nina. Jodi remained on the sofa in the same spot, as Lily watched her without saying a word, she nodded off to sleep.

# Chapter 15

Sam was concerned about Lily. Worried that the day's session had been too much for her, he hesitated to leave. With no memory box to share, she hadn't asked them to stay leading him to assume they were finished taping, and there was no reason for them to remain. After asking Nina to come downstairs, he returned to find that Lily had fallen asleep and that Jodi hadn't moved; she sat rigidly on the sofa in the same spot—he now worried about Jodi also. He felt fortunate that Lily's suggestion had included him to sit in on the day's taping—considering the dramatic turn the interview had taken.

He went into the kitchen to tell Nina that she had fallen asleep. "I'm worried about Lily. I've never seen her like this. I feel bad leaving the two of you alone. I hope she is alright."

Nina quickly responded. "We don't want you to leave. She planned to ask you to stay for supper, and it's all prepared. She's just tired like she said; please stay. She'll be fine after a brief rest. Why don't we let her be, while you and Jodi join me in the kitchen? I have sandwiches and soup, and we can sit and chat a bit."

He was surprised, yet again. "That sounds great, and it makes me feel better. Like I said, I really want to wait for her to wake up and see that she's okay for myself. I'll go get Jodi, and if we can help you with anything, please don't hesitate to ask."

He went into the other room, took Jodi's hand, put his finger to his lips to be quiet, and walked towards the kitchen. "We're going to stay at least until Lily wakes up. Nina has invited us to have a snack with her while we wait. Do you want to freshen up or stretch your legs? You've been sitting for a long time.

"I think I will freshen up a bit. Does Nina need any help?"

"I offered; if she does, I'm sure she'll ask."

When they were seated at the Island, Nina set grilled cheese sandwiches and tomato soup along with chips and cutup veggies before them, and asked if they preferred hot tea or coffee. The hot soup hit the spot. Sam started the conversation by asking Nina how long she had known Lily.

"I've known her about as long as you have. I'm not from New York originally. I'm a born and bred Missouri farm girl, but there's nothing left of that girl in me. Farming had been in our family for generations, but it ended with my father. Our farm had been deteriorating for years, and after my mother died, it hit rock bottom. It was just my brother Danny and I against our abusive alcoholic father. He died when Danny was a senior in high school. The feeling of being free of his abuse was euphoric, and we felt reborn. I had turned twenty-one only months before, so that legally made me my brother's guardian. We were more than ready to pull up stakes and leave the farm and the past behind us.

"Missouri has a long and storied history of riverboat gambling. In the early 1990s, although The Missouri Gaming Commission was established to ensure that licensed gaming operations were not infiltrated by criminal elements, it wasn't long before their power and influence expanded. The Commission began by allowing riverboat casinos to operate while remaining dockside; this did not go unnoticed. In no time, developers descended upon the area and began buying up the unending deserted and failing farms turning them into Las Vegas style casinos.

"We had prayed for a miracle, and we got one. Our farm was purchased by Hilton and in 1996, the Flamingo Hilton Kansas City opened.

"By then, Danny and I were living in New York. He decided to apply to the FDNY Academy to take the written firefighter exam, which was followed by months of extensive in-class and on-field training and took almost a year to complete. By the time he graduated, I was engaged to Eric Butler, a friend who had graduated from the Academy with him; he had introduced us. We were married soon after.

"Ladder Company 10 and Engine Company 10, the **Ten House Ten** are located across the street from the World Trade Center. The only fire station inside Ground Zero—it was Danny's station. They were the first to respond to the attack on the North Tower. At the time, I worked in the North Tower, but on September 11, 2001, Eric and I had taken the day off to celebrate my recent promotion. We picked a weekday, Tuesday, when things were normally quiet both in my office and at the station. Our celebration never happened. When for the first time in over 30 years, all off-duty firefighters were recalled, he headed to the World Trade Center.

"I lost Danny that day. Eric was hospitalized with smoke inhalation and eventually released. A study taken by the Office of Medical Affairs of the FDNY found that firefighters who arrived on the morning of September

11th had the worst impairments, often becoming apparent within the first year after the attack. Eric developed respiratory and pulmonary problems; he endured bouts of depression and anxiety; but in the end it was cancer that killed him. He died in 2012.

"I watched the premiere show of *Profiles* at Eric's bedside in the hospital. When Lily offered to paint portraits of the Heroes of 9/11, I took her up on the offer and dropped off my favorite photo of Danny at her studio. When I went to pick it up, we got to talking, and she learned my story. We became friends. I began helping her out at the studio when I wasn't at the hospital or home caring for Eric. Joe had already passed away when I met her, and we were good for each other. When Eric died, she asked me to come work for the Asher Foundation fulltime and encouraged me to move in with her.

They sat quietly for a few moments. Jodi placed her hand on top of Nina's. "I am so sorry for your losses. I don't think the stories about that day will ever stop being told."

"I agree, though mine pales in comparison to some I've heard. At one point Sam, she suggested that I share my story with you for the show. I told her when she was ready to share hers, perhaps I would consider sharing mine. This hasn't been easy for her; she's lost so much. It is my fondest hope she gets her miracle like Danny and I did, even though ours was short lived."

They looked up to see Lily coming into the kitchen. "My goodness, why didn't you wake me? I think I'll have a bite to eat, and then we can get back to the interview."

"All we had to look forward to was waiting, and waiting was what we did. We decided to honor Nicole's wishes giving her time and space. The days passed slowly; the time of our planned trip to Disney World came and went; we heard nothing from them, nor did they return. Our hearts remained heavy. Time and again, we went over and over the days leading up to their departure to see if we missed anything.

"Had Nicole hinted that she was still burdened with doubt? Not that we remembered. Had Olivia been aware they were leaving? We concluded—absolutely not; there was no way she would leave her Nana and Papa Joe—certainly not without at least saying *goodbye*.

"The years that comprised the decade following September 11th passed in a blur yet there is much that I do recall. Joe and I were inseparable; we clung to one another, as I watched the tall handsome man with the beautiful smile that had captured my heart become old and broken before my very eyes. Year after year, all hope of ever seeing Nicole and Olivia again evaporated. We were beginning to face the reality that they were no longer alive.

"In August 2009, deciding to take advantage of cooler weather that had moved in, we took a walk through the neighborhood and stopped for ice cream. As we got closer to returning to the house, Joe said he wasn't feeling well; he collapsed on the street. The ambulance was there in no time, but Joe was gone.

"I had a private service for Joe laying him to rest beside his parents and Noah. I was the only one in attendance. Friends and associates unwillingly accepted my decision and granted me my privacy, but it didn't stop them from memorializing him in their own way. Donations in his memory poured into the Foundation. I recited the Lord's Prayer, made him a promise that I would never stop trying to learn what happened to Nicole and Olivia, and reaffirmed what he already knew—I loved him from the depths of my being. I laid a single yellow rose on his grave and walked to the car that waited.

"I returned to this empty house alone with nothing but *memories*, and a million *What ifs?* After a week had passed, I took a long, hard *look in the mirror*. I didn't like the Lily Asher that stared back at me. The past was gone; it was time to let go. I was well aware I had much to be grateful for; I was ready to look forward to what was coming.

"I decided to start by renovating and updating the house, ridding it of the old heavy drapes and furniture. I wanted a light airy feeling to permeate with windows that allowed the sun in while allowing one to look out at the New York Skyline whether it was by day or by night. I wanted the house to live again like it had in the early days even before it became home to me. I expanded the Foundation's space, and for the first time, I had an office of my own. I even replaced the old elevator with a new streamlined version.

"I thought about the past as little as possible. I missed Joe terribly; I missed him telling me *I Love You* a dozen times or more a day; I missed simply holding hands. I remained true to my decisions as I stepped into the future.

"The Asher Foundation became my priority by taking a more active part on a daily basis. I got involved in all things associated with the rebuilding of Ground Zero, to which the foundation generously contributed. It had been years since I had an interest in anything having to do with recipients of the many scholarships or funding we awarded each year. I also became more hands-on at the studio. I would pop in from time to time and visit with the students, or the merchants that I knew in and around the streets of West Village. I began painting again allowing me to release a good deal of my pent-up energy.

"As 2011 began, I had reached a turning point in my life. You might say *I came back to life.* I woke up each day with a purpose, and I renewed my promise to Joe that I would never stop trying to learn what happened to Nicole and Olivia. I purchased a Mac for my office, an iPad, and an iPhone, and I hired a young man from Apple's Geek Squad to get me up to par on my new purchases.

"I was well aware that 2011 would mark the 10th Anniversary of 9/11, but I was unwilling to let it deter me with sadness and regret. On an early spring day with bright sunshine in a cloudless sky, trees turning green, and flowers peeking out from the cold hard ground, I met with a young man who not only became my friend, but has gone on to play a significant role in my life.

"Our initial meeting set up to acquaint us with one another and possibly form a working partnership turned out to be more than either of us anticipated. His name was Sam Meyerson. As he introduced me to his new show *Profiles of New York,* defining the word *profile* to extend beyond persons to buildings and events, he revealed a concept that paralleled the very thought behind the very existence of *Portraits by Lily.* It took me back to the time I explained my definition of the word *portrait* to Grace Shepherd as extending beyond persons to include buildings and events.

"I was fascinated by the young man who sat across from me, and I continued to compare his vision for *Profiles* to the vision I once held for *Portraits.* So many years had passed, yet his idea came across as new and fresh. I had no doubt that he would be as successful as I had been.

"*Profiles* was due to debut on the 10th Anniversary of the 9/11 attacks with a two-hour episode honoring the Heroes of that day. Although I had requested the meeting to learn more about the show, by the time it was over, he had invited me to play a small part; I was honored to be included. Certain the show would be seen quite favorably by New Yorkers, and the series would continue, I committed the Asher Foundation's funding for all future episodes.

"Kudos all around to those whose hard work and dedication contributed to the various commemorations planned for September 11, 2011. The premiere of *Profiles* was a huge success. In addition to the annual *live reading of the names*, every major network aired specials that managed to avoid overlapping while covering every aspect. The dedication ceremony for the 9/11 Memorial was held at the site, and opened to the public the following day.

"In the immediate aftermath of the attacks, a memorial was planned for the victims and those involved in rescue and recovery operations. Michael Arad, an Israeli-American architect's winning design—*Reflecting Absence*—features a forest of swamp white oak trees, two square reflecting pools in the center marking where the Twin Towers stood, and the names of the victims of the attacks inscribed on the parapets surrounding the waterfalls.

"In the days that followed, I found myself at peace with having lost Noah. A visit to the 9/11 Memorial the next day was awesome. As I ran my hand over Noah's name etched on the parapet, I somehow felt close to him. My offer to paint portraits of the 9/11 Heroes brought numerous new friends into my life, and I remain in touch with many of them. In particular, Nina Butler and I have become family.

"As I became more proficient on the computer, I was amazed to learn that one could get an answer to just about anything simply by asking someone or something called *Google*. In a matter of seconds, one could choose from any number of choices that popped up. At first, I only turned to *Google* when I was researching something that had to do with the foundation.

"I can't say exactly when I decided to try entering Nicole and Olivia's names and information I thought could bring me a *hit*, but I began *surfing the web* regularly. I didn't have any success, but I did get better at it as I continued my quest.

"Years passed; I was content with my life. The world was changing around me, but it wasn't passing me by. When COVID-19 ascended upon us, we soon realized that we had entered unknown territory. We couldn't possibly have been prepared for something that hadn't existed, and it looked as though nobody had an answer to deal with it.

"The phrase *we are all in this together* became an oxy moron. Of course, we were. That didn't make it any easier to deal with. Politics—something I had steered clear of my entire life—took over. Hatred spread across the country faster than the virus, and at times, a feeling of helplessness enveloped us all.

"In reality, my life changed very little. Although interaction with others outside the house ceased with the onset of the lockdown and mandates, all of my errands and needs were fulfilled via the computer. I found myself asking *why hadn't I done this before?* I called for groceries—they were promptly delivered. I added a new friend to *Google*—it was *Amazon*; they never failed to have an item I wanted and delivered it at warp speed.

"Inside the house, we looked out for one another. As the months passed and mandates and regulations eased up a bit, we cautiously ventured out. We were tested regularly whether we were experiencing symptoms or not, and we looked forward to the vaccines becoming available. In the meantime, the country went through one of the worst presidential elections in our history, leaving many to feel if we could survive that, than we could surely survive the virus.

"When the vaccines became available in early December, I believe we all began to have hope again. More and more businesses opened at larger capacities, and once people were vaccinated, they began to venture out more. I decided not to reopen *Portraits by Lily* until the spring. The Foundation was never shut down, and since the offices were in-house, it was business as usual.

"My *surfing the web* was also business as usual. In September, a friend sent me a link to Jodi Jerome's article in the LA Times memorializing her father Henry Jerome who was one of the first COVID-19 deaths in California. I was mesmerized by her story. I read and reread it until I practically had it memorized. I spent days on end researching the young journalist who had written the heartfelt story."

Lily stopped speaking. She did not motion Jodi to turn off the machine indicating a break or that she was finished for the day. She simply sat there.

Unexpectedly, Jodi's voice began to fill the room. "I woke up so excited and started getting dressed for school. It was the day I was set to announce the contest winner naming my school paper—*PS9 Notes and Notables*. It was actually a combination of two entries. Along with the announcement, the paper having been put on hold after 9/11, was releasing its first issue under the heading of its new name.

"As I bounced down the stairs to have breakfast, I was singing *My Girl*, a song Daddy sang to me and that we often danced to with my feet atop his when I was little. I felt close to him that morning; he had encouraged me to go forward with my idea for the paper and when it was so well received, we celebrated over ice cream, and he sang it to me then too. I always took it to mean he was proud of me.

"At the foot of the stairs by the front door sat three suitcases. I walked into the kitchen but my mother wasn't there. There was no breakfast being prepared. I turned when I heard her coming down the steps.

"She was acting strange and couldn't look me in the eyes. Before I had a chance to ask her about breakfast or the suitcases, she told me we were going away for a while, further telling me she had packed a snack until we could stop for breakfast. She seemed anxious to get going, and impatiently urged me to get a move on.

"My world collapsed in that split second. As she hurried me out the door, my questions began. *What about school and the newspaper? How long is a while? Where are we going? What about our trip to Disney World? Can I call Nana and Papa Joe to say goodbye?* Her answer to my questions was to *stop whining.* She handed me a bag with my snack in it along with a bottle of water.

"We didn't have a car. If we ever needed one to go anywhere, we always used Papa Joe's. Parked directly out front of our house that day was a medium-sized red car; my mother headed straight for it and began putting our suitcases in the back. She told me to get in and buckle up. My next round of questions began. *Whose car is this? Why aren't we using Papa Joe's car?* I had never seen my mother drive; I didn't know if she could drive or not. I never had any reason to think about it.

"As she drove away from the curb, I realized it was really happening. We were leaving for a while. I was ten years old. All I had known my entire life is having been loved—by my parents and by my grandparents. When Daddy died, I hurt so badly, but Nana and Papa Joe were there for me. We were there for each other. For months, my mother existed in her own world offering neither comfort to us nor wanting comfort from us. Things changed after my father's funeral.

"My mother was like her old self. She saw me off to school every morning, and we discussed our days every night. She went back to work. We spent weekends at Nana and Papa Joe's. She even resumed my piano lessons. We spent mother-daughter times together, and we shared plans for my tenth birthday coming up. She told me she and Daddy had decided to get me a cellphone; she had a bright pink one on order. Our planned trip to Disney World was icing on the cake.

"Two weeks after Thanksgiving, I was sitting in a car beside a woman that bore no resemblance whatsoever to the person I called Mom. It was an awful lot for me to digest; I was just a child. I began to cry. The more I cried, the angrier she became. She yelled at me to stop. I could never recall my mother yelling at me in that tone of voice.

"When she finally pulled into the parking lot of a diner along the road, it was lunchtime. I had no idea where we were. It was busy, and she asked if I would rather get something to go. I said I preferred to wait. In my child's way of thinking, I kept hoping if we were closer to home someone would appear, save me and take me back. Of course, that didn't happen.

"As the days passed, we traveled from place to place stopping overnight but never spending more than two nights in any one place. I begged to call Nana and Papa Joe, she responded by saying they weren't expecting us to call until we got to where we were going. When I asked where we were going, all she said was *you'll see soon enough.*

"At our last overnight stop, she told me we were headed to Los Angeles, California, but we would only be staying long enough for her to book us flights to Hawaii. I asked again to call Nana and Papa Joe; she said I could call when we got to Hawaii.

"She started having trouble with the car on our last day as we headed to Los Angeles. A stop at a service station fixed the problem, but I remember the man telling her to see that it was taken care of properly, as soon as possible. She told me we would be in California by late afternoon, and after we checked into a motel, we could go out to a nice dinner and relax. She was in a better mood than she had been in on the entire trip.

"The problem with the car took a long time to resolve. Long enough for her to change moods once again. As we started on the last leg of the trip, it was late afternoon, the time she had originally estimated we would arrive at our destination. She didn't stop for anything to eat, and we only had one bottle of water left. When I asked her when we were going to eat, she didn't answer me. She remained intent on driving with a vengeance to get to Los Angeles.

"It was dark out, but I remember looking up and seeing a million stars in the sky. Since all the businesses we passed were closed, I assumed it was late, how late I couldn't tell. The car's clock wasn't working. One minute she said *we're almost there,* and the next minute the car began making weird sounds and slowing down as if running out of gas. She pulled over to the curb and began banging on the steering wheel saying over and over again *why is this happening to me?* I began to cry really hard. I remember saying, *I don't want to go to Los Angeles or Hawaii; I want to go home.* She grew furious and said, *home is with me; I'm your mother.* I cried harder. She told me to get out of the car, stretch my legs, and sit on the grass while she called for help.

"Finding her phone dead, she started to cry. I began to feel sorry I had behaved so badly; I stood up to go to her, when suddenly the car burst into flames. I froze. I heard sirens in the distance and wondered if they were coming to help us. As they got closer I backed up further away from the car and sat back down on the grass. The last thing I remember was the explosion, and then something hitting me on the head.

"When I came out of the coma three months later, Olivia Asher was no more."

Sam reached over and turned off the recorder. He gathered Jodi in his arms, and she began sobbing. As he held her, through her tears she glanced at Lily who sat stoically except for the smile on her face. Jodi went to her and said but one word—the only word Lily had waited to hear for almost twenty years—*Nana!*

Nina heard everything. Seeing that the time was getting late, she looked in to see how the taping was going to get an idea when to start dinner just as Jodi began to speak. They stood there, the four of them, in a circle with their arms around one another, crying and laughing and crying and laughing.

Nina was the first to step back. "I'm going to start dinner. I'll call you when it's ready."

There were so many questions, everyone speaking at once. Sam smiling the broadest grin Jodi had ever seen said, "Why don't the two of you just be Nana and Olivia for now—no questions, there is plenty of time for that. Twenty years is a long time to catch up on, and it's not going to happen in one night. I'm going to see if I can give Nina a hand in the kitchen."

They took Sam's suggestion—no questions, no explanations for now. They remained with their arms around one another, neither wanting nor willing to let go.

To anyone watching, dinner was a scene that could be anywhere with anyone—laughing and talking while enjoying a meal together.

Sam complimented Nina on the Lasagna. "I'm half Italian, and I must say, this is one of the best Lasagna's I've had. My Mom's side of the family— The Caruso Clan—as I so fondly call them, is quite extensive. Whenever we got together, food played an important part, and my Nonna Gina was the best cook ever. She also made cannoli, and Italian butter cookies that everyone always made sure they saved room for."

Nina blushed. "Thank you Sam; I'm glad you enjoyed it."

Sam smiled. "Hold on just a minute. You're not off the hook just yet. Next time I'll have to test your *Jewish Cuisine* expertise—my father's side of the family—the Meyersons, although I never called them a clan, shared one important common thread with the Carusos—food. To my Grandma Sarah food was the answer to everything from problem solving to celebrating. Whenever I paid my grandparents a visit, I was barely in the door when she would say, *Come in; let me get you something to eat.* Brisket, matzo ball soup, potato latkes, and kugel are a few of my favorites, and if you just happen to make rugulah, that would be awesome."

They all laughed as Lily said, "I don't know about the rest, but I can definitely vouch for her matzo ball soup. You would have loved Joe's mother Arlene; she made everything you mentioned and so much more."

Nobody wanted the evening to end. They all pitched in to clean up after dinner. They retired to the Library for coffee and Italian cookies for dessert.

Sam felt he should take the lead. "This has been quite a day to say the least. I think it would be a good idea for each of us to offer our thoughts on going forward. When we have all had our say, we can make some decisions. It is hard for me to imagine what the two of you are feeling. Twenty years cannot disappear in a day. I am happy to go first and give you my perspective.

"Lily, assuming that you are still willing to complete the interview and go forward as planned, here is my suggestion. The *Profiles* team will begin immediately to review the tapes and determine a format that would best present your story. You will have to determine where your story ends; for example, as of today's taping and your reuniting with Jodi or whatever you have in mind.

"Time wise, we are in good shape. We still have a week to go in February, and I see no problem wrapping the show by June, leaving summer wide open for making plans while allowing Jodi to return to California to tie up any loose ends before officially moving here.

"While I'm working with my team at the office, the two of you will be making decisions of your own. From the beginning, we agreed that you Lily would have the final say. Basically that hasn't changed, but for one exception. That final say must now also include Jodi's thoughts, and just how much of her story she's willing to share and incorporate into the interview. You have endured a separation that has been life altering. You owe it to yourselves to make every minute count from here on down the road. There are so many good things in store for both of you yet to come."

Jodi stood and walked over to Sam and kissed him. Turning to a surprised Lily she said, "Nana, don't tell me you didn't see this coming. Yes, Sam and I love one another, and I know you suspected as much because you told me so.

"I would like to know your thoughts before I make any decisions on my part. As the interviewer, I find myself in a position to compromise the outcome of the interview; it's the last thing I want to do.

"I do, however, agree with everything Sam said. I see it as a good plan, a sensible plan allowing the *Profiles* crew to go forward with finalizing the show. I am part of that crew and should be working with them. On the other hand, as they are determining the beginning of the show, I will be working on finalizing it."

Lily cleared her throat and smiled. "I feel so blessed. You're absolutely right Jodi. I saw that spark between you and Sam the first day he brought you to meet me. In all probability, it was before either of you wanted to admit it to yourselves.

"Sam, I am a woman of my word. There is zero possibility that I would renege on finishing the interview and going forward with the show. When you offered to profile me for the 20th Anniversary episode, you gave Jodi and me the opportunity to find one another, and for that I will eternally be grateful. You're a good man, an honorable man, and although you haven't yet asked, you have my blessing to marry my granddaughter. You were going to ask, weren't you?"

They all laughed. It was good to laugh; it's always good to laugh. They had so much to look forward to. It had been a long day and one they would never forget.

Lily went to bed and as she closed her eyes, she thanked God for having found Olivia and prayed that they would have time to get reacquainted before her journey ended. It was the first time she had prayed for anything. For some reason, she did it automatically as though she had been doing it all her life. She also spoke to Joe telling him she had fulfilled her promise.

Nina, whose Catholic upbringing brought prayer into her life when she was a child, thanked God for granting Lily the miracle she had prayed for.

"Wrapped contentedly in his arms, Jodi and Sam talked long into the night. Her concerns had all been answered, but most importantly, she knew who she was and no longer had to wonder about the first ten years of her life. She wanted that for Sam as much as she wanted it for herself.

# Chapter 16

They spent the next day making a list of pressing issues both business and personal. Sam planned to call a staff meeting at the office. Jodi decided to pack a bag and spend a few days at the house with Lily. With that aside, Sam's #1 priority became how and when to contact his mother and bring her up to date on what was happening.

He knew she would ask about the interview during their weekly call; she always did; therein was his dilemma. There was no way he could tell her about the show and not include Jodi and his plans for the future. It was late February, months away from her scheduled return from Florida, and he didn't see how they could possibly squeeze even a weekend trip to Naples into their busy schedule.

Until now, his mother was the most important person in his life, having grown closer, if that was even possible, since his father died. Their independence was important to both of them and although they lived in the same building, Trudy spent the better part of the year in Florida, or traveling. He had no doubt that his mother would be thrilled at their news. Jodi had pointed out to him that his mother suspected there was something between them, and he had to admit that she alluded as much to him. The fact that she took to Jodi instantly when she arrived in New York, taking her shopping and helping her get settled, was even more proof she would approve and be happy for them.

He simply could not call or Face Time something as important as his love for Jodi; he would have to do it in person. Revealing as little as possible, he would ask her to come to New York. Only Lily and Nina knew of their declared love and plans for the future. If Trudy needed a week or two to clear her schedule and make plans, that would be perfect. By then, they should have the show's format on track and a good deal of the editing behind them.

Sam sat in the conference room waiting for everyone to arrive for their meeting. Greg and Carol, Frank, and Edie, Lou and Sandy arrived and took their places around the table. They had finally received the call from Sam that they had anxiously awaited. The 20th Anniversary Episode was a go. From that point forward, for the first time since the onset of the pandemic, they would be working in the office.

All precautions were in place. Weekly testing was compulsory, as was wearing a mask when they worked closely together. An ample supply of tests and masks were on hand. The kitchen would be restocked with coffee and all the fixings; daily delivery of muffins and pastry for breakfast, as well as sandwiches and salads for lunch would allow them to cover as much ground as possible during normal workday hours. After so much downtime, he didn't want them overextending themselves. He needed everyone to be at his or her best.

Sam produced the tapes and laid them on the table. "I suggest you listen to these tapes from start to finish. If necessary, listen to them again. When you are through, I would like to meet to discuss your thoughts at that point. Of course, I don't need to remind you that this is all privileged information, and we don't want any of it to leak out before the airing. Once you hear the content, you will realize why I'm saying this to the team that I've worked with for ten years—the very core of the show's success. When Jodi first met with Lily Asher, her comment to me was— *get ready for the ride of your life*. Now, I'm passing that onto you."

Leaving the conference room, Sam went down the hall to his office and closed the door. It was a little before noon. He couldn't imagine where his mother might be, certainly not sitting around waiting for him to call. He decided to try reaching her anyway. She picked up on the second ring.

"Hi Sweetheart; to what do I owe this lovely surprise?"

"I hope I'm not interrupting anything. I'm actually calling to extend an invitation that I think you will be interested in."

"Okay, you have my attention. Invite me."

Sam chuckled to himself wondering how he managed to surround himself with women who were always so direct when responding to him. "When we spoke Sunday, I told you the next interview session with Lily was the following Monday, and that she had suggested that I come with Jodi to hear it firsthand. I was quite surprised, but I was also pleased and excited to be included.

"The day's taping was unbelievable. Any preconceived thoughts I may have had went out the window. We're not quite finished with the ending, but she has certainly delivered on her promise to give us the blockbuster we sought. She is an amazing person, and I hadn't realized how fond of her I have grown. I want very much for you to meet her.

"I just came out of a meeting with my staff. They will be working from the office together to listen to the tapes, determine a format, and commence finalizing the show for airing. I thought you might be interested in a preview of Lily's story. The catch is you would have to come to New York for a couple of days. It doesn't have to be immediately. Let's say a couple of weeks—mid-March would be good.

"What do you think?"

"Sam, I actually have tears in my eyes. Thank you for thinking of me to share what looks like is going to be the highest rated *Profiles* show yet. Each time I've spoken with Jodi about the interview, she too seems to have formed an attachment to Lily, and I would be honored to meet her and hear her story. I wouldn't miss it for the world.

"Why don't I make reservations to fly up mid-March as you suggest. I'll text you my itinerary when my plans have been finalized.

"Sam, thank you again. Talk to you soon. Love you."

"Goodbye Mom. Love you back."

That had gone extremely well. Sam's thoughts turned to how they would go about telling his mother they had fallen in love. He couldn't decide if he should tell her alone or if they should tell her together. He decided he had time to mull it over before making a decision.

Before he left the office, he made one last call to set up an appointment at Harry Winston Jewelers on Fifth Avenue to pick out a ring for Jodi. Uncertain as to when he planned to officially propose, he felt it wouldn't hurt to be ready when the time was right.

Pleased with all he had accomplished, he decided to leave the office and run some personal errands. At the top of his list was a haircut. He hated when his thick dark hair became shaggy and unkempt, just as he wouldn't think to skip shaving for a single day. He just didn't think either look was good for him. Craving a good corned beef sandwich, he stopped for lunch at Junior's on 49th Street, topping it off with a piece of cheesecake. When he got back to the Pavilion, he picked up his cleaning they were holding for him, and took the elevator up to his apartment.

Taking a seat on the sofa, he was ready to tackle the final item on his list. When Trudy offered her apartment to Sam for Jodi's stay while she was in Florida, he viewed it as the ideal temporary solution. It turned out to be just that. Still in the midst of the pandemic's unending rules and regulations, working from home and the close proximity of the Pavilion to Lily's house turned out to be not only convenient, but allowed Sam to acquaint Jodi with the area, while allowing them to get to know one another better.

His mother normally returned from Florida the end of May or beginning of June. By that time, if the show was not totally wrapped, it would certainly be in the final stages. Furthermore at the time, Jodi relocating permanently to the city was not yet a given.

A lot had changed since then. Jodi decided to make her move permanent; they fell in love and were planning a future together. To complicate things further, after their first night together and declaring their love for one another, they spent every night since in his mother's apartment. Though they never discussed it, Sam's thoughts were that Jodi would move in with him as they planned their wedding.

With the revelation that Jodi was Lily's long lost granddaughter Olivia, the entire picture changed. The brownstone on Vanderbilt was now hers. Would she want to live there? Would Lily offer or ask that she move into her house with her? Sam soon realized that he couldn't make any plans without Jodi.

She had only left for Lily's that morning, yet he missed her terribly. He somehow felt unhinged. No one to make plans with for dinner, and no one to discuss the interview with. For the first time since Jodi's arrival three months ago, he was alone. He didn't like it at all.

He did make one decision, and that was to dismantle the office he had set up for her in Trudy's den. Going forward, the entire team would be working from the office fulltime. If the need arose to work from home, they could use the office in his apartment. Although May was a few months down the road, he thought it a good idea to begin putting things back in order in his mother's apartment. He made a mental note to have the cleaning crew give the apartment a through onceover before her visit in March. Spending nights together would be put on hold while she was in New York.

With nothing else to do, he thought about ordering in for dinner. Checking his watch, he realized it was a little early so he decided to give some thought to the show. Each episode began with a brief introductory statement about the content, but that was where the similarity ended. Each show featured different formats, different producers, different narrators, but the one constant was that Sam always composed and gave the introductory statement.

It was the one part of each episode that was his and his alone to write and deliver. Rather than go on the computer, he grabbed a pen and pad of paper, and gathering his thoughts began writing. He had been at it a while when his phone rang. It was Jodi.

"Hi, how is your day going with Lily?"

"Wonderful! I went through the entire house a couple of times, and realized it didn't seem familiar to me because it was quite different twenty years ago. She did a major renovation after Papa Joe died and not only were physical changes made but the furnishings and décor were a total do-over. The only room I gave any thought to on our first visit was the bedroom that I assumed was Noah's— even though it appeared more a girl's room than a boy's. It was; it was mine.

"I laid down on the bed and closed my eyes; all kinds of great memories danced in my head. I plan to sleep in my old room tonight. We also went through some photos and items she saved that weren't included in the contents of the memory boxes that she shared with me. Oh Sam, she showed me a copy of the school paper *PS9 Notes and Notables* that my teacher gave her to save for me. Until today I hadn't seen a final copy. I thought I would never stop crying.

"We're planning on doing more of the same tomorrow. I can't wait to share all of this with you. It's so wonderful knowing who I am and learning why no one was looking for us. Above all else, it was the one thought that never left me, and the hardest fact for me to accept.

"I'm coming home Friday evening. However, we have made plans for the day, and they include you. Come bright and early; Nana is making her light and fluffy pancakes. There is someone she wants us to meet, and there are things she wants to show us both together. Afterwards, we're paying a visit to the brownstone on Vanderbilt. I hope I can handle it; if you're with me, I'm sure it will be easier. We can have dinner here before we leave for the apartment.

"Do you miss me? I miss you so much, but I love you more. You understand that I had to do this, don't you?"

Sam hung on her every word. "I'll answer the most important question first. I miss you more than I've ever missed anyone, and I have never felt more alone or lost without you here. I started feeling that way this morning right after you left. I'm excited for you and Lily, and excited to be part of it. Of course, I understand your spending time at the house. I would have been surprised if you hadn't.

"Your plans for Friday sound great and will allow me to coordinate my plans with yours. I had a meeting with the staff this morning, and gave them the tapes. We will all be working together in the office to finalize the show. They were eager to get started, and they did just that following our meeting. Once they listen to the tapes, they can commence formatting and editing. It will be up to us to deliver the ending, but there is no urgency. Time wise we are in great shape.

"Before I left the office, I called my Mom. I invited her to come to New York so we can bring her up-to-date on the interview. She was thrilled and is planning to come mid-March. As certain as we are that she knows about our feelings for one another, hearing it from us is paramount, and we have to tell her in person. She's too important to me to consider anything less—like a phone call or Face Time.

"Although I didn't say anything about us when I extended the invitation, I did say that I wanted her to meet Lily. As perceptive as my mother is, and whether she suspects something is up with us or not, there is no way she could possibly even begin to imagine that you are Lily's granddaughter. I got the impression that she's genuinely interested and eager to see how the interview turns out for both of us."

"Sam, please forgive me for being so preoccupied that I didn't even ask you how your day was. I absolutely agree; we must and we will tell her in person."

"Nothing to forgive. After the past year of COVID, it's so nice to have good things to celebrate and look forward to. Perhaps it's an omen that we'll soon be able to put the virus in the past.

"Friday sounds awesome, starting with Lily's pancakes. The day belongs to the both of you, and it's going to be hard for me getting through tomorrow waiting for Friday to come. If I may, I would like to add one thing. I'll make plans for us to have dinner out, and we can do some early celebrating. I will include Nina, of course. Check with Lily, and let me know what time would be good.

"Thank you Sam. I love you. I'll touch base with you in the morning."

"I love you more. Bye."

A feeling of contentment came over Sam. To him, the best part of their entire conversation was when Jodi said *I'm coming home on Friday.* To her, home was with him; to him, home was with her.

The team was glad to see Sam come into the office Thursday morning and invited him to join them as they listened to the second tape. He was surprised to learn that they opted to go through each tape thoroughly, replaying parts and discussing one another's views before moving on to the next one and doing the same. He thought perhaps their curiosity would lead them to listen—start to finish—then backtrack to the parts they wanted to review.

He spent the entire day at the office sitting in as they listened to Lily's story unfold—watching their reaction was priceless. He thought about his plans for the next day and realized he couldn't be with them to hear the third tape, but he gave serious thought to joining them on Monday for the fourth, which included Jodi's revelation at the end. It would be the perfect time for her to join the team.

Over lunch, they asked why Jodi wasn't with them. He answered them truthfully; she was with Lily. At their meeting the previous day when he gave them the four tapes, he failed to mention it was not the entire story. He decided to fill them in by telling them that in all probability there would be one more. In addition, he told them that he wouldn't be in the office on Friday, but come Monday morning, both he and Jodi would join them in listening to the fourth tape together.

He picked up Chinese Food for dinner and headed home. His mind wandered thinking about what Jodi had said. Lily had someone she wanted them to meet. Who could that be? She also said she had something she wanted to show them together. What could that be? Chiding himself for having an overactive mind, he thought—I'll find out soon enough.

Friday came and Sam set off for Lily's. He decided to walk. Jodi opened the door and flew into his arms. "Wow! So you really missed me." Then he got serious. "I missed you more." He kissed her again, and they went inside.

The table was set for five. Lily was in the kitchen making pancakes. As they walked in, she said, "Jodi Dear if you take over for me, I'll finish putting everything on the table. Nina is still upstairs in the office, and my friend should be here any minute. It won't be long before we can sit down to breakfast."

The doorbell rang and Lily went to answer it. "Hi Charlie. I'm so glad you could join us. Come in, let me have your coat, and I'll introduce you to everyone."

They walked into the kitchen. "Charlie, meet Jodi Jerome who is doing my interview, and Sam Meyerson my dear friend, creator of *Profiles of New York* and Jodi's boss." Turning to Sam and Jodi she said, "This is another of my dear friends, Dr. Charles Hurwitz who is better known as Charlie. I've known him since he was born. His father Stanley Hurwitz was our family doctor. Needless to say, this is not his first time having my pancakes."

Charlie laughed. "And I hope it's not my last. It's a pleasure to meet everyone. Thank you for inviting me Lily. It brings back a lot of good memories when Noah and I were young. Remember how we used to fight over who got the last one?"

Jodi went to get Nina while Sam carried the plate overflowing with *light and fluffy* pancakes to the table. Soon they were seated and everyone began talking at once. Juice was poured, coffee cups filled, and arms reached for pancakes again and again until not a one was left.

Lily tapped her spoon against her glass and suddenly everyone grew quiet. "All of you know me well enough to have surmised I probably have something up my sleeve if I've assembled you here today, and I am not about to disappoint you.

"Jodi, thank you for setting up the recorder; if you will flip the ON switch, I will begin.

"Jodi and Sam, because you have no idea how Charlie fits into all of this, I thought it was time I introduce you to the person most significant in my finding you.

"As I said, his father Stanley was our family doctor and our two families were quite close. Noah and Charlie, less than six months difference in age, were friends from the time they were toddlers. Noah went off to MIT and Charlie left for premed and onto medical school. After they graduated, they both married and had children, but never reconnected on a daily basis. They did manage to keep in touch, and from time to time would meet in the city for dinner with their wives.

"Joe and I remained good friends with Stanley and Sharon and although we didn't see one another as often as we had when we lived in Brooklyn and the boys were younger, we often attended the theatre together and never missed a chance to dine at the many fabulous restaurants in the city. Along the way, Stanley retired. He passed away the summer leading up to 9/11. After the funeral, Sharon went to Florida to spend some time with her sister and eventually she relocated there.

"Charlie and his two partners had a successful pediatric practice on Long Island, living close by. Over a week passed before Charlie found out that Noah had died in the attack on the North Tower. It takes well over an hour to get from Woodmere, where he lived, to the city by train or by car.

"His attempts to reach us by phone in the city, as well as calling Nicole in Brooklyn were to no avail. He finally decided to drive— determined to stay until he got in touch with us. We were not in a good place in the weeks and months following our losing Noah, and to make matters worse, Nicole seriously needed help, and we didn't know how to help her.

"When we finally hooked up with Charlie, I spilled my guts to him. I didn't know what else to do. He offered to talk to Nicole; she refused to speak to him. He and I kept in touch. I was thankful for his help and advice, but mainly for just being there for me when I desperately needed someone to talk to.

"When Nicole and Olivia left, I automatically thought of Charlie and called him. There wasn't much he could do but be there for me when I needed him. He often came to visit and spent hours with Joe who he knew was hurting as well.

"The years passed; Nicole and Olivia never returned. I continued to search; I hired investigators to no avail. When Joe died, I switched gears. I promised him that I would never stop trying to find or find out what happened to both of you. Again the years went by and COVID-19 arrived and soon became a pandemic. The lockdowns, the mandates, the separations, all became a new way of life. What we took for granted was no longer. If you wanted to visit your doctor, you could but only via the Internet.

"Charlie was on a virtual consultation call with Dr. Julius Goodman, a physician at Cedars-Sinai Medical Center, the day Jodi's article appeared in the Los Angeles Times. Satisfied with the advice he sought, he was just about to end the call, when Dr. Goodman shared the article with him stating that he was a long time friend and associate of Dr. Henry Jerome.

"He sent Charlie the link. After reading the article, Charlie sent it to me. We couldn't believe it. Everything fit. The date of the accident, the woman who died in the car, the age of the child that survived, the amnesia—piece by piece the puzzle took shape. Charlie cautioned me to take it slow. He contacted Dr. Goodman who sent him several articles Dr.

Jerome had written over the years about Jodi's case without identifying the patient. It was obvious they related to her. He sent them to me. I read and reread every one.

'He identified her amnesia as one of two types. The more common form is the total loss of memory from before a point in time known as retrograde amnesia resulting from trauma such as a blow to the head. In time, total recall in great detail returns when familiar persons or places jog the memory. On the downside, amnesia can occur in a *fugue state* where one forgets about his or her life, which is sometimes viewed as running away from something too painful to remember. A *fugue state* is rare, but the chance of it lasting twenty years or more even rarer. Most people with amnesia are lucid and have a sense of self.

"Repression is one of the most haunting concepts in psychology. Something shocking happens, and the mind pushes it into an inaccessible corner of the unconscious and amnesia occurs. Recession is one of the stones on which the structure of psychoanalysis rests.

"Another of his reports outlines hypnosis and other tools used to jog the memory into remembering. All of Dr. Jerome's reports end similarly with the fact that throughout almost two decades not one occurrence resulted in the recall of his subject remembering the past.

"I am not a doctor so therefore I did not read the reports to concur or disagree with Dr. Jerome. I read them to get an understanding of what he was dealing with. I believe Jodi was traumatized having to leave her home, people she loved, her school, and her friends so soon after losing her father; it was simply too much for a ten-year old child to deal with. The trip across the country with a mother who she no longer recognized, the tension between them on the trip, and then watching the car explode before her very eyes didn't help the situation.

"Dr. Jerome's conclusion that Jodi was not from the west coast, and should she ever return to where she came from, the chances for a total recall were quite good was music to my ears; my hopes soared.

"Jodi, before I could put any plan into action and move forward to getting in touch with you, Charlie consulted with several doctors to make certain no harm would come to you in the process. I was certain that you were Olivia. I didn't need a DNA test to prove it, and I would never have taken one without your consent.

"When I met you, I saw both Nicole and Noah in you. When you had your hair cut, I saw the same round face, the dark curls, and deep blue eyes as those in the portrait I painted when you were merely weeks old.

"Without Charlie, I don't think we would be sitting here today. There is no way I can ever repay my good friend.

"Without you Sam, I don't think my story would have ever had the chance of being told."

She motioned for Jodi to stop the recording.

The furthest thing from anyone's mind was that the day would result in a taping. They sat absorbing Lily's words, each with their own thoughts.

Sam smiled as once again, there was no doubt whatsoever that Lily Asher was in the driver's seat, and she wasn't about to relinquish that seat anytime soon. Over the past two days, he had given a lot of thought as to how to approach the show's ending. Their original agreement that Lily would have the final say was still in place. However, now, the final say had to include Jodi. There was no way any part of Lily's story that included her would be aired without her consent.

Sam and Jodi both approached Charlie and thanked him. He was about to leave when Sam said, "We're having dinner tonight—*out on the town*—as a small celebration. If you have no other plans, please join us."

He looked somewhat surprised at the invitation. Lily immediately said, "What a wonderful idea Sam. Say *Yes* Charlie; please join us."

His look of surprise at the invitation soon disappeared. "I would be delighted to join you. Thank you for including me."

Charlie took his leave. Sam's reservation at *Match 65 Brasserie* was upgraded to five, and he texted him the place and time. He learned that Charlie lived on the Upper East Side within walking distance of the restaurant. They all pitched in to clean up after breakfast.

Sam arranged for a car service to pick them up and take them to the brownstone on Vanderbilt. They were quiet on the ride to Brooklyn. He was concerned about how Jodi would react to returning to the house she had left almost twenty years ago—the very house she left under the worst of circumstances.

He looked forward to reading the reports that Henry Jerome had written. As Lily summarized his beliefs, the thought occurred to him that her amnesia was possibly a combination of the two types cited. The doctors that had first treated her concluded she had experienced blunt force trauma when she was struck on the head by a part from the explosion rendering her unconscious.

However, the possibility that cutting off all contact with her grandparents was so shocking that her mind pushed them into an inaccessible corner of the unconscious; a situation that was further exacerbated by her mother's strange moods and actions as they travelled clear across the country. He would suggest to Jodi that she share her flashbacks with Lily.

They arrived at the brownstone. Sam helped Lily up the stairs leading to the front door. "I guess I'm showing a bit of a slowdown. I used to bounce up and down these stairs without a second thought, and definitely without holding onto anybody or the railing."

She handed Sam the key; he unlocked the door and stood back allowing them to enter. It was just the three of them; Nina had remained at the house working upstairs.

Jodi's eyes scanned each room on the first floor. It was exactly the same; nothing had changed. The house was neat and clean. She grew sad as she entered the kitchen. Her mind returned to that December day she came down to breakfast and saw the room exactly as she saw it now. Her mother was nowhere in sight; there was no sign of breakfast.

Before they went upstairs, Lily asked Sam to turn the heat up to take the chill out. The rooms on the second floor were bedrooms. Though dated, the larger one was beautifully furnished with drapes and bedding that matched, as did several pillows on the bed. Off of the far end of the room, was a bathroom and another room that held his and her closets and a dressing area. It was her parents' suite.

Across the hall, was a girl's bedroom—everything was a soft pink—the curtains, the spread, the pillows, including the towels in the adjoining bathroom. It was her room. She moved closer to look at the photos tucked in the side of the mirror. She smiled at the faces staring back at her—Mom and Daddy, Nana and Papa Joe, her two best friends—all taken over twenty years before.

The rooms on the third floor were guest bedrooms. They were equally as furnished and coordinated as the rest of the house, but they were seldom used. On occasion, when she had a sleepover with her friends, they would use one of the rooms upstairs.

For the most part, Sam lagged behind helping Lily maneuver the stairs, while Jodi went through the house. Once was enough; she had seen all she wanted to see. When they returned to the first floor, she turned and said, "I'm ready to leave if you are. The house is exactly as I remember it. The only thing missing is the profusion of colors from the flowers in the dirt beds in front of the house—but it's not quite spring yet and in reality, they were already gone when we left that day.

"I'm going to take my time sorting out my feelings for the house, but it's not a priority for me right now." Suddenly, her attitude changed. "It's only one o'clock. Why don't we go to Junior's for lunch? We can share."

They agreed. Both Lily and Sam were concerned when they initially arrived at the house; Jodi seemed sad and anxious to go through the brownstone almost as if to get it over with. She was now in a better mood that only got better as the car distanced itself from Vanderbilt Avenue.

Sam knew the driver from the car service and offered to buy him lunch while he waited for them. He accepted and opted to eat at the counter. There was no one waiting to be seated and only a handful sat scattered at tables. For the most part, the line waiting for pickup was far longer. They were shown to their table and ordered.

As they waited for their food, Sam decided to tell Lily what he had been up to while Jodi was staying with her. "I have turned the tapes over to my team and set the parameters for finalizing the episode. We're going to be working fulltime from the office taking precautions to stay well and testing regularly. They have already begun listening to the tapes.

"Now on a personal note. I have invited my mother to come for a visit in mid-March under the pretext of previewing the show, however I don't consider it a pretext at all. I happen to think it's the best way for her to learn how you and your granddaughter have found one another. I want the two of you to meet.

"My mother is very important to me, and we are quite close. She has a sixth sense and often knows more about what's happening in my life before I do. Just as you have, she has suspected that Jodi and I are more than just business associates for weeks. We plan to tell her while she is here that we have fallen in love. Last but certainly not least, since it's only a matter of time until we become family, I feel getting the three most important people in my life together should happen sooner rather than later."

Lily was elated. "I am so happy for you both. I love you and feel truly blessed. I can't wait to meet your mother. There's so much we have to discuss."

Both Jodi and Sam feigned alarm, as their waitress placed their sandwiches on the table. They were soon on their way back to Lily's. Jodi decided to return to the apartment with Sam so she could shower and change for dinner.

The car service left the Pavilion with its passengers, made its way to pick up Lily and Nina, and pulled up in front of *Match 65 Brasserie* as Charlie approached on foot. They entered the restaurant and were seated at a secluded table in the back.

What an enjoyable evening they had. It was the perfect end to a perfect day.

# Chapter 17

It was good to have Jodi home; it had been quite a week to say the least. Sam suggested they spend the weekend relaxing because they were facing an even bigger week ahead; it was time to get down to work. They were in the final stretch of finalizing the show, but first, more personal thoughts filled his mind—thoughts of their future.

If the two days Jodi spent at Lily's were some sort of test of their feelings for one another, it proved one thing for certain—they were hopelessly in love. Apart, they were miserable. She awoke encircled in Sam's arms, quite content to lie there until he stirred.

At last, he opened his eyes and saw that she was awake. "Good morning, my Love. I don't think I have to tell you how happy I am that you are home, or how much I missed you."

She kissed him. "I missed you too. However, I'm glad that I spent the time with Lily. It has given me a good prospective on finalizing the show. We each had concerns on the more personal parts of the tapings, and we discussed what parts, if any, either of us felt uncomfortable with. There were none. I was Lily's main concern since her story has now become mine too. That aside, I have some great suggestions that I think you and the team are going to like."

Sam continued to hold her close. "I'm impressed. I thought you wanted to spend a couple of days getting reacquainted with your Nana. I didn't expect you to spend your time in work mode. When I filled you in on my plans to have the team work from the office, it was just to let you know what was going on.

"They reviewed the first three tapes, and plan to listen to the fourth on Monday. It's the perfect time for us to join them to finalize the show. When they questioned your absence, I simply told them you were with Lily. Since the fourth tape is quite explosive, being with them when they hear it is imperative.

"It sounds like you've got everything under control, Sam. Monday sounds good to me. I can't wait to get started. I do have a few questions, and like I said, a few suggestions. Is this how episodes are normally put together? Does the entire team work on every episode? And do you only work on one episode at a time?"

Sam laughed. "You're good, or should I say, your questions are good. I'm glad Monday is agreeable with you. I can only imagine how they're going to react when they learn that you are Lily's long lost granddaughter. Get ready for lots of questions, and I'm well aware they won't all be aimed at you. I think their first question is going to be directed straight at me— *How much did I know going into this?*—considering I hired you right before we arranged the interview.

"I know the team, and it's the best. We've been doing this for ten years. They have researched and produced some pretty awesome episodes that have resulted in *Profiles* having won many awards; and we did it all as a team. Of course, it doesn't hurt to mention that each and every one of us is a born and bred New Yorker. I have always felt that the dedication we have invested in the show is the reason it has been such a success. That includes Sandy who came to work for us while still in college. She stayed on after she graduated, and has become quite the researcher.

"Although when I convinced you to come onboard, I had no idea you were a New Yorker, it has turned out to be one of my better choices.

"We've been talking about this episode for over a year. There are many milestones marking the airing on September 11th—Tenth Anniversary of the show, Twentieth Anniversary of 9/11, 100th episode, and now we've learned it is also Lily's Birthday, although we don't know which one. When we started planning, one thing stood out above all else—we had to deliver a blockbuster show. In order to do that, it would require the involvement of the entire team.

"To answer your questions: Who or what we are profiling determines the length of time it takes to produce an episode. The entire team has only worked on one previous episode—the premiere show. We always have several in the works at any given time, and most shows are aired at random. Only the ones that are tied to specific dates are aired in or around those anniversary dates.

"That said; each of us in some way contributes to every show no matter how much or how little. It just seems to work out that way, and I might add, has greatly contributed to our success."

Jodi turned to face Sam. "I told you all along after each taping, that I would ask Lily to share her memory boxes with you. I'm sure she shared them with me hoping to jog my memory with photos of familiar places and people. I wanted you to see them because they tell a story of their own without words, yet when paired with Lily's words have great depth. I asked her if we could use them in the show, and she readily agreed.

"I think streaming photos in the background as Lily tells her story in her own words would be very effective. I told her I would present it to the team, and if they agree, we can pick up the boxes and take them to the office. I'm certain I can identify any photos that are not self-explanatory. If you are in agreement, I can present this to the team following our listening to the fourth tape."

He was so proud of her. Although learning her true identity had barely had time to take root, her first thoughts were professional and centered on delivering for him. "I have never felt more confident about an episode than I feel about this one. We are going to produce a show that will endear our fans not only to *Profiles* but to one *Lily Asher*, as well. And that just might also include you. This, my dear is a fact—not a gut feeling.

"Now that we have the business at hand settled and out of the way, we have more important things to address. *I Love You Jodi Jerome* and nothing will make me happier than spending the rest of my life with you by my side."

"Why Sam Meyerson, are you asking me to marry you?"

"Yes I am; although I'm not quite sure, but I think Lily has already proposed to you on my behalf. I want us to be married sooner rather than later; there is not one reason I can think of to prolong our plans for the future. My Mom will be here in a couple of weeks, and it will be the perfect time to tell both her and Lily. I'm quite certain she will immediately enlist Lily's help, and I have no doubt whatsoever the two of them will make an outstanding team to help us any way they can."

Jodi kissed Sam. "Yes, I will marry you; and I agree *the sooner the better.* Even though they have yet to meet, Lily and Trudy are two of a kind. The relevance each has had on our lives is undeniable, and we are truly fortunate to have them."

They called Lily. Told her they would be working from the office starting on Monday. They promised to keep in touch calling every day to keep her apprised of how the show was coming along.

They made a list and went grocery shopping. They planned to stay in for the weekend and rest up for the week ahead. They talked about everything that came to mind, which was not as much about the show as it was about them. They discussed venues for their wedding; they discussed how many guests they would invite. They joked about how the *Profiles* team would react to their news, while acknowledging how Lily and Trudy would embrace their news. First, they had to pick a date.

Planned reopenings and lifting of restrictions and mandates were months away from any significant return to normalcy as most remained in place. Vaccines were urged for all and were readily available. Home testing was also available and became widely used by those who had to engage in personal contact to do business.

Virtual medical consultations by appointment replaced office visits. Gatherings of family and friends were kept to a minimum, while larger groups were greatly discouraged.

No one knew what the next few months would bring. New cases were reported on a daily basis, and though they had subsided somewhat following the vaccine rollout, the number of cases remained high in New York. Meanwhile, crime throughout the boroughs was at an all time high. It seemed no one was safe anywhere.

After more than 10 years as one of the most powerful governors in New York's history, Governor Andrew Cuomo was inundated by allegations of cover-ups and sexual harassment that began surfacing on a daily basis, along with multiple investigations that posed existential threats to his political career. Dozens of state lawmakers, and nearly the entire New York congressional delegation, including both senators, called for him to resign over the allegations of sexual harassment. He was also under fire for his administration's handling of nursing home residents, who died after being transferred from hospitals, obscuring the full count of those residents who died from COVID-19.

On the horizon was yet another threat—the Delta variant of COVID-19. It was first detected in India and quickly spread to the UK. Deemed to be twice as contagious, causing severe illness in the unvaccinated, and easily spread to others by the fully vaccinated, the country scrambled to be prepared before it arrived from across the pond.

It was hard to make plans under all of these unusual circumstances. They would just have to play it by ear and take it a day-at-a-time.

Monday arrived and Jodi and Sam headed to the office. They had tested negative the night before. When they arrived everyone welcomed them and urged them to grab a cup of coffee and a muffin and take a seat. They were anxious to begin. Aside from Lily's voice, the room was silent. She spoke from the heart and everyone felt her pain. What should have been such a wonderful day of happiness and celebration became a nightmare that would not only affect the Ashers but also engulf thousands upon thousands of New Yorkers.

When the tape reached the point where Lily had stopped, Jodi turned off the machine. "Before we listen to the second half, let's take a break and refresh our coffee. I want you all to be prepared for what you are about to hear." No one had anything to say, but it was evident that her story had deeply touched them all. Taking her advice, they took bathroom breaks and refreshed their coffee cups.

Once again, they were seated around the conference table, and Jodi flipped the ON switch. As they listened intently, they learned that Noah's loss on September 11, 2001, was to become a twenty-year quest for Lily to fulfill the promise she made to Joe and to find closure for herself. Her voice filled the room; everyone sat fascinated by what they were hearing when suddenly she stopped speaking.

After a few seconds, a voice once again filled the room. It was not Lily's voice; it was Jodi's. If they were surprised, they didn't show it; because at first they didn't realize it was she. Their attention hung on her every word until: *When I came out of the coma three months later, Olivia Asher was no more.*

Sam reached over and turned off the recorder. No one moved; no one said a word. Everyone just sat there. Greg leaned back in his chair. "Wow! Sam, you were looking for a blockbuster, and I would say you definitely found it. I have never heard a more poignant and moving story."

He stood up and went over to Jodi. He hugged and held her close. With tears in his eyes, he said, "I am so happy for you and for Lily and although I haven't met her, I feel as though I know her. Your Nana is one special lady—that's for certain."

Once Greg had broken the ice, the questions started as Sam had predicted. "Yes. No. Not exactly." They weren't listening anyway. They ordered lunch and a couple bottles of champagne. They didn't talk about the show; it was all about Jodi.

As the afternoon worn on, they were still at it.

Finally Sam said, "Shall we call it a day? Tomorrow we can exchange thoughts about the show—how to go forward and how to end it."

Jodi offered her suggestion to the team. "During the tapings, Lily shared what she calls her *Memory Boxes* with me. I asked her if she is willing to allow us to use the many photographs she has taken through the years as part of the show, and she has agreed. I thought it would be effective to stream those photos as Lily tells her story in her own words. I think you will all agree that her presentation is powerful, and I don't think we should lose that.

"The main reason I'm mentioning this now and not tomorrow is I would like to pick up the boxes as soon as possible. Sam hasn't seen them either. The photos add so much. Although she used a simple Kodak Camera, she managed to capture the very essence of her subjects, even though many are black and white shots. She could have been a professional photographer, in my opinion.

"I'll add one more thing, and then the newest member of the team will sit down and be quiet. Since her story has turned out to include me, she asked what I would be comfortable including. I don't have a problem with any of it. I do feel strongly, however, in not making the ending about me. I want Lily's story to end with our reuniting. It is totally her story, and that's the way I think it should be presented."

Jodi became cynical. "Of course, if somewhere down the road you want to profile me, we'll talk about it."

Everybody laughed. Sam hugged her, which did not go unnoticed. They all agreed her suggestions were good, and Sam said he would call Lily and arrange to pick up the boxes on his way into the office in the morning. They were all anxious to get started.

It had been a good day, a good start. It was not yet a week since Sam turned over the tapes to be heard, and they were already well on their way. Hopefully, by the time his mother arrived, the show would be in its final stages of wrapping. He didn't know how long she planned to stay. On their call the previous evening, she told him she had booked a ticket to arrive on Sunday, March 14th but had not scheduled a return flight. Once she got wind of their plans, he wouldn't be the least bit surprised if she decided to stay in New York. He would actually love that. He hated to admit it, but he missed her when she wasn't around.

The final days of February finished out the week. They had gone through the first two memory boxes, selected the photos to stream with Lily's first two tapings and were quite pleased with their progress. They felt very little editing was needed; she related her story with few embellishments; they decided to leave them in. Her arrival in New York and the opening of *Portraits by Lily* was the foundation upon which her new life was built, after losing her family in Austria. She had actually managed to make it quite easy for them.

They continued to touch base with Lily each and every day. Whenever they found time during the week, they popped in for a visit. On the weekends, they had dinner together and talked about Trudy's impending return from Florida.

Evenings belonged to them. Although Sam had many questions, he gave her time and space to open up on her own. "I have so many mixed emotions about all that has happened. Of course, I couldn't be happier having my Nana back; I love her. They say the earliest recollections you have are at five years of age; I was just shy of my tenth birthday when we left. The one thing you can never get back is time, and now I have to make every single day count. I will be thirty in December, and I only have five years of memories with her.

"We haven't talked about plans. I think we should definitely wait until your mother is here, though it would be a good idea to have a timeframe in mind. My thoughts say after September but by year's end. Without knowing what COVID restrictions will be lifted by then, I think it would be smart to plan a smaller wedding, and add guests rather than plan a larger event and have to cancel.

"As far as a venue is concerned, Nana's house would be ideal, and I am certain she will be thrilled. This will allow us to have complete control of everything, and we can request that everyone be tested prior to attending. What do you think?"

Sam's broad grin said it all. "Almost my thoughts exactly. I don't know what you consider small, but I thought we could make a list of whom we definitely want to invite, and when my mother gets here, she can fill us in on the Caruso side of the family. Off the top of my head, my aunt, uncle, their three daughters and their husbands, my best friends who also happen to be the office staff, Lily, Nina, Charlie Hurwitz, my Mom, and the two of us are roughly twenty people. Lily may have others she would like to include, and surely you would want to ask Rosy and your parents' friends from California.

"On the other hand, my mother's side of the family is quite extensive. She's one of five children, so the aunts, uncles, and cousins—all married—will certainly increase the guest list. That said, everyone is local; they all live in New York. My father's brother and his wife are the only one's who don't live here; they live in Florida. So there's a very good chance that everyone we invite will attend.

"I have no idea how many people Lily's house can accommodate, but from what I've learned about previous weddings and gatherings they hosted, I think smaller or larger would work."

"Wow! Sam, I had no idea the Caruso Clan, as you refer to them, is so big. Either way, I agree the house can accommodate both choices. We should write all of these thoughts down. I know that Nana and Trudy are going to be a great team, and I love just thinking about it. Weddings should be fun, and I have no doubt ours is going to be the best."

They worked on the show, and continued to make progress. Jodi made notes on everything that came to mind—items they made decisions on, items they sought advice on, as well as questions to be asked.

Sam met with the jeweler at Harry Winston's. The ring—a solitaire round center stone set in a diamond shank—would be ready the following week. Although he had given great thought as to when he would give it to her, he was still uncertain as to when that would be.

As the day for Trudy's arrival grew closer, Sam's introductory statement, and the episode up to the point where Jodi remembered the accident were complete. As the team watched streaming photos in the background and listened to Lily's voice, they were excited and pleased with the progress they had made. However, discussions for ending the show had reached somewhat of an impasse.

They decided to invite Lily to a viewing and get her approval; Sam had made it abundantly clear from the beginning that she would have the final say.

While enthusiastic and eager to see the progress the team had made on the show, she was looking forward to meeting everyone at *Profiles* more. All previous contacts with the show had been with Sam. Lily had an idea for the ending that she wanted to run by them.

The projection room at *Profiles* was ready to go, as they awaited Lily's arrival. The car carrying Sam, Jodi, and Lily was on its way; coffee and refreshments were set up in the kitchen.

When they entered the suite of offices, Lily was touched to see the reception line that awaited her—*Profiles'* staff of young, smiling, and welcoming faces. The woman they saw was one of elegance and grace whose warm aura reflected her successes while defying her tragedies.

Everyone began speaking at once. Jodi took her coat. Sam made the introductions, and took her on a tour of the office space. They ended in the kitchen for coffee and sweets, and finally proceeded to the projection room to view the show. When all were seated, the lights were turned off, and the video began.

Though the room was dark, the light from the screen was bright, and both Jodi and Sam glanced at Lily from time to time to see her reaction. She appeared to like what she saw and smiled during the good times while making no attempt to wipe away the tears during the bad times. It was after the attack on 9/11 that her body became rigid; her expression froze showing no emotion whatsoever. Jodi's article in the LA Times brought back a smile of hope and excitement, only to be replaced by tears once again when she remembered—she was Olivia.

The video ended; the lights came on. No one moved. For a few brief moments there was total silence. Then, Lily began clapping her hands. "Bravo! Kudos to all! I love it! You've captured everything I set out to achieve in telling my story. I might add, streaming the photos in the background is brilliant; it gives the viewer a visual of the times—*a picture is worth a thousand words.*

"Are you happy with it so far?"

Now it was everyone else's turn to clap. Greg said, "We are, but now that we know you are, we're elated. It was Jodi's idea to stream the photos, and although we all agreed, it came out better than we could have ever anticipated. When she initially made the suggestion, none of us had seen the contents of your *memory boxes*—once we did, we considered all those wonderful photographs just as much a part of your story as your words. One without the other was inconceivable."

For almost an entire hour, they took a break. They refreshed their coffee and took time getting to know Lily while she was getting to know them. Sam and Jodi slipped away down the hall to his office. He pulled her close and kissed her. "Well, what do you think?"

Jodi looked suspicious. "I thought you just wanted to get me here to kiss me. It looks like you want my take on the video when you already know that I think it's super."

Sam explained. "No, I want to know what you think about Lily's reaction. She loved it, and that's exactly what I wanted to hear. Were there any parts you felt she might object to or want to change or delete?"

"No, I didn't. I think we did an excellent job editing some of the details that I felt she included for us and didn't necessarily want them in the show. For example, extensive details about the plane crash that killed Allison; or some of the outings with Grace Shepherd acquainting her with the city. I think she expanded on these just to give us background info that really had no bearing on her story."

"Are we going to ask her about the show's ending like we planned?"

Sam thought for a moment. "Yes, as far as I know. Like you said, it's what we plan to do. I think the team wants to know how you feel about the show's ending. You've consistently said that you're all in, and I just want to be sure that you approve of what's aired as much as Lily."

"We'd better get back. I want to order lunch, and we can even talk about this while we're eating. Lily did say that she had an idea, and I certainly want to hear what that is."

They made their way back to the conference room where they found Lily at her best. The team was asking her questions, and she had an answer for each and every one. When Sam offered to order lunch, he was told it had all been taken care of. Sandy had preordered a variety of salads and sandwiches and black and white cookies; a text told her it was on the way and should arrive momentarily.

Lunch lasted longer than expected. The *Profiles* staff loved Lily and she loved them right back. "It is so good to be talking with real live people. I hadn't realized how isolated I've been the past year. I still managed to get out and take walks in my neighborhood, but I missed going to my studio and visiting with the students and patrons of the gallery. It sure has slowed me down quite a bit, but today has been wonderful. In fact the past couple of months have been wonderful too. Seeing Sam and Jodi on a regular basis has brought a tremendous amount of normalcy back into my life.

"Now if I may, I'd like to share my thoughts about the ending to my story. I suggest taping it as we have before. I want to tell everyone how important it was for me to find my daughter-in-law and granddaughter or to find out what happened to them. It went far beyond my promise to Joe; I had to do it for me. And Jodi dear, if there is anything you would like to add, that would be awesome and welcomed."

Lily had done it again. She had been in the driver's seat the entire time. It was perfect; it was settled. They would meet and tape the ending by week's end.

It was almost dark when they left the office. On the ride back to Lily's, she offered to order in dinner if they would like to stay. They eagerly accepted; neither seemed ready to end the day.

Nina joined them for dinner, and they filled her in on the show. Lily was quite generous with her compliments. "If I didn't make myself clear at the viewing of the episode today, I will do so now. I think your team has done a marvelous job, and I owe all of you my heartfelt thanks.

"Sam you have managed to join together a group of people who are excellent at what they do; they bring out the best in one another. I don't know how you chose them or if you previously knew them, but they all fit perfectly like pieces of a puzzle—each with his or her unique talent. I might add that your newest addition to the team is equally as qualified and talented, although I may be a tad prejudiced.

"I touched on how I would like to end my story but that is purely for the show. Now that I have found Jodi, my beloved Olivia, I hope that God grants me time—no matter the length—to make a few more memories together. That will be a gift for both of us.

"I love you too Sam. You've have always shown me kindness and respect, and that my dear is a compliment to your parents. I'm sure you realize how fortunate you both are to have been raised by parents who loved you, supported you, and taught you to put others before you.

"All in all, I'll reiterate—I had a wonderful time today. Thank you."

Sam was touched by her words. "Thank you. I wholeheartedly agree. Now on a lighter note, I would like to share with you some plans we've made. I'm sure you know how close my mother and I are, and although I always miss her when she's in Florida for the winter, it seems more poignant this year.

"As you also know, I have invited her to come up for a visit to view the show. I feel it's the best way for her to learn that Jodi is your granddaughter. I want more than anything for the two of you to meet—in many ways you are so alike. And most of all, I want to tell her face-to-face about Jodi and my feelings for one another, although like you, she has hinted at it for weeks. Throughout my life, she has often known things about me before I realized them myself.

"She is flying up on Sunday, March 14th, and she has an open ticket to return to Florida, so I don't know exactly how long she will be staying. My guess is that if she gets caught up in the excitement of the show, she may just stay in New York. She took an instant liking to Jodi; she took her shopping and showed her around the city before she left just after Thanksgiving. They only spent a little over two weeks together, but she doesn't even try to hide the fact that she looks forward to speaking with Jodi more than she does with me on our weekly Face Time calls.

"She arrives around noon, and I will make plans for dinner that evening. Of course, I will include Nina, as well. After that, there are others I would like her to meet, but I feel that is the best way to start. On Monday following, I would like to take her to the office to view the taping of the show which might be wrapped by then, but if it isn't, what we have completed thus far is sufficient.

"Do these plans work for you?"

Lily was overwhelmed. "Yes, Sam; they do. I am eager to meet your mother; she sounds like someone I could grow quite fond of, as I have her son. However, I would be honored to host dinner for the evening. I have a caterer that I can hire who will take care of everything. After dinner, they can clean up and leave. We can certainly handle coffee and dessert on our own.

"It's a small gathering—only five of us. I will make certain everyone is tested and vaccinated. It will be much easier to be here where we can relax and enjoy our evening. This house has been too quiet far too long. It's about time we start putting some life back into it. It's hard for me to believe that the last catered dinner we had here was the one Nicole planned for the annual Asher Foundation Holiday Party almost twenty years ago."

Sam was excited; he could only imagine what Lily would say when they told her they wanted to be married in her beautiful home. "That would be wonderful. Thank you."

Jodi sat quietly as Sam and Lily laid out their plans. She winked at Nina and said, "If anyone is interested, Nina and I agree. Your plans sound great, and I am certain Trudy will love them as well.

"I've been so engrossed in the show that I haven't expressed my true feelings about finding you Nana, or should I say, you finding me. Although my total recall came at a certain point in your story, I had begun having flashbacks almost from the very beginning of the interviews. It seems as though my father had been right all along, feeling that I was not from the west coast.

"As I told Sam, since one's earliest recollections are around five years of age, I only have five years of memories of my parents, Papa Joe, and you. I look forward to your telling me stories about when I was younger no matter how inconsequential they may seem. We have a lot of time to make up for, and I can't wait. There are a few items I've seen around the house that I have questions about because they seem familiar. There may be stories there too.

"I have a couple of things that I must take care of soon. March 19th will be a year since my father died. I don't know when I will be able to plan a Memorial Service in California; COVID restrictions are still very much in place. I also haven't heard from my parents' lawyer about selling any parts of the estate, and I plan to give him a call and get an update.

"I've decided to write a short article for the LA Times to be published on the anniversary of his death, and indicate that a service will take place in the future when it's allowed. I also plan to call Rosy our housekeeper and ask if she will ship my warmer weather clothing east in another month or so. The boxes have been packed since I leased my condo.

"I too am excited about Trudy's visit or return whichever it may be. We clicked the moment we met. I see nothing but good times ahead, and I for one am ready for them."

All in all, it had been another good day.

For some reason since Lily had reconnected with Olivia, she began having dreams going way back to when she and Joe were first married. For twenty years, she remained steadfast in finding Nicole and Olivia or at least learning what happened to them. When Joe died, she became even more determined to do so. It was only now that she began to realize how much she missed him. She missed his smile, his warmth, his affection, and his *I Love You* a dozen or more times a day.

Her dreams never included anyone else. They were simply dreams of happier times of Lily and Joe, Joe and Lily; she felt truly blessed.

*To whom many blessings are given so too shall sadness befall.*

# Chapter 18

March arrived and found New Yorkers growing exceedingly frustrated with all of the COVID mandates and restrictions that they had anticipated being eased or cancelled still very much in place. Unemployment filings soared as parents, teachers, and students rallied outside the Department of Education headquarters demanding that New York City schools fully reopen.

Newspaper headlines and television program interruptions broke the news that Governor Andrew Cuomo was facing an independent investigation into sexual harassment allegations from two former aides. New York state lawmakers moved to rescind the emergency powers granted to him to handle the coronavirus pandemic, as both Democrats and Republicans alike began calling for his resignation.

On Sunday, March 14th, Trudy flew into JFK International Airport returning from Florida. Sam met her at the airport. As he waited for her in the baggage area, he suddenly saw her coming down the escalator waving to him. She looked great—sporting a tan, and as always dressed to perfection.

She flew into his arms giving him a big hug. "Sam you look good, or should I say, you look happy. You could use a little bit of color; why don't you come down to Florida for a few days and bring Jodi with you. Have you wrapped the show yet?"

He smiled broadly at his mom's unending questions. "Yes, as a matter of fact we have wrapped the show, and it's one of the reasons I lured you back. I want you to see it as soon as possible. So much has happened, and I have so much to fill you in on. I also want you to meet Lily. She is such a treasure. I don't think I've ever met anyone quite like her. With that said, you two are very much alike, and I imagine will become fast friends.

"I'm surprised you haven't asked me why I didn't bring Jodi. Do you know something I don't?"

It was Trudy's turn to laugh. "No, not at all. That was going to be my next question. I considered the possibility that she was waiting in the car, but even with the little I know about her, my guess is if she came with you, she'd come in."

"She decided to remain at the apartment and prepare brunch so that when we get home, everything will be ready. We have a long list of items to catch you up on, including the plans I've made for us while you are here.

Sam retrieved her luggage; there was more than he expected. Perhaps she was planning on staying in New York for the rest of the season. He decided to wait to pose that question after she heard *all of their news*.

He texted the driver to pick them up, and they walked outside just as the car pulled to the curb. Surprisingly, Trudy didn't ask any questions on the ride home. They spoke generally about the weather and the colder and snowier than usual New York winter thus far; how Jodi was settling in at work; and she mentioned once again how happy and content he appeared, alluding to the fact that the outcome of the show was the reason. Sam didn't correct her. She would learn soon enough.

Jodi had gone overboard. The table was beautifully set for three. She put out quite a spread—juice, bagels, lox, cheeses, smoked fish, egg salad (which she made), cream cheese, fruit, assorted sweets, and coffee. It was definitely a typical New York Brunch, one that he had experienced his entire life. Everything was ready to eat and no preparation was required; that way, they could enjoy brunch together. They had a lot to share and wanted it to go as smoothly as possible.

As she was putting her finishing touches to the brunch table, she heard them coming down the hall and quickly moved to open the door for them. Trudy walked in and immediately liked what she saw. It had been a long time since she had entertained at home. Since Al had passed away, it was easier and far more convenient to entertain at the many excellent restaurants the city offered. Even though it was her apartment, she felt welcomed and a feeling of déjà vu came over her as she remembered their house in Port Chester overflowing with family and friends.

Sam took her luggage into the bedroom. Between hugs, Jodi and Trudy had a hard time getting a word in edgewise as each plied the other with questions and compliments. "You got your hair cut; I love it! It suits you. Although we've been chatting face-to-face via the Internet, I thought perhaps you had pulled your hair back. It's much more flattering in person. Does Sam like it?"

Jodi was not disappointed; that hadn't taken very long at all. "As a matter of fact, he does. Everyone has been most generous with their compliments about my hair—the office staff and especially Lily—approved wholeheartedly. I began to think I must have looked pretty bad when I arrived in New York."

Trudy was quick to reply. "No you did not. I just think that short hair is a better look for you, not to mention that it is easier to care for.

"I am so excited about coming back for a visit. In all the years I have been spending my winters in Florida, I've only returned a couple of times and they were for family events. This visit is special because I know how much the anniversary episode means to both of you, and by including me in the loop makes it special for me too. Thank You! I love you both."

Sam smiled to himself. Everything was going as planned. He couldn't believe he had actually pulled it off. His mom had no idea what they had in store for her.

"Mom, unless you want to freshen up or relax a bit, why don't we partake of the delicious brunch Jodi has put together? I'm starving."

"Of course you are. I can relax while we're eating, but I will freshen up a bit. I'll just be a minute. Why don't you go ahead and take a seat at the table. If you would be good enough to pour me a cup of coffee, that would be splendid."

The minute she left the room, Sam pulled Jodi into his arms and kissed her.

When Trudy joined them, once again, they all began speaking at once. "I don't have to tell you how excited I am about my visit because I already have, but it pleases me to no end that I sense the both of you are excited too. I want to hear all about the show and Lily; but first, I want to hear all about the two of you."

Sam began filling her in from the time she left for Florida. December was designated to introducing her to the *Profiles* staff, and acquainting her with the team that she was now a part of. As they embarked on the road back to normalcy, they welcomed the long awaited vaccines, and the home testing kits that allowed them to move forward using every precaution available while remaining solidly in the guidelines of the mandates and regulations in place in order to keep everyone safe and well.

Meeting both in-person at the office and virtually as a team, they planned how to move forward with the anniversary episode. At his suggestion, they agreed to spend the holidays together. It turned out to be the best possible way to put the terrible events of the previous nine months

behind them. Above all else, they began the New Year upbeat with hope
and visions for the future.

January was cold and ended with more snow in the city than it had seen
in years, but weather was the only downside. The upside was far better.
He secured the profile for the show, Jodi wholeheartedly agreed to do the
interview, they began phasing in their return to work from the office, and
slowly but surely businesses continued to reopen on a limited basis.

With the first meeting of the interview only days away, he came up with
a plan to introduce Jodi to New York on a three-day orientation of the city,
Lily Asher, and her new boss. It was a huge success accomplishing more
than he could have ever imagined. Trudy was blown away—especially
when she learned he had taken her to Port Chester.

Sam continued. "I have to admit, it wasn't all business. The truth is
for me it was more personal. Although we had met years earlier, and I had
recruited Jodi to do research for me on a few occasions, there were long
periods of time in between when we were not in touch at all. You really
couldn't say we were friends either. We knew very little about one another.

"That is until I read her article in the LA Times. To me her words
were powerful and proved what I had suspected all along—Jodi Jerome
is one hell of a journalist with the innate talent to read people. At that
point, I became determined to bring her on board *Profiles*. It wasn't easy,
but she didn't resist too much. It was the perfect time for both of us. After
almost ten years, the show was ready for new talent and perspective; after
losing her father to COVID-19, she was ready for a new start or at least a
diversion.

"Mom, as always, you came to my rescue. You offered your apartment
as a place for Jodi to stay; you took her shopping and helped her settle-in
just two weeks before leaving for Florida. When the two of you hit it off
immediately, I felt as though I had hit the jackpot.

"When I met with Lily Asher, and she agreed to be the subject of our
anniversary episode, everything fell into place. We all needed something
to look forward to after the onset of the pandemic that was still very much
at the forefront of all of our lives. There were a few surprises along the way
that popped up, but none presented a problem that wasn't easily remedied.
Lily's request to have Jodi do her interview was genius. She readily agreed,
and we were on our way.

"With Jodi and I living in such close proximity, working together
everyday, and interfacing with Lily on a regular basis, we naturally fell into

the routine of sharing meals together. At times they were working meals, but mostly they were two people alone during lockdowns and mandates and unending regulations sharing not only meals but also past experiences and getting to know one another.

"For both of us, it was a time of more than we anticipated or could have possibly hoped for—we fell in love. In ways we are very much alike, yet in others, we are quite different; it reminds me of you and Dad. We realize that it has been only a few short months since Jodi arrived in New York, but due to the pandemic, we have spent more time together than we would have under ordinary circumstances as a married couple.

"Mom, I simply couldn't tell you over the phone how Jodi and I feel about one another. And I have to admit, I really wanted to get one of your famous hugs, as well as see the look on your face when we told you."

Trudy didn't even need a New York minute; she was out of her chair in a second. She hugged both of them and everyone was crying—a little bit anyway. "I am so happy—happy for the both of you, happy for me, and happy to make the trip back to hear it in person. I told you at the airport you looked happy and content. I should have known that the show wasn't the reason; I must be losing it."

Sam leaned back in his chair. "Trudy Meyerson, this is only the beginning; fasten your seatbelt; you're about to go on the ride of your life. We've put together somewhat of a schedule of what we have planned, but it is not set in stone. How long do you plan to stay?"

"I only booked a one-way ticket; and I'll stay as long as you like. There is nothing urging me back to Florida. Many of my usual activities have been curtailed because of the virus. I have volunteered giving vaccinations and helping out whenever I'm needed, but for the most part, my small circle of friends see each other from time to time—generally we just get together for dinner at a local restaurant with outdoor seating. Truth be told, I've been rather bored. What do you have in mind?"

"Jodi and I both would love you to stay, but it's your decision and one that you don't have to make until we're finished catching you up on all that's happening in New York. We plan to proceed in steps. The first step is having you hear Lily's story. The show is wrapped, however, there may be minor changes made to the end. My first thought was to show you the video of the actual show by airing it in the projection room at the office, but Jodi suggested the better way to go is having you listen to the actual tapings of the interview here in the comfort of the apartment. I agree.

"I'm going to help Jodi clear the table and put everything away. Why don't you unpack or perhaps rest for a bit. There are four tapes for you to hear, and I don't suggest you listen to them all in one sitting. I know once you start, you won't want to stop, but you should take at least a small break between each allowing you to absorb what you hear.

"We have nothing planned for today. We ordered groceries in, and we're cooking dinner for you tonight. So whenever you want to start the tapes, let me know, and I'll set you up."

"Wow! You two are something else. If I thought I was excited before, I don't know how to describe how I'm feeling now. I'm going to unpack; but you know me, I like to get things done sooner than later. Then I'm going to lie down for a while. I've been up since the crack of dawn for my early flight, and I want to be sharp and clear- headed when I listen to the tapes. I certainly don't want to miss anything."

"Sounds like a plan. When Jodi and I are finished putting everything away, I'll set up the recorder. While you're resting, we're going out for a walk as we often do in the neighborhood, especially on nice days. I don't know how long we'll be, but you can start listening to the tapes whenever you're ready. Are you OK with that?"

"Of course, I am. I'll see you when you get back."

With Trudy behind closed doors in her bedroom, brunch cleared and everything put away, Sam and Jodi set off to pay a visit to Lily. Jodi had called and she was expecting them. They stopped along the way to pick up pastries.

When they arrived at the house, Lily greeted them at the door. "Come in. Come in. This is a lovely surprise. With your mother flying in from Florida this morning, I didn't expect to see you today. I made a pot of coffee or I can make tea if you prefer.

Jodi handed her the box. "Coffee is perfect, and we brought pastries from the café near the apartment. Trudy is taking a nap so we decided to come for a visit and tell you what we have planned for her stay. We also have a few items to discuss with you."

Jodi helped Lily bring the coffee and pastries into the library. After they were seated, Sam smiled, took both of Lily's hands in his, and looking directly into her eyes said, "On behalf of your granddaughter and me, I am officially telling you that we are in love, although I feel that you have been aware of this fact before we were or at least before we were willing to admit it. I have asked Jodi to marry me, and she has accepted. She has made me the happiest man on earth. We would like your blessing."

Lily was overjoyed. "You have had my blessing all along. I can't begin to tell you how happy I am for you. I love you both, and though I may be prejudiced, I think you are perfect for one another. What did your mother have to say? From what you have told me, she too sensed there was something in the air between the two of you. Perhaps this news deserves something a little stronger and more festive than coffee."

"Nana, we have plenty of time to celebrate. Sam and I also came here to tell you what plans we have for Trudy's visit. First and foremost, we felt the best way to tell her that I am Olivia and how we found one another is to let her listen to the tapes. That way she will hear your story in your words and mine. She is planning to begin this afternoon after she has rested. We're planning to eat dinner in this evening, so hopefully she can finish the first three today.

"We feel tomorrow would be best to listen to the final tape together. We don't believe she knows anything about your story. She is well aware of *Portraits by Lily*, and she knows you lost your son on 9/11, but it pretty much ends there. And I don't believe she knows that your son was married and had a child. However, Sam has told me that he had a younger sister who died when she was in her teens, and therefore she can certainly equate to your loss. Once the tapes are behind us, we want the two of you to meet. We are going to be family, and we all agree that family is of the utmost importance to all of us."

Jodi smiled to herself and continued. "Now, I'm going to become a true granddaughter and ask my Nana for a favor. We would like to get together for dinner tomorrow evening, and we would like to do it here at the house. You don't have to do a thing. Sam and I will have everything brought in including a couple of people to serve and clean up. We want to be able to talk openly and freely about everything that's going on without anyone having to prepare or watch or serve.

"At first, we considered a restaurant, but it really makes more sense to do it at home. The comfort, the privacy, the lack of dinner noise will all result in a more conducive atmosphere in getting to know one another. Also, we can make certain everyone is tested and feels well even though we have all been vaccinated."

For a moment that seemed to go on forever, Lily did not speak. "My dear granddaughter, there is nothing that I would not do for you. It's been far too long since you came to me saying *Nana will you do me a favor?* I never turned you down even once, and I don't intend to start now. You've brought the love of life back into my heart. Let's have us a party like no other.

"With that said, Sam when you originally told me your mother was coming back, you asked if we could have dinner here, and I agreed. It also makes it much easier for me. At the time, I believe you were planning to show her the video of the episode after we met; I think this is a far better plan. I would rather she learn that Jodi is my granddaughter before we meet especially since we will soon be family.

"Feeling certain that you expect me to, I'd like to make a suggestion or two if I may. If Trudy listens to the final tape in the morning, I would like the three of you to come for a lite lunch and a couple of hours of just the four of us bonding a bit. I'd love to take her on a tour of the house, show her some of the paintings of the family, and perhaps answer any questions she may have. Also, if you agree, I would like to include Nina and Charlie Hurwitz for dinner. That would make six of us, well within the guideline for gatherings."

Jodi and Sam looked at one another. "God Bless you Lily. What would we do without you? Your suggestions are excellent. Some quiet time—just the four of us—is the right way to go. Including Nina and Charlie is the right thing to do. They are both a big part of your life and have become family to you; therefore they are family to us."

On their walk home, for a while they were both quiet. Then Jodi laughed and said, "How did I ever forget all about a force like my Nana? She played such an important part in my life. I actually spent more time with her than I did with my parents. As a child, she was my #1 go-to person. I guess trauma effects people differently. I am so saddened by the fact that I lost twenty years of loving her and her loving me back. Death is final; but miles and years of separation can prove to be a more profound loss; in its own way it too is final."

They held hands, each lost in their own thoughts as they walked back to the apartment. When they entered, they found Trudy in the living room so absorbed in listening that she didn't hear them come in. She was about midway through the second tape.

They decided not to disturb her; instead they set out to get dinner started. Their choice was Jodi's old standby—salad, filet mignon roast, baked potatoes, and roast veggies followed by dessert and coffee. Wine and a charcuterie that she had put together would allow them time to discuss the tapes before sitting down to eat.

When the tape ended, Trudy could not believe that Jodi and Sam had been home for over an hour, and had managed to prep dinner without her realizing it; all that remained was setting the table.

Trudy liked what she saw. She had never seen this side of Sam probably because there had never been a Jodi before. They were so in tune one would have thought they had been together far longer than a few months. Observing the way they looked at one another, it was quite obvious that they were in love. Tears came to her eyes as she remembered her mother's exact observation of her and Al when they came to ask for her parents' blessing. So many years had passed, yet the memory remained fresh.

Sam couldn't resist. "It's not often that I can put one over on you, but I think this time, I have. We're going to set the table, which won't take long, and once dinner is in the oven, we can relax and enjoy the appetizer Jodi prepared and wine, of course. We thought it would also be a good time to get your thoughts on Lily's story. However, if you would like to offer a small *teaser* of sorts, we would both love to hear it."

Trudy gathered her thoughts for a moment. "You were certainly right about once you start listening, you don't want to stop. Aside from the fact that her story captures your attention immediately, one cannot dismiss that her telling it in her own words is priceless. No one can tell it the way she can."

"That's it; that's your *teaser*! Now, can I help with anything for dinner? You know it's not like me to sit idly by and not participate."

"No Mom, you can't. Just this once, we've got everything covered. You've been sitting most of the afternoon. Why don't you stretch your legs?"

"Okay, I will, but let me do just one thing. Let me set the table with my special touch for a very special evening for the two special people in my life. I love you both, and I love the evening you have planned for us."

Trudy set the table in a more formal manner with china she had not used in years, and crystal stemware that had seen many toasts on many occasions throughout the years. She felt it quite appropriate for the evening. Sam left to dress for dinner, leaving her and Jodi to do the same. Less than half an hour later, they were enjoying wine and the charcuterie.

After what seemed like endless toasting, their discussion turned to the tapes. "As I told you in my *teaser*, Lily's voice relating her story is priceless.

The loss of her immediate family, her coming to America alone, and her passion to undertake starting a business of her own—*Portraits by Lily*—was admirable and courageous. I gather she was in her mid to late twenties, and for someone so young to be so determined to succeed, she had to believe in herself and her talent beyond all else.

"The fact that she met and fell in love with Joe Asher was marvelous. You know I'm a romantic at heart, and I couldn't have been happier for her. I hope to listen to the third tape this evening after dinner. Since her story is the subject of your 9/11 episode, am I presuming correctly that possibly the next tape will shed some light on losing her son that day?"

"Yes, Mom, you're absolutely right. I was hoping you would say that you plan to tackle the third tape this evening, and it does lead to the events of 9/11. Jodi and I plan to be with you when you hear the last tape. We would like that to take place tomorrow morning following breakfast, after which we are invited to Lily's for lunch. We wanted you to finish the tapes before we introduced you to one another."

"Oh my, that sounds wonderful and a bit mysterious. I can hardly wait."

The timer indicated dinner was ready to be served.

Dinner was wonderful—formal yet informal, professionally delicious yet homey, and best of all enjoying one another's company. Their banter was light; neither the show nor Lily was discussed. Instead, Trudy lavishly praised them for the meal, thanked them for treating her like a guest in her own home, and plied them with questions about Jodi feelings for her new home in New York, and most of all, what she thought of Port Charles. She had no questions about her feelings for Sam; they were all too evident.

They ended the evening early to allow Trudy to get back to the tapes.

As they were about to leave, Sam said, "Jodi is spending the night in my apartment. We will be back in the morning at 8:00 am to have a light breakfast and listen to the final tape together. That gives us time to answer any questions you might have, as well as make it to Lily's by noon for lunch.

"Remember when I said to *fasten your seatbelt?* As much as you've learned today, you'll see exactly what I mean tomorrow."

Jodi and Sam woke early and decided to go for a long walk before showering and going to Trudy's. It was a beautiful morning but rather crisp. It was the first day of Daylight Savings Time, and the sun was just beginning to rise. There was plenty left over for breakfast so there was no need to stop anywhere except to get Jodi her latte fix. They were both hyped about Trudy and Lily meeting one another.

On their walk back, Sam's phone rang; it was his mother. "I just wanted to let you know that I'm up and ready for you. Breakfast is waiting and so am I with my seatbelt on, I might add."

Sam laughed out loud. "Good to hear. We're just returning from a walk and we'll be there as soon as we shower and dress. See you soon. Love you Mom."

"Love you too Son."

When they arrived at Trudy's, it was just as she had said; she was ready and waiting, and she had the recorder set up and ready to begin. Bagels, pastries, and coffee were just right. They could eat as they listened.

When they were seated comfortably with coffee in hand, before hitting the ON button, she said, "Although the first two tapes disclosed Lily's background and established her as a force to be dealt with, I found the third tape the most endearing. As she spoke of herself as a wife, a mother, and a grandmother, the tone of her voice changed showing her softer side while keeping that force within her in tact."

The tape began. For half an hour, Lily's voice filled the room. Just as he had at the office, Sam stopped the tape when she stopped speaking. Catching Trudy by surprise, she asked, "Is that the end to the story?"

"Mom, the tape is not yet finished. I just wanted to pause and take a break before continuing to allow you to absorb what you are about to hear. Why don't we take a short break and resume in a few minutes?"

They did, and the recording began where it left off. As the voice once again filled the room, Trudy soon realized that Lily was no longer speaking. To her utter amazement, it was Jodi's voice that she heard—clear and precise with the utmost detail of what had occurred almost twenty years previous. She could hardly contain her excitement, but forced herself to remain quietly seated, her eyes locked with Jodi's until the tape ended. She immediately reached for her and pulled her to her breast. They were both crying—crying tears of joy, as Sam looked on with his broad smile of approval.

There were many questions, but it wasn't the time. Was it too much to digest in such a short period of time? Perhaps; but the days that followed would provide the answers and allow them to slowly ease the pain of years of separation and loss by the promise of a future filled with many wonderful tomorrows. Of that, Trudy was certain.

It was a beautiful day, slightly warmer than when they were out earlier, so they decided to walk to Lily's. In her usual manner, she greeted them and welcomed them into her home. For hours, they laughed and talked and cried, and anyone observing would have never guessed that Trudy and Lily had just met. Sam and Jodi were both right—they were definitely two-of-a-kind.

It was almost four o'clock, and they were still going strong. Sam reminded them that dinner was fast approaching. "I think we'd better leave so we can go home, change for dinner and return. The caterers are due shortly, and we don't want to get in their way. Before we go, I'd like everyone's attention. I have something to say."

Everyone immediately grew quiet. Sam on bended knee looking directly into Jodi's eyes said, "Jodi Olivia—I Love You with all my heart and soul. Marry me and make me the happiest man alive. I plan to spend the rest of my life making you as happy as you make me."

Pulling him up and into her arms, she kissed him. "Yes, Yes, Yes—*I Love You* too, but you already know that."

He placed the ring on her finger; it fit perfectly. Lily and Trudy were elated. After a quick glass of champagne and a toast or two, they left for home to get ready for dinner. They could continue celebrating when they returned. Sam had ordered nothing less than a case of champagne to take to dinner.

Walking home arm-in-arm they were a sight to see. Suddenly, Trudy posed a question. "I've only been back a little over twenty-four hours, and I know you warned me, but do I keep my seatbelt on?"

They laughed and laughed. "Yes, Mom; I highly recommend it."

Sam arranged for a car service to pick them up. Not only had the evening grown cold, but he also had a case of champagne and a few other items to take with him. They dressed a bit more formal for the evening. This was a celebration of not only their engagement, but of family and friends and new beginnings. For the first time since the onset of the pandemic, they were looking forward to a normal night with the hope that the months ahead would only get better allowing them to put the hardships of the past year behind them.

They arrived at the house to a party that was already underway. Charlie opened the door and helped Sam with the champagne. When Lily came forward to introduce them, Trudy approached Charlie engulfing him in a big hug. "My goodness I never thought that I would see you this evening. How are you? How long has it been?"

The others stared in amazement. At last, she stepped back, and he chuckled as he said, "Trudy Caruso, you haven't changed a bit. I've missed you without even knowing it—all these years. We have a lot of catching up to do. Time has been good to you—you look absolutely fantastic."

"You don't look so bad yourself; graying at the temples becomes you. In fact I like what I see. I hope life has been good to you too." She turned and said, "Charlie and I have known one another for years. He did his Residency at Lenox Hill where I was a nurse following graduation. We had a small group at the hospital that became fast friends, and we often partied together when we had time off. The only party I missed was the one they threw when his Residency ended. I had a family wedding that I had to attend because I was the Maid of Honor, but I did stop by; I just couldn't stay for the whole evening. That's the last time we saw one another."

Though Trudy had stepped back, he continued to hold her hands in his. "That was quite a party. I invited some of my friends that were not from the hospital who showed up much later. Among them was Noah Asher who I happened to have grown up with in Brooklyn. If you had stayed, I would have certainly introduced you."

"Poor timing on both sides. The very next week, I met Al Meyerson, and as my good friend, I would have certainly wanted your take on him. We married about a year later, and Sam is our son. This definitely gives new meaning to the phrase—*It's a small world after all.*"

As Lily urged them to move from the foyer into the library for appetizers and drinks, she introduced Trudy and Nina.

Trudy leaned in towards Sam and whispered, "Do you have *your* seatbelt on?"

Sam's hearty laugh drew everyone's attention so he decided to take advantage of the moment. Glasses sat ready to fill; champagne was ready to pour. With Jodi beside him he said, "I have asked Jodi to marry me, and she has accepted. Nana and my Mom have given us their blessings, and now Nina and Charlie, we hope you will share in celebrating our engagement as well."

It was impossible to predict how the evening would turn out. What seemed a simple gathering became an *inconceivable night to remember.*

Dinner was served, yet long after the caterers left, everyone stayed. No one wanted the evening to end. Sam's concern for Lily was waived when he suggested the time had come to leave. Instead, she proposed a fresh pot of coffee and what remained of the cheesecake she had made for dessert.

Although the evening had been spent celebrating and reconnecting, they did manage to get the ball rolling with plans for the future. They asked Nana and Trudy's help to plan the wedding, and they asked Nina and Charlie to stand up for them. When they finally left Lily's, it was two o'clock in the morning. The only open item that needed to be resolved was to pick a date for the wedding.

# Chapter 19

Pandemonium could hardly describe the scene at *Profiles* when Jodi and Sam showed up for work the next morning and the team learned they were engaged. After an entire year of zero interaction in person of the closely knit group, they were not only celebrating the engagement but also their recent return to some degree of normalcy allowing them to get back to doing what they did best—*Profiling New York.*

The morning's agenda included the business at hand. Seated around the table in the conference room, each took their turn and updated the others on the progress they had made on the individual projects they were working on. With the Anniversary Episode set to go minus a few finishing touches, they were working on closing out the months of October, November, and December. That would leave the summer open to begin working on 2022.

Since the onset of the pandemic, their profiles were totally concentrated on landmarks, structures, and events deeply embedded in New York history—that is until the Lily Asher interview. They looked forward to the easing of mandates and restrictions that would allow them to return to one-on-one interviews once again.

Sandy having come across an article months earlier—*Secrets of the 20,000 bodies buried under Washington Square Park*—so intrigued her that she began researching the history behind the story immediately. The article featured esteemed New York archaeologist Joan Geismar and her team's findings over the years. Con Edison maintenance workers also found not only bones, but also underground rooms and catacomb-like crypts dating back to the 1800s.

Washington Square is one of New York's liveliest parks, abounding with NYU students, dog walkers, street performers, tourists, and drug dealers crowding the nearly 10 acres of lush sidewalks and meeting spots.

Just below this hustling and bustling humanity lurks a shocking secret:

20,000 dead bodies. Ghost hunters' revelations from the organization NYC Ghosts, the hangman's tree legend, endless reports of ghost citings, and the park's bodies—all serve as a warning that in the event of a zombie apocalypse, avoid the area.

The possibility of interviews with Joan Geismar and members of NYC Ghosts combined with the history and legends of the park would make an especially captivating episode of *Profiles* for October and Halloween, while giving perspective that as we blindly walk the sidewalks of New York, what we see now isn't what it used to be.

Lou suggested looking back from Macy's to the Titanic—The Straus Family Legacy left by brothers Isidor and Nathan Straus and the humble origins of an American holiday tradition—The Thanksgiving Day Parade that in reality does not celebrate Thanksgiving but the next major holiday on the calendar—Christmas.

As America prospered during the *Roaring Twenties*, so did New York City's iconic department store—Macy's. Their flagship store in Manhattan's Herald Square did such a brisk business that in 1924 it expanded to cover an entire city block stretching from Broadway to Seventh Avenue along 34th Street.

To showcase the opening of the *World's Largest Store* and its one million square feet of retail space at the start of the upcoming busy holiday shopping season, Macy's decided to throw New York a parade on Thanksgiving morning hoping to whet the appetites of consumers to do their holiday shopping at Macy's.

At 9:00 am on the morning of November 27, 1924, Macy's gave all New Yorkers—young and old—a particularly special treat. By noon, the parade arrived at its end in front of Macy's Herald Square store where 10,000 people cheered Santa as he ascended from his sleigh.

The 2020 parade during the COVID-19 pandemic might have felt somewhat familiar to those who lived through WWII when the parade was cancelled for 1942, 1943, and 1944—only to come back bigger and better than ever.

Frank and Edie chose a favorite close to their heart. Radio City Music

Hall—the entertainment venue and theatre within Rockefeller Center in Midtown Manhattan, nicknamed—*The Showplace of the Nation.* It is the headquarters for the Rockettes, the precision dance company. Edie's grandmother had been one of the original Rockettes.

A long marquee sign that wraps around the corner of Sixth Avenue and 50th Street displaying the theatre's name is recognized the world over. Radio City Music Hall opened on December 27, 1932, as part of Rockefeller Center's *Radio City* though it later came to apply only to the Music Hall.

It remained largely successful until the 1970s, when declining patronage nearly drove the theatre to bankruptcy. In May 1978, Radio City Music Hall was designated a New York City Landmark; it was restored and remained open. In 1999, the theater was extensively renovated.

Through the years, the Music Hall has hosted televised events including the Grammy Awards, the Tony Awards, the Daytime Emmy Awards, the MTV Video Music Awards, the NFL Draft, as well as graduation ceremonies for NYU and Barnard College. The list grew to include hosting concerts by leading pop and rock musicians, but primarily it will always be known for the *Radio City Christmas Spectacular.*

Sam was blown away. He wholeheartedly approved of the three final episodes of the year. "Wow! You're quite a team, and I am so lucky to have you. It looks like we're in excellent shape and all we can do is wait and see what opens up during the summer to allow us to move forward with a better mix of in-person interviews, landmarks, and events. Great job all the way around."

They took a short break and Sam brought them up to speed on finalizing Lily's story, and their plans for the future. Everyone was so excited for Jodi and Sam, assuring them that they could cover for them whenever the need arose.

For the remainder of the week, they set out to take care of the many items that were on their to-do list. On Friday, March 19th, on the one-year anniversary of her father's passing, Sam accompanied Jodi to St. Jean Baptiste Church to light memorial candles for both Henry and Julia.

Sam had often walked past the church, but had never been inside. They were in awe at how beautiful it was. They walked towards the altar and sat down in one of the pews, holding hands without speaking as they absorbed the serenity and beauty surrounding them. After a while, a priest approached introducing himself as Father Paul. Jodi explained why they were there.

After she lit the candles, Father Paul remained, and they spoke for some time. She explained what Henry and Julia Jerome meant to her and how she owed them her very existence. Intrigued with her story, he invited her back anytime she felt the need to talk. He blessed them and wished them a bright future filled with happiness.

At Lily's invitation, Trudy spent the entire week with her. They had a marvelous time together; Sam was right when he said they would become fast friends. Their excuse— although they did not need one— was they had a wedding to plan. For the most part, Trudy had dinner with Lily and Nina before coming home, so Jodi and Sam were on their own.

The weekend changed the routine. Trudy and Lily wanted to discuss the wedding and clarify what parts they would play. And most importantly, they had to pick a wedding date before they could make any arrangements. When Trudy came home on Friday, she called and asked them to come to her apartment for dinner.

Trudy decided to make dinner informal and more like a picnic. She chose some of Sam's favorites and hoped they were Jodi's also. Hotdogs, hamburgers, homemade potato salad and coleslaw, and she baked chocolate chip cookies to be served with ice cream.

When they arrived at her apartment, a smile lit up Sam's face. "Wow Mom, does the checkered tablecloth tell me what I think it does?"

"It does, and I hope you are pleased. What about you Jodi, are you up to an indoor picnic of carnival food? My Al used to refer to hotdogs and hamburgers as such. To make it an authentic picnic, I would have added fried chicken."

Jodi laughed. "Absolutely; they're my favorites too. This is wonderful. We brought wine, red and white, but I'm not too sure if either goes with carnival food."

"Wine goes with everything, I always say. I'm totally ready; be seated and we can get started. Everything is on the table except the platter of hotdogs and burgers, which I will get while you pour the wine."

For well over an hour, they laughed and talked and thoroughly enjoyed Trudy's picnic fare. After deciding to wait to have dessert, they helped clear the table and clean up, and retired to the den.

"I have missed seeing you all week, but I have so enjoyed my time with Lily. She is quite unique and charming and warm and welcoming, and I could go on and on. I love her as though I have known her forever, and I have the two of you to thank for bringing her into my life. I feel so blessed. As you imagine, we spoke at length about your wedding, and it is one reason for getting together this evening to touch base and determine how to move forward.

"Neither Lily nor I intend to lead the way so to speak. We feel that you should decide if you haven't already, what parts you would like us to play. I don't want you to feel that this meeting is taking place excluding Lily; she simply stated that before the two of us *go crazy*, we want to know how you would like us to proceed."

Looking at one another knowingly, Jodi and Sam both laughed. "Mom, you know me so well; however, I know you pretty well too. We have actually discussed our plans quite extensively, and we were planning on sharing all of it with you and Lily; it's one of the reasons I wanted you to return to New York. In all fairness, it has not yet been one full week since your return, and you have to admit, we are making progress.

"We agree that the most pressing issue is deciding on a wedding date. Until we do, we are well aware we cannot move forward with anything else. If tomorrow evening is agreeable with Lily, we would like to get together. At that time, we will apprise you of the plans we have made that include the date we have chosen. I must add, however, our plans are not final until you and Lily are in sync with us.

"One obstacle and one obstacle alone looms large—the COVID-19 mandates, regulations, and lockdowns that remain very much in place heading into year two. Any and all plans we make will have to consider where we will be in time on the date we choose for the wedding. We view this as requiring plans with backups, while we deal with the uncertainty of what the next few months will bring."

Trudy leaned back in her chair. "Producing and finalizing the show, Jodi and Lily reuniting, and all the many additionally things you both have on your plates, I'm proud of you. You know what you want, and speaking for Lily and myself, we will do everything we can to make your special day *ultra special.*

"I'll check with Lily, but I'm certain tomorrow will be fine. She suggested anytime over the weekend. I think it's easier for us to go there, so we can choose a time and order-in dinner.

"Now, who's ready for dessert—Trudy's famous chocolate chip cookies and ice cream? I can make coffee or open another bottle of wine."

For Sam, it was a good feeling having his mother back in New York, especially to help plan the most important day of his life. She was the only person who really knew him and understood him; that is until he found it uncanny how quickly Jodi had come to know him and understand his innermost feelings after such a short period of time.

For Jodi, she felt as though she had hit the jackpot. After twenty years of not knowing who she was or where she came from, she was reunited with her Nana. The one thing that still puzzled her was how she could have forgotten or pushed aside the memory of someone who was so important to her in her early years—almost more important than her parents. The loss of Julia and Henry Jerome had devastated her, but the circumstances were not the same, and they were actually a part of her life twice as long as Nana and her parents had been.

Jodi and Sam believed they deeply shared a *once in a lifetime* love that many are never fortunate to find. They did not look at their wedding as urgent in any way. They simply took into consideration the ongoing COVID regulations, and decided to pick a date several months away in order to allow ample time to plan. They chose Sunday, November 7, 2021 as their wedding day—marking one year since Jodi arrived in New York. It felt right.

They spent most of the day at Lily's. It was family; it was fun. Jodi and Sam presented their plans, and their requests. Quite amiable and agreeable to all, they quickly took care of the business at hand. It was decided pretty much just as they had planned.

The wedding on Sunday, November 7, 2021, would take place at Lily and Papa Joe's house. They would make two guest lists; one would be shorter depending on COVID restrictions at the time, and the other would include the extended Caruso family depending on the easing of those restrictions. Invitations would be ordered to accommodate the larger list. The entire first floor of the house including a heated tent in the garden area would host a late afternoon champagne wedding featuring an extensive array of appetizers both served and stationed, followed by a wedding cake and sweet table. Music and a small dance floor, cafe tables and chairs throughout, and Lily's choice of a photographer—which was the only request she made—to capture it all completed the package.

It was a bittersweet day for Lily. For twenty years all she ever longed for was to learn what happened to Nicole and Olivia. Not only had she reunited with her granddaughter, but she was also a part of her wedding, helping her plan it, and it was to take place in her and Joe's home. She couldn't have picked a better person for her to marry than Sam Meyerson, and she absolutely adored Trudy.

They placed a call to Charlie inviting him to join them for dinner. Nina who had been out most of the day was home in time to join them too. They ordered in and spent a delightful evening just having fun. Trudy decided to surprise them all, stating that she was staying in New York and not returning to Florida. She would call a friend to pack up what she wanted sent back.

As they sat around the table filled with empty containers and empty wine bottles, Lily said, "Jodi Dear, if you will help me clear the table, we can have dessert and then retire to the library."

'Nana, it's been a long time since I've heard you say that; it used to be *Olivia Dear* or even more often *Joe Dear*. Whenever you needed Papa Joe's help, it was always *Joe Dear* can you help me? Or *Joe Dear* lunch is ready."

"You're absolutely right. You spent a lot of time here with me when you were little. Your Mom used to bring you with her to work at the Foundation offices upstairs. While she was busy working, you used to spend the day with me. We did all sorts of things. We baked cookies; we made my fluffy pancakes; we read books. When you were around two years old, you started to mimic me all the time and giggle and giggle in the process especially when I needed Papa Joe as you called out *Joe D, Joe D* without completely saying the word *Dear* as you ran to get him."

A hush fell over the room. "I was only two years old; I didn't remember. It was the only link that I connected with in my dreams, and when I was hypnotized. It was why they named me *Jodi*. Nana, since getting reacquainted with you I've been having a hard time coming to terms with how I could have possibly forgotten you and Papa Joe. I loved you both so much; you were so important to me. Now I know, I didn't forget you; I just didn't know it."

Everybody was crying. Dessert was served.

As we approached the second year of COVID, New Yorkers struggled not only with the pandemic but also with the contentious election. Unrest and division brought on by demonstrations against the unending mandates and regulations kept businesses either shuttered or open on a limited basis, kept schools closed, and demanded that everyone be vaccinated. Looting and murders were at an all time high, and to add to the dilemma, perpetrators were released within hours of their arrest due to the new laws in place.

2021—a year so many had looked to with hope and a return to normalcy was instead destined to become a year filled with political turmoil, extreme weather, and the specter of the coronavirus—its variants constantly emerging with no relief in sight.

In January, Biden was sworn in with a scaled back inauguration under heavy security. Each month that followed brought a new crisis to deal with. Severe winter storms brought weeklong power outages to Texas killing more than 200 people; New York City saw the worst snowstorm to affect the megalopolis since the January 2016 blizzard.

By the end of March and closer to home, Governor Andrew Cuomo continued to face allegations of sexual harassment, and the nursing home cover-up of underreporting COVID deaths. The New York Assembly called for his resignation and launched an impeachment investigation.

Daily COVID-19 vaccinations peaked in April. The Administration continued to urge everyone to get vaccinated and mandates were handed out to all healthcare workers, the military, pilots, and those dealing with the public—get vaccinated or get terminated. By June, the Delta variant arrived in America. It became a summer of surging virus cases and deaths that continued—peaking in early September. In addition, the CDC announced that booster shots were being suggested six months following initial vaccination.

In July, Nina called Charlie to the house to check on Lily. She was an early riser and by the time Nina came downstairs to grab a cup of coffee and head back up to the Foundation's offices, she could be found sitting at the island in the kitchen reading the paper and drinking her morning coffee. On that particular day, Nina soon realized that she had not as yet gotten up.

When she went to check on her, she found her in bed. Lily readily admitted that she felt weak, lacking the energy to get up, shower, and get dressed, which had been her morning routine for as long as she could remember. She placed a call to Charlie who arrived in record time. After checking her vitals, he announced to their relief that she was simply tired and could use a good rest away from all that had transpired since January when she first met with Sam. The fact was that for almost a year prior, she had been housebound due to the pandemic and very little outside contact with anyone had slowed her down quite a bit just as it had those who were much younger than she was.

Upon learning that Lily wasn't up to par, Trudy proposed a grand idea—an idea that included the six of them. She felt they could all use a little rest and relaxation, and she had the perfect answer—The Hamptons.

Each year, her dear friend Shirley Rosen insisted she spend the last two weeks in July thru the first two weeks in August at her beautiful home in Montauk. Shirley was a widow whose only son died on 9/11 when the South Tower collapsed. As she and her husband were coming to grips with their loss, Rob was diagnosed with Cancer. He fought hard but lost the battle two years later. Trudy and Al were good friends and were by her side every inch of the way.

When Al died suddenly, Shirley was at her side as Trudy had been by hers. In the past few years, her health had declined dramatically and when COVID took over, she became withdrawn preferring to remain in Florida until things changed and restrictions were lifted. She had called Trudy only days earlier to tell her the house was hers for however long she wanted it.

For the remainder of July and for most of August, they were resting and relaxing in Montauk. Only Lily and Trudy remained at the house the entire time. The others returned to the city whenever there was business to attend to. Sam brought laptops and wedding info they could check on and keep abreast of in case any problems arose.

For the most part, the house remained the center of their stay. Because the Delta strain of the virus was still very much in the news, they preferred to eat in except on weekends when weather permitting, they dined outdoors at one of the many restaurants in the area. The cleaning service came once a week to clean, change the linens, and to help with any minor maintenance problems that arose.

It was just what the doctor ordered for Lily, but it was great for Trudy as well. They were *girlfriends* on vacation, and they made the most of it. They donned masks and went grocery shopping together whenever the need arose. They even spent time walking through the town and looking in the store windows of the many quaint shops. When everyone returned for the weekends, the house was ready.

They tried reading; they tried puzzles. They found conversation much more enticing. Lily fondly related stories of Jodi's early years, of Noah and Nicole, and of Joe. At times she became wistful when speaking of Joe, but only because they hadn't been able to find Nicole and Olivia before he died. Sadness was never a factor; he brought only love and joy into their life together. It felt as though she missed him more as time went by.

Trudy's stories of Sam and Al, their love and devotion for one another were uplifting and at times comical as she blended the Myersons with the Carusos, adding she would soon get to meet them in person; stories of the daughter they lost were poignant, but as with Lily love and joy reigned supreme. Unprepared to lose Al so soon, his loss overcame her until she realized that Sam needed her; they got through it together.

Their stay in The Hamptons ended the third week in August. The show was coming up in less than a month; the invitations were on schedule to be mailed; checking and double-checking all the wedding arrangements; and staying on top of the virus updates brought the weeks of rest and relaxation to an end.

August became a month of headlines dominated by the resignation of Governor Cuomo. In a dramatic *fall from grace*, he surrendered to the wave of scandals that engulfed his administration and left him facing impeachment. He resigned on August 10, 2021, by submitting his resignation for Office of the Governor of the State of New York—effective 12:00 am on August 24, 2021.

On August 30, 2021, the last U.S. troops left Afghanistan marking the end of America's longest war. The chaotic withdrawal that resulted in the US backed Afghan government falling to the Taliban, leaving behind American citizens, and billions in US systems, weaponry, and military equipment remained in the headlines for weeks as it was left to private citizens and groups to continue their efforts to evacuate and bring those left behind home.

The long, difficult year of 2021 was almost—but not just yet—coming to an end.

All of the wedding preparations made by Lily and Trudy were arranged prior to their stay in Montauk—they were a great team. Between the two of them, they managed to secure everything that was needed—catering service, music, photographer, and flowers—with Jodi and Sam's approval every step of the way. Deciding to get married at the house was a big factor in their planning; it gave them free reign over the event by allowing them to move forward as they approached November 7th and stay within the guidelines of the current strain of the virus.

Jodi and Sam took care of ordering the invitations adhering to the guest lists that they compiled together. Jodi asked Lily and Trudy to accompany her in choosing her wedding gown. It turned out to be a real adventure. They deemed the gown she chose totally Jodi—elegant yet simple—classic yet fashionable—Iconic Vera Wang.

By September, all of the wedding plans were in place. The invitations were all addressed and ready to be mailed by mid-month. They would decide which list to go with at that time. With their wedding plans in place, they turned their attention to *Profiles* and the festivities they were planning surrounding the 9/11 Anniversary Episode.

# Chapter 20

September 11, 2021 arrived, and the long awaited airing of *Profiles of New York* anniversary episode was good to go. Throughout the day, every major television and cable network featured memorial services annually observed, and numerous specials earmarked to commemorate the 20th anniversary of the attacks. Several were also set to be aired in Prime Time, among them *The Lily Asher Story* on PBS.

Sam thought long and hard about his opening introduction to the show. To *Profiles* the day represented several milestones—milestones that were normally celebrated. Thinking it inappropriate to celebrate on a day that was all about remembrance and loss, he decided to divide his remarks into two parts—an opening statement and a closing statement.

Unwilling to push these milestone aside, and driven by his desire to acknowledge them respectfully and off air in a private manner resulted in a remarkable tribute to his team. He had been tossing around the idea in his mind for weeks, but originally not as a celebration. The idea first came to him as a way to assemble their small group to view the show as it aired. When he realized he could combine the two, his excitement took over.

He let no one in on his plans, not even Jodi, and he made all the arrangements for the evening himself. Viewing the show from the theater at the office had been in place from the beginning, as was the guest list: the team of eight, Lily, Trudy, Nina and Charlie. Sam said he would take care of everything; he did.

Invitations were personally delivered one week prior inviting each guest to cocktails and dinner at precisely 6:00 pm, followed by the 20th Anniversary episode airing of *Profiles of New York—The Lily Asher Story* at 8:00 pm, and followed by a celebration of times past with a look to the future. Dressy casual requested.

The guests began arriving early eager and excited. The smaller conference room was ready with appetizers and drinks including a Bartender. The larger conference room formally set with a centerpiece of multi-colored flowers awaited dinner for twelve. Everyone was in a festive mood.

Trudy had come with Jodi and Sam; the team was all there. Sam sent a car to pick up Lily, Nina, and Charlie, and as they awaited their arrival, compliments galore were heaped upon Sam—once they learned he was solely responsible for what appeared to be the start of an unforgettable evening.

As the elevator opened and Lily stepped out, a round of applause greeted her. She was overwhelmed but not so much so that she quickly responded with applause of her own for everyone else. It was not yet 6:00 pm, but everyone had arrived and in short order, the party was well underway.

When dinner was announced, they took their places around the beautifully set table. Chateaubriand, roasted garlic potatoes, asparagus, choice of Bordelaise sauce or wine-based mushroom sauce—all paired with fine red wine.

There were no complaints. The evening thus far was flawless.

They took a break before going down the hall to the Theatre— featuring plush seating and a giant screen, it comfortably accommodated up to twenty-five guests. They were all seated, eyes forward awaiting the start of the show. Jodi chose to sit with her Nana. Sam chose to sit off to the side so he could observe. Only Trudy, Charlie, and Nina were viewing it for the first time; they chose to sit together. Lily had seen most of it with the exception of the ending remarks by Jodi and herself—though she was well aware of the content.

At precisely 8:00 pm, the familiar **PBS** lead in to *Profiles* began. Sam dressed quite formally in a tux appeared on the screen.

*Good evening and welcome to Profiles of New York—the Lily Asher Story. In our 20ᵗʰ Anniversary episode of 9/11, we are pleased and excited to present to you a different type of narrative—a narrative of life and hope and unending love—that in the end conquers all. Our Profile of Lily Asher fits that description in every sense.*

*To those of you who know of Lily, as well as those who have possibly never heard of her, her story is quite remarkable. It may affect or appeal to you in a personal or emotional way; it may have no bearing on you whatsoever. It may give you hope and strength for the future and perhaps ease your pain.*

*Tonight marks the 10ᵗʰ Anniversary of Profiles of New York having debuted on the 10ᵗʰ Anniversary of 9/11. Beginning with our first episode honoring the Heroes of 9/11, we have dedicated our*

216

*show each year on this date to various aspects of that day. Tonight we*
*have come full circle; we honor a Victim, a Hero, and a Survivor—*
*New York Icon Lily Asher.*

The episode began. It ran slightly longer than the normal two hours.
Up to that point, there was no break in the show. After a brief offering of
items associated with the story, Lily once again appeared on the screen.

*My story is but one of thousands that is connected to that day, a day*
*we will never forget. It robbed the victims of their lives and changed*
*the survivors' lives forever leaving us to wonder what might have*
*been or what if? Sadly, we continue to lose loved ones and heroes as*
*consequences of helping one another.*

*Through the Asher Foundation and personally, I have worked*
*with and supported the many efforts to rebuild Ground Zero and the*
*organizations offering aid to those in need. My offer to paint portraits*
*of the Heroes of 9/11 on the Premiere of Profiles has rewarded me*
*with numerous ongoing friendships including my dearest friend Nina*
*Butler who I consider family.*

*My twenty-year quest searching for Nicole and Olivia was*
*not only to satisfy the promise I made to Joe, it became something*
*I had to do for myself. I didn't do it for closure; I don't believe one*
*ever realizes closure. In my own way, I felt compelled to learn what*
*happened to them after vanishing three months after we lost Noah.*

*Olivia is back in my life and I am back in hers. Yes, I believe*
*in Miracles.*

A split screen appeared with Jodi and Lily.

*I was born Olivia Asher but I have lived the past twenty years as*
*Jodi Jerome. I was a child of ten when the accident robbed me of*
*my identity and all memory of a life filled with love surrounded by*
*people who loved me as I did them. I owe Henry and Julia Jerome*
*my life; they were my Miracle.*

*As I grew older, not knowing who I was and where I came from*
*persistently invaded my thoughts. I hadn't relinquished mourning my*
*mother when my father died. As you can imagine, Henry and Julia*

*Jerome were my entire world, and when I lost them, learning who I was and where I came from became paramount.*

*Providence works in mysterious ways. My article in the LA Times introduced a new guardian angel into my life—Sam Meyerson. His offer of a job at Profiles brought me home, although at the time I didn't know it. The article also found its way to my Nana through a friend Charlie Hurwitz who grew up with my father Noah.*

*My memory has returned, and I recall so many happy times with my Mom and Dad, with Nana and Papa Joe, and with the four of us all together always.*

*I am truly blessed.*

The show ended as credits streamed across the screen.

*The Asher Foundation and viewers like you make Profiles of New York possible.*

No one moved; no one made an effort to leave. Suddenly applause broke out and everyone relaxed and began speaking all at once.

They took a short break and Sam invited them to return to the conference room for dessert and coffee. As they watched the show, the caterer transformed the room into a Birthday celebration for Lily before leaving. With balloons and streamers everywhere and the table festively set, a cake iced with multicolored flowers—precisely like those she planted each year in her yard—sat in the center. There was coffee and tea, and Champagne.

Sam stood and began speaking. "Before we begin the birthday celebration, I would like to say a few words. All of you here tonight are the nearest and dearest to my heart. None of us would be here without one another.

"My original thoughts for the show were to have an opening and closing statement; the latter of which would honor the milestones *Profiles* has reached. I decided that it would be inappropriate for tonight's show and perhaps even a tad disrespectful. Therefore, I decided to keep the celebrating and honors private and in-house.

"To my staff—my best friends—that took a chance with me to follow my dream, I love you all and thank you from the bottom of my heart.

Tonight is the 10th Anniversary of *Profiles,* and tonight's show was the 100th episode. The show has won many awards that are displayed on the shelves behind you—all directly attributed to your hard work and dedication.

"To you Mom—my #1 go-to advisor—who has loved me and supported me my entire life and continues to do so, I love you more. When Dad died, you helped me through one of the most difficult times in my life while in reality you were facing life without your soul mate, the only man you ever loved.

"To Lily—my dear friend—soon to be my Nana too, I love you and thank you for being not only a friend, but someone who genuinely cares about me and has nurtured me along the way without my realizing it.

"To Nina and Charlie—new friends—new family, I love you both and look forward to sharing many happy times while making memories together.

"To Jodi—the *Love of My Life*—you make me whole. I'm a better person because of you. I have but one regret—waiting so long to bring you into my life.

On November 7th, that will be remedied when all of us here will once again be together for our Wedding. Simply put, you are my *happily ever after!*

"We are also celebrating Lily's Birthday today. Before I light the candle for you to blow out and make a wish, Jodi and I have a gift for you."

For a brief moment, a puzzled look crossed Jodi's face leading Sam to explain. "As you all know by now, I planned this evening's *after party* on my own as a *Thank You* and *Appreciation* from me to all of you. The present for Lily, however, was actually Jodi's idea; she just didn't know that I thought tonight would be the time to give it to her."

Immediately, a knowing smile appeared on Jodi's face as Sam pointed to the box that sat on floor next to him. Leaving her seat to stand at his side, she began: "Nana, you would think that with all that has happened to me since the beginning of this year, that it would be impossible for me to consider one gesture, one word, or one day to stand out above all the others, yet I do. It happened on the first day of our interview when after our lunch break, you produced the first of your *Memory Boxes.*

"As much as the *Lily Asher Story* captured my heart and curiosity from the very first word, and before I learned of our connection, the contents of that *Memory Box* made a huge impact on me and set the pace for the Interview going forward. At the time, I didn't realize that it was your way of bringing me home. You did just that. The boxes that followed were no less intriguing to me, and each one brought me closer and closer to finding my Nana."

Reaching down, she lifted a box and placed it on the table. "Sam and I have taken the liberty of starting a new *Memory Box* for you."

As she lifted the lid, she began pulling items from the box. "To get you started, we have included the official DVD of *Profiles—The Lily Asher Story,* an original copy of my article in the LA Times that became the catalyst of it all, several photographs including the *Profiles* crew, our *family* of six, candid shots taken at our gatherings, and an advanced copy of our Wedding Invitation."

Lily was overwhelmed. She remained seated, but quickly regained her composure and lifted her glass. There were no tears just her broad smile. "The best part of my long life has been the people that have shared it with me, the very ones that have made my memories special. As I look around tonight, I feel love from all of you. I want you to know that your love is returned; I am truly blessed. I *Thank You* for this wonderful magical night.

"Now Sam, light that candle."

Everyone laughed. Sam did as he was asked; he lit the candle. Lily stood, blew it out, closed her eyes, and made her wish out loud. "Just one more *Memory Box,* that is my wish."

Containers of assorted flavors of Sedutto Ice Cream sat in the center of the table. After cutting the first piece of cake, Jodi took over and soon plates of cake were passed around to everyone so they could help themselves to ice cream.

The caterer and staff were gone; only the party remnants remained. As midnight approached, Sam called the car service, and they left for home. It was Saturday, and the cleaning service wasn't scheduled for weekends, so the *Profiles* crew stayed behind to clear the conference room before leaving.

Everyone was proud and pleased with everything. They viewed the 20th Anniversary *Profiles* episode and their celebration afterwards as an omen of hope for the future; a future where COVID and its variants were no longer in the picture, where the pulse of New York once again beat with the vigor of old, and where Americans respected one another and our differences. Getting back to basics seemed a good way to start.

In the days that followed, the response to the show was overwhelming. There was no way they could answer the office phones that were ringing off the hook or respond to the thousands of hits on the internet. One thing they all had in common was *they wanted more!* They didn't want Lily's story to end.

Finally, Sam posted a response on the *Profiles* network that they would be giving updates soon hoping to answer their many questions, in particular about Lily's studio and when it would reopen. He was already forming a plan in his mind.

With the wedding less than two months away, Jodi and Sam turned their efforts towards November 7th. Most of the plans and arrangements were in place; the invitations were mailed. Their main concern from that point until the wedding was to monitor the Coronavirus situation in New York in an effort to abide by the rules and regulations in place as the day grew closer.

It was decided that Invitations would be mailed to the extended list—75 guests. They set up a website and all were requested to check the site on a regular basis for updates on the virus and what was required by the State of New York to attend the event. In addition, RSVPs were not due until ten days prior to the wedding. Everyone was asked to take a home test whether they were experiencing symptoms or not 48 hours prior.

The Delta variant peaked in September allowing some relief leading up to their big day as it drew closer and closer. There was excitement in the air as the responses started coming in. For many, it was the first occasion they would be attending since the onset of the pandemic, and they welcomed it with open arms. It was also the first opportunity for many to see one another in well over a year, which was quite unusual for the Caruso Clan whose family gatherings were traditional.

Sam also looked forward to seeing his Uncle Edward and Aunt Ruth who were coming up from Florida. Their three daughters and their husbands responded —*they wouldn't miss it for the world*—they all lived on Long Island.

Jodi's list though short was heartfelt. Her parents' lifelong friends Lloyd and Leslie Buchanan, their daughter and her husband were coming, as was Rosy, her parents' housekeeper who she absolutely loved and adored. They would be flying to New York together. Jodi invited them to arrive a couple of days early so they could have a long-awaited reunion before heading back to California. They accepted.

The days ticked by. As the Delta variant cases began subsiding, everyone who had been vaccinated was encouraged to get a Booster six months after their second shot. The Center for Disease Control continued to urge the unvaccinated to get on board. Even the weather was cooperating.

Jodi welcomed her California *family* to New York. The days immediately preceding the wedding were a whirlwind of activity—introductions to new friends while welcoming old friends. They covered everything from *Profiles*, to their falling hard and fast for one another in such a short period of time, and to Jodi coming home.

Lloyd Buchanan's voice broke as he assured them that his dear friends Henry and Julia Jerome were with them every inch of the way as they looked down from above, further stating that he could hear her father's voice loud and clear: *I knew it; I felt it; I was right. Coming home did indeed bring her memory back.*

Lily and Trudy made all of the arrangements for the Wedding and followed through on the responses. Sam took care of the Honeymoon plans that included a special surprise for Jodi. When they discussed who would perform the ceremony, Jodi agreed wholeheartedly to Sam's suggestion.

Greg, Lou, Frank, and Carol were lifelong friends who grew up together with Sam in Port Chester. They attended different colleges, but remained connected and never lost touch with one another. Ultimately, Greg and Carol married after graduation. Frank met Edie at Syracuse University, and they married a couple of years later. Lou met Sandy at *Profiles;* they hired her part-time while she was still in college. When she graduated, they followed suit and married.

The friends were beyond euphoric when they learned Sam and Jodi were engaged. Sam was right in his assessment that the success of *Profiles of New York,* although it was his idea originally, belonged to all of them. Therein laid his dilemma of sorts. He could not and would not be married without his three best friends taking part in it. He could only choose one as Best Man; and there was no need for Ushers. He decided to research the latest trend—online ordainment.

He chose Greg, Lou, and Frank to perform the ceremony as a team; after all they were not only a team in business but in life as well. It was perfect. In the world of COVID, this also provided a backup if any one of the three was unable to attend. The friends were over the moon and incredibly honored to have been asked. They accepted and took the responsibility seriously, promising to deliver a ceremony like no other. Jodi and Sam were writing their own vows.

The rehearsal was at the house that was well underway in its transformation and almost ready to receive its guests, awaiting only the finishing last-minute touches.

The weeks that followed the broadcast had flown by, but they were ready.

# Chapter 21

Long awaited, November 7, 2021 arrived. It was a partly cloudy fall day with a high of 54 degrees, and for the first time in a very long time, Lily and Joe's beautiful home was ready to welcome guests. Best of all, it was Jodi and Sam's Wedding Day. The excitement in the air was infectious. As family and friends entered the house, they found themselves surrounded by an array of fresh springtime flowers throughout that emanated the illusion of being outdoors.

The Ceremony was set up to take place in the living room. Most of the furniture had either been removed or pulled back to allow a small flower-covered platform to be placed in front of the fireplace. Each guest was offered a glass of champagne or drink of their choice as they were asked to line the large foyer at the foot of the spiral staircase.

Trudy and Sam walked arm-in-arm into the living room where Sam took his place before Greg, Frank, and Lou who awaited him on the platform; Trudy stood slightly behind him. Gasps of delight could be heard as they witnessed Jodi descending the spiral staircase where she was met by her Nana. As they proceeded through the foyer, the guests were guided into the room behind them.

Jodi took her place as Nana stood by her side. Her gown—so elegant yet so simple; his pale grey suit—so classic yet so timeless—offered no competition for the aura of love that engulfed them as they stood side-by-side and repeated their vows.

The Ceremony brought laughter and tears as Greg, Frank, and Lou performed the service that ended with thundering applause of approval as glasses rose high in toasts.

A trio played in the foyer where a dance floor surrounded by small live trees and an abundance of fresh flowers was set up.

Well into the evening hours, guests enjoyed the food, the drinks, and the dancing, but most of all just being together. There were no tears. This was a happy day—long to be remembered. Lily saw to it personally that the photographer she had chosen took pictures of everything—enough to fill not one but two *Memory Boxes.*

By the time everyone left, it was past midnight. Lily fell asleep almost immediately, happy and content; her arms encircled a favorite portrait of Joe.

Their Honeymoon flight left JFK Airport the next morning at 10:00 am—destination Marco Island on Florida's west coast. Landing in Fort Myers, they picked up their leased car and drove to the house Sam rented.

Marco Island, stretching six picture-perfect miles along the Gulf of Mexico, is an ideal destination for guests and residents alike seeking sunny and relaxing days in the calm beauty of its surrounds. The spacious house located on the Gulf offered total seclusion off the beaten track, and included a cook, a cleaning service, and Gabriel who was available to fulfill their every wish. It was their *little piece of heaven* for ten days. There was a cabin cruiser available if they chose to use it; they did on several occasions.

Except for isolated showers one lone afternoon, the weather cooperated fully.

At the end of the ten days, Sam presented Jodi with the surprise that he had managed to keep under wraps—four days in Disney World—to make up for the trip she never got to take with Nana and Papa Joe. She was over the moon. Although the park was not fully open, there was a lot for them to see and do. They became *kids* the instant they arrived and stayed in *kid mode* until it was time to leave. They purchased Mickey Mouse tee shirts for Lily and several others.

They returned to New York the Monday before Thanksgiving. While they were away, the Lily/Trudy team continued. Trudy who normally left for Florida the weekend following the holiday, decided to remain in New York until the beginning of January. Christmas in the City had long been her favorite time of the year, and it brought back many fond memories.

After Al died, she distanced herself from so many of the things they loved doing together; it hurt too much to do them alone. In the past few months, she came to realize how much she missed Christmas and all that came with it. Of one thing she was certain—Al would want her to be the Trudy he fell in love with, the Trudy whose infectious enthusiasm during the holiday season was undeniable.

Once again, she wanted to see the Rockefeller Center Christmas Tree in person and up close, the Dyker Heights Christmas Lights displayed throughout the neighborhood she grew up in, the Radio City Rockettes Annual Christmas Show, Holiday Windows on Fifth Avenue, and the numerous lightscapes throughout the five boroughs—she wanted to see it all. A Broadway show or two would also be nice; she hadn't been to the theatre since the pandemic. Perhaps Jodi, Sam, and Charlie would join her.

Now that they had reconnected, she found herself looking forward to spending more time with Charlie, her longtime friend. She found being with him *comfortable;* they were a good fit, enjoying many of the same things and one another's company immensely.

Charlie's two daughters lived out of state in North Carolina and Texas. Since the pandemic, his limited contact with them and seeing his grandchildren had been on Face Time. The past few months made him realize how much he missed them. He found himself lonely and alone in the most vibrant city in the world albeit a city that was still sleeping, patiently waiting to be reawakened.

After the wedding, Trudy found herself concerned for Lily. Although the year had been one filled with extraordinary delights of reuniting with family and friends that brought her the inner peace she had sought for twenty years, coming on the heels of almost two years of COVID mandates and restraints proved challenging for her, especially at her advanced age.

Fortunately, Charlie lived nearby and though she often joked that her doctor was a Pediatrician, she was thankful to have him care for her. The pandemic managed to change every aspect of her everyday life including in-person medical care—which was Lily's biggest concern.

After her episode of fatigue and lack of energy during the summer, he suggested that she scale back her activities and retire earlier each evening in an effort to build up her strength. She did just that as long as she was in Montauk. However, when they returned to the city, she found it impossible to stick to that schedule or any other for that matter. The festivities surrounding the airing of *Profiles,* and preparations for Jodi and Sam's wedding at the house engulfed her and once again she found herself not quite up to par.

They actually began planning Thanksgiving together as a team. Although the house was back in pre-wedding order, Trudy soon came to the conclusion that there was no need to consider Lily's house as the only place for them to gather. After Al died and she moved to the city, she normally made dinner for Sam and herself allowing them to enjoy one last day before leaving for Naples the weekend following the holiday. Last year, their plans had included Jodi; she considered adding three more people—a piece of cake.

Telling Lily to leave everything to her, Trudy took over and made plans to have Thanksgiving at her place. Her decision to remain in the city through the end of the year at which time Charlie felt Lily would be well on the way to feeling like her old self, allowed him to make plans as well.

He scheduled flights to North Carolina and Texas to visit with his daughters and their families in the New Year. Having accepted Trudy's invitation, he also looked forward to spending time in Florida with her.

Sam arranged for a car to pick them up at the airport. Rested, tan, and happy, they entered the lobby of the Pavilion where Lester welcomed them back. To his surprise, Jodi handed him a small gift bag that contained a Mickey Mouse tee shirt.

Once in the apartment, they made calls to Trudy and Lily to tell them they were home, and that they would touch base later. Sam called the office to say they were back and that they would be there in the morning. They unpacked, put a load of clothes in the washer, and began putting things away. As the saying goes—*the Honeymoon was over.*

They were about to order in something light to tide them over until dinner when Sam opened the refrigerator and saw the note from Trudy welcoming them back. On the shelves were a variety of their favorite comfort foods. The smile on his face said it all. His Mom was the best.

They made plans to meet at Lily's for dinner the following evening. It was a fun laidback evening. They spoke of the beautiful house on Marco Island with emphasis on Maggie the cook and how nice it was to enjoy such fabulous meals eating in. But it was Gabriel who turned out to be a real gem; they were grateful for all of his local suggestions. Jodi excitedly went on and on about Disney World.

Trudy brought them up to speed on plans for Thanksgiving and told them that she was staying in the city until after the first of the year. They all agreed it was nice to look forward to ending the year on a far less stressful note—counting their blessings at Thanksgiving and declaring December a time for family.

On December 1, 2021, the first case of the Omicron variant of the coronavirus in the United States was confirmed by officials in an individual in California who had recently travel to South Africa. The CDC further stated that the person was fully vaccinated against COVID-19, experienced only mild symptoms, and was rapidly improving.

Although the new variant proved to be highly contagious, New York reported 4,592 COVID deaths in January and 1,652 in February, but they were not attributed to the new variant. Almost 90% of those who died were elderly, over 60 years of age, and had underlying health concerns. For the most part, restrictions remained in place but on track to be lifted in the spring.

Following a year of COVID mandates and restrictions having slowed everyone's pace to a crawl at best, the past year proved quite opposite. It was hard to believe that in twelve months time, Jodi arrived in New York, began a new job, fell in love with Sam, married and was now back from their honeymoon. They were well aware that the year ahead would be no less hectic; personal and business decisions loomed large. Though they were adamant about steering clear of work-related issues on their trip, they found themselves easily drawn to discussing the personal conclusions they had already reached while relaxing on the beach.

For the time being, remaining in Sam's apartment seemed the best choice. It was convenient to work, to Lily, and without question to his mother allowing them to check on her unit whenever she was away. The neighborhood offered access to amazing restaurants, coffee shops, food shopping, and anything else they needed within walking distance. The gym in their building had recently reopened and other amenities were on tap to reopen in weeks to come.

As a wedding gift, Trudy arranged to have their apartment repainted and redecorated. The work was scheduled to begin in January when she left for Florida, allowing Jodi and Sam to stay in her place until the work was finished. All the choices were theirs to make, as they would be working directly with the decorator.

Upon their return from Florida, Sam chose their first meeting at *Profiles* to discuss the January through June 2022 episodes. The final shows of 2021 had long been put to rest, with only the December profile of Radio City and the Rockettes remaining to be aired. Knowing they would be busy with personal changes and decisions, Sam thought it best to attend to business first. There were currently several episodes in the works that would carry them through June, and he wanted to make certain they were on the way to being finalized.

As they savored cake and ice cream at Lily's party, profiling the top New York Ice Cream Shops was suggested much to the delight of everyone. From Sedutto founded in the 1920s to Ample Hills who began as a cart at Celebrate Brooklyn in Prospect Park in 2011 to the many smaller and individual newer shops, the episode looked to be a real winner. Who doesn't like ice cream? Sam saw the episode as the perfect way to end the season by airing it in June in time for summer.

The episode profiling Florists and Candy Shops for Valentine's Day looked to be all set for the February airing. Many of the florists also offered a variety of gift packages fitting for the holiday. Li-Lac Chocolates a NYC Icon for almost 100 years, and The Sweet Shop NYC, a fun, full service, nostalgic candy shop, serving handmade ice creams from New York's top makers, delicious fresh-baked cookies, handcrafted chocolates, and retro candy favorites were featured.

But no episode on candy would be complete without including Economy Candy. New York City's oldest retail candy shop opened in 1937, in the wake of the Great Depression, on the lower east side. Today, a third generation, husband and wife team in its original location runs it. Although online orders are accepted, if you want to be *a kid in a candy store,* an in-person visit is a must.

Try as he may to set business aside while they were on their Honeymoon, his vision for the January show never left his thoughts. It was the one business item that he discussed with Jodi, but she didn't mind in the least because she was with him all the way on this one. Following the overwhelming response to the anniversary show, Sam released a statement acknowledging the many inquiries and promising an update in the not too distant future.

Although they only had about six weeks to put the entire show together, he was certain that it was doable. He did have to speak with Lily because only she could answer the questions that were directed to her. He envisioned it as such: *Profiles of New York—Our Story.* The episode would begin with Sam relating his longtime dream of a show that would be all about New York and New Yorkers. Once PBS agreed to air it, he assembled the team—his closest friends—and they hit the ground running. Everyone would be interviewed, and an overview of what taking an idea and turning it into an award-winning episode involves.

He was anxious to present his idea to the team and did so upon their return at their first meeting; they loved it. Carol suggested a less formal approach—an unscripted *Roundtable* format; all agreed. Jodi leaned towards making it more personal by including announcements of their marriage, Sandy having received her Master's Degree, Frank and Edie expecting their first child in June, and Greg and Carol awaiting word to adopt.

Sam thought it a good idea to preview upcoming episodes of *Profiles* to whet the appetites of their faithful fans as a good way to end their segment of the show.

The second hour would belong to Lily Asher and the Asher Foundation. Jodi offered to work with Lily and Nina to include an overview of the Foundation tying it into *Portraits by Lily* and the future of the studio and gallery in West Village.

March, April, and May episodes were still in the early stages. An update on COVID and its variants in New York looked promising for March marking the second anniversary of the onset. Everyone had long awaited the reopening of everything that made New York the most vibrant city in the world. To that point only baby steps had been realized, but the New Year looked toward stepping up the pace.

The April show was on tap to feature the fifteen best parks in New York City—oases of green space where one can enjoy fresh air away from the stresses of any given day. Whether you are looking for a bit of nature, a path for jogging or biking, a spot for a picnic, or a place to walk your dog—parks offer all of that and more. During the pandemic, parks became a refuge offering freedom from masks and distancing.

That left the month of May. All about Love and Weddings, several couples had agreed to be interviewed about the impact of having to reschedule or delay plans for their *Big Day*. Various venues were also being highlighted.

Sam was proud of his team. They never disappointed. He deemed the episodes that were planned excellent, both in choice and content, and he had no doubt that their viewers would embrace them.

With only one day left before Thanksgiving, and having his first priority—taking care of business—well in hand, Sam suggested to Jodi that if available, it would be a good time to meet with the Decorator, introduce themselves, and give her an overview of what they had in mind.

They met for lunch in their apartment, and it turned out to be not only productive, but they instantly took to one another having a fun afternoon in the process. Before leaving, she requested they work on an overview of how they envisioned the redo, asking that they determine any furniture they planned to keep, their color preferences throughout and contrast choices for accessories. Promising to drop off paint swatches over the next couple of weeks, she stated her goal was to be ready to hit the ground running as soon as Trudy left for Florida.

Thanksgiving Day was both serious yet totally fulfilling. The table was set with Trudy's fine china and crystal. A beautiful centerpiece from Jodi and Sam was surrounded by offerings of Turkey and all the trimmings, wine, and six smiling faces holding hands as they thanked God for the many blessings bestowed upon them in the past year. They prayed for those less fortunate and renewed hope for the future.

To Jodi, it seemed not that long ago that she was anxiously looking forward to interviewing Lily Asher and now the year was coming to an end. Where had the time gone and so quickly? She met with Lily and Nina throughout December to finalize answers to the many questions about *Portraits by Lily* and *The Asher Foundation*.

Mid-March would mark 74 years since she had opened the doors of her studio and gallery. While discussing with Nina how to move forward, they soon realized they were on the same page, joking that *great minds think alike*. By the time they met with Jodi, they had a plan in place; a plan that Jodi's gut feeling told her was perfect. They had thought of everything.

The studio would reopen to the public in March on a limited basis no longer offering portraits or art classes but as the *Portraits by Lily Museum*. Nina agreed to manage the studio and offer tours of the premises while relating its history with an overview of Lily's arrival in New York and the opening. Anticipating an excessive amount of requests, reservations would be required.

For the first three months, there would be no charge. Following that initial period, a small fee would be assessed for the Foundation. In the future, art classes would resume, past students could apply to teach, and offer to conduct tours. All of the students' artwork would be available for sale as in the past.

The anniversary episode had generated an unprecedented amount of donations for the Foundation. Lily felt it would be a good gesture to apprise the public of how the various recipients of these funds are determined and identify them. It was duly noted that no political donations are considered.

Lily told Jodi that she was meeting with her lawyers and Board of Directors in January to update The Asher Foundation and streamline its day-to-day business. The first item on her agenda was to move the offices out of the house to an office building setting. She further anticipated several new hires, as the Foundation underwent a complete house cleaning and separation from her personal items.

Feeling that for years her search for Nicole and Jodi had allowed her to neglect her duties to the Foundation, she felt compelled to put everything in order before passing it on to Jodi and Sam. In addition, its worth had increased many times over and was long overdue for an upgrade in status. Her attorneys had advised her through the years to do so; she just wasn't listening.

Lily heeded Charlie's advice and began to feel more like her old self. She no longer waited to drop before she stopped. She rose later in the morning; ate three healthy meals a day; and even began walking in the neighborhood when weather permitted. At his suggestion, she also took a short nap or rest each afternoon.

Christmas Day arrived, and once again, Trudy hosted everyone at her apartment. It was a fun day with everyone wanting to know what Jodi and Sam had planned for their apartment; what Nina was doing to get up to speed on tours for the museum; what Charlie had planned for his visits with his girls and their families; and what Trudy and Charlie were going to do with their time in Florida.

With Nina's help, Lily surprised everyone, including the *Profiles team*, by inviting them to the house for New Year's Day. She promised a day filled with good food and drink, football, family, good friends, and a winter send-off for Trudy and Charlie. She told everyone to come as early and stay as late as they wished.

She had a few surprises up her sleeve that were not totally unexpected, but what the surprises were definitely was. Using the photographer's photos from the wedding, she painted portraits of everyone either individual or as couples. Her wedding portrait of Jodi and Sam was awesome.

While the guys were engrossed in football, she had a treat for the ladies. They went upstairs to her office where she had several memory boxes to show them, as well as several paintings that were her mother's. She wanted their advice about possibly including them in the studio tour.

They were having so much fun, and it had grown dark aside without their noticing. By the time the guys came upstairs to find them, it was almost 7:00 pm.

They went downstairs for a light supper followed by dessert.

Trudy and Charlie agreed they might not stay in Florida long; it was just too hard leaving everyone.

Charlie made arrangements for his friend to look in on Lily, and told Nina not to hesitate to call him if she had any concerns.

With their paintings in hand, the group bid one another goodbye and wished one another the happiest of New Years.

The first day of 2022 had certainly started off on a good foot!

# Chapter 22

January 2022 was busier than anticipated. Trudy left for Florida on the first Tuesday of the month, the same day Charlie left for North Carolina. Their planes flew out of JFK an hour apart. Jodi and Sam drove them to the airport and returned home to begin moving their things out of their apartment to Trudy's. If all went as planned, the decorator was set to begin work on the following Monday.

Millions of New Yorkers looked to the New Year with hope and a return to the old normal, however, the new norm marched on. Many COVID restrictions remained in effect; school attendance was sporadic at best; and the arrival of a new Mayor did little to subdue or tamp down crime, which continued to rise at an alarming rate. Rash court decisions and unending political upheaval only placed more uncertainty on the backs of the average citizen.

The homeless crisis that the Mayor vowed to tackle was interrupted by having to deal with migrants arriving by the thousands. Prices on everything continued to rise steadily affecting the elderly and families with children the most. The blame was placed squarely on transportation and logistics' costs further complicating the situation as inflation continued to soar.

Many continued to work from home, but the service industry required in-person help and this became yet another problem. Food and beverage businesses, hairdressers, etc. continued to operate on scaled back schedules because employees seeking to return to work couldn't keep up with demand.

When the national shortage of baby formula surfaced, frantic parents were faced with a dire situation causing them to travel miles and cross state lines to get nourishment for their newborns. Supply chain problems mushroomed causing consumers to not only face empty shelves of the most basic products, but the rising prices of eggs, milk, and bread when available forced families to consider financial tradeoffs.

As expected, the January episode of *Profiles* was well received. Their audience was quite receptive to their visit behind the scenes. Once again, tributes poured in for both the show's crew and Lily.

Following the airing, Lily enlisted Nina's help to work on a new project. Since being reunited with Olivia, she realized the time was long overdue to upgrade and revamp The Asher Foundation. She envisioned a simpler, more efficient, and totally computerized system. In addition, she wanted to discuss with the Board of Directors her new approach—appointing younger energetic members who could better equate to the recipients of the scholarships they awarded.

She also came to the conclusion that the time had come to move the foundation's offices out of the house to office space in one of the many buildings that remained only partially leased since the onset of the pandemic. She completed her plan on paper, attached her notes, and with Nina's help, set up a meeting the end of January.

Careful not to overdo, she followed Charlie's directions to the letter, but it felt good to have something to look forward to. In addition, as she had promised on the show, she was in the process of reopening *Portraits by Lily* as a museum. She planned to continue to offer lessons by reconnecting with some of her past students, and feature art shows with their work, as well as new artists as she had done in the past. She planned the reopening for the end of March to coincide with the anniversary of 74 years of *Portraits by Lily* in West Village.

Jodi and Sam were busy on their own. They managed to check in with Lily everyday, but they reserved their getting together for brunches and dinners on weekends.

With the second anniversary of Henry Jerome's death approaching in March, Jodi decided to move forward with a memorial service. It took a little bit of juggling and help from Lloyd and Leslie Buchanan, but everything fell into place, and she was quite pleased with their plans. The Service would be held in their church, but it would offer a video hookup for those unable to attend in person. In addition, the ability to participate via video was also offered to anyone who wished to do so.

She and Sam planned to spend ten days in Los Angeles. Hoping to tie up her parents' estate while they were there, and planning to put her condo on the market, she placed a call to the woman who had leased it for the past two years to inquire if she was interested in purchasing. Jodi made her an offer and asked her to think it over and let her know when she reached a decision.

Several days later she received a phone call; she accepted Jodi's offer. They would close on the condo while they were in LA. She also had to go through a myriad of items she left and decide what to keep and what to give away. Her *to-do list* also included spending some time with Rosy, hoping to encourage her to keep in touch and come east for a visit every now and then.

The redo of their apartment was progressing on schedule, and they were due to move back in before leaving for California.

January ended with a snowstorm and February began colder than normal. When the weather was bad, they checked in with Lily and Nina to make sure they were okay, and when possible, they walked over for a short visit bearing pastries from their favorite café.

All too soon, January and February were in the past, and on a cold but bright sunny day, they flew to Los Angeles. The house had not yet sold, so they decided to stay there allowing Jodi one final sweep of its contents to make certain there was nothing she wished to retain.

Returning to Los Angeles was bittersweet for Jodi. After all, she had lived two-thirds of her life there with parents that she loved and adored. She missed them terribly and often wished they had lived to see her total recall just as Henry had predicted. In reality she had many more memories of the Jeromes than she had of her biological parents. She was anxious to put it all to rest and move on with her life—her life with Sam by her side.

Lloyd and Leslie Buchanan were wonderful. They were a great help with setting up the Memorial Service, going over the many aspects of the estate—what had been sold and what remained to be sold—as well as a few personal matters that Lloyd had been waiting for the right time to convey to her. Once he learned of their pending visit, he began finalizing the paperwork and preparing a financial statement for the estate. He planned to obtain her signature on all necessary documents so that any future dealings with closing out the estate would not require her to appear in person. He and Leslie also looked forward to spending time with them so they could get to know Sam better.

Perhaps the person Jodi missed the most was Rosy. She was always there for her whenever she was needed, while knowing that losing the Jeromes was just as hard for her and in some ways more so. She had done wonders with packing up the house and taking care of the place for the past two years, and even Lloyd had to admit that she was a big help to him as he often called on her for clarification of various matters regarding the house.

The Memorial Service was precisely what Jodi wanted. It was well received by all and many who were unable to attend in person were most appreciative that she considered allowing them to participate. Not only did his friends, and fellow physicians come forward, but many of his patients did so, as well. The Service lasted longer than anticipated, but excluded no one. Rosy's tribute was especially heartwarming.

The time they spent at the house with Rosy was fun and upbeat as they recalled so many happy times together. Sam learned about another side to Jodi and the many shenanigans she tried to pull off. But all in all, they did manage to attend to business by packing up items to be shipped east, and identified items to be sold or given away. Accepting Jodi's offer, Rosy had taken several items as well.

As their stay approached its end, they had one last meeting with Lloyd. Once more Jodi was blown away. Her condo was sold; the boat, the house in Malibu, the antique cars, and a portion of the artwork and higher priced items were too. Lloyd anticipated the house and remaining items to sell quickly now that some of the virus mandates and regulations were easing.

She thought their meeting was over, but to her surprise, what she learned next was definitely not what she could have ever anticipated. Lloyd presented her with a financial statement indicating the value of the estate to date and a bank account in her name that held the assets. She stared at the figure at the bottom of the page in awe passing the papers to Sam who was equally as stunned. In excess of ten million dollars, the house, her condo, and additional items to be sold would add millions more.

Lloyd had one last matter to discuss. He thought long and hard how to approach her with what he considered *a delicate subject*. He knew how she felt about Henry and Julia Jerome; he had no idea how she felt about *Nicole*—her birth mother. He learned about her recall on *Profiles;* what he took away from the show was how she felt about her *Nana* and the parts her grandparents played in her life.

Little if any emphasis was placed on her birth parents.

Henry Jerome was one of the finest human beings Lloyd had ever met. They had been friends since growing up together, and he considered their friendship a rare blessing that few are fortunate to realize. Never giving up hope that he would find a way to get Jodi to remember who she was and where she came from, he kept Nicole's ashes so they could be given to her family for a proper burial. Sadly, it was not meant to be in his lifetime.

Once the revelation of Jodi's true identity came to light on *Profiles,* Lloyd was unsure of how to proceed. There was something in her voice as she spoke of her mother and the final minutes before the car exploded that caused him to think and rethink what he was reading between the lines. He purchased a copy of the show allowing him to play and replay her story of how their trip across country began and how it ended. It was so traumatic that for the next twenty years, she had no recall whatsoever of not only that awful last day, but the days before as they wended their way towards Los Angeles.

He placed a small urn containing Nicole's ashes on his desk and simply told Jodi there was yet another reason to be thankful for Henry Jerome. Jodi began to cry, softly at first and then she couldn't help herself as she sobbed in Sam's arms. Although she had no knowledge of Lloyd's thoughts, he was right. She had tried her best to keep her feelings about their trip to Los Angeles in check and dwell on having been reunited with her Nana instead.

Until that very moment, she had managed to do just that. Her world in New York consisted of spending as much time as possible with Nana, her love for Sam, and her job at *Profiles*. In the span of one year, the previous twenty years seemed to evaporate. Her life in New York was a one-eighty compared to Los Angeles.

She sat quietly as thoughts raced through her mind of when she was *Olivia*. What she remembered about the first ten years of her life—which actually translated into five years or a little more—were good memories. They included her parents and her grandparents as a close-knit family that surrounded her with love. She was happy, outgoing, and enjoyed spending time with them together or one-on-one. She had an extremely close and special relationship with each of them. Hardly a day had passed when a word or a gesture did not recall a particular time that brought a smile to her face.

Yet, she was well aware that she had not dealt with those last days with her mother driving cross country and ending in total disaster altering her life for twenty years. By the time, she was reunited with Lily, not only had she lost her father, but her mother and Papa Joe as well. She knew that her time with Nana would not be nearly as long as she would like it to be, and therein was the cause of the ache in her heart that she hadn't been able to erase. Caught up in work, their wedding, Sam and Nana, having to settle things in California, and simply living, she had not given as much thought as she probably should have to come to terms with these feelings.

Once composed, she apologized to Lloyd, explaining that he simply caught her off guard. She thanked him profusely for all his help in settling her parents' affairs, and the time he and Leslie spent with her and Sam. She told him she looked forward to seeing them that evening at dinner.

Jodi and Sam left his office; she carried the urn with Nicole's ashes in her arms close to her heart.

They had arranged a final dinner that evening which also included Rosy. They were due to fly back to New York at noon the following day.

Dinner was a wonderful upbeat evening. Everyone was in a good mood, and all the work and emotional ups and downs of the past ten days were put to rest. There were toasts to Henry and Julia; there were toasts to one another. The food and drink were good; the company was the very best.

Sam continued to extend invitations to come east to visit; they assured him they would. Jodi promised to call Rosy regularly to get the latest on the grandchild she was expecting—it was her first.

As they were leaving the restaurant, Lloyd took Jodi's hands in his and said, "For most of your life, Henry, Julia, Rosy, Leslie, and myself have been your family. Although you often referred to us as your *Guardian Angels*, you were ours. You brought so much joy into our lives. You were a *Miracle* for Henry and Julia; the child they were never blessed with.

"Leslie and I wish you and Sam a life of endless happiness and blessings. You are *family*, and we have every intention of staying close and in touch."

A round of hugs and goodbyes ended the evening.

The next day, the plane left precisely at noon for JFK Airport. Jodi settled back in her seat her arms encircling the urn that held Nicole's ashes. It had been a good trip, bittersweet and nostalgic leaving Jodi with a lot to think about.

Sam looked over at her and their eyes locked. She smiled and said, "I love you Sam Meyerson."

He replied, "I love you Jodi Meyerson."

The evening before Jodi and Sam were due to fly back to New York, Nina and Lily decided on a quiet evening at home. Since the beginning of the year, they had been consumed with arranging for the reopening of *Portraits by Lily*, the revamping of The Asher Foundation, and the many items on her personal to-do list.

It was hard to believe that an entire year had passed since reconnecting with Olivia and all that had transpired since then. Beyond her wildest dreams, she could never have imagined that finding her granddaughter would result in the miracle of *family* so late in her life.

They ordered in their favorite Chinese food and ate at the island in the kitchen, each commenting on how much they had accomplished while Jodi and Sam were in LA. They decided to retire to the Library to have tea and joked about opening their fortune cookies to see what was in store for them.

For a while, neither spoke. The TV was on, but neither paid attention. It was Lily who broke the silence.

"Nina, I know I don't thank you enough for all you do for me, but I want you to know that your friendship has been such a blessing to me, and I thank my lucky stars for you each and every day since you came into my life. You've become the sister that I never had as you filled in for the family I lost. I don't think I could have made it without you."

Nina agreed. "Nor I, without you. I think we were both lucky that day I walked into your studio with a picture of Danny in-hand to take you up on your generous offer. For ten years, I lived questioning how to satisfy my need to stay connected to my brother. In an instant I had the answer—a portrait of him that I could see each and every day seemed the perfect way. By then, Eric was quite sick, and I was unable to work fulltime while taking care of him. Your offer to work for the foundation came to my rescue once again, so I owe you my thanks for that as well.

"For both of us, 9/11 was supposed to be a day of celebration but became a cruel reminder of the evil that can befall us at any given moment. Having earned my accounting degree months earlier, I had recently received a promotion at work. It was Eric's idea to take time off and spend the day together. As promised, the weather was picture-perfect; a sunny cloudless sky and pleasant breeze seemed an omen of only good things to come. I will never forget how excited I was. I had a secret to share; I was pregnant. We were going to be parents in the spring.

"I never got to share that news with Eric. Our celebration never took place. Danny died that very day, and Eric began having health issues almost immediately. I miscarried less than two weeks later.

"In reality, we have been good for one another. And now, sharing your family with me is—using one of your favorite expressions—*icing on the cake*! This past year has been one of the best years of my life thanks to you. Nothing has made me happier than seeing your dream come true and finding Olivia.

"We have blessed one another with our friendship, and I could not love you more if we were sisters. I so look forward to Jodi and Sam's return tomorrow. I miss them. With Trudy and Charlie in Florida, things have become a little too quiet to what we've become accustomed to around here. However, we did get everything done we set out to do."

Lily could equate to Nina's pain; pain that eases when it lies dormant only to return raw and acute without notice. "Although it's been over twenty years, I never really mourned Noah. I don't think Joe did either. We were so worried about Nicole in the weeks immediately following 9/11, but as Nicole began to emerge from her depression, we hoped the worst was behind us. Once they left and seemed to vanish into thin air, all of our efforts going forward went into finding them, but sadly to no avail.

"When I lost Joe, I soon realized that for the first time in my life, I was truly alone. I did take time to mourn Joe, and during the process, the promise I made him is what kept me going. My heart was broken once again, yet this time it was different. I missed him terribly in every imaginable way from hearing him say *I Love You* numerous times a day to simply having him hold my hand or feeling safe and secure encircled in his arms.

"I returned to my studio and painting, took control of The Asher Foundation, and aggressively continued my search for Nicole and Olivia. The pandemic brought everything to a screeching halt. How ironic that in the end, it was the pandemic that brought Olivia home.

"Whatever time I have left on my long and wondrous journey, I plan to enjoy every single minute of it.

"I think we should let Jodi and Sam relax when they return tomorrow. We can ask what day would be good for them to come to dinner. I hope everything went well in LA, and they settled everything with her parents' estate. They seemed to be pleased with the way things were going when we spoke.

"I'm anxious to hear all about their trip, but I'm excited to share with them what we've been up to.

"I don't know about you Nina, but I'm ready for bed. Tomorrow is a new day, and I want to be up for it. Just think, by the time Trudy and Charlie return from Florida, they'll really have some catching up to do."

# Chapter 23

They returned from California the last week in March. It was spring, which had become Jodi's favorite season in New York. She looked forward to Lily's flower garden at the house that transported one to another place and time, and the array of annuals in the beds at the brownstone on Vanderbilt, recalling how she learned her colors from Lily and the flowers just as her father had.

Everything was in place for the reopening of *Portraits by Lily*. While Jodi and Sam were in California, Lily and Nina managed to make all the arrangements. They began by hiring a cleaning crew to give the entire space a much-needed once-over. Next, they hired a handyman to freshen up the paint in areas where needed, and in particular the walls that displayed her paintings. They ordered new supplies for the loft where art classes were held, and posted an announcement online urging those interested to sign up for lessons.

In the Gallery, Lily chose to display not only her own paintings but also a number of her mother's that were her favorites. With Art classes on tap to begin in a month, they interviewed and selected two instructors who were both children when their fathers perished on 9/11, and were previous students of Lily's. They eagerly accepted the invitation to teach but offered to volunteer their time, stating they would not consider compensation, viewing it as an honor to *give back*.

There were also plans to feature the work of local artists during the coming months both indoors and out; in particular, when the streets of West Village become alive with locals emerging from a long cold winter. However, 2022 was different. It would usher in a new and long awaited emergence from the two-year pandemic lockdown. New Yorkers were definitely ready.

In speaking with her neighbor merchants, Lily found them as excited as she was about the reopening, and many joined in by offering specials for lunch, featuring their own goods for sale, or simply celebrating bringing New York and themselves back to life once again.

A press release was sent to local TV stations announcing the reopening of *Portraits by Lily*—The Museum. Local newspapers picked up on the *buzz* and ran articles leading up to the big day. As time grew near, the excitement spread throughout not only West Village but also in nearby communities. Consensus was contagious that the pandemic was at long last making its exit. It was time for rebirth, growth, and change. It was time to reconnect with one another and move forward.

Their plane landed at JFK early evening. It had been a quiet flight home. Jodi even managed to sleep part of the way. As she slept, memories of happy times with her Mom and Daddy invaded her thoughts. Daddy was her *Hero*; he championed her accomplishments and never failed to tell her how proud he was of each and every one. Her Mom was her *Friend*; she treated her as an equal, not a child; those times with her Mom were the best. They loved her, and she loved them back.

Jodi held the small urn containing her mother's ashes securely on her lap.

When they arrived at the apartment, Lester greeted them and welcomed them back telling Sam everything he requested had been taken care of.

Walking into their newly redecorated apartment was wonderful. They were glad to be home. Sam arranged to have food delivered for dinner, and the refrigerator had been stocked with basics until they had time to shop and get back into a routine.

They called Nana to tell her they were back saying they would see her soon. Then they called Trudy in Florida; they hadn't spoken since just before leaving on their trip. The conversation was brief just to let her know they were home.

Deciding to leave unpacking until the morning, they showered and waited for dinner to arrive. Chinese cuisine was a good choice; it was comfort food. As they ate, they discussed the trip in general and agreed that with help from Lloyd, Leslie, and Rosy, they managed to get everything taken care of including the ultimate sale of the house by granting Lloyd Power of Attorney circumventing a return visit once it was sold.

For Jodi, it was bittersweet to see everyone, and revisit the place she called home for most of her life. They found themselves enjoying the time they spent together over dinner including their meetings to take care of business. For Sam, it was the opportunity to get to know Jodi's *family*. Although she was at first taken aback when Lloyd handed her the urn containing her mother's ashes, she was once again reminded how dedicated Julia and Henry Jerome were to helping her find her way home.

"Sam, I know I was quiet on the flight back and although I was a little tired, I was really lost in my thoughts about something I must come to terms with sooner rather than later. My feelings for my mother in those final days of her life weigh heavily on my mind, and now that my memory has returned, I haven't been able to forgive her or forget how her actions traumatized my very existence. I think that most of it comes from the fact that I will never know what made her come to the decision to leave New York, and travel clear across the country without confiding in me where we were going and why. She took me away from everyone I loved and the only life I knew.

"Nana never admitted her feelings to me, but I sensed that she and Papa Joe were deeply hurt by my mother's decision to leave, and ultimately their lives were as deeply affected as mine was. The grandfather that I loved and adored died, and I never saw him again. I lost two-thirds of my life with my beloved Nana. I'm well aware that people mourn differently— different circumstances, different relationships, and different personalities. She had no known relatives or friends in California. She hadn't lived there in years, and yet she left the two people who loved her, supported her, and welcomed her unconditionally into their hearts so cruelly.

"I was caught in the middle. After losing my father, I not only lost my grandparents, I lost my childhood, my friends, my Asher birthright, and in the end the only parent I had left. I can't even imagine what would have become of me if it were not for the Jeromes.

"I've decided not to mention the urn to Nana just yet. I think the time has come for me to explore the brownstone on Vanderbilt. It's long overdue. I'm going to go through the house thoroughly, room-by-room, memory-by-memory, and tackle my demons head on in an effort to find any and all answers to the many questions that continually invade my mind. I have to do this for me. I hope you understand."

Sam stood and gathered her in his arms. "Of course, I understand. I sensed your hesitation immediately when Lloyd handed you the urn. It isn't just a matter of burial. You must find a way to come to terms with your feelings, and I agree that the brownstone is a good place to start. For now, the house on Vanderbilt may be the only place that can offer answers to your questions. Perhaps it may shed some light on questions Lily may have.

"I love you and I want you to know that I am here for you always—to talk, to untangle your thoughts, to share. I'm just suggesting that you take your time and absorb everything slowly and thoroughly. When you're ready, I'm sure Lily will support you, as will I. Laying your mother to rest alongside your father will allow her the elusive and unanticipated closure she has long sought."

Jodi looked up at Sam and smiled. "Have I told you lately how much I love you Mr. Meyerson?"

"Yes, but I will never tire of hearing it."

The days flew by. Lily's reopening of the Studio and Gallery as a Museum was a huge success. She had originally planned to attend a couple of hours each day, but she was so buoyed by the response of so many people stopping by, she spent the better part of each day greeting friends and fellow merchants she had not seen in a very long time. In welcoming new faces and visitors that included many who were not locals, she expressed her gratitude and thanked them for their support. The weather was beautiful, and no mention of the pandemic or COVID was heard.

Each and every member of the *Profiles* crew came, and caught up in the excitement returned a second time. Many visitors were fans of the show eager to see the studio and gallery that had been a fixture in West Village for over seventy years. Those that got to meet Lily in person found her delightful. They marveled at the beautiful paintings she had chosen to show not realizing that her mother's paintings had never been previously displayed.

The streets of West Village were once again crowded like old times. The various eating establishments had visitors waiting on line, and the park was filled with young and old alike including their pets.

The reopening of the *Portraits by Lily* Museum was a total success.

Jodi decided to get started immediately on her project. Monday morning following the reopening, she set off for Brooklyn. The car service picked her up at 9:00 am. She took with her a few basic items to make coffee, bottles of water, and a few snacks. She had no idea how long it would take her to go through the house, so she decided to play it by ear as far as lunch was concerned.

It was a beautiful spring day, and she was anxious to get started. When she arrived at the brownstone, she noticed immediately that the annuals had not yet been planted—it was a bit too early. She put on a pot of coffee, and nibbled on a muffin while it brewed.

She decided to open a few windows allowing fresh air in. Although no one had occupied the house in over twenty years, it was neat and clean and seemed to be waiting for someone to return, perhaps from vacation.

Jodi wandered into the formal living room. It was a room they seldom used, unlike the formal dining room where images of Nana, Papa Joe, her parents, and their many guests quickly came to mind. Her mother was a good cook who enjoyed entertaining so there were many dinners around the long glass table, dinners that often included her friends. Through the glass doors of the hutch, she could see the elegant china and crystal that was used on more formal occasions.

The drawers below the hutch held the silverware, placemats, tablecloths, and napkins. Side cabinets held less formal dinnerware, serving pieces, candlesticks, and smaller items. Alcoholic beverages and glasses of all sizes filled the buffet cabinet. All was familiar to Jodi. She closed her eyes and pictured the table set with the beautiful china and crystal sparkling beneath the chandelier awaiting its guests.

The den was the most utilized room in the house, second only to the kitchen. It was furnished for comfort and use with its oversized plush sofa and Daddy's lounge chair. Once again she closed her eyes and envisioned him relaxed in his favorite space beckoning her to come sit on his lap while offering to read her a story. Tears began rolling down her cheeks. Wiping them away, she went into the kitchen for a second cup of coffee.

When she returned, she walked over to the fireplace. On either side were built-in shelves that contained books. On the left were novels that her mother *preferred* and history books her father favored. She smiled as she looked to the right. On the top shelf, her eyes came to rest on a small sign—*Olivia's Library*; the shelves below held all of Jodi's books from the ones that were read to her as a child to and including the ones she herself chose to read, as she grew older. It was Daddy who often read to her complete with animal imitations meant to amuse her, and they did when she was just a little girl.

A small desk in the den was her mother's. It was an antique lady's desk, a birthday gift from her Daddy. She was with him when he purchased it after seeking her approval of his choice. Jodi opened the drawer; there were stamps, note cards, and several pens along with a small 2001 Hallmark calendar book.

The best way to describe the kitchen was *bare*. The cabinets had long been emptied of any food items. The refrigerator that had been unplugged for years had only recently been turned on. The countertops were empty; any dishes, glassware, cooking pans, and utensils were out of sight behind cabinet doors.

Of all the rooms in the house, the kitchen loomed large in Jodi's mind. The very room that greeted her each day with the aroma of breakfast and her parents' smiling faces was a sad reminder of that last day when it appeared much as it did now etched in her mind as the first inclination that something was wrong, very wrong. Suddenly a chill came over her. Returning to the present, she decided to take a break.

It was just past noon, and Jodi opted to go out to lunch. A walk through the neighborhood would enlighten her to the changes of the past twenty years. She could play it by ear and grab a sandwich or salad along the way, but decided to go to Junior's. She entered the address in her phone as she left the house, and headed down Vanderbilt to Greene Avenue. She walked at a steady pace taking everything in; nothing seemed even vaguely familiar. Cutting over to Fulton, she continued to Flatbush Avenue and Junior's.

At first she found it hard to believe that there was not a single house or business or landmark of any type that she was able to connect to. She realized that having left as a ten year old who returned twenty years later as an adult had undoubtedly changed her perspective about what was, but also her expectations that everything would have remained the same.

The restaurant was moderately busy but she was seated without waiting; she ordered lunch. Her mind kept revisiting her morning going through the first floor of the brownstone. She was overcome with a feeling of having lost what was once a happy time in her life. She loved the house on Vanderbilt and everything about it. She loved the special times with just family and joyful times with guests.

She loved her pink bedroom most of all. With her mother's help, she had chosen each and every item with thought and care. In her eyes, it was perfect. The best part—it was hers. It held all her prized possessions, pictures, and her mementos of the times and many occasions in her life as they were celebrated.

She asked for the check, and on her way out, picked up a couple of muffins for the morning to leave at the house.

The walk back was quicker. She arrived at the house around 2:00 pm, and decided to continue going through the upper floors, which took no time at all. It was sad for her to see that the clothes in her parents' closets and drawers, and hers were still there. Suddenly she thought of Nana and her mood changed. Nana had been through so much. The thought occurred to her that it wasn't necessarily that she hoped they would return—that was certainly not true for her father. If it was consideration for her mother and her, the time had long passed for the clothes to be of much use. Jodi concluded that she simply chose not to deal with it.

She decided to call it a day. For the most part, she had accomplished what she set out to do, but on the other hand, so many new questions came to mind. For the time being, she decided to continue on alone. At some point, she and Nana would have to talk. They needed one another more than ever, and they needed to do this together.

She called the car service to take her to the apartment. By the time Sam came home, she had started dinner and was ready to tell him about her day.

Tuesday and Wednesday were pretty much the same. Jodi spent the day at the brownstone on Vanderbilt. She went through each room again and again recalling times that brought smiles and others that brought tears. For the most part, Jodi found nothing to help her understand her mother's decision to leave that awful day.

There was a small safe in the dressing area of the master bedroom, but its open door proved it empty. She was certain that Papa Joe and Nana had removed all valuables such as jewelry and important documents when it became apparent that they would not be returning as expected. Not a single place in the house came to mind where *secrets* might be kept. In fact, there appeared to be no *secrets* on Vanderbilt Avenue. Once again, Jodi got the feeling that her mother had made a last minute decision totally on impulse.

Arriving at the brownstone Wednesday morning, Jodi decided that it would be her last day searching for answers at the house. She decided to go down to the cellar to see what she could find, estimating that she could be finished by lunchtime and head home. It was actually Sam who brought up the cellar over dinner as she related how frustrated she was at not having found any answers to her questions.

She was glad to see that the cellar was well lit, and that it had been cleaned regularly like the upper floors had been. There were no cobwebs, no musty smell, and little dust. Several rather large brown boxes were neatly stacked along one wall. Upon closer inspection, she saw that they were all addressed to Lillian Asher, and had never been opened. One smaller box rested atop one of the larger ones; it too was addressed to Lillian Asher and never opened. Although the tape on the boxes had yellowed with age, the contents of each box remained firmly sealed. The return address on all of the boxes was the same—Zurich, Switzerland.

The first thought that came to mind was *How long have the boxes been in the cellar?* Immediately followed by *Why were they here at the house that belonged to her parents? Why had they never been opened?* And more importantly, *Did Nana know the contents of the boxes?*

Jodi could not believe that the thought had not occurred to her to check out the cellar. She couldn't remember the last time she had been downstairs. She knew her crib and other baby items were stored there; decorations for holidays like Christmas and Halloween also. And she recalled her father bringing the cushions from the outdoor furniture and smaller items in for the winter to be stored until spring. She had seldom been in the cellar and did not recall seeing the boxes.

She stopped to think things through. Finding these boxes put an entirely new perspective on her project. At Nana's behest, her lawyer transferred her parents' assets to her before she and Sam were married. The package he delivered contained the Deed to the Vanderbilt house and a list of its contents, her Birth Certificate reissued with the name Jodi added to it, her parents jewelry, their bank accounts transferred to her name, a copy of Nana's revised Will leaving the house on the Upper East Side and its contents to her, the education trust account Nana and Papa Joe set up for her when she was born, and control of the Asher Foundation.

Technically, she owned the contents of the house, and the boxes were in the cellar, but they did not belong to her and there was no mention of them on the list. Perhaps Nana had forgotten about them. She couldn't imagine that with everything else she had to deal with that the boxes would have come to mind. The little she knew about her Nana's life before she came to America only added to the puzzle. She knew for certain that she had an aunt and uncle in Switzerland who she went to live with after losing her family. That was seventy years ago. It was hard to imagine that these boxes have been in the cellar all this time and were never opened.

She checked out the remaining items along the far wall, and she had been right. The decorations, the baby furniture, and the outdoor items were all there neatly stacked and covered.

Jodi went upstairs, turned off the lights, and closed the door behind her. She headed straight for the kitchen and another cup of coffee. She went to the den and sat down in her Daddy's lounge chair, closed her eyes, and tried to make sense of the thoughts that had overtaken her. She would ask Sam for help. She desperately needed some of his good old common sense and gut feelings. Then she and Nana would have their talk.

After dozing off, she awoke feeling better and somewhat refreshed. Sitting in her Daddy's chair was comforting; she felt his arms wrapped around her keeping her safe and close to his heart. It brought back memories of how she felt as a child. She stared at the bookcase and the sign that read *Olivia's Library*.

Wanting the feeling to last, she remained in the chair. She turned her attention to the bookcase that held her parents' books. Her father favored New York history. He often took her to see what he called *New York's Treasures*, making each outing an adventure. She felt certain he would have been a big fan of *Profiles*. He particularly enjoyed sharing with her the books that were written about the projects he worked on.

Her mother preferred novels based on true experiences. She was a big fan of and liked nothing better than happy endings. Suddenly Jodi noticed a dark blue book on the top shelf. It didn't have a colorful jacket like the others, and the spine was blank. She got up from the chair, walked towards the bookcase, and reached for the book. Several small notes fell out and landed on the floor. Picking them up, she returned to the chair.

Slowly she lifted the cover. On the first page in her handwriting was:

Nicole Robins
New York Journal

Jodi's curiosity peaked. She began turning the pages of the Journal that were lined, but there was no calendar. All of the entries were dated by hand. The first entry dated October 14, 1983 was written on her flight from Los Angeles to New York. She wrote of having graduated from UCLA with a degree in Accounting, losing her mother to cancer, selling their house, and heading east to a new start. Her entries in the beginning were frequent. She found an apartment; landed a job with a prominent New York estate attorney; and enrolled in classes to prepare for the CPA Exam.

Weeks and months separated some entries and many were just one-line updates on her job and classes. An entry in 1984 stated that she passed the

CPA Exam on her first try, earning her a promotion. Her boss and his wife took her to dinner to celebrate and offered to keep an eye out for possible job openings to launch her career.

Her entry in 1984 two months after passing the CPA Exam stated that she had secured a position with the Asher Foundation. Her excitement at having landed what she called *the dream job of a lifetime* was evident in every word she wrote.

1984 proved to be a memorable year as subsequent entries outlined her meeting Noah Asher and their immediate attraction to one another, how they began dating, and ultimately falling in love.

Throughout 1985, her entries included their engagement, redecorating of the brownstone on Vanderbilt, and their wedding at Lily and Joe's home on the Upper East Side on September 11, 1986.

There were several entries during their idyllic Honeymoon in Hawaii, how happy they were, and their return to New York to settle into married life.

At times, entries were far and few between, but when an occasion or happening earned an entry, they were about her personal life. Business successes or occasions that occurred along the way were not mentioned.

There were entries of family dinners marking birthdays and anniversaries with special emphasis on times that were celebrated solely by Nicole and Noah. These entries were particularly heartfelt as she declared her profound love for Noah. She definitely felt loved in return.

Spring 1991—multiple entries documented they were expecting; their long awaited *addition to the family* was due in December. She revealed how they shared their news with Lily and Joe over dinner, describing their joy as *over the moon.*

Throughout the summer and fall entries detailed each visit to the doctor and how the pregnancy was progressing. When they learned they were expecting a *girl,* she mentioned a gift that a student of Lily's had given them—a pink sweater set complete with hat and booties that she had knitted.

They readied the nursery for the arrival of their first child along with grandparents-to-be—Lily and Joe. Each new addition to the nursery was documented down to the very last detail allowing one to envision the room although the entries were brief and to the point.

There were entries describing how she felt carrying the child she and Noah had longed for over the past five years since they were married. She wrote humorously how her constant *craving* for ice cream became a frequent adventure to seek out new places to try in the neighborhood.

She wrote of growing impatient waiting for the birth, but Noah assured her that their baby would arrive when the time was right.

The entry for December 17, 1991 was heartfelt and showed her excitement of becoming a mother. She and Noah were parents. She expressed her feelings in a poem called:

*A Mother's Love*

*How do I measure a Treasure?*
*Your eyes, your smile, your button nose*
*Your tiny fingers and toes*
*A complexion fair, curls of dark hair*
*All perfectly framed*
*And named—Olivia!*
*How will I measure my Treasure?*
*In a million ways*
*In a lifetime of days!*

Entries in the months immediately following Olivia's birth were jam-packed with excitement and awe of the beautiful daughter their love had created. Lily's gift of the picture of the three of them was recorded in a special thank you and tribute to both Lily and Joe.

Throughout the years leading up to 9/11, there were many entries mostly about Olivia. Jodi duly noted that not a single entry was one of disappointment or sadness. Only love and happiness and achievement filled the pages of the Journal.

Nicole's last entry was August 2001. Upon returning from a week's vacation in the Hampton's, she wrote that she looked forward to September—the month that was always *special* to the Ashers was *super special* in 2001. September 7th was Lily and Joe's Anniversary, and September 11th was Lily's 80th Birthday and Noah and her 15th Anniversary. In addition, she shared Olivia's excitement to return to school and her pet project—the school's newspaper.

To Jodi, it was apparent that the Journal was totally personal, and certainly not meant for anyone else's eyes. At times, it was as if Nicole was speaking to herself. At other times perhaps she was speaking to her mother

252

letting her know how well her life was progressing. Could she have felt guilt that her mother who worked so hard to provide for her had died just as her life was beginning?

The entries though brief and specific did not appear to be jotted down, so as not to forget. They were heartfelt and written with love that reflected her happiness. The entries that contained words of thanks and appreciation were particularly confusing since it was obvious the recipients of the words were never meant to see them.

Jodi began looking through the notes that had fallen out of the journal. To her surprise, the notes were quite the opposite of the entries. Many were in the form of questions that indicated insecurity, questions that threatened her happiness.

Although in her final entry, she wrote of looking forward to a *super special* month of celebrations, Jodi found no mention of any plans to celebrate Lily and Joe's Anniversary, their Anniversary, and Lily's Birthday. Previously, her entries of the pursuit of the perfect anniversary gift for Noah each year, were prominent, yet there was no mention of a gift in 2001 for their milestone anniversary.

Jodi found one note rather puzzling. It was an appointment with the Rabbi at their Temple dated almost three months after 9/11 and only days before their sudden departure to LA. She was unaware and surprised that her mother would seek to meet with the new young Rabbi who had only arrived and been introduced to the Congregation in early September. They had all attended Services that evening and Jodi remembered vividly Papa Joe's sadness that Rabbi Solomon was retiring and moving to Florida. They were longtime friends. On the other hand, there was no indication what the appointment was about or that she kept it.

Jodi was exhausted mentally and physically. It had been quite a day. It was 4:00 pm, and she realized that she hadn't eaten all day. Her love of coffee was entirely a morning thing; she needed that cup or two to get going. Anticipating that she would be finished at the brownstone by noon, she made no plans for lunch. She was more than ready to head home.

Before she left, she decided to return to the cellar and take pictures of the boxes as addressed, capturing the return address and any visible postal markings. She took one final shot of the boxes stacked along the wall. Returning to the den, she picked up the Journal, tucking the loose notes securely among the pages. Returning to the kitchen, she pulled a plastic bag she had noticed earlier from its container and placed the Journal in it, zipping it shut.

The car service was on the way. As she got into the car, Sam called. He had just arrived at their apartment.

Surprised that she was not yet home at 6:00 pm, he grew concerned. He had not heard from her all day, which was unusual. They agreed that she would call him so as not to disturb her in case she was onto something. However, in and out of meetings for the better part of the day, time eluded him. Relieved when she answered her phone on the second ring, he cheerfully asked, "Are you standing me up for dinner?"

Jodi laughed. "Never my love, would I do such a thing. I've had an amazing yet perplexing day, and I can't wait to share it all with you. Engrossed in what I found and learned, not only did I neglect to call you, I haven't eaten all day. Coffee is all that I have ingested. Needless to say, I'm starving and a bit wired.

"Some cheese and crackers, a bottle of wine, and a welcome kiss would be fantastic when I get home. I will tell you all about my day. We can make dinner together; I have everything we need ready to go. And to peak your interest further, I am even more excited about what I have to show you."

It was Sam's turn to laugh. "You have a deal. I can't wait. I promise by the time you arrive, cheese and crackers, wine, and my kiss will be waiting for you, although not in that exact order. Love you. See you soon."

As the car headed towards home, Jodi decided a change of plans was in order. She calculated that it would be close to 7:00 pm by the time she reached their apartment and well after 8:00 pm by the time dinner could be ready. She reached for her phone and called Luke's Lobster placing an order for their favorite—Noah's Ark—a Maine feast big enough for two, a large order of Lobster Bisque, and Sea Salt Kettle Chips. Then she told the driver they would be making a quick stop.

When Sam opened the door, he was surprised to see Jodi with a rather large brown bag that smelled delicious.

They decided to forego the cheese and crackers, stuck with the wine, and sat down to bowls of Lobster Bisque that were still hot. The soup was delicious. Jodi cleared the bowls and placed the *feast* in the middle of the table. As they ate, she started telling Sam about her day.

She began in the cellar. In telling it, she realized there wasn't much to tell. She found several large boxes and one smaller box stacked against the back wall. It was when she revealed that the boxes were all addressed to

Lillian Asher, all had the same return address—Zurich, Switzerland, and all had never be opened that Sam stopped eating.

"Did I hear you correctly? They were never opened? Are you certain? How long do you think they've been there?"

"Exact same questions I asked myself. None of the tape on any of the boxes though yellowed with age shows any sign of having been removed and reattached. Each box is firmly sealed. They are all addressed to Lillian Asher; the return address has no name, just a street address in Zurich, Switzerland. My first thought was that the boxes do not belong to me, although when Nana transferred the Deed to me, she stated that the contents of the house were mine, as well.

"I think she forgot about the boxes. I thought it odd that they remained at the brownstone after Nana no longer lived there. Why didn't she move them? Having never opened them, I would assume she knows the contents. I took some pictures before I left. I'll show them to you after dinner. The postal markings are very faded and barely visible, but maybe you can notice something I missed.

"I've been thinking a lot about the house that was the only place I lived with my parents. I loved every inch of it, especially my pink bedroom. I recalled so many happy memories all week as I visited each room. Although I was only ten years old, everything came flooding back to me. I could picture so many happy times with Nana, Papa Joe, my friends, my parents, and their guests—personal and business.

"That said, I don't see myself living there again. I don't think Brooklyn fits into our lifestyle. We are pretty much tied to Manhattan, and I like it here. I like the neighborhood, the convenience, the amenities; it's comfortable. What are your thoughts?"

Sam thought for a moment. "Honestly, I haven't given it any thought at all. I agree; we really have no ties to Brooklyn. I do understand what the house meant to Joe's parents, and it seemed perfectly natural to pass it on to Lily and Joe, and they in turn passed it on to your parents."

"The first day, I decided to walk to Junior's for lunch. I wanted to see if anything seemed the least bit familiar to me. Nothing did. Along the way, I stopped to speak to a man who was overseeing a delivery of appliances. He told me most of the brownstones on Vanderbilt, and the adjacent side streets have been converted to multi-family condos. The older families were long gone, replaced by young singles and couples investing in their futures.

"It must have cost Nana a pretty penny to maintain the place all these years, going so far as to continue having annuals planted each year in the front beds. My heart breaks for her and what she endured. She lost so much yet she carried on.

"I'm getting off-track here. My priority is to sort out my feelings towards my mother and lay her to rest beside Daddy. He was her whole world, and I don't think she'll rest in peace until that happens. I will deal with the boxes afterwards.

"It's getting late, and the rest of my day has revelations you could never have imagined. What is your day like tomorrow? Would it be possible for you to go in late? I really would prefer to show you what I found with a clear head after a good night's sleep."

"Tomorrow is good; my morning is pretty clear. I have a tentative appointment in the afternoon, but there's a good possibility it may not materialize. We did an excellent job with dinner. There's nothing left but the trash. If you take care of cleaning up, I'll take a look at the pictures you took of the boxes."

Jodi pulled up the pictures on her phone and handed it to Sam. He was right; there was very little cleaning up to do. She joined him in the living room and sat down next to him on the sofa. Neither spoke as Sam continued to zoom in on the postal markings.

All of a sudden, an excited Sam exclaimed, "Jodi, have a look. Am I seeing this right? It looks like they were shipped in March 1953. It's the same on two of the boxes. Assuming they were all shipped together, they arrived not long after Lily and Joe were married, and before Noah was born."

The markings were faded, but between the two you could see that the month and year were visible. "Wow. That was almost seventy years ago. Do you think the boxes have been there all this time? I wonder why she never moved them with her to the Upper East Side. That raises another question. What did my father know about the boxes?

"Let's go to bed Sam. I'm exhausted."

# Chapter 24

Jodi awoke to daylight and a sunrise that promised a beautiful spring day. She gently eased out of Sam's embrace and was almost to the door when he said, "Good morning my Love. Did you sleep well?"

"Oh Sam, I'm sorry I woke you. I tried my best not to. I thought I would put on a pot of coffee and see what we have for a quick breakfast before tackling what I have to share with you from the brownstone. Why don't you sleep in for a while? It's still early. I don't anticipate my discovery to be a long drawn out guessing game. My plan is to tell you my thoughts and then get yours in return, after you read what I have to show you."

"Okay, but I'm up, and I would just as soon get started. You have definitely peaked my interest with what little you have said, and if the situation were reversed, you would be bugging me to death to tell you everything—immediately."

Jodi threw her head back and laughed. "You're absolutely right; I would. I admit it; I have less patience than you do and my curiosity never fails to get the better of me. So let's get going. I'm going to brush my teeth. I'll wait until later to shower and dress."

Once in the kitchen, she removed milk, butter, and eggs from the refrigerator and placed them on the counter. Then she started the coffee. When Sam came in, she was seated on the sofa waiting for him. "Slight change of plans, but I'm sure you'll approve."

She motioned for him to sit down next to her. Removing the Journal from the plastic bag, she went through the pages and gathered the loose notes she had tucked in to keep them from falling out. "After going through the cellar, I went upstairs to the den and sat down in Daddy's lounge chair. Fond memories came flooding back of the times I spent on his lap as he read to me. It wasn't long before I fell asleep.

"When I awoke, it felt so comfortable sitting there that I made no move to get up. As I gazed about the room, I noticed a book on one of the shelves that was unlike the others. It had no cover like the novels and was unmarked. I got out of the chair and reached for it. As I did, notes on post-its and scrap pieces of paper fell to the floor. I picked them up, returned to the chair, and spent the entire afternoon going through what turned out to be my mother's Journal.

"You'll see, the lined pages are not a calendar, and entries cover a period of about eighteen years. It chronicles her early days in New York, meeting my father, my birth, occasions, and milestones in her life up to and including her last entry in August 2001. Her first entry was written on the plane as she flew east to begin her new life.

"I read all of it. I'm certain when I read it again, I may find something I missed, but for now I'd like you to go through as much of it as you can and get a feel for her words. Then when we compare notes, we can see if we both came to the same conclusion.

"While you are going through the Journal, I'm going to make Nana's pancakes. We can discuss it as we eat if you like. In the meantime, I'll bring you a cup of coffee and get started on breakfast."

Sam leaned over and kissed her. "You never fail to amaze. Sounds like a plan to me."

The pancakes were a big hit. Sam could not put the Journal down for even one minute. Jodi suggested he reread certain parts, in particular when her mother was pregnant, and especially the poem her mother wrote when she was born.

After clearing breakfast, Jodi joined Sam in the living room and began going through the notes again trying to connect them in some way to the entries she read in the Journal. They seemed removed and random, and indicated items needing attention. They almost appeared to be reminders of some sort.

They spent the entire morning quietly, reading, and engrossed in their own thoughts. As Sam continued reading the Journal, she decided to take a shower and get dressed. She called Nana to check in and told her she looked forward to getting together over the weekend.

It was noon by the time Sam finished reading. For a few moments, he sat quietly before speaking. "I did as you suggested; I reread several entries. I found her words to be poignant, heartfelt, and loving. Throughout, she expressed her gratitude to everyone who believed in her and helped her achieve her dreams. Without a doubt, she loved her family deeply—Lily, Joe, the *Love* of her life Noah, and you. The poem she wrote when you were born is beautiful.

"To me, it seemed more like a Diary. Her entries were personal making it clear she wrote them for herself. I don't think she meant it to be read by anyone else. I remember my sister keeping a diary; it was locked at all times. I'm sure she poured her heart out about each and every boy she liked, and would have destroyed it before sharing it with anyone, including her best friend.

"Perhaps she decided to document her new beginning because when she moved here, she had no friends and no one to confide in. At times, it also seemed like she had a plan, a type of bucket list. As she crossed off item after item, she simply entered it into the Journal.

"We haven't spoken about your feelings; I though it best to give you time and space knowing that when you felt ready, we would discuss it. When Lloyd handed you the Urn with your mother's ashes, I sensed the time had come. I don't know what you're looking for. Do you feel up to talking now?"

Jodi sat in a chair opposite Sam. "That day at Lily's when my memory returned, and I was once again with Nana was wonderful in every way. Yet when I listened to the replay, I heard hostility in my voice. Each and every question that I had asked my mother over and over and over all the days of the trip across country emerged clear and remained unanswered.

"For over a year, I have held onto that hostility unable and almost not wanting to let go. The mother I knew and loved, loved me back. I had only the best memories of her, that is until the trip. I didn't understand her actions as a ten-year old child, and I don't understand her actions now as an adult.

"The Journal does not answer any of my questions because it doesn't mention the trip, and there are no references leading up to it. Her last entry was four months prior to our leaving. That brings me to another thought. Although she mentions September 2001 as a month of milestone celebrations for the Ashers, no further entries are made. I found this odd and inconsistent with previous years.

"The Journal confirmed to me how much my mother loved me. I guess that's what I was hoping for above all else. Even if I never learn why she made the choices she did, I feel better knowing that our lives were not a lie. We were truly a happy and blessed family until 9/11 changed everything. Now Nana and I are reunited, and I'm looking forward to each and every day we have.

"I called her after I got dressed and told her we would get together over the weekend. I'm going to tell her about the Urn and ask what she would like to do. It's important to me to lay her to rest with Daddy. They had a special love that many never know, and she can finally rest in peace.

"We both came to the same conclusion that the Journal was personal. I noted that the entries documented happy, positive events and occasions. None were sad or disappointing. The notes on the scraps of paper are quite the opposite, so I may spend some time trying to decipher any clues they offer. At one point, I thought she was writing to her mother telling her of her new life and all she had accomplished. The entries though brief were genuine and heartfelt. If expressing her thoughts and feelings on paper made her happy, then I'm glad she did."

Sam put the Journal down. "Well, I'd say the days you spent at the brownstone were a success. I'm glad that you decided to do it, and I think it was best that you did it alone. For now, I think we should set aside making any decisions on the house. I agree; I can't see us living in Brooklyn.

"If you're wondering how Nana would feel about your selling it, I really don't think she would mind. I don't believe that the house meant as much to her and Joe as it did to his parents. I recall her once mentioning that Lou wanted to hold on to it because it represented their last ties to Brooklyn.

"I'm going to take a shower and get dressed. Then I'm going to call the office and tell them that I'm not coming in. It's a beautiful day, why don't we go for a walk and stop along the way for a light lunch? We can make what you planned for dinner last night together, and then spend a nice relaxing evening just the two of us.

"I almost forgot. You'll have to decide if you're going to ask Nana about the boxes in the cellar. I can't imagine that their contents are so insignificant that they have remained unopened for almost seventy years."

"The boxes do puzzle me somewhat. Although at first I wasn't sure, I'm now certain she knows the contents. I do think she may have forgotten about them, although she's as sharp as a tack so I may be wrong about that. At any rate, we'll ask and see what she says.

"I'll put the Journal away while you shower and dress. There's nothing I would like better than to spend the remainder of the day with you Sam Meyerson."

Jodi returned to Vanderbilt Avenue to go through the brownstone one last time. For now, all would remain as is. There was no urgency to sell or make any other decisions as far as she was concerned; the contents were memories of her childhood that she wasn't quite ready to let go of. By noon, her mission complete, she decided to move on. Locking the door behind her, she opted to walk through the neighborhood once again and headed toward her old school.

The streets were lined with well-kept brownstones and an abundance of trees whose foliage was about to burst welcoming the arrival of spring. Soon the landscaper would fill the flowerbeds of not only her home but also others with a bright array of colors. The image in her mind brought a smile to her lips.

A satisfying feeling came over her. She felt comfortable here on the streets of Brooklyn; the very same streets she knew as a child. It all seemed so long ago. She wondered what Nana's thoughts would be of her days as a bride moving into the brownstone on Vanderbilt eager to begin her new adventure with Papa Joe. Youth has its advantages—the best of which is optimism allowing us to believe that all is possible, within reach, and looking good.

Before she knew it, she was on Atlantic Avenue near the Barclay Center. She crossed the street and decided to have lunch at Applebee's. Before calling the car service and heading home, she crossed back over, entered the mall, and followed her nose to Auntie Annie's. Just out of the oven, she opted for two Almond Pretzels—her favorite. Taking the escalator, she went outside to wait for the car service to pick her up.

Saturday came quickly. Jodi had made arrangements to spend the day with Nana. Since returning from California, the reopening of her studio, and Sam having to get back to work, they hadn't seen much of one another. They made plans for the entire day; it would give them the opportunity to fill her in on their trip.

They arrived at the house to a warm welcome, breakfast ready and waiting, and the heavenly aroma of brewing coffee. Nina was headed to West Village and the Museum but she stayed to eat and visit with them for a while.

Jodi thought Nana looked a bit tired, but when she questioned her, she assured her she was just fine. They retired to the library with coffee refills, and they began telling her all about their trip to California.

Nana was happy to learn that they had accomplished so much, knowing that although the Memorial Service was Jodi's #1 priority, she managed to put her entire list to rest. She and Nina had watched the service along with the others who couldn't attend in person.

Finally, Jodi felt it was right. "I can't tell you how wonderful it was to spend time with Rosy and the Buchanans. We laughed a lot, cried a little, and though Sam was still getting to know them, it was as though they were old friends. Before we ended our last meeting, Lloyd took me totally by surprise. He handed me a small Urn that held my mother's ashes. Once again, Henry and Julia Jerome showed me how much they loved me, and even though they were gone, they continue to watch over me in the hopes of connecting me to my past.

"Sam will tell you, I was more than a little shaken by the gesture. Since you don't miss a trick, you may have noticed my hesitation whenever we spoke of my mother, especially about the last days we spent together. They were quite traumatic for me, traumatic enough to have blocked my mind from remembering the first ten years of my life for twenty years.

"When we returned to New York, Sam and I discussed the issue. I decided that the time had come to deal with these feelings by coming to terms with them as an adult not as a ten year old child. After determining that I could only do this by revisiting the past, I focused on Vanderbilt Avenue. My early years were totally connected to the brownstone; it was my only home, my school, my neighborhood, and the three of us were happy there.

"I spent this past week at the house going through the rooms and picturing our life; immediately wonderful memories came flooding back. I was optimistic that I might find even the slightest clue that would explain my mother's decision to make our ill-fated trip clear across the country; I did not.

"I was apprehensive that the house would evoke sadness or loss of what might have been; it did not. I love the house, and it was wonderful to recall the many dinners and celebrations we had around the big table in the dining room— always at its best to greet our guests. The only thing missing to make it picture perfect are the flowers that have not yet been planted.

"The best part was sitting in Daddy's lounge chair; I felt comfortable and secure imagining being wrapped in his arms with me on his lap as he read to me. In fact I fell asleep. When I awoke, I stayed there unwilling to break the spell that had come over me. As I glanced about, I noticed an unmarked book on the top shelf of the bookcase. It turned out to be a Journal that my mother kept on her new life in New York.

"After reading the entire Journal, and asking Sam to do so, we came to the same conclusions. It is extremely personal, written in the form of a diary, and not meant for anyone's eyes, other than her own. The entries are not daily; they are brief and to the point while documenting her successes, her happiness, her appreciation and thankfulness to those she loved and cared for. When I read her entry about becoming a mother on the day I was born, I cried.

"Her decision to go to California no longer mattered. I know that she loved me, and for whatever reason she chose to go, her love for me did not give her the choice to leave me behind. She lost my father, and the thought of losing me was probably more than she could deal with at the time.

"I brought the Journal with me, and I'm going to leave it for you to read. Nana, she loved you and Papa Joe so much. I hope after reading it, you will feel as Sam and I do. I would like to bury the Urn beside Daddy so that she can rest in peace eternally united. We don't need a Rabbi. Paying our respects followed by the Lord's Prayer will be heartfelt, and allow us to move on. We can plan for the burial sometime soon."

Lily smiled to herself. She was so proud of Olivia. "I'm glad you spent time at the house. I know you love it, and I still recall how excited you were when your parents told you your bedroom was due for a makeover totally at your discretion. I never knew they made so many things in *pink* until you and your Mom started buying furniture and accessories.

"We owe the Jeromes so much. They thought of everything. Laying your mother to rest will indeed be good for both of us. I'll call the cemetery on Monday and make the arrangements. I agree it should be only for family.

"I look forward to reading Nicole's Journal. We were extremely close yet somewhere deep inside, she felt the need to express herself on paper. Although in the beginning you sense that she wrote to herself, perhaps she altered her thinking and meant the Journal for you after you were born. If she did, it all worked out because now it is yours. You can read it whenever you have the urge to do so, and I am certain you will feel close to her when you do. When you have children of your own, you may even equate to some of her entries."

Jodi walked over to Nana and kissed her. "Thank you. It means so much to me that you understand my feelings, and that I had to deal with them on my own terms.

"Before she left, Nina told me there are several choices for lunch in the refrigerator. Why don't we eat at the island, and after lunch, there is one more item I would like your thoughts on. We can also decide which lucky restaurant will get our dinner order. Nina will be here for dinner won't she?"

"Yes she will. The Museum closes at 6:00 pm. She may be home sooner, but once you're there, you quickly get caught up in the enthusiasm of our visitors, and it's not easy to break away and leave. Before you realize how much time has passed, you've reached the end of the day."

They laughed at all the food that Jodi continued to place on the island. They opted for sandwiches; there were several choices and each made their own. Sam preferred a beer while she and Nana chose coffee. A large bowl of fruit and small cups were set aside for dessert.

While Sam and Jodi put everything away and cleared the dishes from the island, Nana returned to the library to wait for them. When they walked into the room, they found she had fallen asleep in her lounge chair. Jodi picked up the throw and covered her. Joining Sam on the sofa, it wasn't long before she fell asleep in his arms. He smiled as he looked down on her and made a mental note to ask his mother when she was planning to return to New York during their weekly call on Sunday. He missed her.

As they slept, Sam's thoughts were of the brownstone as he tried to imagine how almost impossible it would be for Jodi to connect to any of it. The fact that her life in the house had been as a child and seen through the eyes of a child would offer an entirely different perspective than how she would view it twenty years later as an adult while taking into consideration all the changes that had occurred in the surrounding neighborhood.

He felt Jodi had managed to accomplish her mission. Although she originally sought answers to her questions and none were answered in her findings, the Journal gave her insight to her mother she could have only grasped as an adult, and for that Sam was pleased; it allowed her to forgive, and by doing so, move on.

By the time Nina came home, and the sleepyheads awoke, it was late afternoon. They remained in the library talking about having turned *Portraits by Lily* into a Museum and incorporating it into the Asher Foundation. The nominal fee charged for visits would be used solely for art supplies for their students. All services such as art classes were offered gratis. There were no employee salaries; all teachers and guides were volunteers.

They planned to host art shows on the street during the spring, summer, and fall months by inviting local unknown artists to participate and sell their works, planning also to include their students. The property held Landmark status. *Portraits by Lily* would be her legacy of both personal achievement and to the colorful history of West Village.

Having made the decision to move the Asher Foundation out of the house to commercial office space was an excellent decision. The foundation had grown to such proportions that its day-to-day business could no longer be properly and efficiently conducted by a handful of people. Plans were in the works to increase the number of Board members, replace several current members, extend the legal and accounting departments, and introduce new and fresh ideas.

The move was planned to begin during the summer months with the goal of their first Board Meeting in their new space projected to take place after Labor Day.

At Sam's suggestion, a last minute decision was made to go out to dinner. They chose The Gray Hawk Grill—offering a variety of excellent dishes. The car service picked them up for early seating, and they were soon on their way.

Once they were seated and had ordered, Nina commented. "This year seems to have flown by. With all the changes and taking care of business that's been going on, we haven't been out to dinner for months. This evening is a real treat. Thank you Sam for suggesting it."

"You're quite welcome. And, you're right. The four of us haven't dined out since the end of last year. Of course, that doesn't mean we haven't eaten together because we have. By the way, lunch was delicious."

Their upbeat banter throughout dinner was fun. Nina was excited about all that was going on with the museum and the foundation's move. Jodi and Sam spoke of their trip to Los Angeles. They made plans to have Lily and Nina over to their apartment to see the redo, and Lily was quite pleased with her decisions to tie up loose ends. Dinner was excellent.

When they returned to the house, Jodi and Sam decided to stay for coffee. He let the car service go. It was a nice evening to walk back to the apartment.

When they were seated at the island with coffee in hand, Jodi said, "Nana, I want to ask about what I found at the house. At Sam's suggestion, I went down to the cellar. I don't remember having been there very often when I lived there, so the thought never occurred to me.

"The few items that I knew were stored there are pretty much where I remember them to be. However, along one wall there are several large boxes and one smaller one. They are all addressed to you, from Switzerland, and none have been opened. Upon closer examination, the mailing dates though faded and somewhat unreadable indicate they were shipped in March 1953.

"Do you know the contents of the boxes? Why have you never opened them? If this is none of my business, just say so. I'm sorry, am I overstepping here?"

Nana was not in the least surprised or upset. "Instead of answering your questions one-by-one, I'll just tell you about the boxes. Joe and I were married in September 1952. My Uncle Gus whom I lived with after I lost my family was supposed to join me in America, but circumstances prevented that from happening. He declined the invitation to our wedding stating poor health; shortly after we were married, he passed away.

"The boxes were sent to me by his attorney when they settled his estate. I was his sole survivor. From what I was told, the boxes contain artwork. My uncle owned a successful art gallery in Zurich. Before the war, he was an art broker doing business all over the world and frequently in New York. In fact, he had been to the United States several times. He set me up to come here, and it was with the help and guidance of his friends at the bank that enabled me to establish *Portraits by Lily*.

"I assume that the artwork in the larger boxes are paintings from his gallery that he still owned at the time of his death. After the war, he began selling off his vast collection in anticipation of our moving to America. The smaller box contains paperwork that includes sales receipts that prove ownership of the paintings. Without paperwork, genuine art cannot be sold legally.

"All financial transfers of funds, etc. were handled separately.

"When the boxes arrived, we had just moved into the brownstone; we were newlyweds, and the contents were the furthest thoughts from my mind. There just never seemed to be a need to open the boxes. Honestly, I haven't thought about them in years. I haven't been down to the cellar in years. I would never have moved them without opening them; since they were never opened, they were never moved.

"Let's plan to have lunch next week. When you can, go by the brownstone, pick up the smaller box, and bring it with you along with your recorder. We'll go through it together. Knowing how precise Uncle Gus was, I feel certain among the paperwork is a list of the contents of the larger boxes."

Jodi and Sam did not move. It was so quiet you could hear a pin drop.

On the walk home, they both spoke at once and Sam said, "You go first."

"I cannot believe it. Every single minute of every single day, I regret missing those twenty years with her and now after tonight, I keep thinking what if I hadn't gone down to the cellar and found the boxes? I can only thank God that she has lived this long and that all her faculties are in tact. I don't know if I can wait until next week."

Sam laughed. "It looks like you're going to have to. Maybe we should go to Brooklyn tomorrow and pick up the smaller box. That way, we'll have it at the apartment if she decides to move up the meeting. Do you think I'm included in the invitation? I would love to be there."

It was Jodi's turn to laugh. "I'm sure you're included. We're a package deal. Sometimes I think she loves you more than she does me. But that's okay in my book. How many different scenarios do you think I can come up with between now and our meeting? Sam, this is going to drive me crazy!"

# Chapter 25

Wednesday morning of the following week finally arrived. With the smaller box and recorder in-hand, they left the apartment and headed down to the lobby to await their Uber. With little traffic, and no weather problems, their short ride to Nana's took less than ten minutes. She invited them into the library where coffee and Danish sat on the table. Sam set up the recorder, and when they were seated, Lily began speaking.

"Located right on the Austrian-Hungarian border in the small town of Sopron the Sisters of the Holy Cross Convent had long been a significant part of the community. Established by the Catholic Church in an abandoned building, it was converted to a hospital, orphanage, and school run by the Sisters most who were assigned there as novices. Free standing and adjacent to the main building was the Chapel newly constructed during the original conversion, and although the Convent was privately operated, the locals often attended services on Sunday, took Confession, and sought advice from the Priests. All were welcome; no one was turned away.

"A week before Christmas in the year 1897, Sister Agnes entered the Chapel through a door behind the alter, to prepare for the morning Mass. To her surprise, beside the last pew at the far end of the aisle sat a German Shepard. At first glance he didn't appear to be hurt, and as she slowly continued to approach, he made no effort to stop her or to leave. As she grew closer, her eyes were drawn to the basket on the pew where a newborn swaddled in pink lay sound asleep.

"An envelope tucked into the side of the basket contained a note that she removed and read: *I am entrusting the Sisters of the Holy Cross with the care of my daughter until such time as I am able to return. Her name is Adele after her mother who died giving birth to her. I must report to my Unit, but I will return as soon as I possibly can. Please see that her birth is recorded in the church—December 19, 1897 born to Adele and Luca Kruger. I have enclosed what little money I have. If you could find it agreeable to allow Max to remain with you as well, I assure you, he will be no trouble. He is a loyal and good companion.* The note was signed *Lt. Luca Kruger.*

"Adele Kruger was my mother. She grew up at the Convent, and Max was able to stay with her until he died. Sadly, her father never returned. A cholera outbreak ended his life and resulted in the death of almost his entire Unit. Upon his passing, the Convent received his personal effects, which included a watch, two rings, and a faded picture of his wife, Adele's mother. The packet also contained a sizeable amount of money for her future. Adele was five years old.

"Sister Agnes was the one constant in my mother's life at the Convent. She took it upon herself to be personally responsible for her until her father returned. When she learned of his death, she became more determined than ever to take care of her, to teach her, and to encourage her.

"From a very young age, it was evident that she had artistic ability far beyond the norm. Her pictures hung throughout the Convent and visitors often commented on them. She was known to give what she called *feel better drawings* to patients in the hospital when she went on rounds with the Sisters and thought they could use cheering up.

"The years passed and Adele blossomed. She was a good student; she played the piano; she continued to expand her artistic ability; and everyone at the Convent adored her. She was a free spirit with only love and kindness in her heart.

"Sister Agnes came from a large Austrian Catholic family, whose many siblings lived in and around Vienna. As Adele approached the end of her schooling at the Convent, she discussed with her what she wanted to do with her life, what she saw in her future. She was overjoyed when Adele chose to study Art History. Her eldest brother was a professor at the University of Vienna, and she called upon him for his help.

"The Academy of Fine Arts Vienna would have been preferred, but at the time, women were not admitted. Through his contacts at the University, Sister Agnes's brother submitted her application, and she was accepted as a student of Art History, scheduled to begin her studies in the fall of 1914.

"The timing could not have been worse. The assassination of Franz Ferdinand on June 28, 1914, at the hands of a Serbian terrorist group led to the beginning of World War I. Exactly one month later on July 28th, the Dual Monarchy of Austria-Hungary declared war on Serbia. The war endured the entire four years she was a student at the University, ending on November 11, 1918.

"Before leaving the Convent, Sister Agnes told her how she had found the basket guarded by Max. She told her what she knew about her parents, gave her the note that her father left, and told her of his untimely and sad demise. Along with his personal belongings, there was a gold chain with a Star of David that had been in the envelope with her father's note indicating that her mother was perhaps Jewish. Left at the Church, she had been raised Catholic.

"The money that her father left her and additional funds that came from the Convent provided for her living expenses and tuition. It was sad saying *goodbye* to the only home she had ever known, but she eagerly looked to the future.

"Although she had been denied admission to the most traditional and prestigious art university in Vienna, Sister Agnes could not have been happier. They had found the perfect place for Adele.

"Vienna was not a combat zone, and its population was therefore never confronted directly by the war. It nevertheless left its mark on the city following the armistice in many different ways that challenged its inhabitants to endure great sacrifices as they found themselves caught up in a vicious cycle of uncertainty.

"To Adele, Vienna could be summed up in one word *freedom*. She quickly adapted to her classes eager to learn. She made friends her own age and together they explored the city as best they could under the circumstances.

"Sister Agnes's brother managed to get her an apartment adjacent to the school making it safer for her to attend classes. He implored his good friend Professor Anton Bruner to watch over her. They were student and teacher who quickly became good friends. She absorbed all that he taught her; he lauded her artistic ability and told her she had a bright future ahead of her.

"As they grew closer, they soon realized their feelings for one another were far stronger than friendship. As her professor, he agonized risking his entire career by getting involved with a student. He was fifteen years her senior, and he didn't want to appear to be taking advantage of her.

"Although Adele was young and naïve, he adored her. He was falling in love with her and didn't want to lose her. Anton confessed his feelings, and she admitted she felt the same way about him. They agreed to table their affections for one another until she graduated. At that time, if they still felt the same, they would enter into a proper courtship.

"Their love endured. Adele graduated. The war ended on November 11, 1918, and Anton was offered the position of Curator at Vienna's prestigious Museum of Art History as the city began its post war recovery.

He left the university; they were married in a small intimate ceremony with only Gus, Petra and a few close friends in attendance, and Adele became Frau Anton Bruner. They moved to the beautiful house where I was born and grew up. I was their firstborn, and they named me Analiese. Five years later, my brother Alexander was born.

"After my birth, my mother preferred to set aside her career and take care of me rather than hire a nanny. I had a wonderful childhood and to this very day, my memories of my life in Vienna are near and dear to my heart. My parents' love and care always made me feel special. Perhaps growing up in the Convent instilled in her the need to give her children a life of family.

"We were extremely close. She taught me to play the piano; she encouraged me to express myself by doing what I liked best. I never played with dolls, other toys, or had tea parties like most little girls. I only wanted to draw. She often packed a picnic, and we spent the day at the park or other public place where we could relax and sketch pictures together.

"One day in the park, I drew the baby asleep on the blanket near us. When I showed it to her, she was amazed at the detail and likeness that I had captured. I was only four years old at the time. After showing the drawing to my father, they agreed that I had a rare artistic ability, and they were determined to see that I had every opportunity to nurture my talent, if that was what I wanted. I did.

"During the time my mother spent with me at home, she became interested in art restoration. She researched the possibility of finding someone who could mentor her in Vienna and advise her how to move forward. My father suggested contacting one of the restorers at the museum. Karl Gorman and my mother hit it off immediately and under his guidance, she came into her own.

"By the time, Alexander was born, she was ready to return to work. When he was three months old, Hannah Spitzer joined our household. To Alexander, she was Nanny Spitzer but to me, she was a friend, and I called her Hannah. I started school, and although my mother was working, and I had my studies, we continued to have our outings whenever possible. At times, I would also accompany Hannah when she took Alexander to the park. She enjoyed watching me sketch as he slept.

"I lived in a world of privilege. My parents were dedicated to their work at the museum and their lives revolved around it. They were invited to galas and balls which were always formal affairs attended by the elite

271

of Vienna. Their closest friends were all connected in some way to the museum. Each year, my parents hosted a Christmas Ball at our home. Alexander and I had a secret place where we could watch the festivities. Closing my eyes, I can picture them waltzing; they were perfect together.

"My best friend was Tessa Gruber. We were inseparable; we did everything together. As teenagers, we experimented with makeup; giggled about the boys we had crushes on; and followed the trends in fashion that were liberating. We lived close to one another so we attended the same school. Her father appraised and authenticated artwork for the museum. Our parents were close friends, and our two families often spent time together. It was as though nothing outside the art world could penetrate our lives.

"When I was sixteen, my parents presented me with a choice of schools. My mother researched schools that offered dedicated art programs and found one in Zurich that stood out above the others. Although it was a boarding school, my Aunt Petra and Uncle Gus lived in Zurich which would allow me to spend weekends with them, making it easier on me leaving home for the first time. I was quite excited even though it meant being separated from Tessa.

"I loved my aunt and uncle; we spent holidays with them, and having no children of their own, doted on Alexander and me. They owned a small art gallery in the Zurich business district, but my uncle was better known as an art dealer brokering the sale of valuable paintings and art collections worldwide. His clients were the wealthy, the famous, the museums, and the institutions that paid him handsomely for finding what they sought.

"For the most part, my life was far removed from politics; my parents tried their best to keep it that way. Unfortunately, it was not meant to be. March 1938 saw the Annexation of Austria. I was at school in Zurich, and when I came home for the summer break, my mother had a surprise for me. She gave me a camera. She came up with the idea while using one in her art restoration process. It was an American-made Kodak—made right here in New York, a fact I didn't learn until I moved here.

"With the Nazi presence throughout Vienna, my parents urged caution wherever Alexander and I went. Originally, my mother's concern stemmed from noticing the attention the young soldiers paid the young women they encountered on the streets, but her concerns quickly grew far more apprehensive by their sinister treatment of the Jews.

"In the fall of 1938, I returned to school in Zurich; Hitler's anti-Jewish policies fell on fertile soil in Vienna on Kristallnacht November 9ᵗʰ. The city began changing overnight and though hostilities to-date had been solely against the Jews, my mother grew wary and worried constantly, not only for us but also for their Jewish friends.

"As Christmas and the end of the year approached, my parents made a decision about our holiday plans. For years, our routine was to spend Christmas Day at home in Vienna, and the week following skiing in the Swiss Alps with my aunt and uncle. As a family, we all looked forward to spending time together.

"My mother called Petra and Gus to tell them that I was to remain with them when school closed. They planned to spend Christmas Day in Zurich before leaving for our ski trip together. I never forgot the hesitation in my mother's voice when she called to tell me their change of plans. By the time the holidays were over, and my parents and brother returned to Vienna, I had set my worries aside. We had a wonderful time together as always.

"At the end of June 1939, I returned home to Vienna for the summer. I wasn't prepared for what I saw. The Nazis seized Jewish businesses and looted their belongings, while leaving in their wake shuttered stores and buildings, streets scattered with debris, and Austrians hurrying on their way with heads lowered.

"That summer, I grew up overnight. Horrified at what I saw and with a feeling of dread, I worried for my parents, for my brother who was attending school in the city, and the only way of life that I had ever known—one of kindness and love.

"I stayed close to home. When I told my mother I planned to call my friend Tessa and see if we could get together, she told me they no longer lived in Vienna. Her father was transferred; they had moved to Berlin months earlier. Other than that, they knew very little about the situation. I could not believe that she had not written to me to tell me of their move. The last time I had spoken with her was at Christmas.

"The summer seemed to drag on forever. Having broken his foot playing soccer, Alexander was frustrated with the cumbersome cast that kept him immobile. We both felt like prisoners in our own home. In August, my parents surprised us by renting a lake house in Salzburg for two weeks. It was wonderful. Alexander's cast had been removed, and the Lake Region was beautiful for sketching. There were no soldiers, and we all relaxed and enjoyed those final days before returning to school.

"By the time Christmas came, my parents decided to stick with the previous year's plans and spend Christmas Day in Zurich. I would go directly to Gus and Petra's from school, and my parents and brother would join us at their home for the holiday and then off on our ski trip. The only deviation would be a brief stop in Berlin for a meeting with Tessa's father.

"At the museum, my father was inundated with requests for inventory after inventory of artwork on loan to the museum and artwork that had been loaned out, in addition to the vast collection of famous and valuable artwork owned by the museum. All requests came from Berlin; all requests came from Tessa's father. My mother and brother would accompany him, spend the night in Berlin, and travel to Zurich the following day.

"On December 22, 1939, they boarded a heavily laded D180 Express train from Berlin to Genthin, Germany, where they would change trains and travel on to Zurich. Christmas Day 1939 fell on a Monday, which many families and soldiers planned to use as a long weekend.

"As the train approached the Genthin Station, the preceding D10 Express was late leaving, having been delayed by patchy fog. The D180 slammed into the rear of the D10 with such force that coaches were hurled upwards, landing on top of the locomotive. There were 453 injured and 278 fatalities—my mother, father, and brother included.

"It wasn't until the next morning that my uncle learned what had happened. As we waited for them to arrive, and it grew later and later, there wasn't much we could do about it. The electronics we take for granted today were unavailable—a part of the distant future. And we were at war.

"If it weren't for Petra and Gus, I cannot imagine what would have happened to me. It took weeks to learn what happened; it took months to settle their affairs. They were cremated; we scattered their ashes in Switzerland; we said our goodbyes.

"I returned to school, and threw myself into my art; it kept me close to my parents. The three of us settled into a quiet way of life. Removed from the horrors of war was a blessing. The headlines were dominated by Hitler's invasion and occupation of country after country. Although Switzerland was neutral, there were Nazi soldiers everywhere.

"I had but one goal—finish school. I had entered the art program at the University of Zurich in the fall of 1939. I tried desperately to live in the present, but the past never left me. The ache in my heart never subsided. I missed my parents and brother with every ounce of my being. And the business meeting my father had in Berlin haunted me without end.

"What could have been so important in the art world that would require him to travel to Germany mere days before Christmas? If not for that meeting, my parents and my brother would still be alive. Tessa's father had requested and scheduled the meeting. I had no idea what his new position was or why he would be meeting with my father.

"It was a beautiful fall day in late October, and I had been running a few errands between classes. I decided to take a break and stop at the café in the next block for a coffee. As I approached, I noticed a small party of soldiers seated at the corner table. One whistled; another asked me to join them; and a third called my name. As I heard, *Analiese, is that you?* I turned, and there stood Theo Gruber, Tessa's older brother, in a Nazi uniform.

"The sight of him in the uniform left me speechless. He invited me to sit with them. When I didn't respond, he asked if he could get a table for the two of us, and I simply nodded. Once we were seated and our order was taken, he offered his condolences. Much to my surprise, he didn't stop there but continued telling me that he had seen my parents and brother when they were in Berlin. In fact, his family and mine had dinner that evening.

"The meeting my father attended was to inform him that he too was being transferred to Berlin and assigned to the team that would be acquiring and assessing artwork for the Fuhrer's grand vision of Germany's place in the world of art under The Third Reich.

"Again, I was speechless. I had no idea that the situation had grown so bad. It seemed as though my father had not been given a choice; it was an ultimatum that he couldn't refuse. The sunglasses I wore shielded the pain in my eyes from Theo's sight. I was devastated. After all the weeks and months of wondering about the ill-fated trip, I had the answer that I longed for. It didn't ease my pain; it added to it.

"Suddenly, I stood. I had to get away from there. I needed time to think things through. Excusing myself, I told Theo that I had to leave; I was due back at school. He was visibly upset at my reaction to his news, but he mistakenly attributed it to mourning for my family. I hurried off without looking back.

"Two days later, he showed up at my uncle's gallery inquiring about me. I was due home that evening for the weekend. Without knowing about our meeting, Petra invited him for dinner. There were many occasions when my aunt and uncle while visiting in Vienna were in the company of his family. They knew him, and they knew that his sister Tessa was my best friend. In fact, she had visited me in Zurich before the war.

"He was not Jewish; he was an Austrian who was now living in Berlin. To Petra and Gus, the sight of Theo in a Nazi uniform seemed perfectly logical. In the back of their minds, they thought perhaps getting reacquainted with Tessa would be good for me and help ease the pain of losing my family. As teenagers, we had shared everything including our deepest thoughts.

"Theo was there when I arrived home. Surprisingly, I was not as unsettled as I had been earlier, and dinner was nice. We spoke of random things that had nothing to do with the war, and shared more laughter around the table than we had in a long, long time. Petra was an excellent cook, and as each bottle of wine was emptied, Gus quickly produced another.

"We learned that Theo was only in Zurich on assignment. He was due back in Berlin in two days. He promised to keep in touch, and said he couldn't wait to tell Tessa. Thanking my aunt and uncle profusely, he thanked me as well for welcoming him. He left. After he had gone, I helped Petra clear the table and put everything away. As we worked together, she commented on how grown up and handsome he looked in spite of the Nazi uniform. I was thinking the exact same thing.

"I received a phone call from Tessa days later, and it was wonderful. I missed my old friend more than I realized. She promised to call again soon, and we gave thought to meeting for a visit possibly after the first of the year. Two months passed before I heard from Theo again. He told me he would be in Zurich the second week in December and invited me to return to Berlin with him for a visit. He was aware that Christmas would be the first since the accident, and assured me that I would be home in time to spend the holidays with Petra and Gus.

"I was pleased at the prospect of seeing Tessa, her family, and Theo. I promised to discuss it with my aunt and uncle and get back to him. At first, they were apprehensive. They had no idea what it was like in Berlin. They only knew what they saw and heard from news reports, and one could never be certain of their accuracy. However, they felt my excitement and agreed to let me go.

"The Gruber home in the Westend neighborhood of Charlottenburg, a district that sits in the central-western part of Berlin, was beautiful. It reminded me of Vienna and the home I grew up in. It was wonderful to see the Gruber family after all the time that had passed. Tessa and I were so happy we couldn't stop crying. I travelled to Berlin with Theo in an official

Government car. During the trip, he told me that he was elated that I came and promised surprises beyond my imagination.

"He certainly did not disappoint. The first night, we ate in. In addition to the Grubers and myself, another guest, a young man by the name of Karl Kessler joined us. Invited by Tessa, she considered him her *boyfriend*, and had been seeing him for several months. The next day as we shopped for last minute gifts, Tessa gushed with the news that she was in love. He too wore a Nazi uniform and was currently on duty in Berlin.

"Never one to hold back her thoughts, she openly stated that Theo and I were a beautiful couple. Our dark hair and blue eyes suggested we might be sister and brother, but we were not. When I protested saying that Theo and I had never been on a date, and that I had no idea that he saw me as a potential romantic interest, she laughed, reminding me that it was he who had extended the invitation to visit.

"When we returned home from shopping, I learned that we were leaving the city and travelling overnight to the Obersalzberg, a scenic mountainside spot above the town of Berchtesgaden, where we would be staying overnight. Saturday evening we would be attending a holiday party. Tessa gave me a choice of dresses for the event and told me not to forget to take my camera.

"In the 1930s, after becoming the German chancellor, Adolph Hitler was looking for the perfect spot to establish an official mountain retreat—a Camp David for his Nazi regime. He chose Obersalzberg, a few miles uphill from the town of Berchtesgaden. The region of Bavarian territory juts south into Austria, long considered one of the classic Romantic corners of the world.

"For his official retreat, Hitler had a modest chalet renovated into a supersized alpine farmhouse and named it the *Berghof*. He considered it the ideal setting for crafting his public image. By 1936, German media was awash in photos of the Fuhrer in Obersalzberg, surrounded by nature, gently receiving flowers from adoring children or fraternizing with farmers in lederhosen. No modern arms industry, no big-time industrialists, and no ugly extermination camps existed.

"Party leaders soon took over the rest of Obersalzberg as their own vacation spot. It was home to a huge compound of 80 buildings connected by extensive bunkers where the major decisions leading up to World War II were hatched. Hitler himself spent about a third of his time as chancellor at the Berghof, hosting world leaders in the compound, and later had it prepared for his last stand.

"The town of Berchtesgaden is synonymous with Hitler's *Eagle's Nest*, which actually refers just to the small lodge itself, perched atop the summit of the Kehlstein amid spectacular scenery like a villain's lair. Built in 1939, it was Hitler's 50th birthday gift from his inner circle. Afraid of heights, it is documented that he only visited a total of 14 times. While Nazi officials met and hosted diplomats, and Eva Braun was fond of sunbathing on the terrace, it never had any beds.

"Until that night, I could not remember ever being as excited as I was dressing for the party at the Berghof. The dress I had chosen to wear was a steel blue that accented my eyes. When Theo arrived to pick me up, he stood staring at me for what seemed longer than it actually was before he finally told me I was beautiful, absolutely beautiful. I never had a boyfriend. It was a new feeling for me, and I loved it. Although he wore his uniform, he truly was quite handsome. I smiled as I briefly recalled Tessa calling us a beautiful couple.

"The chalet was decorated for Christmas. There was more than ample music, food, and drink. There were women in beautiful dresses and men in uniform everywhere. I had my camera, and I began taking pictures. As I angled to take a picture of Eva Braun, a voice spoke to me. I turned and there beside me stood the Fuhrer. Theo quickly came to my aid and introduced us. At first, I thought he was going to ask me to put my camera away, but he did no such thing. Instead, he asked that I take a picture of him with Eva Braun.

"After I took the picture, he asked me about my photography. We spoke at length about my art studies, how my mother introduced me to painting from a photograph, losing my parents and brother, moving to Switzerland with my aunt and uncle, and the Grubers who were our neighbors in Vienna.

"When I thought our conversation was over, he began to tell me about himself and actually compared his experiences to mine. He too was born in Austria. His father envisioned a job in civil service for him but it was not to his liking. At the age of six, he began attending school, but he was uninterested in a formal education, and he left school with a poor educational record of achievement. The death of his father when he was 13, released him from the pressure of seeking a government job.

"He found himself free to pursue his preferred choice of study, that of art. He attended art school and regarded himself as an artist, absorbing diverse cultural influences such as opera, theatre, reading, and drawing. He moved to Vienna with the aim of attending the Vienna Academy of Art, but his application was rejected. The very school my mother could not attend because women were not admitted.

"His disappointment was compounded by his failure to get into the Vienna School of Architecture due to his inability to provide a school leaving certificate. He struggled to survive in Vienna, living in a men's hostel, and selling postcards, which he drew of famous sights. At the outbreak of World War I, he volunteered for service in the German army. He distinguished himself in service, was promoted to corporal, and decorated with the Iron Cross. He never returned to study art, but his love for the arts never waned. The opera, theatre, reading, and drawing remained with him always.

"One could say I was naïve or possibly just plain stupid. In my defense, I was unaware of the extent of Nazism and only learned years later what Hitler's Third Reich inflicted upon the world. The man I spoke with that evening could have been anyone.

"For that night and that night only, I was on top of the world. I fancied myself in love with Theo—my first love. I had reunited with my best friend. Being with her family brought back good memories, and I welcomed them with open arms. The past year had been a nightmare. I was doing well in school, and my aunt and uncle were doing the best they could under the circumstances to keep us together and safe.

"When I returned home, I had my film developed. I painted three small portraits of the Fuhrer and Eva Braun. I had them framed and set aside to give to Theo to deliver for me. I told my aunt and uncle about my weekend and showed them the photographs that I had taken.

"As I relived minute by minute my reunion with Tessa, the party at the Berghof, and the days I spent in Obersalzberg, I noticed the horrified look on their faces. Staring at the pictures of the high-ranking Nazis that surrounded Hitler was terrifying to them. As my uncle put it, what possible good could come from my associating with the likes of the Third Reich? We were not Nazis, and he reminded me that my parents had not embraced Hitler's coming to power either. He didn't have to remind me how concerned and worried my parents had been when Austria was annexed.

"In no uncertain terms, he told me there would be no more trips to Berlin. He apologized for having welcomed Theo into our home when it was quite evident that he was one of them. Petra agreed with him, and they both implored me to stay away from him.

"I was taken aback at their reaction. There was nothing in the pictures that had anything to do with the war. It was a social gathering to celebrate the season. It reminded me of what life was once like in Vienna before I lost my family. For days, I sulked. I hated to admit it, but I really had feelings for Theo. If they objected to my going to the Nazi parties, I could accept that. What I didn't want to accept was not seeing Theo again.

"Several weeks passed before I heard from him again. He was in Zurich for a few days, and we met at the Café. Without revealing Petra and Gus's true feelings, I told him they felt I was too young to attend such parties. Admitting that he liked me and wanted to continue seeing me, he agreed there would be no more parties. I gave him the paintings, and he assured me he would deliver them.

"From October 1940 when I ran into Theo in Zurich and my last visit in the fall of 1941, I travelled back and forth to Berlin a handful of times. My aunt and uncle were not happy about it, but I went primarily to visit Tessa and stayed at their home. For the most part, Theo was not there. However, whenever he learned I was in Berlin, he came to see me and we went out—to dinner, to cabarets, to local parties. We were with young people like ourselves, and we had fun.

"As we were dancing one evening at the Eldorado Cabaret, the most famous in all of Berlin, Theo told me he loved me. As he held me close, he told me he looked forward to the war ending. He had earned a degree in Accounting at the university just prior to the war, and although he was now using his skills working with his father on the Fuhrer's Art Program, he preferred to open his own practice. Suddenly, he stopped talking, stepped back, and said: Analiese, *do you love me too?* I answered with my kiss. I was over the moon.

"I hated myself for it, but I did attend gatherings at the Berghof and even a couple at the Eagle's Nest. The events were social, never official business, and although high-ranking Nazi officials attended them all, to me they were entirely celebrations with good food and drink, and fine music offered simply for the guests' enjoyment. I justified my attending with the fact that each time I went, I was Theo's guest. I was never invited on my own.

"I never had another conversation with the Fuhrer other than him thanking me for the portraits I had sent. Eva Braun thanked me as well. I continued to take pictures but began including shots of the buildings and surroundings. I did make it a point to send copies of photographs of certain high officials and their wives that I thought they would perhaps enjoy. I was of no consequence.

"As in all conflicts, there is a turning point, a point of no return. As Germany continued its aggressions, their successes mounted until June 1941; ignoring the peace pact, Hitler instituted Operation Barbarossa and attacked Russia, opening itself to a two-front war. When Japan attacked Pearl Harbor in December 1941, America entered the war on both Asian and European fronts.

"My last visit to Berlin was in early December 1941; they ceased for several reasons. Shortly after the holidays, Petra was diagnosed with cancer; it brought me back to reality. I was ashamed for having betrayed my aunt and uncle's trust. It was no surprise to learn that they had suspected all along that my visits to Berlin were not to see Tessa. I threw myself into taking care of Petra. Gus stayed with her when I attended my classes and left for the gallery when I came home. I took over running the house; I ordered groceries, cooked, and followed the doctor's instructions to keep her comfortable and as free of pain as possible.

"When Petra passed away, Gus and I clung to one another. I promised him that I was not going anywhere. I was on course to finish school the following year. As we waited for the war to end, we agreed to spend our time getting the gallery and our belongings in order so we could make plans for the future. From time to time, my uncle began talking about the two of us going to America. He had numerous contacts in New York and told me endless stories about his visits to the city. He told me repeatedly that I would love it here, and he could think of no better place for my career.

"As Germany began retreating, Hitler became enraged and trusted no one. In the final months of the war, Tessa called me and I learned that Theo had been sent to the front to fight. I never heard from him again; I never heard from Tessa again. I learned their beautiful house in Charlottenburg was destroyed when the Allies bombed Berlin in May 1945.

"On May 8, 1945, World War II came to an end in Europe. As news of Germany's surrender was celebrated around the world, the real horrors of The Third Reich began emerging. When the rumored concentration camps proved unbelievable reality, the Allies moved quickly.

"The Nuremberg Palace of Justice was established. Known as the Nuremberg Trials, the crimes charged before the court would include crimes against humanity, and conspiracy to commit any and all war crimes.

"Many felt that the Nazi's highest authority, the person most to blame for the Holocaust was missing at the trials. Adolph Hitler had committed suicide in the final days of the war, as had several of his closest aides. Others were never tried. Many fled Germany to live abroad, including hundreds who came to the United States.

"As my uncle began clearing the gallery in preparation for our move, he enlisted my help. He kept impeccable records of the artwork sales he brokered, as well as paintings sold in the shop. In the early days of the war, Jews that had relatives in America or elsewhere they could flee sold artwork to raise funds for their passage. Unable to deny anyone that came to him, he purchased over two-dozen paintings.

"Each had a recorded bill of sale and each identified him as the legal owner. I was tasked with researching the possibility of reaching out to the original owners to see if they were interested in buying them back. As impossible as it first seemed, it turned out rather well. Attorneys that were trying to retrieve artwork that was stolen were happy to work with us resulting in not all, but most of the paintings going back to their original owners.

"The house was far more difficult. There were too many memories, and it was the only place Petra and Gus called home. We decided we would go room by room, but it didn't work out that way. He was reluctant to pack anything up, and we continually moved on without finishing.

"That is until he came to a small room that I used to store my things. We began opening box after box of the hundreds of photographs I had taken at the Berghof and the Eagle's Next. I had never shown them to him and Petra because I wasn't supposed to be seeing Theo, and they had basically forbidden me to attend the Nazi gatherings. I promised I wouldn't. He noticed that the photographs of the rooms clearly displayed artwork and various collectible items of great value.

"After looking so intently and commenting on the artwork, I was quite surprised when he asked if I could identify the people in the pictures I had taken. For the most part, I could. The attendees at the parties I attended were always the same. Perhaps a new face here or there at most.

282

"From that day forward, Gus came up with a new plan. He contacted the American Headquarters in Berlin and arranged for a meeting in Zurich. Capt. John Montgomery arrived two weeks later. He introduced himself and asked that we call him *Jack*. He was quite personable. He was tall and handsome with a smile that lit up his face. He hailed from Austin, Texas, and I was fascinated by the southern drawl he had picked up, telling me he was not originally from the south.

"Before coming to Zurich, Gus had explained to him why he was requesting a meeting so we got down to business without further delay. Jack listened intently as my uncle told him our story, and how I came to take the photographs. Although I had not been privy to any inside information regarding the Third Reich, he thought my photography was excellent.

"Not only were the pictures of the Nazi officials useful, but the ones of the rooms and the surrounding areas of both the Berghof and the Eagle's Nest attracted his interest immediately. As he explained, they were quite rare. They were a first for him, and he assured me would be useful.

"The Berghof was completely destroyed by the RAF in a daylight raid in April 1945, less than a week before Adolph Hitler and Eva Braun committed suicide in their bunker below. During the same raid, the Eagle's Nest, which proved too small and elusive, managed to survive the attack without damage.

"Over the following months, there were additional meetings, and Jack brought others with him. All were in Switzerland; my uncle explained that he wanted to spare me returning to Germany. Jack understood and respected his wishes. I identified the high-ranking officials who were well known and others whose names were known but not their faces. Some were in custody; many had left for places unknown.

"It was evident that Jack and Gus liked one another immediately. At one point, my uncle took him to the Gallery and explained how he was working to get the artwork he had purchased back to the original owners. I think Jack not only liked Gus, he respected him and admired him for what he was doing for me—something I knew nothing about.

"The best known of the Nuremberg trials was the Trial of Major War Criminals, held from November 1945 to October 1946. Subsequently, the United States held twelve additional trials of high-level officials.

"Jack requested that we remain available during that time in case we were needed. I continued to pack up my things. Whenever I questioned Gus about his lack of interest in clearing out the house, he simply deferred to biding his time until we could make plans and book passage to the States.

"1947 arrived and with it came the realization that Gus' plan was not to my liking. On a cold January evening as we ate dinner, he told me what he had done. In exchange for my photographs and information, he had an agreement with the United States Government that would assure my future.

"For my protection, I would be given a new identity and relocated to New York. My uncle through his connections would put me in contact with friends who would help me get settled and embark on my new life. Stating he needed more time to close up the house and gallery, he would join me as soon as he could. I knew deep in my heart, he would never leave Switzerland, Petra, and his memories.

"In September 1947, as Lillian Austin I flew to New York on a military plane to begin my new life. I had a Passport, Birth Certificate, Social Security Number, and a Chase National Bank Account—all bearing my new name. An apartment awaited me at the Barbizon Plaza Hotel for Women, and I had the name and phone number of the person I was to contact—John Shepherd. I never saw my Uncle Gus again, although I did speak to him by phone, and corresponded regularly. He came to my rescue when I lost my family, and for a second time, he gave me a future, a life—and what a life it has been.

"My Uncle Gustav Bruner was my father's older brother, and I loved him like a father. The only downside to my leaving Zurich was that he was not coming with me, but I promised him that I would make him proud. He never left my thoughts during my early days in New York. I wrote him regularly and kept him apprised of every step I took. My letters were posted through Chase Bank with their return address and my new name was never written on them. Each was signed using my father's nickname for me—*Schatzi* meaning *Little Treasure*.

"He was too ill to come to our wedding when Joe and I were married. Once I left, and he was alone, his health deteriorated. He died two weeks later. It wasn't until the following March that his house and gallery were sold, and the boxes in the cellar were shipped to me. Along the way, I recall being told that the larger boxes held paintings, and the smaller box held paperwork. I don't have a reason why I never opened them. I just didn't. I didn't want anything from the past to mar the happiness in my new life, or open old wounds."

Lily stopped speaking. Sam turned the recorder off and said, "Are you okay? Let's take a break and stretch our legs."

Lily sat quietly, her mind a million miles away. She closed her eyes and envisioned Theo in his uniform. She loved him so. When she was with him, she felt safe and protected, especially encircled in his arms as they kissed or danced. He couldn't possibly have been like them. Not her Theo. Suddenly she began to cry. As Jodi came towards her, she motioned her away.

"I never learned what happened to Theo or to the rest of the Gruber family. I've carried the burden of having identified Theo, Tessa, and their parents in the photographs I gave the Americans, perhaps sealing their fates. I followed the trials while in Europe, but once I came to New York, I thought it best to leave my past in the past.

"In the spring of 1952, an article appeared in the New York Times stating that the remains of the former political residence of Adolph Hitler known as the Berghof had been destroyed. On April 30, 1952—what would have been Hitler's Birthday—a massive explosion leveled the bombed out shell of the building.

"Only once did I speak of what I have related to you today. I told Joe when he asked me to marry him; we had no secrets between us. We never spoke of it again.

And now that I have told you, it is my wish that we do the same. Analiese has been gone for longer than she existed. I think it is safe to say there is no one alive today that would know her or know of her.

"The tape has all the facts. It's important to know your roots, and where you came from. Growing up in the Convent left my mother knowing virtually nothing about her background. I lived my life as Lily Austin Asher and that's the way I want to be remembered. For almost 75 years, I have called New York my home; Vienna and Zurich have faded away.

"Even after all these years, there are some memories that are best left in the past. The blessings in my life have far outweighed the losses. Joe's death was by far my greatest loss because I was left alone to deal with it. When I lost my family, Petra and Gus were there for me. When we lost Noah, Joe, Nicole, Olivia, and I had one another. Losing Joe could have broken me, but somehow it made me stronger and more determined than ever to find you and your mother. Now here we are.

"We have definitely earned a break. There are several choices for lunch in the refrigerator. After we eat, I'll open the box you brought from the brownstone."

285

# Chapter 26

During lunch, Lily was not her usual self. She sat quietly at the island as Jodi and Sam removed salads and sandwiches from the refrigerator. Plates, napkins, utensils, chips, pickles, and a pitcher of iced tea covered the island surface.

"Nana, did we miss anything? I can put on a pot of coffee or tea if you like."

She looked up, smiled and said, "Everything looks good. I don't know about you, but I'm famished. We can make coffee after we finish eating."

They were all hungrier than they realized, and left little to be put away. A pot of coffee brewed as Jodi and Sam cleaned up. Jodi took the coffee and pastry into the library. Sam retrieved the box from the foyer and placed it on the floor beside Lily's chair. He cut the tape and carefully opened it. Although they referred to it as the small box compared to the others, it was more medium in size, and its weight indicated to Sam that its contents held more than paperwork.

The items were neatly packed in envelopes and individual boxes. Jodi and Sam sat quietly as Lily began opening box after box placing the items on the coffee table. She immediately recognized her mother's jewelry box that played a Viennese waltz when the lid was lifted. Inside were the beautiful broaches, earrings, necklaces, and bracelets that her mother wore to the balls and galas they attended. She had totally forgotten about it. It was one of the few things they took from the house in Vienna.

Another box yielded several exquisite jewelry items that had belonged to Petra. In particular, a sapphire and diamond ring that she admired as a child, and that Petra had promised to her because sapphire was her birthstone. A pair of Murano glass birds from Italy, an antique fan from Le Lido Club in Paris, and a 14K Gold Statue of Liberty—all purchased on their many trips—brought tears to Lily's eyes.

Yet another box contained several exquisite pieces of jewelry unknown to her. A small envelope contained sales receipts indicating her uncle had purchased the items from Jews fleeing Europe in an effort to help them.

There were envelopes that contained sales receipts for the artwork in the larger boxes. A list identified each painting, the artist, and when it was purchased.

The sizes ranged from 18x24 to 20x24 to 30x40. There were 10 pieces of Impressionist Art listed—1 van Gogh, 2 Monet, 1Pessarro, 2 Renoir, 2 Cezanne, and 2 Degas; one additional painting by Symbolist Artist Gustav Klimt was also on the list. The entire collection belonged to her mother. The Klimt painting was of a young woman that bore a unique resemblance to her mother, and had been a gift from her father. She had no idea that Gus had them shipped to Zurich when they emptied the house in Austria.

One envelope contained pictures, of her father and Gus's parents and an aunt that she never knew—their sister who died in infancy. The pictures were old and brittle but the backs identified the subjects and year they were taken. A picture of Petra and Gus on their wedding day made Lily smile; they were so good together.

One last envelope remained. Although it was the first item she had removed, Lily set it aside because it had a name on it—Analiese. The box was empty; she had not commented on any of the items aloud. Jodi and Sam sat observing her reactions. For a moment or two, she continued her silence, gathering her thoughts, and clutching the unopened envelope. "I feel like such a fool. How could I have been so negligent? I should have opened these boxes 70 years ago when they arrived. I will never forgive myself. How could I have closed the door on such a wonderful part of my life?

"I'm going to lie down for a while. If you have no other plans, please stay. Nina will be home soon, and we can have dinner together. Feel free to look through the items if you like. If you're hungry, help yourself. Nina always leaves something in the refrigerator to snack on."

Jodi helped her upstairs and told her they would stay. She left her sitting on her bed still clutching the envelope with her name on it.

Returning to the library, she found Sam deep in thought gazing into space. She came up behind him and began massaging his shoulders. "Do you want to talk or just continue thinking? What about thinking out loud?"

"I am so totally blown away. I don't know what to think. Do you realize that for almost 70 years, the boxes were relegated to the cellar on Vanderbilt? Boxes whose contents are worth millions? For twenty years, the house stood unoccupied. Aside from the cleaning crew, I can't imagine Lily or Joe spending any time there once your mother and you left.

"What if you hadn't decided to go through the house? What if I had not mentioned the cellar? I hope the paintings have not been damaged in any way. I can't imagine storing them in an unheated and possibly damp place was the best decision. Knowing the larger boxes contained valuable paintings, I am amazed she didn't reconsider leaving them in the cellar. Unless she knew, she must have given some thought to what paintings were in the boxes, and that puzzles me even more.

"Another thought that crossed my mind was when the boxes arrived, she was in a pretty good place. She was newly married; *Portraits by Lily* had taken off and was doing well; Noah had not been born; and yet, she chose not to deal with the death of her uncle at that point. I would have thought that she would have embraced the opportunity to close the book on her past once and for all."

"I agree with you Sam, but my heart breaks for all that she has been through. Don't get me wrong; I don't see her as a victim at all. In spite of all the tragedies, she has had a wonderful life, a privileged life, and she got to share it with the love of her life. I think her strength came from Papa Joe. When he died, I believe the one thing that kept her going was the promise she made to him—to learn what happened to my mother and me. It gave her a reason to live.

"In hindsight, perhaps it would have been better if she had opened the box alone. Although it didn't seem to deter her, we were observing her pretty intently. I wonder why she chose not to comment on the contents. It was evident that she recognized the items and reacted to them. Last but not least, the letter she chose to read in private concerns me most of all.

"I'm really worried about her wellbeing. I can't wait until Charlie and your Mom get back from Florida. She's overdue for a complete checkup. It's evident today has been really hard on her. Somehow, I guess we never completely sever ourselves from the past. In a way, I feel I'm to blame. If coming to terms with the boxes causes her any undue stress, I'll never forgive myself for questioning her about them."

Lily opened the envelope slowly and removed the letter. Gus's familiar writing filled the pages.

*My Darling Analiese,*

*I can't begin to tell you how much I have loved you since you came into our lives. You were the daughter that Petra and I never had. Your father and I remained close though we lived a distance apart and for that I will always be grateful.*

*When Petra and I first met your mother, we could not have been happier. Your parents were so in love and so good together. Memories of family trips, and watching you and Alexander growing up have sustained me in my old age. When tragedy struck, we managed. Many times, I have wondered how different things might have been if not for the war. Until then, we had a wonderful life— a life of love and family.*

*I bless the day that Capt. John Montgomery, or as he liked to be called—Jack, came into our lives. He secured your future, which I could never have done on my own. Each letter you write to me confirms that I made the right decision.*

*New York has been good for you. Petra and I visited several times and often wondered what living there would be like. You have found your home and the love of your life. How happy I am for you. You deserve nothing less.*

*I won't deny that it has been lonely for me since you left; five years have passed quickly. Jack has returned to the States, to Texas I believe. He did stop by to see me and inquire about you on several occasions, stating that he was in Zurich on business. I don't know if I truly believe that or not, but it was good to see him.*

*Three years after you left, I had a visitor one evening. At first I couldn't recall why he seemed vaguely familiar but when he said, "I'm Theo Gruber, Analiese's friend." I realized who he was.*

*At the time, he was in Switzerland for medical treatment. He had been injured in the war and suffered burns on his face and left arm. His injuries on the mend, he was in Switzerland for plastic surgery for his burns.*

*I inquired about his family, and he told me they were killed in the final days of the war when the Allies bombed Berlin. Their home was completely destroyed. He told me Tessa was married, expecting, and living at home awaiting war's end and her husband's return. He didn't make it.*

*When he asked for you, I simply told him you no longer lived in Switzerland. I was grateful he didn't question me further, grateful that I didn't have to lie to him. The war changed us all.*

*He told me he planned to be in Switzerland only long enough to have his surgery and recuperate. I asked if he needed anything, and he thanked me but said he had access to an account set up by his father at the bank in Bern. He offered no further information. I wished him well; he wished me the same. We said our goodbyes.*

*I agonized over telling you at the time, but reasoned what good would it do? I couldn't reveal your new identity, and I didn't want to risk upsetting you. I had no way of knowing how you felt about him.*

*With my health failing and acting upon my doctor's advice to get my affairs in order, I made an appointment at my bank to arrange the transfer of my assets to you. To my surprise, I ran into Theo. He looked good and said he was doing well. Upon his release from rehab after his surgery, he secured a job at his bank in Bern in the accounting department. He had recently married. He did not ask after you. I thought it best to let it be.*

*The time has come to let you know what happened to your friends.*

*When you get this letter, I will have joined my beloved Petra and reunited with your parents. Know that we will watch over you and yours eternally as we are there for you always guiding you in the right direction.*

*God Bless Schatzi!*

*Your loving Uncle Gus*

Lily held the letter to her heart as tears streamed down her face. She lay back on the bed, pulled up the covers, and surrendered to sleep.

Jodi looked at the clock and saw that it had been over an hour since Nana had gone upstairs. "Do you think I should check and see if she's okay?

Sam smiled, "Of course; I'm surprised you waited this long. Don't wake her; just look in on her."

She found Nana fast asleep. She decided to sit with her for a time and sat down on the chair in the corner. She did not seem stressed; her breathing was even; and she appeared to be dreaming as a smile crossed her face. Jodi rose and returned to the library just as Nina came in.

They left everything in the library exactly where Lily had placed it, including the empty box. They had no idea what Lily planned to do with the items, but felt certain that she wouldn't pack the items back in the box.

Lily came downstairs to find them sitting at the island in the kitchen. She looked refreshed and ready to return to the box and its contents. "My little rest lasted longer than I anticipated. I apologize for abandoning you."

"No apology necessary Nana. I checked on you and you seemed to be resting quite comfortably so I came back downstairs just as Nina got in. Everything is as you left it in the library. Can we help you put it all away?"

"Good idea. But first, I'll tell you about the items, and I will need your help to deal with the paintings. Come, it won't take us long and then why don't we call an Uber and head out for dinner?"

Lily picked up her mother's jewelry box and lifted the lid. Just as she had remembered, the strains of a waltz filled the room. "These magnificent pieces of jewelry were all gifts from my father to my mother. Whenever they attended a social event, she carefully coordinated her jewelry with the beautiful gowns she wore. She often held up two choices and asked me which I thought went best with her choice of gown for the evening. I loved to watch her get ready and then see my father's approval when she joined him. We took this box and its contents with us on the train to Zurich when we left Vienna. I remember my uncle was terribly nervous traveling with the jewels on the over-crowded train. Thankfully, we made it home with no problems.

"These items belonged to Petra and Gus. Of course, I recognize everything and can even picture where the items were in their home. Petra's jewelry though not quite as extensive as my mother's is also beautiful. The sapphire and diamond ring is my favorite. When I was small, she always let me try it on telling me that it would be mine when I was older because Sapphire is my birthstone. We were very close, and after I lost my mother, I was fortunate to have her love and support.

"The papers and receipts are self-explanatory. My uncle was straightforward and honest and kept meticulous records even before the war, in order to circumvent any misunderstandings. The artwork he brokered was extremely valuable, and the one-of-a-kind pieces left no room for error. I know he purchased a number of paintings from Jews seeking to raise money for passage to America at the beginning of the war; my father also referred a few of their close friends to him. His records served him well enough to allow him to contact the original owners or their relatives and sell back the paintings after the war, by working with the American law firms that sought to reclaim artwork stolen by the Nazis.

"The jewelry items that he purchased are unknown to me; I only knew of the paintings. This ruby and diamond necklace with matching earrings belonged to my mother's good friend Sarah Freed. I saw her wear it many times. Only the wealthy owned art, but everyone owned jewelry. Many pieces were custom made and one-of-a-kind. Jewelry was also easy to hide among their belongings, so many took what they didn't sell with them.

"I truly regret having waited a lifetime to open the boxes. As I said before, I have no explanation or justification for having done so. I hope that I have not ruined the paintings by leaving them in the cellar. My uncle never told me that he had made arrangements to have them shipped to Zurich; perhaps he too had forgotten them. The eleven paintings belonged to my mother. She purchased all of them with the exception of the Gustav Klimt *Portrait of a Young Woman*. The resemblance of the young woman to my mother caught my father's eye; he purchased the painting for her as a birthday gift.

"I lost 70 years of enjoying the artwork my mother cherished, the sapphire and diamond ring Petra saved for me, and all the other pieces of my past that Gus so generously kept and passed on to me. Time I will never get back. He also left me a letter, which I chose to read alone when I went up for my rest. I didn't have to read it to know that he loved me as I did him. Ironically, opening the boxes years ago would have lifted the burden I carried for most of my life regarding the fate of Tessa and Theo Gruber and their parents. I learned that the entire Gruber family except for Theo was killed when the Allies bombed Berlin in the final days of the war.

"Although Theo had worn a Nazi uniform, he had been a small fish in an enormous pond of evil of which he basically had no part. His hobnobbing with the higher ups of the Nazi Party was solely through his father and his father's job to manage the artwork stolen from the Jews to create Hitler's personal art collection under the Third Reich. He was sent to the front to fight as the war was nearing its end. In Switzerland for medical treatment, he contacted Gus looking for me. Of course, he couldn't tell him where I was.

"I don't imagine he is still with us today, but if I had read the letter sooner, I would have learned that he was alive and well, living and working in Bern, and married. How nice it would have been for me to know that I had caused him no harm. In the end just as I had, he lost everyone. I can only hope that he had a good life.

"After all these years, it seems a bit presumptuous of me to unbox the paintings as soon as possible, have them evaluated and checked for damage, appraised, and insured. However, it is what I must do immediately. Then we can decide what to do with them. I need your help to do that, and I'm open for any and all suggestions.

"The safe upstairs is big enough to hold the jewelry. I can call my jeweler and see about getting everything appraised and insured. The other items and the paperwork can go in my office.

"Now, if everybody is as famished as I am, we can go to dinner."

As the 2022 calendar peeled off month after month, the country remained unsettled. It appeared as though *politics* affected every aspect of our lives. The economy remained dismal; crime continued to rise; and our past came back to haunt us. To make matters worse, it was an election year, and the midterms were relentless with candidates entrenched in hatred of the opposite side causing further division. Unity was nowhere in sight.

New Yorkers were no different than the rest of the country; many lived paycheck to paycheck and were forced to make dire decisions on a daily basis. The sinking economy saw the demise of many longtime businesses after barely making it through the pandemic. Hit by out-of-control costs of supplies, and the inability to get people to return to work, they had no option but to close their doors; many left the area. Since the onset of the pandemic, the exodus of half a million people from the state was unprecedented.

Many seemed to think that children were the biggest losers. Locked out and continued postponement of their return to in-person classes caused parents to scramble looking for alternatives. New York City's public school system is the nation's largest school system; in the spring of 2022, it had yet to reopen.

To compound things further, the Administration's border policies opened the floodgates allowing drug cartels easy access to distribute fentanyl leaving a wake of violence and death in our neighborhoods. The millions of migrants entering the country were distributed throughout placing an undue burden on states at a time when they were already in crisis attempting a recovery from COVID. New York was one of the hardest hit.

On a brighter side, New York was back to a large extent. Broadway was up and running; the food industry offered numerous choices; service businesses were good to go; and gyms were once again available. Weddings that had been postponed for over two years were making a big comeback as venues were booked solid. For the most part, young and old ventured out and about; public transportation was back in use; and everyone was trying their best to get back to basics.

As spring arrived, Jodi and Sam were endlessly busy—together and separately. Sam had been considering the pros and cons to expand his company for some time. Since its inception, his company consisted of one entity—*Profiles of New York*. Immensely popular and having won many awards, it was a total success from the very first episode. Although the show had been his *baby*, there was no doubt in his mind that its success belonged to the team. The time had come to move forward.

He met with his attorneys and drafted a proposal for expansion. With *Meyerson Media Group* at the helm, *Profiles* would become an entity under the new company but would remain unchanged. His vision going forward would allow them to produce documentaries, educational programs, and foster newcomers to the Arts.

He further proposed establishing *Meyerson Media Group* as a partnership. Greg and Carol, Frank and Edie, Lou and Sandy would each be given a 15% share. Sam and Jodi would own the controlling interest of 55%. A Board of Directors would be established as a formality, but as they had in the past, they would continue to work together as a team for day-to-day operations. He saw no reason to change what had worked so well in the past.

To be determined was selecting the company's premiere show, new hires, and new office space. What would be the perfect place for *the team* to start? Sam had no doubt that he could count on the team to add their suggestions to the mix.

Sam arrived home first allowing him to set up everything for dinner. Jodi had been busy helping Nana sort out the paintings, and he had been working on the partnership for the past few weeks. He wanted to show the proposal to Jodi and get her thoughts before presenting it to the team. He hoped everything would be in place so they could launch their first show—whatever they chose that to be—as early as the fall. September would be devoted to a *Profiles* episode for the 9/11 Anniversary; there would be no change to that. However, October would be an excellent month to launch a documentary if that was the choice.

Dinner arrived before Jodi; he placed it in the oven to keep it warm. They hadn't spent much time together recently because of their busy schedules, and his mother and Charlie were due back from Florida in a couple of weeks. Summer was usually a slow time, and he hoped to use that time to get *Meyerson Media Group* up and running.

Sam heard Jodi at the door and went to meet her. "I was beginning to worry about you. Where have you been?"

She kissed him. "No need to worry. Today was a really good day. We heard from the people we contacted to evaluate the paintings, and it was all good news. They had been packed professionally to protect them. Evidently, even though the cellar at the brownstone wasn't heated, the temperature sustained year round was not harmful in any way. It was suggested that the frames be cleaned to restore the wood to new; then they would be ready to be appraised and insured. In the meantime, we could give thought to what to do with them.

"The jewelry has all been taken care of. Her mother's items and Petra's have been appraised and insured. The items that Gus purchased took a little more time to resolve. The jeweler suggested that although many years had passed, it might be a good idea to break up the pieces selling the stones and the gold separately. Nana agreed.

"Something smells mighty good. Can I help get dinner on the table?"

"Yes you can. I ordered Italian food, three different entrees. I though it would be fun to share. After dinner, I have something I want to show you and get your thoughts on."

As usual, Jodi kept asking questions about what it was that Sam wanted to show her. As usual, he told her she'd have to wait.

When dinner was over and all had been put away, they settled in the living room. On the coffee table was a very official looking folder; Jodi eyed it curiously.

Sam smiled to himself. He knew her so well; she never disappointed.

Jodi sat quietly listening to Sam present his proposal for *Meyerson Media Group*. She loved it; and she never loved him more. What a wonderful thing to do. It went far beyond appreciation. The friends had grown up together, but instead of going their separate ways, they bonded for life. They were family.

"I love it! I love it! I love it! They are going to be blown away. When are you going to tell them?"

"Well, I have a plan for that too. I thought we could spend the weekend at the cottage in Port Chester. Next weekend would be best if that's doable for everyone. My mother and Charlie will be back by the end of the month, and I'd like to have this all wrapped up by then. Edie and Frank's son will be here in six weeks. Carol and Greg's adoption is on track for late August; it's a little girl, and they couldn't be happier. Sandy's sister is getting married in June, so she and Lou will be upstate for a week of festivities.

"I like the atmosphere at the cottage. It will be a nice relaxing weekend that we can all use before returning to a summer that's lining up to be jam-packed for all of us. We could bring groceries for breakfast and snacks. The Roadhouse is only one of a number of good restaurants nearby that we could visit for lunch and dinner. I don't know if Edie will be up to it, but the boat is available, if we want it. I checked and the weather is looking good."

"Oh Sam, they are going to be so surprised. I just know it. I also think this is the perfect time. All of us are married; four of us are becoming parents; and we are going to be partners. I say we go for it. I hope everyone can make it next weekend. If you like, we can have dinner with Nana on Thursday and tell her and Nina about your plan. I'm certain they will be happy for us."

"I guess we're all set. I'll speak to the team in the morning."

It was definitely *a go*. Everyone was so excited about getting away for the weekend together. The thought never entered their minds that Sam had plans—big plans for all of them. They decided to meet at the cottage late afternoon on Friday and stay until late afternoon on Sunday. The guys and Carol had grown up in Port Chester and Greg and Lou still had relatives in the area so no directions were necessary.

Jodi and Sam left midday, and picked up groceries at the local supermarket. They stopped in at the Roadhouse and ordered dinner, arranging to have it delivered at 6:00 pm. The weather was perfect— warm, dry sunny days and cool nights were expected through the weekend.

The cottage had four bedrooms; a living room-dining room area that they referred to as the *great room* featured a big picture window that overlooked the harbor. The expanded table was set for dinner; afterwards over coffee and dessert, Sam planned to kickoff his presentation.

The team arrived and settled in. The food delivery was right on time, and it wasn't long before everyone was digging in and offering kudos to the Roadhouse that only seemed to get better with time. The girls told Edie to relax as they cleared the table. Jodi put coffee on and left the desserts to be served later.

When they were all once again seated around the table. Sam cleared his throat and began speaking. "The past year has been a banner year for all of us. In the midst of one of the worst times in our lives, we managed to not only survive, but to do so and help others in the process. As born and bred New Yorkers, we have always taken pride in *the city that never sleeps*; dealing with a city forced into a coma by mandates and regulations one would think unimaginable became our reality.

"During that time, we never slept. *Profiles* continued to not only produce new episodes throughout, but some of our best work emerged earning the team praise and awards that I humbly agree we deserved."

Everyone laughed; Sam continued. "I do not by any means think that *Profiles* has reached the top and can go no higher. We have a wealth of resources at our fingertips, and I envision nothing less than providing the same excellence in broadcasting in all future episodes for our loyal audience that continues to grow.

"*Profiles of New York* was a dream that I nurtured for a long time. All about New York, all about my love for New York, and all about why so many come to New York to visit and to live was a subject near and dear to my heart. This made it all so easy to succeed. When I added my best friends, also born and bred New Yorkers, to the mix, it was the second best decision I ever made. I don't have to remind you what my best decision was."

Again everyone laughed and Sam continued. "I have always viewed *the gift of friendship priceless*—you gave me that gift; a gift I might add that keeps on giving.

For me personally, the past eighteen months could not have been better. Jodi, I never knew how incomplete my life was until you became a part of it. Now, as I look around this table, I see family because family is what we have become.

"You all know me, and you know me well. You also know that the wheels in my brain are constantly turning and churning out new ideas. So without further ado, I present to you *my* vision for *our* future."

Sam handed each couple a folder. "You hold in your hands my proposal for *Meyerson Media Group* which is an expansion of the company. *Profiles* is not going anywhere, but will become an entity of the parent company, continuing to operate as it has since its inception. *Meyerson Media Group* will allow us to expand the shows we produce to include documentaries, educational programs, and foster newcomers to the Arts.

"Now comes the best part. *Meyerson Media Group* will be a partnership that is fully vested immediately upon execution. I want you to read the proposal *carefully* and let me know if you have any questions. Of course, you can discuss it among yourselves as well. It is concise and to the point; there is no hidden agenda. We can move forward as soon as the proposal is accepted.

"We have some busy months ahead of us both personally and businesswise. Setting up a new company will be a challenge, but we are up for it. Remember what Coach Powell used to say whenever we had a big game coming up—*With every challenge comes the chance to succeed!* We didn't always come out on top but it taught us that if we didn't try, we would never win. He was a great guy. I used to stop in to see him whenever I was up this way. He passed away during the early days of COVID and the funeral was private.

"As partners aside from sharing our successes, we will also be sharing the *not so fun things* such as looking for new office space, hiring additional personnel, and long brainstorming sessions aimed at choosing a paragon subject for our premiere show. So any and all suggestions are welcome.

"Jodi and I will get the coffee and dessert while you begin to look through the proposal. Don't worry; I don't need your answers tonight nor do I anticipate them. I wanted to get this out of the way so that we can relax and enjoy the weekend. We haven't done this for a while. The weather is cooperating, and the boat is ready and waiting. The new boat came in right before the pandemic, so none of you have seen it; she's a real beauty."

Over dessert and coffee, the proposal was put aside and the guys began joking about growing up in Port Chester. Starting off with stories about their elementary school days was amusing, but as they eased into dating, sports, driving, and senior year heading towards graduation, the dialogue became hilarious. The girls laughed uncontrollably unable to believe they had never heard the stories before. Jodi smiled to herself wondering if they knew how fortunate they were to have one another.

It was almost midnight before they finally called it a night and went to bed.

Sam pulled Jodi close and kissed her. "I had forgotten how much fun we have whenever we're together. What I like best is the fact that it gets better with each passing year. I hope it never ends."

The next morning, Sam awoke to the aroma of coffee brewing. That meant only one thing—Greg was up. He went into the kitchen just as he was pouring himself a cup. Grabbing a mug, he joined him. "Last night was like old times. I'm so glad we have each other. We're adults now but we are still crazy together."

Greg laughed. "I know. Carol kept asking me if we were making those stories up. She finally agreed they were too coordinated not to be true.

"I want you to know how much Carol and I appreciate your offer. I can't imagine a life that wouldn't include all of us in it. I have long felt that *Profiles* was only the beginning of what we could accomplish as a team. The best is yet to come my friend." He pulled Sam into a bear hug.

In short order, everyone was up. Jodi decided to serve breakfast on the deck. She had bagels, lox, cheeses, and the works for a typical New York breakfast. As they ate, Jodi laid out their plans for the day. "When I learned for certain we were coming here for the weekend, I looked into a few things to do. They are not set in stone but are merely my suggestions.

"I thought we could split up for the day. Guys out on the boat talking business, sharing some more Port Charles growing up stories or whatever you guys do when you're on your own. Girls on a shopping trip—equivalent to guys on the boat. Soon-to-be Aunts, Sandy and Jodi taking soon-to-be Moms, Edie and Carol to the greatest children's store in the area—Sammy + Nat. Furniture, toys, clothes—they have it all."

Before Jodi had a chance to continue, everyone started clapping and whistling including Sam who knew nothing about Jodi's plans. "Okay. Okay. Calm down; I'm not finished. I'm sure you guys can figure out lunch for yourselves."

Again, Jodi was interrupted, this time by Lou. "Yes we can. I vote for Pat's Hubba Hubba. I haven't been there since before the pandemic."

Jodi had no idea what he was talking about, but soon learned it was a chili house only the bravest could handle. "Fine as long as your friends agree. We will be lunching at The Barley Beach House. For the evening, I have tentatively chosen Garcia's for dinner prior to attending the Capitol Theatre to see Jessie's Girl. The show is at 8:00 pm. Garcia's is close enough that I thought a 6:00 pm reservation would be good. What do you think?"

Sam said, "I think I really picked a winner. Jodi you outdid yourself. I don't think we locals could have chosen better."

Everyone started talking at once; everyone was excited. The weekend was turning out to be better than anyone could have imagined. There were three bathrooms at the cottage, but it still took a while for everyone to shower and dress.

The guys went first. Over second cups of coffee, the girls talked babies. Edie and Carol were both looking forward to being moms, and embraced the shopping trip wholeheartedly. They also talked about Sam's proposal. Sandy had a fantastic idea. She had been trying to figure out a way to produce her idea for a *Profiles* episode but try as she may, it was not a good fit. Once she realized it could only be presented as a *documentary*, she considered it tabled until an opportunity arose for her to go forward with it. Sam's proposal presented her with both the opportunity and the time for the subject matter.

Sandy's mom taught school in the New York public school system for forty years prior to retiring during the pandemic. Since then, she kept a close eye on the harsh mandates, unending regulations, and total disregard for the wellbeing of all children. She commiserated not only their treatment, but also the total disregard for the rights of their parents, and the lack of a plan to move forward. New York was not alone. Throughout the country, state after state, town after town, it was a total shutdown.

Whenever Sandy and her mother spoke, the subject came up. She began researching the facts and figures. She didn't like what she saw.

"When we get back to the city and back in the office, I'm going to gather the team together and show you what I have. It's quite a lot and although it's nowhere near completion, if we decide to go with it, I think we could be ready for a fall airing. The schools in New York have not yet reopened fulltime and many jurisdictions are still pushing homeschooling and video participation.

"From what I've learned, they are planning a full reopening for the fall which would coincide with the documentary. I can't think of another subject more appropriate or of more interest to the greater community at this point in time. It affects us all.

"My question is if Broadway, restaurants, sports and other entertainment venues are up and running, why are the students still in lockdown? I can only imagine how frustrating it is for the children and their parents. If children are the future, our future doesn't look good."

Although their conversation had turned serious, they were proud of Sandy. "Wow! From the looks on their faces, I think I can safely say that Edie and Carol agree with me; we are really impressed. My God Sandy, Sam is going to be blown away.

"I'm going to suggest that as hard as it might be, we follow your lead and not speak of this until we return to the office. The first order of business is to accept the partnership and establish *Meyerson Media Group*. Let's not put the cart before the horse. We'll go shopping and have ourselves the weekend we need to deal with all that's coming our way."

The weekend was great. Sunday, Jodi rose early and treated everybody to a breakfast of Nana's pancakes. The guys accused the girls of putting Sammy + Nat out of business by buying out the store. They decided to hang out at the cottage for the day, and eat an early dinner before heading back to the city.

Sam insisted on putting business aside deferring all discussions to the office.

Having driven separately, each couple took leave on their own.

After packing up the few perishable items to take with them, Jodi and Sam went through the cottage checking to see if anything was left behind. Before leaving, Sam pulled Jodi into his arms. "Thank you. Never ceasing to amaze me, you really made the weekend perfect. I might add that this weekend definitely qualifies for a memory box. Come with me; let's take a walk along the harbor before we head out."

Hand-in-hand, they walked without speaking. Sam was content knowing his friends were on board for the partnership even though they had not officially said so. Jodi was bursting at the seams knowing that Sam was going to welcome Sandy's documentary with open arms.

It was an easy ride back to the city; there was very little traffic. Trudy and Charlie were due to return to New York the following Saturday. The cleaning service had been scheduled, and they would see to it that the refrigerator was stocked with the basics.

# Chapter 27

Signed, sealed, and delivered started off the week. Officially *Meyerson Media Group* was a done deal. As soon as the lawyers left, Sandy took the opportunity to present her idea to the team. As Jodi had predicted, not only Sam, everyone was blown away. Lou knew she had been working on a project, but he had no idea of the hours of research and effort she had put into it. It was unanimous. With Sandy taking the lead, they were off and running.

The months ahead were on track to be jam-packed. Aside from the list of priorities required to launch their new company, the team's individual personal lives awaited the arrival of two babies, while Jodi's commitment to get Nana's business affairs settled was ongoing. The conversion of *Portraits by Lily* to a museum, and the expansion of the Asher Foundation were no small feats. Determined to assure that her wishes for both entities were closely followed to the smallest detail, Lily's hands-on approach was steadfast.

Although Lily and Nina had done an unbelievable job in coordinating both the reopening of *Portraits* and restructuring the Asher Foundation with guidance from their legal staff, they also managed to get the ball rolling to acquire new office space allowing the foundation to relocate and move out of the house. Although they accomplished it all while Jodi and Sam were in California, Lily insisted that they would not be moving forward without their input. It was tabled until their return.

Trudy and Charlie's return the last weekend in May officially signaled summer was just around the corner. As always, the first business at hand was to catch them up on what was happening in New York. Sam picked them up at the airport, dropped Charlie at his condo, and headed home. They made plans to have dinner together and spend a quiet evening filling them in on what he and Jodi had been up to.

When Sam and Trudy were alone in the car, he casually asked, "How are things going with you and Charlie?"

Raising her eyebrows, Trudy replied, "What exactly is it that you're asking?"

"Come on Mom. I can see how happy and content you are, and we all noticed that you were in no hurry to come back to New York. I'm happy for you. I know how much you miss Dad. With his two daughters living out of state, Charlie is alone here; reconnecting has been good for both of you."

"It has been wonderful. Having become friends back in the day allowed us to bypass the *getting to know you* phase which is awkward at any age. We couldn't be more in sync with one another. Above all else, it just feels right being together. His children were warm and welcoming to me when we visited, and agreed it was nice to see their father happier than he has been in a long time. We actually stayed longer for both visits than we planned to.

"Less than a year after retiring, losing both his mother and his wife was hard on Charlie. Alone here in the city, he was glad Lily reached out to him to look after her during the pandemic. Ultimately, it led to helping her learn what happened to Nicole and Olivia resulting in a win-win for all of us, especially for Lily and Jodi.

"We had a good winter, but we are happy to be back. Home is where the heart is, and for both of us that's New York. For now, we are just enjoying what we have while counting our blessings. Living together is an option that we are considering. He owns his condo, but it is smaller than mine, so my apartment is the obvious and sensible choice.

"Looking forward to summer, I've made arrangements for the house in the Hamptons for the month of August. And I'm determined to do what I can to have a reunion of sorts; I've been working on it for months. We haven't had a big family gathering since before the pandemic other than your wedding, and I miss my Caruso clan. We always had such good times. I'm very close to finalizing my options."

"Thanks Mom. That's all I wanted to know. Your happiness means the world to me, and Charlie is definitely one of the good guys. We have so much to tell you, and many plans are in motion that include both of you. As you may have guessed, Lily has plans of her own that include you too.

"I don't want you to draw any wrong conclusions when I say that Jodi and I have an announcement to make; we've been saving it to tell everyone upon your return. We are not expecting, so channel your thoughts elsewhere. We will tell you everything when we are together for dinner tomorrow evening.

"On another note, we are somewhat concerned about Lily; thank goodness for Nina who until now has managed to ground her somewhat but not totally. In this case however, the two of them have teamed up, and you can't begin to imagine what they have been up to since you left.

"Although Nina is with her and takes excellent care of her, Jodi and I will feel much better after Charlie gives her a much-needed checkup. Surprisingly, she agreed when we suggested it."

Jodi popped in to welcome Trudy home when they arrived at the apartment, leaving her to spend the afternoon unpacking and settling in.

At 5:00 pm, Trudy and Charlie arrived at Jodi and Sam's for dinner. They had not seen the redo of the apartment, and Jodi thought a light supper of rotisserie chicken, chopped salad, and roasted vegetables at home would be casual and relaxing as they filled them in on the past five months.

The redo was Trudy's wedding gift to them; her decorator had not disappointed. The conversation started with the apartment, but soon moved on to California and their trip. They had participated in the Memorial Service from Florida, and were aware that they had finalized her parents' estate, sold her condo, and were savoring the time spent with Rosy and the Buchanans. Having declared the trip a *fait accompli*, Jodi revealed that Henry Jerome left her one last gift—her mother's ashes. We buried her beside Daddy.

The conversation shifted to Lily as Jodi began relaying what she and Nina had undertaken and managed to pull off largely on their own. "The promised reopening of *Portraits by Lily* was a huge success. Sporting its new look, as a museum, was genius on her part evidenced by the overwhelming response it received from the community. West Village returned to pre-pandemic status with a vengeance, and Lily was there for all of it.

"Meanwhile in her spare time, she initiated the groundwork to reorganize and relocate the foundation. Meeting with the Board of Directors and their attorneys to update and accommodate the foundation's growth didn't deter the two of them from personally visiting building after building with available office space to lease."

As Sam observed Trudy and Charlie's looks of disbelief, Jodi reiterated concern for Lily's wellbeing by raising the subject of a complete checkup, adding that when she suggested it to her, she was in total agreement. Charlie promised to see to it as soon as possible.

Moving on to lighter and more personal happenings, they mentioned parenthood ascending upon *Profiles* and the two babies that would soon be here. Everyone was excited looking forward to welcoming the next generation.

Returning to the gift of her mother's ashes, Sam elaborated on Jodi's feelings. "Upon our return from California, I urged her to spend several days at the brownstone on Vanderbilt in an effort to come to terms with her mother's final days. While revisiting her past, she fondly recalled the days when the house was her home, and her school and her friends were right up the street. She soon realized that she grew up surrounded by people who loved her and she loved them back.

"Finding a journal that belonged to her mother lifted the burden she had carried for the past year, and gave her the insight to forgive her. Although many of the answers she sought in an effort to understand her mother's choice to embark on their fatal trip remained elusive and unanswered, she found her mother's handwritten words too powerful to ignore. She realized that the ashes were truly a gift not only to her, but also to Lily.

"In the process, she came upon boxes in the cellar of the brownstone that had been shipped to Lily when her uncle passed away in Switzerland; she had never opened them. They contained artwork, jewelry, personal items from her parents' home in Vienna, and items from her aunt and uncle's home in Zurich."

The look on their faces when Sam expressed utter disbelief—that unbeknown to anyone, the cellar was home to millions of dollars of artwork and jewelry unsecured and uninsured for seventy years—was priceless.

In retelling all that had transpired in their absence, Jodi and Sam realized that perhaps they should have planned more than one catch-up session. It was a lot to digest in one sitting. They were glad they had chosen to tell them about *Meyerson Media Group* the following day.

As they enjoyed dessert and coffee, surprisingly Trudy and Charlie had no questions. It was totally out of character for Trudy. No mention was made about *Profiles*.

As the hour grew late, Trudy and Charlie prepared to leave. "What is the plan for tomorrow?"

Jodi and Sam glanced at one another. "I'm sorry. We were so wrapped up in today that I totally forgot about tomorrow. I spoke to Lily this morning, and as you would guess, she and Nina are anxious to see everybody. I told her we were spending the evening at home, and that tomorrow the day belonged to her. Without hesitation, she claimed it, and decided we should make a whole day of it.

"We are expected for breakfast. Jodi has graciously agreed to make

Nana's pancakes to start off the day. As I have hinted, aside from the news we plan to share, Lily has news of her own. Nina said she would take care of lunch and dinner. That leaves us the entire day to catch everybody up to speed.

"Mom, it will also give us the opportunity to discuss spending time in the Hamptons, and the possibility of a family reunion. I love the idea. You can count on us to help any way we can. I must admit, the Carusos know how to have a good time, and I can think of no better way to start putting the pandemic behind us."

"We don't have to leave too early. There's no rush. Is 8:30 am good for you? We can all lend a hand setting up breakfast while Jodi is whipping up pancakes."

It was settled. "It's good to have you both home; we missed you."

It was Memorial Day weekend, overnight showers had cleared out, and the sun promised a beautiful day. They arrived at Lily's a little earlier than anticipated, but she and Nina were ready and waiting. All ingredients to make the pancakes were on the countertop. Jodi turned the griddle on to heat, and went to work.

The table was set. The choices were many—bacon, sausage links, a variety of fruit toppings, syrup, and whipping cream. Juice was poured, and a small tray held cream and sugar for the coffee. Jodi called for Sam, and he promptly placed the heated tray of pancakes on the table. Following behind him, Jodi carried the coffee. Everyone dug in.

As they chatted among themselves or as a whole, Lily sat back and smiled. It was hard to believe that not too long ago, she had no family. This was better, far better.

Jodi accepted kudos for her pancakes, but added that it was after all her Nana's recipe.

When breakfast was over and the kitchen back in order, they assembled in the library. Sam anxious to share his news motioned Jodi to sit beside him.

"I find that my name has been expanded, and that more often than not when I have a statement to make, it starts with *Jodi and I*. So here goes.

"Jodi and I are pleased—no ecstatic—to announce our new venture— *Meyerson Media Group, LLC*. Fueled by the amazing success of *Profiles of New York*, it is undoubtedly clear that our future lies in expansion. The time has come to challenge ourselves further. The *team* who made all of it possible made my decision to form a limited partnership a no-brainer.

"It's hard to put my finger on any one particular reason for our success. The fact that five of us grew up together, or that we share similar goals, or that we are insanely loyal to one another have definitely all contributed, or perhaps along the way we were fortunate to meet others who have impacted our lives beyond imagination. All of the above apply to us.

"Going forward, *Meyerson Media Group* becomes the parent company and *Profiles* an entity. Our plan, which is not set in stone, is to produce documentaries, a wide range of educational programs, and to foster and mentor students in the arts.

"We are hoping to launch our first program in the fall. Since children are our future, we have chosen for our premiere show a topic that touches every aspect of the future. It will be aired as a documentary and expose the devastating impact the pandemic has had on our children's education and what it will take to help them get up to par and beyond going forward.

"Although we have only begun to scratch the surface, all signs indicate the documentary could become a limited series. The benefits of home schooling versus traditional classroom attendance, and addressing the needs, the choices, the costs, and the rewards of pursuing higher education as opposed to trade schools or a career in the military are all subjects closely related.

"With two of the couples on the team about to become parents, and all of us having family members who are teachers, the subject of education is long overdue for discussion. The pandemic simply brought the subject to the forefront.

"My vision for *Profiles* was my dream. I asked my best friends to come on board and they did. By believing in my vision and me, their hard work and dedication made my dream come true. The new programs will allow us to explore subjects that affect all of us to some degree, and give a voice to many who have not had one in the past.

"The papers were signed this past week, so we are forging ahead. We are also in the process of looking for new office space and considering new hires as we await becoming parents or aunts and uncles. It's all quite exhilarating."

The applause was totally unexpected. Jodi and Sam were pleasantly surprised and humbled at their reaction. Congratulations, kisses and hugs all around followed.

They took a break and decided to visit for a while. It was a beautiful spring day, sunny and breezy; they opted to take Lily's suggestion and have lunch outside in the garden. The early spring flowers were in full bloom, and the smell of the few lingering lilacs was heavenly. It was nice just being together.

Observing that Charlie never left Trudy's side, Lily considered them a good match and couldn't be happier for them. She had known Charlie his whole life and felt as though she had known Trudy far longer than she actually had. She recalled fondly that Sharon and Stanley, Charlie's parents, had been their good friends for many years even after they moved from Brooklyn to the house on the Upper East Side.

Noah and Charlie had grown up together in Brooklyn and didn't go their separate ways until college. Noah went off to MIT and Charlie went to medical school, ultimately opening a pediatric practice on Long Island. It was losing Noah that brought Charlie back into Lily's life and what a godsend he had proven to be.

It was so nice and relaxing in the garden, they decided to continue their discussions there after lunch. Charlie was about to see what Jodi and Sam had implied about their concerns for Lily's wellbeing.

"You might say I've been busy getting my affairs in order. It's no secret; I'm no spring chicken. When Nicole left, the Asher Foundation lost the one person whose vision transformed our idea of a small family funded entity into a force to be reckoned with. What her experience lacked in length, she made up for with ingenuity. As our reputation grew, it afforded us the opportunity to give back to the community by helping others.

"Although I managed to stay involved and continued to take a hands-on approach, there were times when the demands were overwhelming. We hired several people, but no one seemed a good fit and no one stayed on for very long. Our Board Members came to the rescue by fulfilling our promises—the annual scholarship awards and commitments never defaulted. Financially, we were sound, but growth had definitely slowed, so we maintained our status quo while biding our time.

"After we lost Noah, and then Nicole and Olivia, Joe lost interest in just about everything. He never formally retired; he simply eased into it. I was still painting and spending as much time as I could at *Portraits*. It was the only way I could deal with my overflowing plate.

"I viewed losing Joe as a wake-up call. As I buried him, I promised to continue my quest to learn what happened to Nicole and Olivia. In reality, it was probably one of the best decisions I've made in my entire life, because it gave me back my life, a reason to live. Somewhere deep inside of me, I knew that Olivia and I would be reunited on earth, not in heaven.

"I was no longer counting days, weeks, and months—only years. I threw myself into work and took on a more active role in the foundation. When Nina came into my life, my offer to help her landed me the better end of the deal. She came to work for the foundation, helped me at the studio whenever she was needed, and eventually took over many of the responsibilities here at house. More importantly, I was no longer alone.

"Over the years during the times we spent together, Nina learned my story. Ever by my side, my quest became hers. When the pandemic engulfed us, we made a plan to ride it out together. Our goal was to stay home, stay safe, and use any and every precaution to stay well. I called Charlie and asked if he would check in on us, and he became our sole contact with the outside world. We eagerly looked forward to his every visit.

"How ironic that my search would come to fruition during one of the worst times in our history because of one of the worst times in our history, and that Charlie would be the catalyst.

"Today, the Asher Foundation has reached new heights. Since my story was featured on *Profiles*, contributions have never waned. After the holidays, Trudy and Charlie left for Florida, and Jodi and Sam began planning their trip to California. I showed Nina my list of priorities and enlisted her help. Together we made all the arrangements to reopen *Portraits by Lily* as a museum, and scheduled the festivities.

"The Asher Foundation was a far more in-depth undertaking, but we had the help and advice of longtime friends, board members, and our attorneys. I told them what I wanted to accomplish and for the most part, they took over. We have leased office space, hired personnel, and legal papers have been prepared to transfer leadership. The Board of Trustees is in place, I have named Jodi and Sam Co-CEOs, and as of September 1st, our new office space will be ready for occupancy.

"The lone open item left is to appoint additional members to the Board of Directors. As Co-CEOs, Jodi and Sam have been added automatically. Trudy and Charlie, if you accept, the Board will be complete.

"Now that you all know what Nina and I have been up to, and our job is done, I look forward to a relaxing summer and taking time to smell the roses, something I've never found the time to do in the past. I've been given the heads-up Charlie, and I'm expecting your call to schedule my checkup."

What a day it was turning out to be. Jodi and Sam's news followed by Lily's made Trudy declare, "I don't think I'm ever leaving town again. I can't believe all that has happened, and we are not yet at mid-year. Yes, I accept the honor of serving on the Board of Directors. Thank you."

Charlie once again recalled Jodi and Sam's concerns for Lily. How was it possible that she and Nina had accomplished the impossible? "Thank you my dear, dear friend. I too am honored and humbled, and I accept as well. By the way, you can expect my call after the weekend."

As it had become routine in recent weeks, Lily excused herself and said she was going upstairs for a nap. Urging her guests to relax, enjoy the garden, or watch TV, she stated that she was not quite finished and promised one last revelation before the day ended.

Lily got into bed and fell asleep almost immediately.

*Joe, it seems as though I am constantly tired as of late. I miss you more than ever. If you have been keeping an eye on me as I suppose you have, you know all that I have been up to recently is enough to make a much younger person tired.*

*Along those lines, I feel the need to talk to you. There were never any secrets between us, but following our return from our trip to Europe, I spoke truth to you when I said that revisiting Vienna was a gift that I never expected. We never talked about it again, and I always had the feeling that you suspected there was a "but" that I never explained.*

*The year is 1976. We Ashers are in a good place. Noah is in his third year at MIT and looking forward to his summer internship in Manhattan.*

*I'm apprehensive about our impending trip to Europe. Sharon and Stanley Hurwitz have convinced us to accompany them to Vienna, but as the time for departure grows closer, I begin second-guessing my decision.*

*We learn Stanley's father immigrated to America with his parents when he was three years old. The Hurwitz family has a lengthy history in Austria boasting a close family of highly respected achievers ranked among the elite of Vienna. Family members include professionals and entrepreneurs alike, Hurwitz Jewelers among them. Stanley's father and his parents are the only family members who live in America.*

*On the brink of war, his father's Aunt Sarah who has recently lost her husband reaches out to him to help her leave Austria. Only weeks before the annexation, she arrives in New York. She is up in years by then, but Stanley remembers her as a kind and loving woman whose endless supply of cookies follows him to college and beyond.*

*When she passes away, his grandfather tells him that helping her come to America in all probability saved her life, but most of all, having a Hurwitz relative in New York and getting to know her meant the world to him. Stanley decides to research the possibility of a trip to Austria and trace his roots.*

The thought of ever returning to Vienna has never occurred to me. At first I am adamantly opposed to the trip, but after you reason with me, as only you can, pointing out that in reality Vienna holds only good memories for me, I begin to reconsider. You are right. When I left to live in Zurich, the Nazi presence was largely soldiers, void of the destruction yet to come.

I found myself thinking it would be nice to see The Art Museum; I know it is still there. My old neighborhood and my schools are probably long gone, but the parks and public places my mother and I frequented could possibly still exist. The more I think about it, the more excited I become. We make plans to meet for dinner, and to Sharon and Stanley's delight, we accept their invitation to join them on the trip.

Sharon and I spend days shopping and preparing. Over dinner, Stanley gives you our tickets and a copy of the itinerary. We are due to fly out of JFK in two days. When we get home, I look at the itinerary. Based in Vienna, nine days in Austria include daytrips, and one overnight stay to nearby attractions.

On day ten, we are set to depart Vienna by train to Berlin, Germany. My hands begin to shake, and I freeze. That is how you find me when you come out of the bathroom. Again you reason with me. However, this time, I have managed to upset you, and it upsets me. I apologize profusely.

I will not hear of your offer to cancel the trip. I don't think that is fair to you or to our good friends Sharon and Stanley who have no idea whatsoever of my circumstances. They know that I was born and grew up in Vienna, moved to Zurich when I lost my family, and immigrated to New York after the war. They have no reason to believe that I left relatives in Austria, ever had relatives in Germany, or lost anyone in the Holocaust. I didn't.

Two days hence, we embark on our trip. I am truly excited about visiting Vienna where memories of my childhood abound. As each day passes, we are enjoying the trip immensely. The accommodations are excellent, the food superb, and visiting the museum that had been such a presence in my life is wonderful. I actually picture my parents walking throughout the rooms as they once did on a daily basis.

Stanley knows that I want to find the street we once lived on, and he confides in me that he wants to see where his Great Aunt Sarah lived. One morning after breakfast, with map in hand, we set out on foot. We have no problem finding my street. The house *is no longer there but the neighborhood is beautiful, and new houses stand in place of the old. It is May; the trees and flowers are in full bloom. I feel the presence of the old neighborhood all around me. The old stately well-manicured homes of the elite of Vienna are very much alive and well even though they have been replaced.*

As Stanley searches the map, he realizes Sarah's street is two blocks over in our same neighborhood. Suddenly, he too is excited. Never having seen her house, he has no idea if the one that stands before them is hers or its replacement. *I know immediately it isn't the original house because I have been there many times with my mother to visit her good friend Sarah Freed.*

*For the first time since I left Zurich to relocate to New York, a feeling of apprehension comes over me. I find it hard to imagine what would have happened if I had met Sarah on the streets of New York. Would she have recognized me? Would she have approached me asking if I am okay? Of course I am. Our paths never crossed, and she is no longer with us.*

Throughout the day, Stanley repeatedly states his disbelief that I actually knew Sarah. When I tell him I have also been a recipient of her cookies, he claims I have made his day. We find the park where my mother and I spent hours drawing. It is not too far from our house, and the perfect place for a picnic. *If you and I had been alone, I would have definitely insisted on treating you to a picnic.*

For nine days, we travel throughout Vienna and various neighboring towns. Any destruction from the war has long been removed, rebuilt, and replaced, while many of the small towns manage to retain an aura of the past.

*You being a stickler for detail inquire earlier in the day about our train the next morning. Upon learning that it takes over ten hours to reach our destination, you deem it totally unacceptable. You call Stanley and together you set out to make plane reservations to fly instead.* Our train departure scheduled for 6:00 am means rising at the ungodly hour of 4:00 am. By changing to a later flight, our arrival in Berlin is close enough to leave our accommodations in place.

Over dinner, I wholeheartedly thank Sharon and Stanley for inviting us to join them. My earlier concerns about the trip have all but vanished. *Best of all Joe, I got to show you where I was born and grew up.*

Berlin is totally not what I expected. With the exception of certain landmarks, it could be anywhere. The time I spent in the city was limited, and I actually have nothing to compare to present day. I know the Grubers' house and surrounding area better. We inquire and learn that the Westend neighborhood of Charlottenburg is only ten kilometers from where we are staying.

Our morning tour of the Bode-Museum on Museum Island in the historic center of Berlin is in the general area of our hotel. Afterwards, we opt to remain and have lunch at the Bode Café. Our discussion begins with the museum, but before long, our comments turn to Berlin. Stanley states that since none of us have previously been to Berlin, there are no comparisons to be made as in Vienna.

I have given thought all morning as to how I can approach the subject of a possible visit to Charlottenburg, and he gives me my opening. I tell Sharon and Stanley that I have been to Berlin on a handful of occasions to visit with my best friend from Vienna after she moved. In the early days of the war, my aunt falls ill causing my visits to end. I am needed in Zurich to help my uncle. I tell them that my friend's home in Charlottenburg is merely ten kilometers from where we are staying, and ask if they are up to paying a visit to my friend's old neighborhood.

Their neighborhood totally demolished during the war is gone. The Charlottenburg Palace has been rebuilt, as were other buildings such as museums, theatres, and various public places. Unlike Vienna, the area is as unknown and unrecognizable to me as it is to you, Sharon, and Stanley.

For some reason, a tour to the Eagle's Nest on the itinerary did not evoke any reaction from me. From time to time, articles concerning WWII and the rebuilding of Germany appeared in newspapers and periodicals; I read them all. I saw no harm in learning about places that had played a part in my life.

I read with interest about the massive bombing attack on the Berghof and Obersalzberg that occurred during the last weeks of the war. The Eagle's Nest, regarded as a relic of the Third Reich, barely survived. After the war, it was going to be razed like many of the Berchtesgaden area buildings with Nazi associations, but intervention by the Bavarian District President saves it. It becomes one of the few local buildings from the Nazi era that still remains.

After breakfast, we leave our hotel in a bright red tour bus. For most of the ride, you, Sharon, and Stanley talk about a myriad of things. I close my eyes, and you assume I am sleeping. A million thoughts run through my mind, thoughts of Tessa, Theo, and my visits to the Berghof and the Eagle's Nest. I secretly wish I had saved just a couple of pictures of my old friends before the war when we were young and innocent, the way I have chosen to remember them. I wonder how long my memory will serve me.

When we arrive at our destination, a tour guide is assigned to take us through history as he points out pictures that adorn the walls, and items of interest from the past.

I find my trip back in time not the least bit disturbing, and since I haven't anticipated what I would find, I am neither elated nor disappointed. I am, however, totally surprised to find not one but two pictures taken by me hanging on a hallway wall. It is easy for me to identify both; I recognize the clothes. In the photograph of Eva Braun, she is wearing a lace dress taken on my very first visit to attend the Christmas *party. The photograph of Hitler and his German Shepherd Blondie along with Eva Braun and one of her Scottish Terrier Dogs Stasi was taken outside at a later visit.*

*Other pictures that hang on the walls throughout include watercolors of the rooms painted by Hitler himself. One can easily see that very little if anything remains from one of the worst periods in history. Although it is documented that Hitler only visited his retreat 14 times, Eva Braun spent far more time there entertaining her friends and family. A social event of note that took place at the Eagle's Nest was the wedding of Eva Braun's sister Gretl in 1944, long past my last visit. Hitler was not present at the party, but he did attend the reception at the Berghof.*

*Open to the public from mid-May through the end of October subject to weather conditions allowing accessibility, we learn that our tour is the first of the season.*

*Before heading back to Berlin, our bus stops in Berchtesgaden where we lunch at Kehlsteinhaus that has also recently opened for the season. It is delightful. It is late afternoon as we board our bus and head back to Berlin.*

*At dinner that evening, we all agree that the past two weeks have flown by as we enjoyed each and every day with special emphasis on the company and the food. We fly back to New York the following morning.*

*It is the only trip we take out of the country. It is a trip that I wish we had taken alone. Revisiting my childhood, tracing the life of the Bruner family, and sharing my memories with you firsthand would have been ideal. I would have liked to research any mention of my parents in the museum's records and perhaps learn about what happened to our neighbors and friends. I couldn't do that with Sharon and Stanley present.*

*Joe, I did the best I could and made the decisions that I thought best over the years since I lost you. I'm afraid I made a terrible decision in not opening the boxes Uncle Gus sent me. From time to time, you urged me to do so to no avail. Seventy years is a lifetime, but now that I have opened them, I have been given a second chance, the opportunity to give their son Charlie a priceless gift.*

*My recap of our 1976 trip was more for me than you. I just wanted to get everything straight in my mind before going downstairs and rejoining our family. Once again there is happiness and laughter in our beautiful home. What more could I ask for?*

*I so look forward to reaching for your hand and feeling the familiar warmth of your hand holding mine. I love you so my Joe.*

Lily awoke suddenly as if coming out of a trance.

A change of clothes after freshening up felt good. The nap was just what she needed. Lily stopped in her office before continuing downstairs to join the others.

∞

As Lily slept, the others remained in the garden enjoying the beautiful afternoon while sharing the excitement of playing a part in all that was to come. Nina elaborated on the museum relating how so many previous students and friends had came forward to volunteer their time to man the studio, as well as provide lessons. With the reorganization of the foundation, Nina opted to take on the day-to-day operations of *Portraits*, which included not only the museum, but also the lessons, and the handling of all financial matters.

As the afternoon wore on and the breeze kicked up, it grew cool. With everyone's help, they soon had all the furniture back in place, and the remnants from lunch put away.

The dining room table was set for dinner. Charlie and Sam returned to the library to watch television, and Trudy and Jodi followed Nina to the kitchen. They plated the appetizers and placed them in the refrigerator ready to be served. Dinner that had been preordered would be reheated as they enjoyed the appetizers and wine. There was no rush. They awaited Lily.

They were all in the library when she came downstairs. Her lounge chair awaited her. "My apologies for my impromptu departure. However, my little nap is just what I needed to get a second wind. It has been a long day for me."

Jodi assured her, "Nana I am certain that I speak for all of us when I say no apology is necessary. We're going to bring in the appetizers and drinks, while Nina puts dinner in the oven. Are you okay with that?"

"Of course, I am. Somehow whenever we're together, we never miss a meal. I think our ethic backgrounds have something to do with that."

The passing around of appetizers, and the filling of glasses prompted several renewed toasts of *Thank You* and *Congratulations*. When all were seated, Lily smiled contentedly and said, "Today has been a very fulfilling one for me. Surrounded by family and the people I love could not be more gratifying. Today is more than just a stop away from tomorrow. Though brief, each day is filled with hope and potential. No one knows better than I do that our todays are precious and are for us to enjoy.

"All too often the return of what we have put to rest reminds us that despite our efforts to the contrary, our past has a way of claiming far more than its fair share of attention. However, our past is our history and history speaks truth unaltered.

"Our future demands our focus to set our goals and nourish our growth so that we may realize our dreams. Our lives are too often interrupted by fate of which we have no control. Life offers us choices, but there are no guarantees.

"I am proud of all of us; not only of what we have done in the past, but what we have planned for the future, and sharing it is what has made today outstanding.

"Charlie, I don't know if you recall, but when you and Noah were in your third year of college, Joe and I took a trip to Vienna with your parents. When your father first brought up the subject, I admit I was a bit apprehensive, but as Joe pointed out to me, by the time the destruction of war came to Vienna, I had been living in Switzerland with my aunt and uncle for several years. The thought never crossed my mind to return probably because I left no one there.

"Your father explained that a travel brochure sparked his interest, and on a whim, he looked into it. He knew very little if anything about his family's deep-rooted history in Austria. At the beginning of the war, when your father arranged for his aunt to immigrate to New York, he saved her life. Other than your grandparents and your father, she was the only other Hurwitz to leave Austria. After the war, Sarah's attempts to learn if there were surviving members of the Hurwitz family were futile.

"Knowing that I was born and grew up in Vienna, he invited Joe and I to join him and your mother on the trip.

"On the other hand, I had total recall. I was eighteen when I lost my family so I knew Vienna quite well. I remembered every detail of my childhood, my parents and brother, the house where we once lived, the schools I attended, and The Art Museum where my parents worked. I would come to think of that trip as not only a gesture of kindness, but as a priceless gift from your father. I had never given thought to returning to Vienna or to Switzerland; without your parents' invitation, I never would have.

"The only information your father had was Sarah's address. What a day that turned out to be. The map your father picked up in the hotel gift shop was perfect. We had no trouble locating my old street; the neighborhood was as beautiful as I remembered. Our house had been replaced, as were all the others on our block.

"Your father produced a piece of paper with Sarah's address. With your grandparents and Sarah gone, there was no one to ask for additional information. As your father perused the map, he was pleasantly surprised to learn that her street was merely two blocks over from ours in the very same neighborhood.

"After a short walk, we stood before the house bearing Sarah's address. Your father wondered out loud if the house we faced was the original or if it had been replaced as those on my block had. It had been replaced; I could attest to it. Gartenweg 12 was the home of Sarah Freed, one of my mother's dearest friends. I had been to the home many times. Learning that I had actually known Sarah pleased your father to no end.

"We continued on. Visiting the University of Vienna and The Art Museum made me feel close to my parents. The park where my mother and I spent hours sketching, my schools, a government building or two, and a café or restaurant though replaced bore the names of old. The afternoon was nostalgic for me to say the least. I was overjoyed that Joe got to see where I lived and grew up.

"When we returned home, we reminisced for awhile, and moved on. I hadn't thought about our trip in decades until a few weeks ago. Upon returning from California, Jodi decided to pay a visit to the brownstone on Vanderbilt and go through the house. In the cellar she came across several large boxes shipped to me seventy years ago; they had never been opened. When she asked me about them, I told her they were sent to me from Switzerland after my uncle passed away, a few months after Joe and I were married.

"When asked if I knew the contents, I realized that I did not know exactly, but assumed they held paintings from his gallery in Zurich, along with personal items he left me. There was a smaller box that his attorney said contained paperwork.

"My decision to put off opening the boxes has proven to be one of the worst decisions I have ever made. I opened the smaller box first and found it held paperwork related to the contents of all of the boxes. I was right in assuming there were paintings, eleven in all, but they were not from his gallery; they belonged to my mother and came from our home in Vienna. There was additional paperwork and sales receipts regarding the purchase of several items of jewelry that were totally unknown to me.

"We unpacked the boxes. The paintings were as the list stated. My mother's jewelry box that we had taken from our house in Vienna was there and contained the beautiful jewelry my father had given her. I had totally forgotten about it.

"A separate box contained jewelry items that were mostly unknown to me except for one broach in particular that I had seen many times. In matching the receipts with the items, I realized what they represented. As war loomed, the Jews who had relatives in the states began considering their options to leave. Several friends approached my uncle to purchase their artwork to provide funds for their passage. He also helped my parents' friends at my father's request.

"The owners of artwork were far fewer than the many who owned jewelry. Everyone owned at least one piece whether they were wealthy or not. Somehow my uncle began purchasing jewelry in addition to artwork. Receipts contained details of each item, a brief description, the seller, and the amount paid. Listed with the broach were two additional items, a ruby and diamond necklace and a pair of matching drop earrings."

Lily stood and walked over to retrieve the box she had brought down from her office. Handing the box to Charlie, she said, "These belonged to Sarah Freed."

The silence was deafening. Everyone's eyes were on Charlie as he lifted the lid to reveal the beautiful items as they sparkled under the overhead light.

"If I had only opened the boxes sooner, I could have given your father as grand a gift as he gave me."

Overwhelmed, tears ran unashamedly down Charley's face as he hugged Lily.

Stepping back, she added, "I had all of the pieces cleaned and appraised. I suggest you insure them as soon as possible. It might be a good idea to leave them here in the safe until you do so."

From total silence to utter chaos, Nina announced, "Dinner is served!"

# Chapter 28

Sam smiled to himself as he fondly recalled his Nonna's words. *Don't rush time; it will pass fast enough when you grow old.* He was far from old, yet the previous two years had come and gone without hesitation despite the pandemic's mandates and regulations that brought everything to a screeching halt. Time marched on in quick- time without missing a step.

*Meyerson Media Group* was a work in progress. He took Lily's suggestion to checkout the available office space in the building where she had chosen to relocate the foundation. It was one of several new buildings nearing completion in the months prior to the city's lockdown, and although it was almost fully leased at the time, it remained largely unoccupied since the onset of the pandemic.

When the agent ushered Sam into the Penthouse, he knew immediately that his search was over. Large enough and fully equipped to accommodate their needs, it was actually the view of the city he loved and that *Profiles* was based on that sealed the deal. A fall move-in date looked promising.

The team hadn't missed a beat; shows through the end of 2022 were either complete or nearing completion. Carol had taken the lead on the anniversary episode prior to having received the news of their impending adoption in August, but the timing couldn't have been better. Normally, the show due to be aired in September was a wrap by the end of June, and this year was no exception.

Known as the *Children of 9/11,* there were more than 100 still in their mother's womb at the time of the attack; they were born in the immediate months after their fathers died. Unlike previous shows that concentrated on single digit participation, Carol aimed to interview and include everyone who came forward, and rather than single out individual experiences chose to treat them as a group.

To many who had spent twenty years feeling cheated for not having known their fathers or having a single picture of the two of them, Carol's approach was welcomed and opened up a long overdue conversation. She found her interviewees to be truthful, straightforward, and extremely loyal to the memory of their fathers, fathers they actually had no memory of.

With Lily's plans for the museum and the foundation nearing completion, Nina found herself with too much time on her hands. Although she was managing the day-to-day operations of the museum, she had chosen to step away from the foundation seeking only to take part when needed. The foundation's growth and reorganization demanded far greater expertise and participation going forward.

On a whim, she volunteered her help to Sam, adding that her experience in working with Lily for so many years was solid and far reaching. He decided to take her up on her generous offer and inquired if she had a background in human resources. It turned out she did. A team meeting to network and determine a priority for hiring additional personnel ended with the team's unanimous decision to bring Nina on board as a part-time employee of *Meyerson Media Group.*

Wasting no time, Nina hired a receptionist to replace Sandy. She suggested implementing an interim intern program for research positions by offering internships to college students during the summer months, as well as part time during the school year. Students of history, museum studies, historical preservation, archival management—to name a few— would qualify. Nina saw her vision as allowing them to learn from the bottom up while challenging them to excel in their individual preferences, as a win-win for everyone.

As the days of June peeled away, New Yorkers welcomed the easing and cancellation of COVID restrictions as the White House reluctantly stated that the pandemic was over. The midterm elections kicked off in earnest promising a *red wave* until the Supreme Court overturned *Roe vs. Wade*, ending 50 years of abortion rights by paving the way for individual states to curtail or ban abortion rights entirely. The ruling quickly became the focal point in the upcoming midterms.

Charlie arranged for Lily to have a complete physical at Lenox Hill Hospital as promised. Amazingly for the most part, she passed with flying colors. They did find that she was slightly anemic which could explain the fact that she frequently complained of being tired. He prescribed iron supplements and added iron-rich foods to her diet. With all that she had been up to since the beginning of the year, he felt alleviating herself of the responsibilities of the foundation, while transferring her estate holdings and commitments to Jodi and Sam would be treatment in itself.

On Father's Day, June 19, 2022, Edie and Lou welcomed Christopher Reed Collins. The blond-hair, blue-eyed cutie who weighed-in at 8 pounds exactly, announced his arrival with a lusty cry. Edie's mother came up from Florida to help the new parents settle in and get acquainted with her first grandchild.

With the reconfiguring of the new office space, the placing of orders for additional office furniture and equipment, and all *Profiles* programming through the end of the year complete, Sam and Jodi looked forward to Trudy's family reunion that was on target for being one of her best ever. She booked the second weekend in July for the event at the Rocking Horse Ranch Resort in Highland, New York. Less than 90 miles from the city and closer to those who lived in other parts of the state, it was a good choice. The resort catered to young and old alike.

When the weekend drew to a close, the Caruso Clan unanimously proclaimed the gathering a huge success. Lily, Nina, and Charlie had never seen anything like it. Since it was a first for Jodi too, it was unanimous; they thoroughly agreed.

Carol and Doug left the city for Upstate New York to await the birth of the daughter they were adopting in mid-July. Although she wasn't due until early August, the doctor indicated at the mother's last appointment with the baby in position, she was on track to deliver early.

They moved into their new condo in February—all of the rooms including the guest bedroom were complete. They were, however, slightly superstitious about finishing the nursery. Upon their departure, Jodi, Sam, Sandy, and Frank went to work with list in hand. They began by scheduling the wallpapering and installation of the window treatment. Next, they arranged for everything for the nursery to be delivered. While Sam and Frank set up the room according to specific instructions, Jodi and Sandy stocked the shelves and filled the drawers.

Carol and Doug brought their beautiful baby girl home on August 22, 2022. They named her Makayla Aubrey Cutler. Carol's parents were there to welcome them.

The house in the Hamptons was theirs for the entire month of August. Trudy, Charlie, and Lily were the only ones that stayed the entire time. Charlie's daughters and their families were invited and both came for a week. For the most part, Jodi, Sam, and Nina stayed until something arose that required their return to the office.

Charlie's watchful eye on Lily embraced her new *not a care in the world* attitude.

The Asher Foundation moved into their new home the end of August and officially opened their doors the day after Labor Day. In hindsight, the Foundation and Meyerson Media Group based in the same building turned out to be pure genius. Not only was it convenient for those involved in both entities, their interaction and support of mutual projects was never more apparent than with the upcoming airing of their premiere documentary in mid-October.

With Lily's Birthday approaching, Nina suggested a low-key celebration for the family, which would include a tour of the foundation's new offices followed by cake and ice cream in the conference room. As Lily ushered everyone around and received kudos for a job well done, Nina set up the refreshments. The plaque at the entrance to the conference room read: *Studio A—In Memory of Anton, Adele and Alexander.* To Trudy and Charlie, it was the perfect touch. Only Lily, Jodi and Sam knew it also included *Analiese.*

On September 8, 2022, New York City's public school students returned to class hopeful for a more stable year as the nation's largest school system aimed to overcome a 36% chronic absenteeism of the previous year. For the most part, masks and testing were suggested but no longer mandated.

September also put an abrupt end to rest and relaxation. Normally a busy month for the team, this year promised far more. *Meyerson Media Group* moved into their new office space. *Profiles'* 9/11 Episode was an instant hit. The Children of 9/11 were heroes in their own right as they moved on with their lives by honoring the fathers they never knew. They found strength in being presented as a group rather than individually and from a viewpoint unlike any other survivors.

In October, Sandy delivered a solid documentary on a subject that was particularly at the forefront of the new school year. *Education in Crisis* was the most viewed show in the history of PBS to-date. Not only did the audience consist of parents and grandparents, but also the number of students whose interest was peaked was overwhelming and unanticipated. The show was dedicated to Christopher Reed Collins and Makayla Aubrey Cutler.

As the midterms approached Election Day, the frenzy grew. No longer were our elections final on that day, but dragged on for weeks and weeks. There was no *Red Wave.* The Conservatives won the House by the slimmest of margins, but lost the Senate. The midterms had solved nothing. The nation remained divided with unrest and disappointment on both sides.

Jodi and Sam spent a quiet evening celebrating their first anniversary.

With their busy schedules, it was a wise choice. Thanksgiving was a family affair. Never had the Asher home been so blessed. At times, Sam felt guilty that while they were enjoying so many positive things in their lives, there were many who were suffering with no end in sight.

Our elected officials absent and derelict in their duties; the midterms yet to be determined; and no relief on the horizon for millions, did not deter the 2024 elections from becoming front and center. In the wings were numerous candidates champing at the bit to announce their candidacy for *President of the United States.*

December was a month devoted to family and holiday festivities. Sam and Charlie worked together to start off the month with an *evening to remember.* Both Jodi and Trudy had birthdays later in the month. Securing tickets for opening night of *A Beautiful Noise*, Sunday, December 4, 2022, and reservations for dinner at Sardi's in place, they announced their plans at Thanksgiving.

Created in collaboration with Neil Diamond himself, *A Beautiful Noise* is the uplifting true story of a kid from Brooklyn who became a chart-busting, show-stopping American rock icon. Much to everyone's delight, Diamond showed up and performed as the audience sang and danced in the aisles to his songs. Everyone agreed wholeheartedly with Lily's comment, "His music is in my DNA."

The remainder of the month flew by. Their holiday party at the new offices—Makayla and Christopher included, visits to holiday light shows, Christmas light decorations in Dyker Heights and throughout New York City kept them quite busy and on-the-go. Christmas Day was dinner at Trudy's. Bypassing gift giving to one another, they arranged for dinner with all the trimmings, toys, and gifts to be sent to a local shelter.

New Year's Eve was a quiet dinner for Trudy, Charlie, Jodi, and Sam. New Year's Day started with breakfast at Lily's, and was a repeat of Christmas Day devoted to family, just being together, and reflecting on the past year.

It was hard to imagine that a year that had only just begun was ending. It was a year of progress on many fronts. Certain issues had been put to rest while others had only just begun. The New Year would usher in the third anniversary of the onset of COVID-19. New Yorkers continued to face far too many challenges as they strove to recover from the pandemic.

∽

A *changing of the guards* at the Asher Foundation indicated that the reorganization was well underway, and everyone on board was eager and excited to set in motion the aggressive agenda that was planned for the New Year.

The first item of business was a dual event. It began with Lily personally honoring the retiring board members for their hard work and devotion. The foundation had been through unprecedented hard times and could not have survived without their loyalty and expertise. A catered lunch followed.

After lunch and the departure of the retiring members, the Foundation's first Board Meeting of new members was called to order. They began by going around the table and introducing themselves adding a brief background statement. A folder was given to each attendee outlining the programs in place, and an agenda going forward that was quite impressive. The folder also included a list of all employees on site, as well as outside legal and accounting services, although they were very close to finalizing both in-house legal and accounting departments.

All members were urged to familiarize themselves with the programs, request clarification if needed, ask questions, and feel free to offer suggestions.

As the conference room emptied, Lily asked Nina to remain behind. When they were alone, Lily took Nina's hands in hers; there were tears in her eyes. "The day we found one another was truly one of the best days of my life. I can't thank you enough for the plaque in memory of my family, but when I saw that you arranged to have my mother's paintings displayed on the walls of this room, I was speechless.

"Since handing over the reins to Jodi and Sam, I am well aware that any time I spend here will be limited to very special occasions. However, as I sat in the room today, the most wonderful feeling came over me as I looked at each and every painting and recalled how my mother fondly told me why she chose them. She truly cherished them."

Nina smiled to herself. "You're welcome my dear friend. I too bless that day, but there have been many more throughout the years that I also cherish. The Klimt painting is at the house. Since it was a gift from your father, I thought it too personal for the office."

A car was waiting to take Lily and Nina home.

New to the Board of Directors and never having served in that capacity previously, Trudy and Charlie decided to stay at the office and go over the information in the folders they had been given. They were excited to be a part of the foundation. Starting out as a small, low-key entity, it had grown substantially. Lily had given them an overview in the weeks leading up to their first meeting, but her assessment was modest at best.

The Asher Foundation of 2023 was well on its way to becoming one of the largest in the country. Headquartered in New York, and dedicated to promoting education and the arts, it was not only financially sound, but also prudently administered by a relatively small number of employees while keeping overhead at a minimum. Although originally expansion costs elevated, the decision to bring legal and accounting in-house indicated that they were leaning to a break-even point or slight reduction instead.

The dozens of scholarships, and financial support given to any project were awarded solely to New York institutions and groups to further education and the arts in all forms. The shows the foundation backed were aired on **PBS** and were tied to New York. Under no circumstances whatsoever would *Politics* or anything to do with *Politics* be considered. It was the one stipulation that Lily was adamant about. It was Joe's decision, and she never waivered from honoring it.

Everything they read about the foundation added to the rush of excitement at having been asked to be a part of it. They had delayed making plans to leave for Florida until after the meeting. By deciding to stay in the city until month's end, it afforded them the opportunity to spend time with the family while taking in a few Broadway shows with friends they had not seen since the pandemic.

As holiday decorations disappeared from view until next time, the weather fluctuated between cold and warmer days, rain and dustings of snow. Waiting for the holidays to pass, Edie and Lou scheduled Christopher's Christening for the second week in January. It was hard to believe, he was seven months old. Jodi and Sam were his Godparents.

February began with much colder weather, accompanied by warnings from the CDC for the sick and the elderly to stay indoors whenever possible. With the foundation no longer in the house, and Nina working part time for *Myerson Media Group,* Lily found herself with an excess of *alone time.* Each day without warning *Memories* invaded her thoughts.

At times it seemed as though she was in a trance, spending the day with her mother in Vienna sketching in the park, and the picnic basket with its contents so real, the aroma of cheese penetrated her nostrils. She heard her mother's voice loud and clear complimenting her work. That she could have so vivid a recall of such a young age was quite extraordinary.

On other days, her memories of Noah provoked strong and clear images as well. She could hear his voice, his calling *Mama* as he ran to her and she scooped him up in her arms covering him with kisses. Though he was born at a time *Portraits by Lily* often demanded her presence, rather than leave him behind, she included him taking him on an adventure. He loved the studio and all the attention lavished on him by the students who were enchanted by the rambunctious little boy who could stand before a painting for several minutes as if studying it.

More than anyone else, she recalled memories of Joe. Their early days together, their marriage, and especially when Noah was born, the strong and clear impressions on her senses filled her with love, happiness, and contentment. In all the years they were together, they never had a disagreement; their faith and trust in one another was unwavering.

Each memory occurrence was unique; each recalled a single person and her interaction with that person. Absent were family members and gatherings. Most notably was the absence of memories of Olivia. Perhaps recent months and having her back in her life left no need for memories.

For the first time in her adult life, she felt totally free, and while she embraced the feeling, Lily found herself in a place she had never been before. With the responsibilities of the foundation and the studio in the hands of others, and having fulfilled her promise to Joe to learn what happened to Nicole and Olivia, she chose to relish her newfound family while enjoying her blessings for whatever time she had left, a subject that was ever on her mind.

The month of March brought a break in the ever-pervasive memories. With spring just around the corner, she set up a series of meetings with the landscaper and other services needed for the house. At the top of the list, was a good spring cleaning, missing since the onset of the pandemic. Her office emptied of all business items, would remain an office with all the furnishings that she had so carefully chosen. The two additional rooms used for the foundation would remain empty for the time being.

Her landscaper needed no special instructions. He had taken care of both the house and the brownstone for many years. Flowers would be planted after the last frost, and the outside furniture wiped down and placed in the garden area.

Nina having overseen the hiring of the interns, and having submitted her proposal for the program to Sam, found herself going into the office only one or two days a week at most. The opportunity arose for Lily and her to spend time doing things they enjoyed that abruptly stopped three years ago.

She approached Lily with the subject. Lily was delighted. "Oh Nina, you read my mind. I would love to get out and about, with restrictions of course, and not go crazy, but there are so many things we can do."

They made a plan. They would use the car service for transportation, and outline their days to encompass more than a single place to visit but not so many as to be exhausting. They wanted to savor each and every choice.

For the most part, their excursions kept them in and around Manhattan; there were unending resources but Lily had certain places in mind. Broadway shows, favorite restaurants, the Ice Cream Factory, and West Village were all on the table. They devoted two days to DUMBO and Brooklyn.

Jodi and Sam wholeheartedly approved, but kept a very close eye on Lily. Nina assured them she would take every precaution to make certain that she would not overdo. With Paul as their driver, they stuck to their plans and only on one lone occasion did the weather dare to interfere.

New Yorkers found it hard to believe that three years of COVID, mandates, and masks had passed—that is until they woke up each day to the reality of the sad state of the economy, rising crime, and a multitude of other concerns. An additional and more pressing item raising concern was the open Southern Border and the ongoing migrant situation, which had reached unprecedented numbers. The city was in distress to say the least, as the Mayor warned they were headed to bankruptcy.

As Paul maneuvered around problem areas, his #1 priority was to see that Lily and Nina were safe. He dropped them off at each place they visited, and picked them up at the door. The pandemic that curtailed Lily's daily walks through the neighborhood ultimately became non-existent. But as of late, she found she lacked both the energy and the will to resume them.

By mid-March, they had completed their adventure; Nina who thought she knew Lily quite well learned a few new things in the process. When they visited DUMBO, she was surprised to learn that Lily had once considered opening a second studio there. Upon realizing that what made *Portraits by Lily* unique was its location in West Village, she quickly dismissed her thoughts never to be considered again.

Trudy and Charlie were returning the following week for a Board Meeting and a wedding and would not be going back to Florida until next season. They had made the decision to live together. Charlie planned to contact a real estate agent and put his Condo on the market. It was a beautiful unit that he had totally renovated when he purchased it; the building with a doorman 24/7 was secure; and it was located in a desirable Upper East Side neighborhood. He felt he would have no problem selling.

Jodi and Sam had lunch or dinner with Lily several times a week. They didn't want to come across as overbearing, but they worried about her constantly. Nina shared their concern when she discussed with them her feeling that their adventure seemed more like a farewell tour on Lily's part. Each place they visited, she had a story to tell and many of the places were a part of those memories.

Sam reasoned that at her age, she came to the realization that she wanted *one last visit and one last look* at her past even though her memory was as sharp as ever, and there was no way she would forget any of it.

With their adventure at an end, Lily began finalizing her plans for the upcoming anniversary of *Portraits* marking 75 years in West Village. The extensive reopening in 2022 announced that the Gallery would become a Museum showcasing many of her works, as well as her students' who wished to participate. In an effort for their community to mark the end of the pandemic, merchants throughout offered specials on food and goods to lure customers back into the shops. Widely advertised, it was a total success.

Lily thought a low-key Thursday through Sunday event with a street art show and refreshments would suffice. When her mother gave her that first camera, she had painted a portrait of herself from one of her very first photographs. In the years that followed at certain milestones in her life she continued to paint the self-portraits, which were all 5x7 in size and framed in identical wood frames.

Starting with the first portrait, which she painted when she was sixteen, there was only one additional painting just before she left Zurich. All of the others were painted in New York at times she deemed memorable. They began with the day *Portraits by Lily* opened in March 1948. The series included her and Joe's engagement, their wedding, Noah's birth, Noah's graduation from MIT, Noah and Nicole's marriage, Olivia's birth, and her 80th Birthday (painted just days before 9/11) among several others.

Frustrated and unable to come to terms with losing Noah, Nicole, and Olivia, her next painting was almost a year later followed by a longer period of many years before she painted her next one. It wasn't until Joe died and her hair turned gray overnight that her image in the mirror urged her to once again continue the series. Since that time there were five additional paintings; most recently when she and Olivia were reunited, Olivia and Sam's wedding, and the final one that she finished only days before.

She considered displaying the self-portraits for the 75th Anniversary and came to the conclusion that it would be a nice surprise for the family as well. She had never shown the paintings to anyone, not even Joe. Of course, she would have to confide in Nina her *partner in crime* in order to get them to the Museum and displayed.

It was an early spring, and March began with unseasonably warm weather. Last fall and for the very first time, her landscaper had planted tulip bulbs in the flowerbeds at the brownstone. The unexpected early warm weather created a magnificent array of color that was so breathtaking, he urged Lily to find time to visit and see for herself.

Lily and Nina awaited the car service to pick them up. They were going to the brownstone, stopping for lunch, and then they would be off to West Village where Lily would tell Nina her plan for the anniversary. Upon their return to the house, she would show her the portraits.

It was a wonderful spring day. The landscaper was right; the tulips were breathtaking. Lily smiled to herself. She always felt that the house came to life each spring when the annuals were in full bloom. Even when it stood empty or when times were sad, the magic of the flowers was heartwarming. The brownstone on Vanderbilt had been in the Asher family for over a century, but she alone had been the one responsible for the flowers.

They returned home in time for a short rest before meeting Jodi, Sam, Trudy, and Charlie at their favorite Chinese Restaurant for dinner. Trudy and Charlie were going to be Upstate for a wedding over the weekend; they planned the impromptu dinner to touch base.

Lily went up to bed. Nina checked to see that everything was in order, but before going upstairs, she decided to pop into the office and take a second look at the paintings that were lined up on the table in the order in which they were painted. Lily's eyes in each portrait revealed positivity, peace, passion, prosperity, perseverance, and pain coinciding with every aspect of her life. To Nina they were windows into the soul of the most beautiful person she had ever known. She was as beautiful in the last as she was in the first. What a precious gift to leave her family. She would never be forgotten. You don't forget someone like Lily Asher.

In the morning before going downstairs, Nina looked in on Lily. She was still sleeping. They didn't have anything planned for the day; Nina wasn't expected at work. Perhaps they could make a few calls to arrange for the art show and refreshments for the anniversary at month's end. A couple of calls should do it. A few days prior, the portraits would be taken to the Museum and displayed.

Nina poured herself a cup of coffee, turned on the TV, and sat down at the island to read the paper. Before she knew it, the clock on the stove read 10:00 am.

It was not like Lily to sleep this late. In her day, she had been an early riser wanting to get a head start on the busy day ahead. During the pandemic, with no place to go and nothing pressing to do, she normally arose at 7:00 am or by 8:00 am at the latest.

She walked into her room and immediately she knew. Lily was gone. Lying next to her on the bed was her favorite picture of Joe. Suddenly Nina began to cry uncontrollably as she sat at her bedside. After a while, she stopped crying but found it difficult to collect her thoughts. She just sat there unable to move, unable to think, unable to imagine life without Lily.

She began speaking aloud. "Goodbye my friend, my sister. I love you; I owe you for bringing me back to life. You picked me up and showed me the way when I had no one else. I will miss you every minute of every day until the end of my days. Rest in peace." She leaned over, kissed her on the forehead, and recited the Lord's Prayer. Then she went downstairs to call Sam.

They were in shock; they had been together mere hours ago, yet now she was gone. They would not mourn Lily. They would celebrate the person, her life, her successes, and the legacy she left them all.

It was agreed that she would be buried privately next to her beloved Joe with just the five of them in attendance. This would also allow the family almost two weeks of privacy and time to begin the process of coming to terms with moving forward without her.

The self-portraits were yet another surprise they never anticipated. Though Lily viewed them as personal, Jodi considered them among her best and meant to be shared.

In order to allow as many as possible to take part, a celebration of her life and the 75th Anniversary of *Profiles by Lily* was to take place in Washington Square Park in West Village by hosting a virtual live streamed memorial service.

Jodi prepared a press release announcing the passing of Lillian Asher.

# Chapter 29

Washington Square Park is a public park in the Greenwich Village neighborhood of Lower Manhattan, New York City. It is one of the best known of the City's public parks as an icon of meeting places and cultural activity. Having long been a gathering spot for avant-garde artists and a battleground for chess enthusiasts, it has served as an outdoor energized living room for generations of its bohemian-rooted and student-infused community. It was their venue choice for the Memorial Service.

Never before in its long and colorful history of lingering, playing, celebrating, or demonstrating had the park attracted a crowd of such diversity, loyalty, and devotion that spanned generations. There were police on hand to contain the huge number of people who had come to pay their respects, but they weren't needed.

Everyone's eyes stared upward as face after face appeared on the big screen eager to tell what Lily Asher meant to them. Lasting over three hours, the crowd remained in tact until the last voice went silent and the service ended.

Jodi and Sam graciously thanked everyone for coming in person, as well as those participating by video. An invitation was extended to everyone to visit the museum to view the premiere showing of Lily's self-portraits on display for one year. At that time, they would become a permanent part of the Museum.

The people who came up to her, introduced themselves, and professed their admiration for Lily overwhelmed Jodi. Grace and John Shepherd's grandson came with his wife. He had taken art lessons at the studio when he was a youngster. Although they had never met, he had been in touch with Lily from time to time. He had long treasured the original painting she had given his grandmother when she first came to New York.

It was a wonderful afternoon and although the crowd dissipated throughout the streets of West Village, few left the area until it grew dark and shops began to close.

The day had been a tribute to a New York icon whose legacy of love and giving back would forever remain in the hearts of millions of New Yorkers. As she had wished, she was not mourned; she was celebrated.

Jodi decided to take a couple of weeks to gather her thoughts. Sam thought it was an excellent idea. So much had happened since her move to New York, it was almost unbelievable.

After Lily's passing, Trudy had insisted that Nina stay with her rather than alone in the house. At first she resisted, but was glad that she reconsidered. As always, Trudy was a breath of fresh air, and just what she needed. Aside from being a nurse whose job it was to provide for the needs of others, she genuinely cared about people especially those she loved.

They reunited Lily with Joe in Mount Hebron Cemetery in Queens on a beautiful cloud-free morning filled with an abundance of sunshine and birds heralding the beginning of spring. The five people in attendance were her family. Each spoke from the heart—not of her but to her—what she meant to each of them. They concluded by reciting the 23rd Psalm.

The car service took them to brunch at Maman's in Soho. Over a mishmash of her favorites—Quiche Lorraine, chocolate croissants, and nutty chocolate chip cookies—their memories and comical stories filled them with laughter while reminding them of what a force of nature Lily Asher had been. Although she never got the recipe for nutty chocolate chip cookies, one could say that she certainly tried.

Both the burial and the memorial service were a team effort, and they were pleased with the outcome. The time had come to move on.

With Nina back at the house, Jodi called to set up a schedule. "Good morning! I hope I didn't catch you at a bad time. As I told you, I'd like to spend some time at the house, but only at your convenience. There is no need for you to rearrange your schedule for me."

Nina laughed. "Jodi, I don't really have a schedule these days. I realize that you want some alone time, and I understand completely. However, if you have no objection, I would also like to spend some time with you sorting through my thoughts, since there's a good possibility that there are many we share. At any rate, the house is certainly big enough that my being here the same time you are wouldn't present a problem."

Jodi was in total agreement. "You're absolutely right. I would like nothing better than the two of us working together."

Well into the month of May, they got together every weekday. Nina was the best link possible to Nana; she spent thirteen years working closely alongside her while living with her for over ten of those years. They discussed a myriad of things concerning the house, the museum, and working; before long, it became personal.

Jodi thought carefully before proceeding. She didn't want Nina to get the impression that she was urging her to make decisions that she was not ready to make. That was not her intention. "I guess I shouldn't be surprised that Nana took care of so many things before she died. The tulips at the brownstone were awesome; and the garden here is complete along with the spring-cleaning.

"Sam and I are concerned about you. You are officially part of our family, and we want to help you move forward any and every way we can. During the summer months when things are not quite as busy at work, I thought we could make some headway unless you have plans to the contrary."

Nina thought for a moment before replying. "I knew the decision to work as a team was the right way to go. You are extremely insightful. I have been privileged and honored to live in this wonderful house. Being in a position to help Lily manage the overall day-to-day care of a large home, as well as overseeing such mundane duties as groceries, laundry, and housekeeping was a responsibility I eagerly accepted as my way to give back for all she gave me. Many times this Kansas farm girl had to pinch herself to make sure it wasn't all a dream.

"Of course, I knew the day would come when we would lose her. However, I viewed that as a *future* not a *now* concern; however, *now* is here. As you know, Lily was quite generous providing for me in her will. I did not expect it; I honestly never thought about it. Our relationship was unique. For many years, we were one another's only family; we were best friends; we worked together; and we lived together. I might add we got along splendidly.

"With the Asher Foundation offices moving out of the house, it looms larger than ever. In no way does it qualify as a residence for one person. The reason I came to live here is gone. The only sensible decision for me to make is to move on."

Jodi tried to inject her thoughts, but Nina stopped her and continued. "It should be no surprise to anyone, and I don't believe that these surprises will stop anytime soon, but once again Lily took care of family. I don't know if she had a premonition that her final days were near, but her actions indicate to me she did. She spoke to Charlie and made arrangements to purchase his condo for me. She included a total renovation of the unit to my liking and Trudy added the services of her decorator.

"Since Trudy and Charlie are remaining in New York for the rest of the year, coordinating his move with the renovation should go smoothly. In the meantime, if you and Sam are in agreement, I will remain here. I don't know if you've given any thought to the house; I'm quite certain, you have no intentions of selling. Do you?"

"My goodness. Leave it to my Nana; what can I say? I am absolutely thrilled that your plans are solid and ready to go. Charlie's condo is perfectly located; it's convenient to the office, to the house, and in a neighborhood that you know well and has so much to offer. Selling this house will never happen. I see it staying in our family for generations to come. Sam and I have no problem whatsoever with you staying until the condo is ready. In the meantime, perhaps you and I can go through the rooms and pack up or give away items we don't need."

They enjoyed their days, just the two of them. They didn't confine their thoughts to Lily. For two and a half years, they had been in one another's company consistently getting to know one another and growing closer by the day. Now that Trudy and Charlie were on the foundation's board, and Nina was working for *Meyerson Media Group,* they were all working together.

In mid-May, Nina headed back to the office to get the summer intern program up and running. She scheduled orientation, and introduced the six participants. They were given an overview of how an episode of *Profiles* is produced. Explaining that once a subject is chosen, the importance of their job begins. Research is the engine that drives each and every aspect of the story—from the history to its individuals to the events to their impact on New York.

During lunch, the excitement that filled the room was infectious. The students were anxious to get started although the program was not scheduled to begin until June 1st. Depending on the number of episodes in the works, they were told that at times they would be working together while at others each would be on his/her own. They were all in agreement that the internship at *Profiles* looked to be a true learning experience.

In the past, the summer months had offered somewhat of a break at work. By June, episodes for the remainder of the year were either complete or very close to completion. In 2022, the first documentary they produced—*Education in Crisis* was a huge success. Sandy had taken the lead and discovered early on that the subject was too important and too vast to limit it to one episode. The series of four shows delved into the urgency of educating our children.

On tap for the fall of 2023, was a follow-up series of three episodes that explore options not only for higher education but for primary education also. With the student interns on board for the summer, Sandy planned to task them with the research of a subject near and dear to their own hearts. She also felt it would give their audience the perspective from their view.

Jodi and Sam looked forward to tackling several major decisions that although not pressing required some initial thought at least. While the office kept Sam busy, Jodi and Nina spent time together. Most of the time, though their discussions were all about Lily, they neither mourned nor celebrated her; it was simply an attempt to gently ease her out of their daily lives. They soon found that wasn't going to happen any time soon.

For the most part, Lily had seen to everything. The museum was up and running, fully staffed, and solvent. The foundation's reorganization was on track to award a record number of scholarships for the fall. The boxes found in the cellar at the brownstone had been unpacked and the contents at long last put to good use.

With Lily's passing, Jodi and Sam now owned two houses and all the contents. They decided to discuss how to move forward while vacationing in the Hamptons away from the city. For the time being, the apartment was convenient and suited their needs, but two empty houses requiring maintenance and upkeep indefinitely was simply not practical. The brownstone on Vanderbilt stood empty for over twenty years and as unbelievable as that was, the thought of Lily and Joe's beautiful home unoccupied and abandoned even for a short period of time, was totally unacceptable. Their problem was soon to be solved.

They were over the moon when they learned early in May that they were expecting. The baby was due in mid-December around Jodi's Birthday. Too soon to let everyone in on their news, they considered the Hamptons a better time and place to make their announcement. Jodi was fortunate that she felt pretty good. A couple of queasy mornings offered no inconvenience, and her appetite remained as robust as ever.

On their second visit to the doctor, they received news that put an entirely different perspective on things. They were expecting fraternal twins—a boy and a girl. While they were enthusiastic and eager to share that they were going to be parents, with their departure for the Hamptons only a few weeks away, they decided to keep their original plan in place.

The Hamptons house is quite large; with six bedrooms and six and a half bathrooms, there is more than ample room for guests. Sam decided to invite the team for a long weekend. It would be a nice vacation for Christopher and Makayla too, and a shared one-year birthday party for them would be fun. They could announce their good news when they were all together.

As Jodi's pregnancy grew more apparent with each passing day, Sam reconsidered and brought up the subject over dinner one evening. "Have I told you lately how much I love you Mrs. Meyerson? You look more beautiful than ever; being pregnant certainly agrees with you."

'Are you saying you think I look good with the added weight I'm carrying, or is it that special glow all future mothers have? Either way, I've never been happier, and I love you too Mr. Meyerson."

Sam laughed. "No, but it's getting to the point where your being pregnant is quite obvious, and I think we should reconsider and tell the family now. By the time we leave for the Hamptons, it won't be a secret any more.

"We've been busy and haven't gotten together much with the family especially in the past two to three weeks. My Mom and Charlie were away; you are still on hiatus from work so you haven't been to the office; and Nina returned to set up the intern program ending your daily get-togethers. We can still keep it under wraps for the team, but the minute they see you in the Hamptons, it's going to be apparent to them too."

"You're right. I think I saw Nina eyeing me one day as I was stretching. My normally flat stomach hasn't been flat for weeks. What do you suggest?"

"Simple, arrange for a family dinner. I feel kind of guilty keeping our news from Mom in particular, but from Charlie and Nina too. I know she's going to go ballistic and start shopping immediately so be forewarned and prepared."

Jodi gazed down at her stomach. "It's settled then. Let's have dinner this weekend. Do you want to have it here or at a restaurant?"

"Before I answer that question, I have another subject that I have given some thought to, and I'm thinking you might like and agree with what I'm thinking."

"Okay Sam, I'm listening. What's been on your mind? What have you been up to? Should I be concerned?"

"First, I want to thank you for all your hard work getting the house cleared out and helping Nina move forward with her plans. I know it couldn't have been easy especially when we first learned we were expecting, and you were not feeling well, yet you managed to soldier on and get everything done before Nina returned to work.

"Just as Nana took care of so many things before she died, you followed in her footsteps. With the twins due in December, we have sufficient time to dismantle the office, set up a nursery, and make the entire apartment *baby friendly* before their arrival. For the first few months, I think it will be easier on us to be where we are. We will be closer to them when they need feeding or changing, and I know Mom will be there for us if we need her and Charlie too. How lucky are we to have a nurse and a pediatrician right down the hall?

"That leads me to my next thought. When Nina is settled in her new condo, and I think that should probably be by late summer or early fall, we can begin planning a total renovation of the house. Spring would be the perfect time to move our family into our new home. The house means too much to both of us to leave it vacant for any period of time. As far as I know, it has never been unoccupied since Lou and Arlene moved in over seventy-five years ago.

"That's what I have been thinking. What do you think?"

Jodi walked over to Sam and kissed him. "I love you so much; I love your thinking too. My thinking is telling me to have dinner at the house this weekend and along with our news of the twins, we can tell them our plans for the move."

Jodi and Sam took care of everything. They invited everyone; they ordered dinner partially prepared and added the finishing touches; and having asked Nina to come with Trudy and Charlie, they awaited their arrival.

Jodi wore a billowy top with maternity Jeggings and actually looked slim. Appetizers and champagne awaited their guests. It was their first time together in the house since Lily died. Over the previous two years, the house was the core of their family; it not only brought them together, it tied them together. To all of them, Lily's presence would forever be felt throughout every inch of the home she loved and shared with Joe.

Of the many occasions celebrated within its walls, none held more meaning than three generations of weddings—Lily and Joe, Nicole and Noah, and Jodi and Sam. In the spring, it would welcome a new generation, not with a wedding but with the birth of the twins—Lily and Joe's great grandchildren.

When their guests arrived, they were ushered into the library where champagne and appetizers awaited. Sam asked everyone to take a glass of bubbly before speaking. With Jodi's glass of apple juice and Sam's glass of champagne raised, they spoke in unison. "We are proud and happy to tell you that we are going to be parents in December. We are expecting fraternal twins—a boy and a girl."

The small party of five managed to be quite vocal as everyone hugged and congratulated one another. As Sam had predicted, Trudy went ballistic but that was a good thing. They looked forward to her help and guidance. Over dinner, they discussed their plans to move into the house after a complete renovation. For the first time since Lou and Arlene's days, it would be solely a residence. The only events celebrated would be family oriented and have nothing to do with the foundation or *Meyerson Media Group.*

With August approaching and their departure for the Hamptons on tap for the following week, Sam called a team meeting to go over the fall programming schedule. The 9/11 episode complete and ready to be aired is dedicated to the 343 New York Firefighters that lost their lives that day, and delves into the 11,000 plus FDNY members who are suffering from World Trade Center-related illnesses. By year's end, it is predicted that the same number of firefighters that died that day will be matched and undoubtedly surpassed.

On a lighter and sweeter note, October *Profiles* the story behind Manhattan's oldest chocolate house, formed in 1923. In 1914, a young Greek immigrant with the rare skills required to create chocolate stepped off the SS Laconia at Ellis Island. Nine years later, that same young man would make his mark and rise to become the proprietor of the New French Candy Company at 120 Christopher Street in the heart of Greenwich Village. Later to be known as Li-Lac Chocolates, *Timeless Tradition* is the 100-year history of what has become one of New York City's premier chocolate houses and one of the few old-school chocolate companies to survive into the modern era.

Their Documentary—*Education in Crisis*—thoroughly covered *The Negative Effect of the Pandemic on Our Children's Education, their Social, Emotional, and Mental Wellbeing, and How the Pandemic Exacerbated Educational Inequities.*

The fourth episode was a roundtable of experts offering ways to move forward.

Although the 2023 series continues the discussion of education in the United States, it is not a documentary. It is a look to the future, a look to customizing education to the student, and a revisit to the concept that higher Education is a *one size fits all*. Costs and a guide to available scholarships, and counseling are just a few of the topics discussed. With input from parents, teachers, and students alike, it is meant to offer a wide range of options.

The final episode is set to announce a new entity entitled *Paths* funded by the Asher Foundation that offers counseling to high school students; *Paths' Mission Statement—Helping you choose the right path in life.* Everyone's definition of *right* will be different. Guidance offered will include choice of college versus vocational training, student loans vs. financial support, and following your passion versus what is expected of you. The free service will be accommodated by appointment only on a first-come, first-served basis.

November *Profiles* features fall fun at the Great Jack O'Lantern Blaze in the Hudson Valley at Van Cortlandt Manor in Croton-on-Hudson for the 19th year, and Old Bethpage Village Restoration in Old Bethpage, Long Island for the fourth year. Both experiences feature thousands of hand-carved Jack O'Lanterns in elaborate displays, along with annual favorites like the Statue of Liberty, the Pumpkin Planetarium, and the country's first-ever pumpkin Ferris wheel in Hudson Valley.

December *Profiles* visits American Christmas, largely responsible for many of the decorations throughout Manhattan. A seasonal stroll along Holiday Lane in Mount Vernon, NY, their indoor walkthrough experience, transports visitors of all ages to a world of wonder and holiday enchantment with over 100,000 lights, 100 animatronics, 9 themed areas, and so much more. For a nominal fee, reserved tickets are a must; 100% of which is donated to local non-profits.

Sam was pleased that everything was going well at the office. With their trip to the Hamptons coming up, he looked forward to just chilling out and clearing his mind of all things pertaining to business. He hoped that he and Jodi could reach some decisions about the renovations to the house, so they would be ready to get started once Nina moved to her condo. He was also looking forward to the crew's visit and spending time with Chris and Makayla who were both walking.

With the car packed to the gills, they set off for the Hamptons on a beautiful sunny morning the first week of August. Trudy and Charlie left two days previous and had taken Nina with them. When they arrived at the house, Trudy had lunch waiting on the patio overlooking the pool.

After unloading the car, they joined the others who awaited them. Lunch was relaxing and enjoyable as they talked about a myriad of subjects. Trudy surprised them by asking, "What do you think about Charlie and I buying this house? Shirley Rosen hasn't really used it for years, and she told me before we left Florida that she plans to put it on the market."

"Mom, I think that's a fantastic idea. I love this place; it's a beautiful piece of property. Charlie, your kids seem to like it here too. It would certainly serve as a gathering place at least once a year; it's family friendly and good for kids of all ages."

Trudy seemed pleased. "That's what we thought. She refurnished the house just a year before the pandemic and upgraded all the appliances, and she's selling it with all the furniture, so there's very little if anything to do. I love it here too and really look forward each summer to spending time away from the city at the shore.

"I told her that we were definitely interested and that we would give her an answer at the end of the season. Jodi, Nina any thoughts?"

Jodi spoke first. "I agree with Sam. I love it here too, and it would definitely be a great place for the twins particularly their first couple of years."

Nina chimed in. "It's unanimous; I love it too. Lily used to say she could totally unwind here; I totally agree with her. Being together is the best part."

Trudy clapped her hands and laughed. "Then it's a done deal. Charlie and I already decided we were going to buy the place. It's been easy to notice how much coming here the past few years has meant to all of us."

The next day the team arrived. Everyone was excited about Jodi and Sam expecting twins. Greg was funny when he said, "You guys never do anything the easy way, but don't worry; we're all here to help if needed."

Christopher and Makayla gave Jodi and Sam a preview of what to expect.

The days passed with one group of guests leaving and another arriving a day or so later. All too soon August ended, and it was back to the city, to work, and to waiting for the arrival of the twins.

∞

As the month *Profiles* premiered, September is always crucial with the 9/11 episode setting the pace for the beginning of a new season of programming.

The anniversary show was a solid winner and received kudos not only from their fan base, but also from the thousands of victims and their families that continue to suffer and die from 9/11-related illnesses. From time to time, articles appeared in various periodicals but were never reported to any extent.

The excitement surrounding the premiere Documentary—*Education in Crisis*—was rewarded with an unprecedented number of viewers, and was lauded by parents, students, and educators alike when it aired in October 1922. A series of three segments to further explore the subject, and offer options to higher education was set to air the first episode—*College Isn't for Everyone*—in the early weeks of October 2023.

New Yorkers began to breathe easier as the pandemic faded from the headlines. Flu shots and the new COVID vaccine became available and although highly recommended urged all to check with their own physicians first. While many still worked from home; slowly but surely more and more began returning to their offices at least on a part-time basis.

For the most part, New Yorkers were easing further and further away from the pandemic and its confines. A colder and snowier winter was predicted for the northeast but the National Weather Service had been wrong before, so it was of little concern. For the first time in almost four years, feelings of hope, optimism, and family emerged.

Jodi and Sam were good. Their plans for renovating the house, and converting the spare room in their apartment to a nursery were in the works and both were on schedule.

As Jodi grew more cumbersome, Sam became more protective. There was no reason for her to go to the office, and he didn't like leaving her alone. He made the decision to work from home and only go to the office if the need arose.

# Chapter 30

The first episode of *Profiles'* education series aired in early October, and as the week drew to a close, the Palestinian group Hamas shocked the world with a full-fledged surprise attack on Israel waged by air, sea, and ground by hoards of Hamas militants. Within hours of the attack, Israeli Prime Minister Benjamin Netanyahu called it a *dark day* for his country and declared war on Hamas. A veteran Israeli military official deemed the assault *Israel's 9/11*.

In the days immediately following the attack, the Israeli Defense Forces unearthed the trail of unimaginable slaughter resulting in over 1400 deaths, 3400 injured, and over 200 taken hostage and held in Gaza, among them 27 Americans killed, 17 taken hostage, and at least 14 missing. Entire families were shot as they slept in their beds; infants were beheaded; and women, children, and the elderly were driven into Gaza as hostages.

The mere mention of a comparison to 9/11 brought back memories of a day that New Yorkers had spent 22 years coming to terms with. Eleven percent of the State's population is Jewish, making its Jewish community the largest in the world outside of Israel. Approximately half a million Americans live in Israel.

As the calendar peeled off day after day of October, Israel vowed to defeat

Hamas once and for all. They prepared for a ground invasion of Gaza. Throughout the month, demonstrations for both sides raged across the country. In New York, as tempers flared and tensions ran high, thousands took to the streets.

For the first time since the Holocaust, anti-Semitism reached an unprecedented level rearing its ugly head and spilling over into the streets and onto the campuses throughout calling for the annihilation of all Jews and the destruction of Israel. Though the protests spread across the country, nowhere were they more concerning, unending, and disruptive than in New York.

November, a month Sam looked forward to preparing for the twins arrival and finalizing their plans for their move to the house was upended by the war in Israel, as day after day disheartening headlines dominated the news. He was worried about Jodi. For the most part she didn't share her thoughts, but he saw the deeply troubled look in her eyes as she watched relatives of the hostages pleading for their safe return.

Until now, morning sickness early in her pregnancy had been the only issue she faced. Weeks away from her due date, she found it frustrating and unable to get comfortable sitting or lying down. Many nights, she tossed and turned keeping Sam up in the process.

Sam continually searched for ways to keep her occupied otherwise and continue forward with their plans. Trudy helped order the seemingly endless items for a newborn times two. The office had been dismantled, painted, and stood ready to receive the deliveries to come.

One evening after Jodi retired early, Sam decided to look at the plans for the house one last time before turning in; they had a meeting in the morning with the contractor. After checking and rechecking to make certain he hadn't omitted anything, he placed the papers and notes in the folder. Everything was good to go.

Rubbing his eyes, he leaned back in his chair and let his mind run away with a million thoughts that invaded his senses to a point beyond reasoning. Over and over, he kept asking himself, *how did we get here?*

He considered himself an average citizen, a proud American who loved his Country. He considered himself fortunate, perhaps lucky, to have great parents that raised him with love and taught him to be honest, to treat others with respect, and to always help anyone he could if the need arose. His life was middleclass America; he attended public schools until he went to college, and his friends came from an eclectic background. They were his schoolmates, his peers, and his neighbors; they became friends through the interests they shared. Race, religion, and the color of one's skin were never factors in his choices.

He was a good student, and one of his favorite subjects was History. He often attributed that to his teacher Mr. Marks who awakened in him the desire to learn all that he could about America and then about New York. Upon graduation from high school, he pursued a career in Journalism. It was from Mr. Marks' teachings that *Profiles of New York* was born. In retrospect, he could have become a teacher, but a media audience allowed him to reach far beyond a classroom in both scope and age.

Politics were a part of his life only to the extent that he always voted, priding himself on the fact that he was an informed voter. Registered as an

Independent, he felt it gave him the freedom to approach each election with an open mind and thus far, he stood by his choices. He made his decisions based on a candidate's record, policies, and vision for the future. He paid no attention to political smear ads, to rubberstamp voting, to identity politics, or to encouragement by groups or individuals to support their choice. Only the candidate's voice caught his ear.

November 7, 2023 was *Voting Day* in America for statewide elections. It was also their second Anniversary. They voted early to avoid the crowds, and opted to spend a quiet evening at home to celebrate.

Once again, a predicted *Red Wave* did not materialize; once again, setting aside the economy, unending and unpunished crime, and the illegal migrant crisis on course to bankrupt not only New York City, but also cities all across the country, voters prioritized abortion issues above all else.

Before marrying Jodi, his sole responsibility had been himself. He now had a wife, and was mere weeks away from becoming a parent, and everything that had shaped and given meaning to his life was in peril.

For over twelve years and 123 episodes, each month millions tuned-in to watch *Profiles* air an episode of *New York* history. New York City long ranked #1 in the country to visit with its variety of cultural attractions, extraordinary culinary offerings, landmarks, museums, and robust nightlife continually led the way drawing millions of tourists each and every year.

Headlines like *NY, NY—IT'S A SHELL OF A TOWN; THE BIG APPLE IS ROTTING AWAY; NEW YORKERS WHO NO LONGER LOVE IT ARE LEAVING IT*—are but a few of the many that portrayed the city's current declining state of affairs.

The facts that were staring everyone in the face had been denied too long. New York—the greatest city on earth where everyone wants to come is indeed rotting away and becoming a shell of a town with high rents, high taxes, the smell of Pot, crime through the roof with no accountability, vagrant-filled sidewalks, no support for seniors and veterans, overwhelming support for migrants, English becoming a second language, businesses closing up, people packing up, and the middleclass? Gone.

If that isn't enough, anti-Semitism has taken over the streets, the schools, and the media. It has infiltrated every part of our lives with disruptions, demonstrating, and hatred aimed at America. Within the halls of Congress, we stand divided, our elected officials unable, perhaps unwilling to defend and support the very people who elected them.

Sam suddenly sat upright visibly shaken by his thoughts. It pained him to realize how bad the situation had become. The 2024 elections loomed large; they were only weeks away from the Iowa Caucuses that would kickoff the primaries. Although all elections are important, as they should be, both sides were touting 2024 as the *most* important one in our lifetime. The one truth they agreed upon.

He firmly believed that an informed voter was paramount and that one should vote as an individual. He never accepted politicians who went after the *black vote, the Hispanic vote, or the Jewish vote,* anymore than he felt a person should be appointed or hired for a position because of *gender, skin color, or religion.* In his mind, political positions were not suited for on-the-job training. He believed in voting for people for their qualifications.

Suddenly an idea came to mind that he and Jodi could work on from home. It would help pass the time while keeping them productive as they awaited the birth of the twins. It was also right in line with furthering their documentary subject matter.

Sam looked at the clock and saw it was almost time to get up, and he hadn't gone to bed yet. He brushed his teeth, changed into his pajamas, and quietly slipped into bed.

Their first stop was at the doctor's for what had become weekly visits. The babies and Jodi were fine, and she confirmed once again that they were on schedule to arrive the second week in December.

Although they were early for their next stop to meet with the contractor and sign off on the renovations to the house, they decided to proceed on the chance that he was free and could see them when they arrived. He was glad that they did. The few questions that Jodi and Sam had were quickly resolved; they signed off on the corrections; work was scheduled to begin immediately.

As they rode the elevator to the lobby, Sam asked, "Are you up to an early lunch? I'd like your opinion on my newest and most enterprising idea."

Jodi smiled to herself. "Of course, I am. When have you ever known me to turn down food or a meal when I wasn't eating for three? Now that I am, there's no chance whatsoever. And I'm curious about your idea which you're not going to tell me about until we're seated and ready to dig in, right?"

It was Sam's turn to smile to himself. One thing for certain, they knew one another quite well. "Right you are. I'm not being evasive; it's a serious subject, and I need your undivided attention when I present it to you."

Sam called and made a reservation at Match Brasserie; close by, it was a short walk away. After they were seated and had ordered, Sam began. "I won't keep you in suspense any longer. Last night after you went to bed, I turned off the news, closed my eyes, and tried to get a handle on all the thoughts raging through my mind. No matter how hard I tried, I could not dismiss the fact that what is happening in America is deeply troubling.

"Closer to home, what's happening in New York is downright frightening. Have we lost our minds? Through all the trials and tribulations New Yorkers have gone through both in my lifetime and before, it gets harder with each passing day to see a way out of the mire we find ourselves in. We are about to become parents, and I find our present situation both urgent and difficult to accept.

"For me, the overwhelming support for the terrorist group Hamas on our college campuses is the most disturbing issue. After becoming highly invested in higher education through our *Crisis in Education* series, it is unsettling to me that so many students have no clue whatsoever what this country was founded on, what we stand for, what freedoms we have, and why so many have risked everything and continue to do so to come here for a better life, a new beginning. The responses from the American-born students interviewed at the protests indicate they either don't know why and what they are demonstrating for, or they know little if anything about the great country we live in. Sadly, I'm inclined towards both.

"Without any relief in sight, and to make matters even worse, we are a few weeks away from the start of the 2024 elections. The history of recent elections in far less dire circumstances is not in the least encouraging and does not offer even a tiny glimmer of hope that this time things will be better, or that we will get it right.

"Void of politics, *Profiles* has always been and always will be about history based on fact which translates into truth whether we are profiling people, places, or events. Unfortunately in today's culture there are many who deny history thereby denying fact resulting in less and less truth.

"With *Meyerson Media* now at the helm, our shows have concentrated on education, and I foresee this line of thinking extending into the future. It is more urgent than ever that voters do not act on hearsay or become sheep and simply follow the crowd.

"With the 2024 elections coming up, and the 250th Birthday of the United States two years away, *Educating America—Getting Back to Basics* would make an excellent documentary for us to develop. I see it as a three-part limited series to be aired the second week in January on three consecutive evenings just ahead of the primaries.

"My initial thoughts are that you and I can start the process working from home and develop the first episode. We could then present it to the team and hand it over to them to develop the second and third. I sense the wheels spinning in your brain. So what do you think?"

"Oh Sam, I love it. I have gone over and over many of these same thoughts as I watched the horrors of the past month dominate the headlines. I welcome the opportunity to be useful and work on something near and dear to my heart at a time when it's getting harder and harder for me to get around. Working from home will be much easier for me, and I promise not to overdo.

"It reminds me of what a good team we were when I first came to New York and was about to embark on my interview with Nana."

They talked and talked during lunch, and Sam loved seeing her so excited about their project. Everything for the arrival of the twins was in place; and working together leading right up to the births seemed the perfect diversion. Certain that things would become chaotic once the babies arrived, he felt strongly that keeping her occupied would deter marring this joyous occasion in their lives.

They hit the ground running by taking a day or two researching on their own before comparing notes and deciding how to proceed. Having offered his line of thought, Sam encouraged Jodi to come to her own conclusions.

When the day arrived to put their heads together, it was obvious Jodi was enjoying every minute of their collaboration. It was just what she needed to make time pass, while allowing her to be a part of what Sam envisioned for *Meyerson Media's* next offering. It was a good feeling to be useful and needed.

After breakfast, they settled in the living room to begin comparing notes. Jodi offered to go first. "Before I give you my thoughts, I just want to say *Thank You.* I'm terribly excited about your idea, and humbled that you asked me to be a part of what I consider an extremely important first step forward. On a lighter note, I'm willing to bet that not many pregnant women in their eighth month get offered such an opportunity. With that said, here are my thoughts.

"The title you gave the documentary said it all to me. I took *Getting Back to Basics* to mean way back to the founding of our great nation and our Constitution—a first of its kind document that remains so to this day.

"I came across a pocketsize book distributed by the Commission on the Bicentennial of the United States Constitution. The goal of the Commission was to stimulate an appreciation and understanding of our national heritage—a history and civics lesson for all of us—by reading and grasping the meaning of the document. That was almost 50 years ago, yet I feel it is even more significant today.

"The Commission consisted of 24 members. Warren E. Burger, Chief Justice of the United States was designated Chairman. When I read the FORWORD he wrote for the book, I was terribly moved. His beautiful words encompassed what our great nation stands for and why our democracy had endured for almost 200 years up to that point.

"If possible, I suggest we consider reissuing an updated pocketsize book of the Constitution and its Amendments, and distribute copies prior to the airing. Am I on the right track with your thinking or have I blown it?"

Sam was speechless; she was good; no she was excellent. He had forgotten how thorough her research had been when he sought her help in the past, long before she came to live in New York. "Wow, you amaze me. You're my *wonder woman* eight months pregnant or not.

"Your ideas are similar to what I have in mind, and you grasped where I'd like to begin perfectly. Why don't we take the next couple of days and the weekend working together to come up with the first episode?

"Although I have never entertained producing a show about politics, I want to stress the importance of our right to vote. For the most part, I'm leaning towards younger Americans whose curriculum no longer includes history or civics. It is disturbing to me to hear the students that are interviewed at the protests unable to reply to basic questions about our history.

"It reminds me of Jay Leno's *Jaywalking* segments where he would ask people on the street random questions about our country. American-born college students didn't have a clue when asked what a particular holiday celebrated, to name the current Vice President, or what country we defeated to win our independence. The segments were always good for a laugh, but in retrospect, it was rather depressing.

"By energizing young and old alike to return to basics, the goal is to impress not only the importance of our right to vote but equally as important to become an informed voter. For decades, we have elected and reelected politicians who have not served the very people who elected them. We are at a point in history where we have never been more divided. We need to elect strong, capable leaders who will not only reunite us but also return our country to its glory.

"The second episode could open with the history of voting and the four governing Amendments. Registering to vote, early voting, mail-in voting, voting accessibility, voting locations, etc. would be addressed. In addition, how to become an informed voter, and what a voter has the right to expect from a candidate seeking their support would shine the spotlight on the importance of each and every vote.

"I haven't given as much thought to the final episode, but during my research the past two days, the idea of addressing new, first-time candidates occurred to me. In line with this, we could interview first-time voters and also get their thoughts.

"After we present the series to the team, we can determine if we've covered everything we set out to accomplish; I'm certain they will have an abundance of suggestions of their own.

"Next Monday after our weekly doctor's appointment, I can set up a meeting at the office, and we can present our ideas at that time. That way we can get everyone working on it. Do you think my goal to air the series the first week in January is realistic? The Iowa caucuses are Monday, January 15th, followed by the New Hampshire Primary on Tuesday, January 23rd.

"You're probably thinking, is he done yet? I am. What are your thoughts?"

"Sam, I love when you're so passionate about an idea that the wheels just keep on turning in that brilliant mind of yours. I agree with everything. The first episode is powerful and would be a fantastic documentary on its own. I do feel, however, we should tread very carefully in our presentation of voters and candidates in the second and third episodes so that no bias or political party becomes a part of the story.

"With that said, I think we're good to go. Our team is unstoppable. There is no doubt in my mind that we will deliver the series in your timeframe. Your choice just happens to be the perfect airtime with the Iowa caucuses less than a week later. Just imagine the hype factor kicking in. That's really what we're trying to do here, isn't it? When is the last time anyone was excited about an election? Let's do it."

Sam stood, walked over to her and kissed her. "Let's take a break. If you feel you need to lie down for a while, you should. We have soup and sandwiches for lunch whenever you're ready, and leftovers for dinner that only need to be heated up. I suggest we each work on our own for now, and we can talk about our progress over dinner."

Sam welcomed the chance to work with Jodi on their project. It was a diversion from the sadness that engulfed him as each passing day brought pro-Hamas demonstrations throughout the city he loved. No longer could they be labeled pro-Palestinian. To make matters worse, they spread to state campuses. Although the protestors claimed to be peaceful, they were not as people could not deny what they saw with their own eyes. Police were attacked and injured, arrests were made but they were released immediately, and vile chants were aimed at the Jews decrying their very existence.

Jewish students on the campuses involved felt threatened and unsafe and looked to their schools' hierarchy to intervene. At first, many had *no comment*, but as longtime Jewish donors began calling them out and distancing themselves from their Alma Maters, they were forced to issue statements, perhaps too little too late.

The demonstrators demanding a ceasefire in Gaza targeted New York members of Congress and the Governor's home, Biden's home in Delaware, and the White House where red paint was smeared on the gates. Who could have ever imagined this happening in our country?

By contrast, in early November, a pro-Israel march on Washington, DC drew 300,000 peaceful advocates that included members of Congress, celebrities, Christians, Jews, young and old; many spoke eloquently from the heart. Their sole request was to free the hostages.

The day following the march, a post on TikTok of the 2002 Osama bin Laden *Letter to America* justifying the killing of Americans on 9/11 and criticizing US support of Israel added fuel to the fire. The video went viral. Most disturbing were dozens of young Americans posting expressions of sympathy for Osama bin Laden.

Although politicians and influencers immediately condemned the users creating the posts and called for a ban of the App, the families of 9/11 victims emerged victims once again—22 years hence. Most of the posts were taken down, but not before they spread and expanded on other social media sites.

As protests continued, they grew to include anti-American policies. Negotiations were ongoing to free the hostages, and a brief ceasefire to allow food and medical supplies to be delivered to Gaza, made little progress.

New York faced additional problems. The Mayor under investigation for the misuse of campaign money, favors, and possible foreign influence presented a budget cut of 50% across the board urging tax payers to help by contributing funds to the city. A new headline emerged—*THE BIG APPLE IS NOW THE BEG APPLE!*

Sam was invigorated by their project. Although Jodi was also, she found it impossible to deny how offended and deeply hurt she was by the young Americans who readily dismissed 9/11—the deadliest terrorist attack on American soil in US history. 9/11 had changed the course of her life, but she was not alone; almost 3,000 people died and thousands were injured that day while many continue to die from related illnesses.

Though each approached the planned documentary from different viewpoints, their thoughts to present it were one-in-the-same. They worked diligently to present the show as *history* translating into *truth* and the need to educate future generations.

Sam set up the meeting with the team on Monday at noon, and ordered lunch to be delivered. He advised them that there would be nine people in attendance including a special guest, and requested they clear their calendars for the afternoon.

His enigmatic side was not wasted on his friends; it excited them. They never knew what to expect when Sam's creative juices began to flow.

Their appointment went well. The babies weighed over four pounds each, and Jodi's due date remained on schedule. Although she had reached the final uncomfortable and stressful weeks of pregnancy, the doctor found her upbeat demeanor and uncomplaining nature refreshing.

The car service awaited them as they left the doctor's office. They had one stop to make before heading to the meeting—to pick up their guest. She smiled as she imagined the look on everyone's faces when they entered the conference room.

Guy Marks, or *Mr. Marks* as Sam continued to call him, was not only his favorite teacher, he was the one person he credited with guiding him towards a career in Journalism. He had briefly considered becoming a teacher himself, but Mr. Marks saw a special talent in him—*writing*—his ability to express in words the enlightenment of any subject he chose to write about.

Carol, Greg, Frank, Lou, and Sam had grown up together in Port Chester, New York, and attended Port Chester High School. They had all been Mr. Marks' students in US History and Civics.

Sam contacted him when the idea of *Profiles* first began to emerge. From time to time over the years, he continued to reach out for his knowledge, advice, and opinion on the two subjects that were near and dear to his heart—history and civics.

On the other hand, Mr. Marks was proud and honored that he had made such an impression on Sam and often called to extend praise for an episode of *Profiles*.

When the thought occurred to Sam to call Mr. Marks, it was not to seek his advice. It was to include him in the episode. Presented as a lesson, he could think of no one more suited to the job than the person who had taught him. Embracing Sam's idea for the show, he eagerly accepted the invitation to once again play a part he had played most of his life—US History and Civics Teacher.

When they entered the conference room, the smiles that lit up the faces of Carol, Greg, Frank, and Lou were priceless. They began with lunch, and as they ate, Jodi and Sam gave them an overview of the project they had been working on. They began with the headlines that encompassed the world while expressing urgency for the headlines that concerned New York.

Their documentary suggestion: *Educating America—Getting Back to Basics* received unanimous approval. Jodi began the presentation by explaining their thoughts. "Opening remarks by Carol, Greg, Frank, Lou, and Sam followed by a brief explanation of the contents and ending with the introduction of Mr. Marks lays the foundation for the first episode—a history and civics lesson taught by Mr. Marks. The Constitution of the United States will be read in its entirety as the viewers participate by following along."

Sam explained further. "Our goal is to encourage everyone to better understand and appreciate the principles of government that are set forth in America's Founding Documents by embracing these great gifts from our Founding Fathers.

"Mr. Marks will teach our viewers as he taught us. History is fact; fact is truth. It is not for you to like or dislike; it is there for you to learn from. If it offends you, you are less likely to repeat it. History is not anyone's to change or destroy.

"Jodi came across a pocketsize booklet issued by the Commission on the Bicentennial of the Constitution of the United States to stimulate an appreciation and understanding of our national heritage. It was presented as a history and civics lesson for all of us that cannot be learned without first reading and grasping the meaning of the document—the first of its kind in all human history. As we now approach its 250th Anniversary, not only has it endured, but without the principles of the Constitution, the principles of a free society are impossible.

"Normally we do not *market* our programs, but in an effort to reach as many viewers as possible by encouraging hope and optimism in the future of the greatest nation on earth, I propose the distribution of 500,000 pocketsize booklets of the Constitution throughout the state of New York with the help of the 755 public libraries, their outlets, neighborhood branches, and bookmobiles prior to the airing in January. Any out-of-state requests will be honored promptly, and every effort will be made to keep up with demand.

"Not only could this create hype for the show, it could become a *movement* for the entire country to get back to basics.

"Our outlines for episodes two and three are simply our thoughts for you to consider in creating the shows. We will work with you as much as possible as we await the birth of the twins. After that, we aren't promising anything."

Everyone laughed. It was a good meeting. The viewers' overwhelming acceptance of their first documentary had set a high bar. All were in agreement Jodi and Sam's idea more than qualified; the time was right for a much needed wakeup call to every American and in particular to our public servants. It was definitely time to get back to basics.

As Thanksgiving loomed in the not to distant future, Sam took the lead on the first episode. Together they met and prepared an opening statement. A brief summary of growing up in Port Chester, attending Port Chester High School, and having been students whose teacher made US history and civics a class they looked forward to attending were offering viewers a chance to return to class taught by their very own teacher, Guy Marks, for the same experience.

A brief bio and his introduction would turn the program over to Mr. Marks. There was no planning or rehearsing needed on his part; he had taught thousands of bright young minds before retiring five years earlier. He could do it in his sleep. The Constitution of the United States would be read from start to finish including the Amendments, with comments and explanations accordingly.

Filming was coordinated and scheduled; 500,000 pocketsize booklets were ordered; January 10th, 11th, and 12th were chosen to air the three episodes. As they waited an availability date of the booklets, the plan to distribute them was finalized. Sandy, Carol, and Edie were tasked with promoting the upcoming series while urging viewers to get a copy of the booklet before the airing preparing them to take part in the class.

Working on the documentary proved to be the best medicine for Jodi. She was more relaxed than she had been since the Hamas attack on Israel in early October. As a career, she had chosen Feature Journalism, which focuses on human-interest stories. The plight of the hostages weighed heavily on her mind as families emerged begging for their release.

Hope and optimism in the days leading up to Thanksgiving were rewarded when Israel's cabinet approved a deal for the release of the hostages in exchange for a pause in the fighting in Gaza; the ceasefire was slated to begin on Thursday morning. The agreement would see the release of at least 50 hostages—women and children—in exchange for a four-day truce in Israel's air and ground campaign. It held out the potential for an extension.

On Wednesday, as final negotiations of the agreement continued in Israel, a vehicle exploded at the Rainbow Bridge border crossing between the US and Canada. The car driving from New York to Canada at a high rate of speed was headed for the border office building when it suddenly crashed into a barrier, exploded, and burst into flames. Both the driver and one passenger in the car were killed. It was 11:30 am.

For weeks, travel for Thanksgiving 2023 was on track to reach record high numbers as Americans headed for family gatherings for the first time in four years. As COVID eased out of the picture, travelers turned their attention to the weather.

With tensions running high, the FBI immediately identified the incident as a terrorist attack prompting a temporary shutdown of all four bridges between Canada and the US near Niagara Falls on the busiest travel day of the holiday weekend.

The Governor headed for the scene. By dinnertime, she held a news conference announcing to New Yorkers and all Americans: *At this time there is no indication of a terrorist attack.* Although questions remained, investigators believed the man who died had plans to attend a KISS concert in Canada; when it was cancelled, he went to a casino in the US instead. The crash occurred after the couple left the casino.

Also on the news Wednesday evening was the announcement that the ceasefire and hostage release was rescheduled to begin on Friday.

Jodi and Sam started Thanksgiving Day by watching the Macy's Parade. After breakfast and once comfortably settled on the sofa, they were prepared to exchange memories of having viewed the parade with their families. They agreed that the parade was a part of every New Yorker's DNA.

The parade not only commemorates a piece of our country's history but also New York history. Demonstrators had different ideas. In an effort to disrupt and tarnish the time-honored and family-friendly Macy's Thanksgiving Day Parade, they inserted themselves into the parade route and glued their hands to the pavement. They were quickly cuffed and hauled away, and the parade continued while others defaced the New York Public Library leaving the taxpayers with a $75,000+ tab to clean up after them.

Trudy and Charlie hosted Thanksgiving, and as always, it was the best. They had been somewhat preoccupied with finalizing the purchase of the house in the Hamptons before the babies arrived, while Nina's time was consumed with overseeing the Museum and the intern program, as she settled into her new condo. As a result, numerous phone conversations between the five of them replaced in-person meals and conversation.

They began dinner giving thanks for their many blessings. They talked about the arrival of the twins that although the doctor said otherwise could actually happen at any time. When questioned if they had decided on names, Jodi and Sam changed the subject.

When Trudy remarked that Jodi's demeanor belied the usual final days of discomfort and anxiety in a single pregnancy while carrying twins, she and Sam looked at one another knowingly and began to tell them about the documentary.

The evening ended early. To Jodi, It seemed ironic that a total day of relaxation could exhaust her more than the adrenalin rush and effort that went into creating a documentary series.

They had their work cut out for them. Their goal was to wrap up the first episode by the end of the month. It was very doable, and Mr. Marks was set to begin filming the following Monday. With everyone working on the second and third episodes, Sam felt good about everything falling into place and keeping them on schedule.

In New York on Black Friday, as shoppers headed out to kickoff the Christmas Season, protestors continued their interference. They closed a Manhattan bridge, blocked streets, and waved anti-Semitic signs as they shouted slurs against Israel, and against America for supporting them.

In Israel on Friday morning, hours after the four-day ceasefire took effect, the first hostages taken captive by Hamas on October 7th were released from Gaza. The group of thirteen consisted of women and children. All were Israelis; there were no Americans. Continuing on Saturday, Sunday, and Monday, a total of 50 Israeli hostages were released—all women and children. At the end of the day, a two-day extension of the ceasefire was agreed upon.

Tuesday and Wednesday, the ceasefire and hostage release continued, as the world watched families being reunited while learning of the horrible conditions the children and women endured for over fifty days at the hands of their captors. Another two-day extension was agreed upon.

In New York, hundreds of protestors clashed with police Wednesday night as they swarmed Rockefeller Center in a mindless effort to derail the annual Christmas tree lighting. They attempted to knock down the barricades NYPD put up to separate them from the crowd taking in the holiday tradition, but they failed to break through.

Prevented from getting to the Christmas tree, the protesters targeted smaller trees outside the News Corp. Building while waving signs to *Free Palestine* resulting in multiple arrests, as they were jeered for interrupting the time-honored tradition.

In Israel, Thursday saw additional hostages released. At the end of the day, authorities learned the names of four hostages that died in captivity; there was no mention of arrangements to return the bodies to the families. In the early morning hours of Friday, Hamas broke the ceasefire by firing a rocket into Gaza that was intercepted by Israel's Defense System. Only eight hostages were released, not ten that had been agreed upon.

After a week, the temporary ceasefire in the war between Israel and Hamas ended on Friday and hostilities resumed. An estimated 137 hostages including the 14 Americans remained in Gaza.

For New Yorkers, the month of November had been harsh, unbearable, and burdensome on many fronts. Hoping that December and the holiday season would change people's mindsets was a long shot that many didn't see happening. They were right. The protests continued as wary New Yorkers were met with closed streets, blocked bridges, and property damage to Jewish owned businesses as they tried to simply go to work, do a little shopping, or enjoy a night out.

According to plan, all deliveries began the first week of the month. Within a matter of days, the nursery was good to go. Sam's arms were around Jodi as they stood in the doorway of the room and surveyed their handiwork. They were pleased. It was just as they had envisioned it—*two of everything!*

Although *warp speed* does not exist in the real world, it seemed as though the documentary was proceeding close to it. The team decided to continue the series in the same mode—lessons taught by Guy Marks.

The second episode—*The Voter*—covers everything about voting from *who can vote* to *where and ways to vote* to *what matters most individually.*

The third episode—*The Candidate*—covers everything about the candidate from *their qualifications* to *their history and track record* to *what they stand for and their vision for the future.*

Both episodes were well on track to be completed by Christmas at the latest.

The final week leading up to the twins pending arrival was bittersweet. Jodi and Sam decided to enjoy the last days of calm and quiet enjoying the present while looking to the future. Other than their weekly visit to the doctor, they had no plans.

Each morning they awoke and while having breakfast decided what they wanted to do that day. For the most part, they played it by ear taking the weather into consideration. If the weather was nice, they went for a walk. Sitting and lying positions had grown terribly uncomfortable. Preferring to take meals at home, Sam cooked or ordered in. Trudy and Charlie stopped by everyday, and Nina came by almost as much.

Sunday evening, Trudy and Charlie invited them to dinner. It was a lovely evening. Everyone was in good spirits; all world problems were set aside. Trudy was *over the moon* at becoming a grandmother—not once but twice. Jodi and Sam though *overjoyed* hoped they were up to the task of being good parents. As Nina assured them that no one gets it right all of the time, but having had the parents they had, she was certain they were up to the job; it was in their genes.

The week started with their Monday morning visit to the doctor. As she began the examination, she asked Jodi how she was feeling. "Except for the rather sharp pain in my lower back, I feel pretty good. Is something wrong?"

The doctor smiled. "No. Nothing's wrong. You're in the very early stages of labor. Rather than send you home, I will call ahead, and they will be expecting you. Sam, it's time to take Jodi to Lenox Hill; you're about to become parents."

Jodi and Sam looked at one another astonished. "Wow! I guess I won't be able to take you to lunch today Mrs. Meyerson, but I promise you a magnificent celebratory dinner when you're up to it."

When they got to the hospital as they were checking Jodi in, Sam called Trudy promising to keep her updated throughout the day. He asked her to call Nina and let her know.

And so the wait began. For the first few hours, it seemed as though it was a false alarm. However, when her water broke and the pains began in earnest, Sam called Trudy, Charlie, and Nina to come to the hospital.

At precisely 7:11 pm, December 11, 2023, Andrew Noah Myerson was born; equally as anxious to come into this world at 7:18 pm, Analiese Nicole Meyerson arrived. At over five pounds each, they were healthy and beautiful, and Jodi was fine and exhausted. Sam though elated was overwhelmed.

The babies were placed in Jodi's arms and a warmed blanket covered them in the first, precious golden hour following the births. Beaming as she held them close, Sam's heart was about to burst. Never had he experienced such love and pride. What a beautiful family he had been blessed with; becoming a parent was a feeling like no other he had ever experienced or could have possibly imagined.

For Trudy becoming a grandmother was bittersweet, making her miss Al more than ever. How proud he would be of Sam with all that he had accomplished, but one look at these beautiful babies would have eclipsed everything else, of that she was certain.

Charlie who had grandchildren of his own told Trudy that based on his own experience, being a grandparent was far more fun. Loving them, spoiling them, and simply enjoying them without the responsibilities of being a parent was the best.

Nina's smile lit up her face. While she couldn't help wishing that Lily was here to see her beautiful family, she felt her presence.

Sam slipped away and headed towards the bank of elevators. Exiting on the fourth floor, he approached the multi-faith Chapel and entered. Finding it empty, he chose to sit in the first row; bowing his head he thanked God for blessing them with the twins and asked for guidance in parenting. Making no move to leave, he began speaking aloud.

> *Dad, I have never missed you more. How I wish that you were here beside me. You and Mom were the best parents a kid could possibly have, and I could sure use your help and advice now that I'm a parent. I might add Mom hasn't missed a beat; I call her my #1 go-to advisor for a reason. She always has the right answers and comes up with the right solutions.*
>
> *Please watch over us. I'm counting on you to let me know when I'm heading in the wrong direction. Just send me a sign; I'll know it when I see it.*
>
> *Love you forever and miss you always. Amen.*

Trudy came up behind him and tapped him on the shoulder. As Sam stood and turned, she gathered him in her arms and held him close. They didn't speak.

Trudy stepped back and broke the silence. "Sam what you said to your father was beautiful. You know he loved you more than he could ever tell you. Just the thought overwhelmed him with emotion, and that started on the very day, the very moment you were born. I often found him watching you as you slept, his smile lighting up his face.

"He would have been so proud of you and all your accomplishments both personal and business. He would have loved Jodi too, and been more than happy to welcome her into our family. He was a good man, but he was a fantastic husband and father.

"I'm sure if he were here, he would tell you that nobody is a perfect parent. Nobody gets it right 100% of the time. Being a parent is definitely on-the-job training, but somehow our love guides us and points us in the right direction. Until you actually hold your own child in your arms, there is no way you can anticipate the feeling. It comes from within, and has been known to melt the strongest of hearts.

"Like you, I came here to talk to your father. You said it so eloquently for both of us. I think we should head back. Jodi and the twins will be in their room soon, and we should be there when they arrive."

They exited the Chapel together and took the elevator to the sixth floor.

Jodi and the twins entered a room of smiling faces, a dozen red roses from Sam, pink and blue balloons from Trudy and Charlie, pink and blue hand knit sweater sets from Nina, and a note from the desk asking what to do with the multitude of flowers that continued to arrive.

The hour had grown late and was approaching midnight. Jodi and the twins had settled in and all were sleeping. It had been quite a day. Trudy and Charlie offered to drop Nina at her condo on their way home.

Sam was spending the night. He was quite comfortable in the chair wrapped in one of the blankets the nurse brought him. Although getting a little rest while the opportunity presented itself was the goal, he found it impossible to take his eyes off of Jodi, Analiese, and Andrew as they slept.

# Chapter 31

The following Thursday, they said goodbye to the wonderful nurses and left Lenox Hill Hospital. Andrew and Analiese were in their car seats, and Sam and Jodi sat on either side as the car service took them home. In eleven days, it would be Christmas Day. It was easy to get wrapped up in the excitement of becoming parents; however, first-time parents do not anticipate the emotions, the anxiety, and the panic that normally comes with the job.

Jodi's initial attempts at breastfeeding did not go well. The day before she was due to be discharged from the hospital, her frustration and growing apprehension led to a meltdown as she broke into tears proclaiming herself a failure.

Gathering her in his arms, Sam kissed her. As he dried her tears, he gently began to speak. "I've never known you to fail at anything in the past, and it's much too soon to consider yourself a failure now.

"Jodi Myerson—take a step back and look at what our love has created. Don't ever lose sight of the fact the you just gave birth to two human beings and nurtured them for nine months before that. To me you're not a failure you're a *Rock Star!* Even if you don't agree with me now, I promise you, one day you will look back and realize that I'm right.

"It's going to take a while to get our ducks in a row, but we will. We've been given sound advice going forward, and to second-guess ourselves before we even start isn't going to solve anything. Sleep and rest for you are critical. We must take advantage of each and every opportunity to take care of *you*. When the doctor mentioned *don't forget to eat,* I chuckled to myself. No chance of that on my watch.

"We are so fortunate to have all the help we need. My Mom, Charlie, Nina, and the whole crew at *Profiles* are there for the asking. Limiting visitors to our inner circle and sharing meals together is a great way to ask for their help while keeping everyone involved and close.

"Last but not least, take time to breathe. With each passing day, nursing will get easier, diaper changing will get easier, and parenting will get easier."

They sat quietly without moving. "You're right as usual. Sorry for the tears; I feel foolish. I have so much to be thankful for. *I Love You* Sam."

They took the doctor's advice and made a plan. They would tend to the babies' needs together as a team. They would ask Trudy and Nina to be in charge of meals. Charlie's role would be backup. They felt fortunate to have not only an in-house pediatrician in Charlie, but also a grandmother who was a nurse. Not living in their building allowed Nina the opportunity to run errands and/or pick up supplies on her way to and from their apartment as needed.

It was a solid plan, and by the time Christmas Day arrived, Jodi and Sam were in a good place. At two weeks of age, Analiese and Andrew were thriving. Early insecurities and self-doubts had all but disappeared, and they approached the holiday as a day to be spent as family.

They invited Nina, Trudy, and Charlie to spend the day at their apartment. Beginning with breakfast, Jodi offered to make Nana's pancakes. Nina was tasked with lunch. Dinner would be a group effort with everyone pitching in. A belated Birthday cake and ice cream for Jodi and Trudy was delegated to Sam. Throughout the day, Jodi could rest and relax between feedings. Analiese and Andrew were expected to spend some *awake-time* getting to know one another.

The invitation was Jodi and Sam's way of getting back to normal. Jodi eager to regain the energy she once had grew stronger with each passing day. Although they were not yet ready to relinquish the help and support they sought after the twins were born, they wanted to express their thanks and gratitude.

As Jodi fed the twins, everyone pitched in and cleared away the breakfast remains. With Sam's help, Analiese and Andrew were changed and dressed and placed in their snuggle seats. To everyone's delight, they were wide-awake sizing up their surroundings and the people staring back at them.

Jodi smiled. "This is the first *routine* day we've had since the twins were born. It seems like old times getting together and enjoying one another's company. I feel good, not exhausted like many of the past fourteen days when I found it hard to tell when one day ended and another began.

"We haven't had a single chance to simply talk during that time, and I've missed that most of all. Although I spent a good deal of the time sleeping, when I was resting, the wheels in my brain were constantly spinning.

362

"When Nana and I were reunited, the one fact that affected me the most was the realization that the first ten years of my life equated to only five years of actual memories. Never was that fact more evident than when I learned that the only recall I had in twenty years was that of Papa Joe when I was around three.

"Nana eagerly shared many memories of the first five years of my life, and as I began to reconnect with my parents and Papa Joe, I felt reborn. I felt loved and wanted. For twenty years, I yearned for those feelings without even realizing it.

"That brings me to my project that includes all of us. I have started journals for Analiese and Andrew that I want us all to contribute to documenting the first five years of their lives. A poem on the first page of each journal is the exact poem my mother wrote when I was born, changing only the name."

### A MOTHER'S LOVE

How do I measure a Treasure?
Your eyes, your smile, your button nose
Your tiny fingers and toes
A complexion fair, curls of dark hair
All perfectly framed
And named—Analiese Nicole!
How do I measure my Treasure?
In a million ways
In a lifetime of days.

### A MOTHER'S LOVE

How do I measure a Treasure?
Your eyes, your smile, your button nose
Your tiny fingers and toes
A complexion fair, waves of dark hair
All perfectly framed
And named—Andrew Noah!
How do I measure my Treasure?
In a million ways
In a lifetime of days.

"Analiese for Lily—Nicole for my mother; Andrew for Sam's father—Noah for my father—is how we chose the twins' names. We opted to give Andrew a name of his own to avoid any confusion when speaking about his was-one-of-a-kind Grandpa Alvin.

"Without even knowing it at the time, named Jodi by the Jeromes forever honors Papa Joe, the sole person that remained in the corners of my mind.

"And last but certainly not least, Sam and I owe you a debt of gratitude for your love and support." She glanced at the twins who had fallen asleep.

Jodi managed a short nap before their next feeding. The best way to describe dinner was fun. Trudy shared stories of Sam before he was five that he had never heard before. Jodi related a few of Nana's recollections. It was a *family* day all the way around.

With one week left in 2023, thoughts turned to ushering in 2024 and the end of the first quarter of the twenty-first century.

Every year as the clock nears midnight on December 31st, the eyes of the world turn once more to Times Square the symbolic center of New York City that has become a global tradition ringing in the New Year, and more than just a celebration.

The world holds its breath and anticipation runs high as the New Year's Eve Ball begins its 60-second descent from atop One Times Square. Countless people nationwide and throughout the world gather to bid a collective farewell to the departing year and express hope for the year ahead.

Having long been New York's symbol of celebration, the ball will have a new design this year based on the actual shape of Times Square. The square forms the shape of a bowtie from 44th to 47th streets. It is 12 feet in diameter and weighs 12 tons.

Since early November, people from all over the world have stopped at the Wishing Wall in Times Square to jot down on colorful pieces of tissue paper their hopes and dreams for 2024. These same slips of paper will be among the 3,000 pounds of confetti that will fall from the sky after the ball drops at midnight on New Year's Eve.

This year, the Wall on Broadway between 45th and 46th Streets has collected over 130,000 wishes from residents of 140 countries, including online submissions. Hopes range from the basic to the ultimate. Most are personal and optimistic. World and political wishes are almost non-existent.

Jodi and Sam submitted their wishes online.

After an early dinner at Trudy's, Jodi and Sam returned to their apartment. They welcomed the time alone and planned to watch the ball drop on television. After the twins managed two feedings and a nap in-between, Jodi and Sam donned pajamas and tuned into the festivities that were well underway. The weather was cooperating with a clear brisk evening for the revelers in Times Square.

Nestled on the sofa, safe and secure in Sam's arms, Jodi's thoughts turned to the New Year. "Do you have any gut feelings about 2024 to share?"

Sam smiled to himself. She is a treasure, his treasure. "I do, but they are not personal. I've spoken to the team about the upcoming documentary series, and all indications lean towards another big-time winner. The Constitution booklets are almost gone, and were reordered before Christmas."

Jodi sat upright. "Wow! Why didn't you tell me? That's fantastic."

"Well, you've been a little busy the past three weeks, and it didn't occur to me that you might have any thoughts of business on your mind."

Sam ducked as she hit him with the pillow. "I'm never *not interested* in *Meyerson Media*. Who knows when I'll be able to work on the next big project? This might have been my *last hurrah* until the twins go off to college!"

He grabbed her, enclosing her in his arms and kissed her. "I love you Mrs. Meyerson with every fiber of my being; I will never stop telling you that. And you underestimate yourself. The way I see it, you should be more than ready about the time they start kindergarten. I wonder if Analiese will have her mother's fiery personality."

"Excellent comeback. I kind of hope she does. It comes in handy at times. I do hope Andrew is exactly like you. No improvement needed."

At 11:59 pm, the ball began its descent to the dazzling lights and bustling energy of Times Square, where if for only a brief time, the problems of the world are replaced by confetti of hope and wishes of better days to come.

As Fireworks lit up the sky, they kissed.

Both speaking at once—*"Happy New Year!"*

# New York—2023

On Thursday, December 28, 2023, people hoping to shed burdens, bad memories, peeves, and disillusionment converged on Times Square for *Good Riddance Day*, a promotional pre-New Year's Eve event that offers New Yorkers a chance to do just that, at least symbolically.

Previous iterations of ***Good Riddance Day*** have involved shredders and dumpsters. This year, magician Devonti Rosero used a grill lighter and a flourish of his hand to incinerate pieces of paper on which many had written down all they wanted to put behind them.

New York is in crisis. The list is long and unending: the economy, crime, lawlessness, thousands of illegal migrants, a city on the brink of bankruptcy, effects of the Israeli-Hamas War on the state's Jewish population, the uptick of anti-Semitism throughout academia, anti-American demonstrations, defacing and destruction of public buildings and businesses, the exodus of hundreds of thousands of New Yorkers, and a pandemic that has yet to be put entirely to rest.

2023, a year whose every aspect was defined by division, ended with the addition of ***the death of humanity*** to the list.

To many, the lack of leadership is the most disturbing. The people that we have given our most precious of freedoms to—***our vote***—are nowhere to be found.

2024 is a Presidential Election Year. With no rest for the weary, the primaries begin two weeks into the New Year. Until Election Day November 5th, we will be inundated by ads, by robo calls, by mailed flyers, and by rallies promising ***to fix all*** for our vote. We will be criticized, ostracized, and disrespected by those who disagree with us. As much dirt and negativity as possible will be dredged up by each side against the other.

The time has come to take responsibility and reevaluate our future as we listen without judgment, care without hating, and love no matter what. The choice is ours and ours alone.

How nice it would be if we no longer felt the need for a ***Good Riddance Day***!

This ***is*** New York. Anything is possible.

# Epilogue

In April 2003, an international competition to choose a design for a permanent Memorial at the World Trade Center was launched. It yielded 5,201 submissions from 63 countries that were judged by a 13-person jury that looked for designs that honored the victims, spoke to the needs of families who had lost loved ones, and provided a space for healing and reflection.

In January 2004, the design submitted by architect Michael Arad, an Israeli-American who was living in the East Village on 9/11, and saw the second plane hit the south tower from the roof of his building was selected.

He called it *Reflecting Absence*. His design was to become an eight-year battle that was at times nasty and politically filled with drama and delays but that ultimately stitched the site back into the everyday life of the city.

The focal points of the Memorial are two pools. The walls of each pool are thundering 30-foot waterfalls cascading to a subterranean shallow and to a second void within to an unseen bottom. The pools are ringed by parapets containing bronze panels into which 2,983 names of the men, women, and children killed in the attacks of 9/11 (in New York, Pennsylvania, and the Pentagon), and an earlier attack on the World Trade Center on February 26, 1993 are etched.

Per Arad's own assessment: *Its scale is massive and personal, its impact individual. It is meant to make that absence tangible, physical, something that when you walk up to the edge of that void, you feel it. It's not just in your head; it's in your heart.*

*Reflecting Absence* opened to the public the day following the tenth anniversary of the 9/11 attack. Since Nina's first visit to the site that very first day, she returned many times in the ensuing years.

The 9/11 Memorial Glade was dedicated on May 30, 2019, the 17th Anniversary of the official end of the recovery effort.

The Glade's design includes a pathway flanked by six large stone monoliths, ranging from 13 to 18 tons that are inlaid with World Trade Center steel accompanied by an inscription at either end of the pathway. The Glade honors all who are sick or have died from exposure to toxins in the aftermath of the 9/11 attacks.

∞

367

2024 was no longer just around the corner it was here. Nina was in a good place. She was happy with her new condo, her new family, and her new job at *Meyerson Media Group.* She looked towards the future with hope and optimism as she did every year, but somehow she had a gut feeling this year would be better.

On a beautiful sunny but brisk morning the first week of January, she awaited an Uber to take her to the 9/11 Memorial. She carried a florist's box that contained her special order for four yellow roses with eight-inch stems.

Her first stop was at the Memorial Glade where she placed a rose in her special spot for Eric. At times, her visits were brief, but for some reason she stayed longer than she intended recalling how happy they were, how optimistic for the future they were, and how together they felt they could conquer the world. It wasn't meant to be.

From the Glade, she walked to the North Pool. Finding Noah's name, she placed her hand on it and smiled. Instead of standing beside her, she felt Lily beside Noah looking down on her. Removing a rose from the box, she wedged it upright into the etched name.

As she walked to the South Pool, she observed others who had come to pay their respects and took notice that most were alone. Suddenly sadness overcame her. Realizing that for the first time in her life she was living alone momentarily stopped her in her tracks.

Remembering she had come to the Memorial to observe Danny's 50th Birthday, she snapped out of it, and picked up the pace as she headed toward the parapet that held his name.

It was hard to believe. Her baby brother Danny Russell was born fifty years ago on this very day. They were always close even though she was almost four years older than he was. Growing up with an abusive father, she became his protector and all too often endured their father's wrath for having done so.

Their life in New York, no matter how brief, was the best, and for that she would always be grateful. It was through Danny that she had met Eric; she was grateful for that too. She ran her hand back and forth over his name several times before removing the third rose from the box and wedging it into his name as she had done for Noah. Tears filled her eyes as she whispered, *Happy Birthday Danny! I love you and miss you more each day.*

Wiping away the tears with the back of her hand, she looked down and saw a penny at her feet. Picking it up, she smiled; Danny was thinking of her too.

Turning to leave, she bumped into a man who asked, "Are you okay?"

Caught by surprise, she replied, "Yes, thank you. I'm fine. I apologize for bumping into you. I didn't see you. Sorry."

"It is I who should apologize. Not that I was spying on you, but you seemed a bit upset, and I came towards you to see if you needed help. That's why we collided."

Suddenly Nina laughed. "I think collided is a bit strong a word. I do thank you however. It is most kind of you to offer to help a stranger especially in these times. I'm Nina Butler, and you are?"

The man laughed also. "Hello Nina Butler, I'm Jack Montgomery. It is a pleasure to make your acquaintance."

"And I yours. I'm afraid you caught me at a bad moment. I came here today for my brother Danny's 50th Birthday. I lost him on 9/11; he was a firefighter and among the first responders to the North Tower. He was so young and hadn't really begun to live; it was all over much too soon. I miss him."

"I'm here to pay respects to my father who died in the South Tower. He was a visitor to the building that day. He was in the wrong place at the wrong time. I miss him too; we were quite close.

"Would it be presumptuous of me to ask you to join me in a cup of coffee? I can show you some identification if you like. I'm a physician, and although I am somewhat retired, I'm still affiliated with Lenox Hill Hospital."

What a small world Nina thought. "Do you happen to know Charles Hurwitz?"

"I do know him. We are not close friends, but I have had the privilege of working with him and attending his lectures. He's a Pediatrician, and I'm in Pediatric Research; our paths have crossed many times. How do you know Dr. Hurwitz?"

"That's a long story best told over a cup of coffee or two. I accept. I have an extra rose if you would like to place it in your father's name."

"Thank you. I accept as well."

Arm-in-arm they walked to the Parisienne Café a short distance from the Memorial. For over two hours, two total strangers found they had more in common than they could have ever imagined.

Jack learned about the Kansas farm girl turned New Yorker, losing

Danny and then Eric. How an offer from Lily Asher to paint a portrait of the brother she lost on 9/11 led to a new beginning, a new life unlike anything she could have envisioned while allowing her to give back. But best of all a family, something she never had was now once again a new beginning, a door to the future.

Nina learned about the grandson of General John Montgomery who preferred to be called *Jack*, and the son of Col. John Montgomery, both graduates of West Point. How he couldn't become third generation military because of a heart defect he was born with which led him to become a physician dedicated to research childhood illnesses. He too had taken a photo of his father to Lily for a portrait.

Jack was a widower having lost his wife three years prior. After his father perished on 9/11, he grew quite close to his grandfather. Fascinated and extremely proud of him, he never turned down an opportunity to listen to stories about his life in the service of our country.

On one occasion not long before he passed away, Jack learned that his grandfather had been in charge of the team that gathered evidence for the Nuremburg Trials in Germany following the war. Somewhere along the way, he came in contact with a young girl from Zurich who painted a portrait of him all too similar to those painted by Lily Asher.

After his grandfather died, he spent hours on the internet in an effort to learn about Lillian Austin (her maiden name) in Switzerland, on the chance that the artist was one in the same, but came up totally empty handed and eventually decided to abandon his search.

They exchanged phone numbers and agreed to share an Uber home even though they lived in slightly different directions, neither wanting their time together to end.

It had been quite a day. You could say their meeting was a coincidence. You might even say Danny had a hand in it. Perhaps 2024 was going to be Nina Butler's Godwink year.

*When God winks, the power of coincidence guides your life!*

**Coincidence is God's way of remaining anonymous.**

**Albert Einstein**

# Author's Notes

I was born in Brooklyn Women's Hospital on Eastern Parkway near St. John's Place four miles from where I live today. When I was six months old, my parents moved to Washington, DC where I grew up, went to school, married, and raised my children in the nearby Maryland suburbs.

In 2000, my late husband Jack and I moved to Cape Cod, Massachusetts. He continued to work while I newly retired pursued my lifelong dream of writing a novel. In 2005, my first *The Dollmaker* was published followed by my second *Clattering Sparrows* in 2010.

Jack passed away in 2014. At the time, my daughter and her family lived in Maryland; my son and his family lived in Massachusetts an hour away. Finding myself alone on the Cape never evoked thoughts of leaving and moving elsewhere. I continued to write; my third novel *A Diamond in the Rough* was published in 2017.

The arrival of COVID-19 and its impact on all of our lives forever changed all of our lives forever. My son and his family moved to Brooklyn the year before the pandemic, and finding myself not only alone on the Cape but in all of Massachusetts, cutoff from family and friends, inundated by mandates and restrictions, and the inability to get basic medical help jolted to the core my independent existence.

Hijacked by politicians and others seeking to empower themselves, the pandemic showed no signs of ending. After passing the two-year anniversary of the onset, and at the urging of my family, I took the leap to move to Brooklyn. My new adventure began on June 15, 2022.

Although I left when I was merely six months old, New York never left me. My mother's family lived in Brooklyn and growing up, no holiday passed without my grandmother coming to DC or my family going to New York. Jack's father was a New Yorker. He had aunts and uncles living there, and being in the Jewelry business, we frequently attended Jewelry Shows in Manhattan. The lure and love of Broadway, and the city's unrivaled eclectic cuisine often found us on a getaway weekend.

Through the years, I never lost interest in hearing about what was happening in or my feelings for *the city that never sleeps*. Though I grew up in DC, many memorable times in my life are tied to New York: Macy's Thanksgiving Day Parade, the Easter Parade, ice-skating at Rockefeller

Center, the Rockettes, Coney Island's Cyclone and Nathan's Hotdogs, carriage rides in Central Park, Broadway shows, the Copa Cabana, the Russian Tea Room, Lindy's Cheesecake, the Automat, and Stage Deli are but a few.

I've welcomed-in the New Year in Times Square, visited the Empire State Building numerous times, toured Ellis Island and Liberty Island home to the Statue of Liberty, cheered to victory the Brooklyn Dodgers at Ebbets Field, and been totally captivated as I walked through the doors of FAO Schwartz and Economy Candy on the lower east side as a child and as an adult. What a ride it has been!

When I walk or ride down the streets of Brooklyn today, nothing is familiar; only the street names remain the same. The old neighborhoods that were so much a part of my past are gone; too many years have passed. New is good; I don't compare; I accept and enjoy. I love every minute of it. *I Love New York!*

So many blessings have been a part of my new adventure. I have attended and taken part in three of my grandchildren's weddings, and I have become a great grandmother, having welcomed three great grandsons. Not only do I get to enjoy my family living here, my daughter, son-in-law and family have visited often.

When I first moved to Brooklyn, I lamented all that I could not bring with me. There is no comparison space-wise from a seven-room house with a full basement and double garage to a one-bedroom apartment.

I no longer feel that way. Each time I look out my living room window at my piece of the New York Skyline—*The Freedom Tower*—I feel pride for what it stands for and how it defines us—both as New Yorkers and Americans. It represents a time when as a country, we were at our best.

Requiring no packing, no moving, no lamenting, my *Memories* are with me always, alive and well in Brooklyn. I have come home.

There is not a day that has gone by that a fond memory of my childhood hasn't pervaded my thoughts. Many of these memories are of times, things, and places that no longer exist making them all the more precious.

I look to 2024 and pray that the world will right itself once more, and we will somehow in someway figure it all out as we have time and again in the past.

As New Yorkers, it is in our DNA ***to expect the unexpected!***

***Marilyn Land***

Printed in the United States
by Baker & Taylor Publisher Services